FIFE'S TIN BOX
A NOVEL

First Published in Great Britain 2021 by Mirador Publishing

First edition: 2021

Any reference to real names and places are purely fictional and are constructs of the author. Any offence the references produce is unintentional and in no way reflects the reality of any locations or people involved.

A copy of this work is available through the British Library.

ISBN: 978-1-913833-58-9

Mirador Publishing
10 Greenbrook Terrace
Taunton
Somerset
UK
TA1 1UT

Fife's Tin Box
A Novel

By

Peter Copley

DEDICATION

THIS NOVEL IS DEDICATED TO my best friend, Kathleen, my wife of 53 years, all my family and friends and to all seafarers past and present

OTHER NOVELS BY PETER COPLEY

Diomed's Ghosts
Blue Sea Brown Rivers Red Blood.

CHAPTER 1

BLACKSTONE VILLAGE, LANCASHIRE, ENGLAND. JANUARY 1940

A BITTER NORTH-EASTERLY WIND blew down the cobbled street of terraced houses as Kevin Fife made his way towards his pal's house. Seemingly oblivious to the cold, he wore short pants and a hand knitted grey wool pullover, his socks down around his ankles. At number 6 Princess Street he knocked on the door. With his hands thrust deep into his pockets, he looked up at the grey clouds scudding across the early evening sky, whistling a tuneless tune while he waited.

A woman answered the door wiping her hands on her floral wraparound pinafore.

"Is your Tommy playing out, Mrs Daggers?

Ida Daggers smiled at seeing Kevin. "Hello, young Kev. Come on in, he's just finishing his tea."

Kevin Fife followed Tom's mum into the parlour.

"Be with you in a minute, Kev," Tom called as he finished off his meal.

Kevin glanced at Tom's dad sitting hunched by the fireplace. "Hello, Mr Daggers."

Brian Daggers barely glanced up from poking at the coal. "Oh, hello," he grunted and continued staring into the fire.

"Guess what, Tommy?"

"What?"

"I've just been up to see Mr Stansfield. He said we could use his old house for our chickens."

"Oh, wow. That's great. Does he want any money?"

"No, he said we can have if for free, well, until he pulls it down. He said, if we fix up the windows and what not, we could use it as long as we want, and he said if we keep chickens it will help the war effort. He even said he'd buy eggs off us. Come on, Tommy, get your coat on. We'll go over and have a look at the house."

Tom took his coat off the hook and put on a felt cowboy hat.

"Where you off to now?"

"Just goin' out for a bit, Mum."

"Well, don't be home late, be home for 9. It's school in the morning … and don't forget your gas mask. And put your scarf on, it's cold outside."

"Yes, Mum."

Ida Daggers looked at Kevin's shorts and jumper. "Aren't you cold, Kevin? It's freezing outside."

"No, I'm warm enough, thanks, Mrs Daggers."

"Alright." She looked at her son. "And, think on, no playing with matches or breaking windows, just don't get into any more trouble. You hear?"

"No, Mum."

"Kevin. You keep out of trouble too; I don't want the Police or Fire Bobbies coming here again. I'll let them lock both of you up for the night if they do."

"Yes, Mrs Daggers. We won't get into trouble. My mum said she'd kill me if the coppers come to our house again."

"Hmm," Mrs Daggers murmured. "Take your torch, it'll be pitch black at 9 and mind when crossing the road; little Angela Roberts was knocked down last week in the blackout…Right, lads, be off with you then."

Tom picked up his gas mask and slung it over his shoulder, he put the flashlight in his jacket pocket. The two boys left the house and headed towards the old house on Cobden Road.

"Keep out of trouble - keep out of trouble. What trouble?" Kevin moaned. "Flippin' heck, Tom, I didn't deliberately set fire to Farmer Davey's field, the camp fire *accidentally* spread to the field. I tried to put it out and help the firemen…" Kevin paused, thinking about the night they raided the vicar's pear tree. "And, we were only scrumping. Pinching a few pears from the vicar's pear tree."

"It wasn't just the pears, was it? It was the greenhouse windows you broke chucking that stick up at the pears."

"Erm, well, yeah, but what a fuss they made. No need for the vicar to call the cops." Kevin altered the position of his gas mask box. "I don't know why we have to carry these masks around with us all day. The Germans won't bomb our village. There's nothin' here to bomb. Anyway, they reckon the war will be over by Easter."

A single snow flake hit Tom's face, he looked up at the sky. "Do you think it'll snow again?"

"I don't know, my dad says it's too cold to snow."

"How can it be too cold to snow?"

"Dunno. Dad says it's the coldest January since 1895." They continued chatting as they made their down Sheffield Road, kicking a small chipping stone between them. Walking alongside the boundary wall of the municipal allotments they could see a couple of old men tending their vegetable plots. The ground was frozen with just the odd cabbage and a few sprouts left on their stems.

"You see that pigeon coop?" Kevin said. "The dirty red one in the middle."

Tom looked over at a line of lofts. "Yeap."

"That one belongs to Stig Marron and Flogger Links. They have about ten pigeons. Racing pigeons. Flogger's always boasting about his racing pigeon, he even had a name for it... Bongo."

"Bongo! What a silly name. How do you race birds, anyway?"

"I'm not sure. They have a clock or something and they time the bird over a certain distance and the fastest bird back in the coop wins the prize. Anyway, Bongo landed on that pole." Kevin pointed to a telegraph pole. "But it wouldn't return to the coop, so, guess what Flogger did?"

"I dunno. What did he do?"

"He got his air rifle and shot it down."

"You're joking! Why would he do that?"

"To clock it home. If his bird wouldn't land in the coop, he'd lose the race. The pigeon cost him two shillings and the prize was ten-bob. So, he thought it worth it to shoot the bird down, clock it home and win the prize."

"Did he win?"

"No... He was as mad as heck."

Tom smiled briefly. "I don't like Flogger. He's a real pratt, he stole my bike and threw it in the canal. It took me all week to clean and oil it."

"Yeah, he's a numbskull alright. One day he'll get his comeuppance. He belted me last month and ripped my shirt just because I laughed at him for shooting his prize bird for nothing. I'd like to give him a good hiding."

"Yeah, me too. But he's too big. I wouldn't like to have a fight with him. He's cock-of-the-school, you know. He beat up 'Big Bithall' t'other day."

"Yeah, I know he did, but one day I'm going to get my own back on him." Kevin pointed towards the coop. "I'm going to pinch his pigeons, and his air rifle. That'll teach him not to steal your bike."

"Steal his pigeons!" Tom scoffed, "are you tired of living? Flogger would murder you if he found out. He's a pig. He even looks like a pig. I'd like to flatten his piggy nose. And Marron, he's as bad. He sits in front of me in school, he stinks of fish."

"That's because his dad's a fishmonger. All the Marron's stink of fish, even his sisters. Flogger's the one who started calling me, 'Five-foot-Fife'. Now everyone in school calls me 'Fifefoot'"

"I don't call you Fifefoot. You are nearly as tall as me. Why did you take him on anyway? He's twice your size."

"Because he's always taking the Micky out of me for being small and he kept shoving me over in the playground. My mum said, never let anyone bully you, always stand up for yourself. When she found out that I'd had a fight with Flogger she gave me sixpence. Dad showed me a few self-defence tricks he learned in the army, he said all bullies are cowards and if you stand up to them, they won't come back for more. And you know what? Flogger never bothers me now, although he gave me a black eye and made my nose bleed, and ripped my shirt."

"I wish my dad was like your dad. If I'd come home with a ripped shirt, my dad would have gone mad and belted me."

"Erm, I'm sorry about that. How's your dad doing anyway? Is he getting any better?"

"No not really, he's okay some of the time, then he gets these violent mood swings. I think the shrapnel in his head moves from time to time. He screams out in the middle of the night; it takes mum ages to calm him down." Tom bent down to pick up the chipping they'd been kicking and threw the stone towards the allotment. "You're not serious about stealing Links' birds, are you?"

"Maybe, I don't know. I promised mum I'd keep out of trouble, but the best way I can get my own back on Flogger is to nick his prize birds." Kevin chuckled. "Can you see his red piggy face when he finds out all his pigeons had flown the coop."

Tommy smiled, shaking his head, "yeah, I'd love to see phooey Marron's face too."

Laughing at the thought of seeing Links' and Marron's fuming, puffing faces, they walked on towards Stansfield's old house. Five minutes later they arrived outside the front gate. They both stood by the railings checking out the building. The old square-four was derelict, the house had no windows, slates were missing off the roof and a broken drainpipe stuck out from the wall at 45 degrees. It was surrounded by an overgrown garden, bordered by 10-foot-high bushes. A rusty wrought iron gate hung onto one of the two stone gate posts. Carved on one pillar was the word COBDEN, on the other, the word HOUSE. Kevin pushed at the gate and headed up to the front door. The door was unlocked and slightly ajar. Pushing at the door, it creaked open. He turned to his pal.

"Come on, Tommy, let's go inside and check it out."

Inside they found themselves in the hallway. The brown paint had peeled off the walls. Crumbling plaster exposed laths under the plaster. The house was cold and smelled damp and musty. At the end of the hall a staircase led up to the first floor, several stair treads were missing. The door to the front lounge hung off its hinges. Inside the lounge the boys looked around the empty room. The cast-iron fireplace was full of rubble, ashes and soot.

"Clean out that soot and we can have a fire. It's freezing in here."

Tom pulled a couple of bricks from the fire grate, scraping out the fallen soot and muck. Searching around the ground floor he found an old newspaper and scraps of wood. He stacked the fuel in the grate.

"Have you got a match?"

"Err, no."

A noise from the first floor made them both look upwards. Staring up at the ceiling they froze, listening to footsteps on the floorboards above.

"Who's that?"

"Shush. It might be a tramp."

The footsteps moved across the floor heading towards the stairs. Kevin and Tom stood motionless watching through the open door, wondering who was coming down the stairs. They breathed a sigh of relief when two girls appeared, creeping carefully down the staircase. The girls, dressed identically with grey cardigans over gingham skirts, white socks and black leather shoes, looked as nervous as the boys. Both girls had a gas mask box slung around their shoulder.

Breathing a sigh of relief, the bigger of the two girls said to her friend, "Oh, it's only Tommy Daggers, he's a bell ringer at our church." She looked at Kevin. "What are you doing in our house?"

Kevin equally relieved that the girls were not tramps, said, "what do you mean, your house? Mr Stansfield said we could use the house. We are going to keep our chickens here."

"Chickens? What chickens?"

"We ain't got 'em yet. We'll get them when we've fixed up the windows and put some chicken wire outside."

"Well, this is our house, we've been coming here all last summer. Mr Stansfield didn't mind."

"What have you been doing here all year anyway? Mr Stansfield said the bedroom floorboards are not safe."

"We've made a den up there, we just play 'house'. And we smoke. Cigarettes," she added as if boasting about smoking cigarettes.

"You're too young to smoke."

"No, I'm not. I'm 14. And you are too old to be wearing a cowboy hat and a toy sheriff's badge, Tommy Daggers." She stabbed her finger at the tin star on Tom's shirt; a silver star with the word SHERIFF across it. "Do you think you are a cowboy or something?"

Tom, in embarrassment, wagged his head. "I got it for Christmas with a cowboy's six-shooter. I just forgot to take it off, that's all." He looked at the other girl and said, "you're not 14. I know you, Maureen Dawson. You go to Blackstone Primary School."

"No, I don't, I left there last year. I go to the Grammar school with Jane now."

Kevin turned to the older girl and asked with a slight frown, "Is your dad the vicar? I've seen you playing in the vicarage gardens."

"Yes, so what?" she said defensively, tossing her head, causing her long dark brown plaits to swing around her shoulders.

"Oh... Nothing...What's your name?"

"Jane. What's yours?"

"Kevin."

"I've seen you around, playing near the vicarage." Jane looked at Tom. "I know you. You go to our church; you joined the church bell-ringers just before the war started."

"Yeah, I started last August, the war put a stop to bell ringing in September. I bet your dad doesn't know you smoke?"

"No, he doesn't. You'd better not tell him either."

"I thought you were stuck up; you going to the Grammar school and singing in the church choir, looking so innocent."

"Stuck up? I'm not stuck up. I'm not innocent either." She laughed lightly, raising her eyebrow. She pointed to the fire place. "What are you doing there?"

"We were just going to light a fire but we haven't got a match."

Jane rummaged in her gas mask box. "I've got a match." She handed a crushed matchbox to Kevin. There was a single match in the box.

"Oh, boy. Thanks, let's light the fire it's getting cold and dark in here."

"Wait on," Jane said. "We have some candles upstairs. I'll fetch them."

As Kevin lit the paper, Jane sprung up the stairs, two steps at a time, avoiding the broken treads. By the time she returned to the fireplace with a couple of candles, flames were licking up the chimney.

"Are these from the church?" Kevin asked, grinning as he lit one of the candles from a spill.

"Don't ask questions and I'll tell you no lies." Jane smiled at Kevin.

The earlier animosity between the four had by now vanished as they squatted on the bare floorboards, bathed in candlelight, watching the flames, sparks, and smoke curl up the chimney.

"What else are you planning to do here?" Jane asked.

"We're going to turn the bedroom into a pigeon coop and we're going to breed white mice."

"Mice? I hate mice. They're a pest."

"Not white mice. They make good pets; we can breed them and then sell them for 6 pence each."

"Ugg, who'd want mice as a pet? The vicarage is overrun with them."

"My dad says people are having their pets put down because of the war and you can't take pets into the shelter," Maureen said. "Anyway, who would want to keep mice in war time?" She looked up from poking at the burning sticks. "Do you think the Germans will bomb us with gas bombs? I'm scared," she said fretfully. "Do you think they will invade us?"

"No, the army will stop them in France at the Maginot Line. The war will be over by Easter anyway."

"Well my dad said Churchill is a warmonger and will want or keep on fighting," Maureen said. "Can we help you with the chickens?"

Kevin looked at Tom. "I don't know, what do you think, Tommy?"

"I don't mind, they can help if they want. Do you want to join our gang?"

"Gang? I've never been in a gang. Who else is in the gang?"

"Just us two...and you two, if you want to join?"

"I'd like to join," Jane said

"Me too," Maureen agreed.

"What shall we call our gang?"

Kevin gave it a thought, looking at his dirty hand. "Black Hand Gang?"

"No, that's rubbish," Tom said. "How about The Four Cowboys?"

"No, because us two are girls," Maureen said.

"How about the Cobden Gang? Cos, this house is called, 'Cobden House'," Jane suggested.

"Yeah, that's a good name. Okay then, we'll call ourselves the Cobden Gang."

The four, sat on the floorboards, their knees drawn up to their chests, watching the flames in the hearth die away. The candles fizzled out leaving the room in semi darkness.

"We'd better get going then, my mum gets worried," Jane said. "Will you walk us home? I hate the blackout."

"Yeah, sure. Come on, Tommy, it's getting late. We'll take Jane to the vicarage then take Maureen home."

The youngsters left the old house headed off towards the already blacked out village. Tom shone his torch on the pavement.

"Keep that light down," the ARP warden, who appeared out of nowhere, called officiously. "That light can be seen by German planes."

"Oh, alright, Mr Webster. Sorry." Tom then whispered to his friends, "silly bugger, as if they can see this torch. It hardly lights up the pavement."

"Keep that light down," Kevin said in a gruff voice, mimicking the warden.

"Put that light out," Jane scoffed, also trying to imitate the self-important warden.

The four Cobden Gang members giggling, laughing and friendly jostling, hurried off into the darkness.

~ * ~ * ~ * ~

Mr Cyril Parkinson, Class 4A's teacher, noticing Tom Daggers chatting to his classmate, swung around from the blackboard and flung a piece of chalk across the classroom. The chalk bounced off Tom's head causing him to squeal and look up at the teacher.

"Next time I catch you talking, Daggers, I'll give you the cane."

Tom Dagger's rubbed his head. "Yes, sir, sorry, sir."

Parkinson turned back to the blackboard and continued chalking the date.

"Today is Friday 12th January and we have been at war with Germany for nearly five months. You boys will be leaving school this year so now is the time to decide what job you're going to do when you leave. Also, I want to know what you are doing or what you plan to do to help the war effort." He put the chalk on his desk and sat facing a classroom of 40 boys. "Durkin, what job are you going to do when you leave and what are you doing for the war effort? Stand up, Durkin."

Durkin unwound his legs from the chair and stood up.

"What are you doing to help win the war?"

"Err, sir, err. I'm going down pit with me dad."

"Good. What else are you going to do to help the war effort? "

"Err, sir, err. What yer mean?"

"The government expects us all to chip in and help do things to help the war. Such as joining the LDV or fire-watching or collecting metal and glass."

Kevin Fife leant across to Tommy Daggers and whispered, "my dad says LDF means Look, Duck and Vanish."

Tom grinned.

Durkin, still standing, stammered, "err, sir, I'm collecting jam jars. I get h'penny for the big jars and a farthing for the little jars."

"You lying fat fucker, Durkin," whispered Stig Marron, who was sitting just behind Durkin. "You're just collecting nits from your scabby sister."

Durkin turned and pointed his finger into Marron's face and mouthed, "watch it, Marron, or I'll put your lights out."

The partially deaf Mr Parkinson didn't hear the muttering coming from the class.

"Very good, Durkin. Sit down."

Parkinson called on each boy to ask what job they intended doing and what activity they intended to do to help the war effort.

"Going down the pit, sir, and joining the Boys Brigade as a messenger boy."

"Going down Bankhall pit, sir, filling sand bags, and a messenger boy."

"Goin' into Harvey's cotton mill, sir. I'll be fire watchin' wiv me dad an' fillin' sand bags."

Most of the boys in the class were either going down the coal mine or planning to work in the cotton mills as well as collecting jam jars, old newspapers or scrap iron. None of it, as far as they were concerned, for the war effort, just a new found way of earning a little pocket money.

"Daggers, what are you going to be when you leave school?"

Tom, still rubbing his head from the chalk strike said, "I'm going to be a cowboy and raise chickens, sir."

The whole classroom erupted into hilarity and hoots of derision.

"Tommy 'the Cowboy' Daggers! What a plonker," called Stig Marron. "He still plays cowboys and indians, sir."

"All you play is doctors and nurses with girls from St Maggie's," Tom retaliated.

"Alright, settle down." Parkinson frowned and asked, "what do you mean by a cowboy raising chickens? Are you going to work on a farm, Daggers? A farm hand, herding cows and feeding the hens?"

Daggers screwed his nose and puckered his lips, "no, sir, I'm going to be a cowboy like in the pictures. Like Tom Mix."

The classroom burst into giggles again.

"Alright, class, calm down. If Daggers wants to ride the range chasing chickens, he can."

"Fife. What job are you going to do when you leave school this summer?"

"Err, sir…"

"Stand up, Fife."

"I am standing up, sir."

The classroom burst into laughter again. Flogger Links sniggered from the back row, "Five-foot-Fife!"

Kevin Fife's face blushed but he didn't respond to Flogger's taunt. "I'm going to join the Merchant Navy, sir."

"Merchant Navy? Not many folks around here join the navy. What else are you going to do until you join the navy?"

"For the war effort, me and Tom Daggers are going to raise chickens and eggs." Kevin didn't mention breeding white mice as pets.

Parkinson nodded and said, "going to sea is dangerous at the best of times, Fife, but in war time it's very dangerous. Do you know the war at sea started on the first day war broke out? The liner 'Athenia' was torpedoed and sunk on the first day, when the war was only twelve hours old. The war in France is being called the phony war, but war at sea is a very different kettle of fish. In the last four months the German U-boats have torpedoed and sunk dozens of our ships. If you go down the pit you will be exempted from the army and navy."

"I know that, sir, but I want to go to sea."

"Where do you get that idea from? We are 40 miles from the nearest sea port."

"My granddad was a seaman. He told me stories of life at sea, adventures and so on."

"Oh well, Fife, if that's what you want, good luck to you. Alright, Fife, sit down."

Just as Fife shuffled his chair to sit down, the school's assembly bell rang for the lunchtime break.

Kevin and Tom ate their school dinner quickly; they planned a trip to the pet shop during the dinner hour. After handing in their empty plates to Mrs Dean, the formidable 'Dinner Lady', they left the school grounds and meandered through the town. Wasting time, the two boys looked in shop windows on the village High Street. The shops were getting more threadbare each month the war went on. By 12.45 they stood outside the pet shop window looking in. The animal cages were empty. A notice in the window stated no cats or dogs for sale here for the duration. Another notice stated, 'White mice – 6d each'. The boys went inside and spent five minutes choosing which mice to have.

The shopkeeper pointed out the mice. "Them two are males, those two are females."

"We've only got a Bob. Can you let us have them for threepence each? Four for a shilling?"

"Go on then," the shop owner said without much hesitation. "You can have them for a Bob. I'm glad to get rid of the mice. The war is having a real bad effect on my business. Have you got a box to put them in?"

"No, we'll keep them in our pockets, 'till we get home. We have built a little playhouse for them."

"Okay, boys, just be careful they don't escape from your pockets or you will have a job on to catch them again."

On the way back to school Kevin glanced up at the Town Hall clock. "Crikey, it's nearly one-o-clock. Let's get a move on. Come on, run, old Frosty Knickers will go mad if we're late, and we've got her all afternoon."

~ * ~ * ~ * ~

The English teacher went by the nickname 'Frosty Knickers'. Her real name was Miss Janet Frost. Frost, a stern looking spinster type, called the register.

"Daggers."

Tom groaned as he heard his name being called, he couldn't open the classroom door quickly enough, he turned to face Kevin who was holding one of his mice up to his lips. "Hurry up, Kev. Stop admiring your mouse."

"Thomas Dagger. Where's Daggers?

"Don't know, miss. I think he and Kevin Fife went into town after dinner."

She was about to mark them absent when the two boys returned to the classroom.

"I'm here, miss. Sorry we're late, Miss Frost," Tom apologised. "We had to do an errand for my mum. I had to call at the clinic for orange juice for my little sister."

"Take your hands out of your pockets when you speak to me, Daggers. Where's the orange juice now?"

Tom reluctantly released the mice he had ensconced in his blazer pocket, one in each pocket. "I had to take it home, miss, that's why we are late back."

Miss Foster then looked at Kevin. "You too, Fife. Take your hands out of your pockets."

Kevin Fife also reluctantly released the two tiny white mice, hoping they would stay put in his pocket.

"Alright, sit down and open your book. Tale of Two Cities by Charles Dickens."

Looking over the rims of her spectacles, she called to Fife, "Fife, read aloud to the class, the first two paragraphs of Chapter 1."

"Err, hum," Kevin cleared his throat. He looked at the book. "Err...It was the best of times. It was..."

"Stand up, Fife." Miss Frost interrupted.

Kevin cast his eyes upwards. "I am standing up, miss."

Once again, the 39 boys in class 4A laughed and chortled.

"Five-foot Fife," sniggered Flogger Links again.

"Be quiet, Links. Carry on, Fife."

Kevin Began again, "It was the best of times, it was the worst of times, it was..."

Two tiny noses peeped out of Kevin's blazer pocket. One disappeared back inside while the other dropped from the pocket to the classroom floor.

"Mice," screamed Marron. "Mice, miss, on the floor."

Miss Frost gave out a stifled shriek, scrambling onto her chair.

"Mice! Where?"

"There, miss. There, under Fife's desk."

During the scramble, the second mouse escaped from Kevin's pocket and ran across the floor towards the front of the classroom.

Miss Frost, now standing on her chair, shrieked again, "there! There it is, catch it someone."

The whole classroom was now in uproar as 38 boys scrabbled around the floor trying to catch the mice. The only two boys not involved in the scramble were Tommy Daggers and Kevin Fife.

"Don't tell miss that they are ours, Kevin," whispered Tom fretfully. "She'll know I was fibbing about the orange juice."

"I won't," promised Kevin. "Just hold on to your two."

Tom's hands slipped back into his blazer pockets. He searched around, feeling around in panic. "Oh bugger, they've gone too." Tom searched all his pockets again. His two mice had also escaped.

"There's two, miss. Look, another!"

"There's three, miss."

"I've caught one, Miss Frost, look." Marron held the captive mouse up by the tail to show the teacher.

Miss Frost recoiled in fright. "Kill it, Marron, kill it."

Before Fife could stop him, Marron had no more ado than throw the mouse at the classroom wall. The mouse with all its bones broken, slid down the wall.

"You bloody bastard!" blurted Fife, unable to stop himself from swearing. "That's my mouse, you've killed it, you bastard."

"What do you mean, your mouse?"

Fife was almost in tears. "It's mine, I bought it today."

"I've caught another one, miss." Joe Durkin held the little mouse by the tail. The mouse clawing at thin air.

"Kill it, kill it," screamed the teacher. "I hate mice."

Fife and Daggers looked on in horror as Durkin, following Marron's example, threw the tiny mouse hard against the blackboard. The dead mouse slid down the board leaving a wet trail.

The classroom now was in turmoil. Durkin, the only fat boy in the class, was trying his hardest to stamp on the third mouse scurrying around on the floor boards. Tom and Kevin watching the frenzy, had resigned themselves to the fact that the four mice, bought at lunchtime for 3d each, were goners. Kevin just hoped that Miss Frost hadn't heard him swear and admit that he had brought the mice into the classroom. Bringing livestock of any description into classrooms was strictly against school rules. This could lead to getting six-of-the-best from the ever-ready cane for sure.

When all four mice were well and truly dead, Flogger Links presented them to Miss Frost laid out in a neat line on a drawing board.

"Take them away, Links. Get rid of them. Put them in the dustbin outside." Miss Frost was now slightly calmer and climbed down from her chair, checking there were no more mice under her desk. "I hate mice."

"Miss, Fifefoot said he bought the mice this dinner time from the pet shop," Marron snitched on Fife deliberately, dropping Kevin in it.

Miss Frost stared at Kevin. "Stand up, Fife."

"I am standing up, miss." Kevin was getting fed up of repeating himself, wishing he was a bit taller.

"Get out here," Miss Frost said fiercely. "Get out here and explain yourself."

Kevin walked slowly to the front of the classroom, head down, looking like a man condemned to death.

Frost glared at him. "Is it true what Marron said, that you bought the mice this dinner time? Is it true that you lied to me that you went with Daggers to the clinic for orange juice and that you went to the pet shop instead?"

Kevin hung his head. "Yes and no, miss."

"Yes and no? What do you mean, yes and no?"

"Well, miss," Kevin began to lie about his dinner time trip. "We collected the orange juice, took it back to Tommy's house and on the way back to school we called in the pet shop and got the mice."

"Daggers came into the class with his hands in his pocket. Did he bring mice into class?"

"No, miss. I brought all four in. Sorry."

Miss Frost looked at Fife for a few seconds, not quite believing him, but secretly admiring Fife for taking all the blame. "Alright, Fife. Stand there, clear of my desk." She turned to the cupboard and brought out the cane. The cane, two-foot long and 2 inches around was hard and inflexible. "Hand out."

Kevin raised his right hand turning his head to the left. The cane swished through the air cutting hard into his palm. He drew a sharp intake of breath but didn't cry out.

"The other one, if you please."

Kevin held out his left hand. The cane swished again, hard across Fife's hand. Miss Frost was renowned for how hard she could cane a boy. Once again Kevin flinched but didn't cry out, hoping he wasn't going to get two more strokes. The usual punishment was two strokes of the cane, occasionally, depending on the mood of the teacher or the seriousness of the offence, four strokes were given. Six-of-the-best were only administrated by the Headmaster.

"Alright, Fife. Go back to your seat."

Relieved to get away with two strokes, Kevin returned to his desk, blowing into his palms and glaring at Marron with an, '*I'll get you back, Marron,*' expression on his face. The class eventually got over the brief excitement and settled down to the rest of the lesson.

~ * ~ * ~ * ~

At four pm the assembly bell rang for home time. The boys stood up scraping and banging their chairs, happy and looking forward to the weekend.

"Fife!" Miss Frost called above the racket. "Here, please."

Kevin wondered what else she wanted. He stood next to her desk.

"Kevin Fife," she started. "To look at you, you would think butter wouldn't melt in your mouth. You look much younger than you are, freckles and glasses, a cheeky little boy face. But for all that, you are always getting into trouble. Always up to some mischief. It was you who put that cat in Mr Olney's cupboard, nearly gave him a heart attack when it jumped out onto his head and clawed off his wig." Miss Frost struggled to hide a smile. "Also, Fife, I heard that the police called at your house last autumn for vandalising the vicarage."

"Vandalising the vicarage, miss? I was only scrumping pears and accidently broke a greenhouse window. My mum paid for the damage; it was only half a crown for the glass."

Miss Frost's frosty face and voice softened. "Erm," she said and was silent for a moment. "Mr Parkinson told me that you are determined to go to sea when you leave school."

"Yes, miss."

"Well, Kevin..." Miss Frost hesitated, as if remembering some distant memory. "My little brother James was lost at sea in the last war. Jimmy was in the Royal Navy though. He was only 16 years old. It killed my mother, she died of a broken heart. In the Great War, over 44000 Royal Navy sailors were lost and 15000 British merchant seamen went down with their ships, nearly 60000 mothers to mourn them. I should imagine in this conflict with modern U-boats and whatnot, there will be many more ships sunk." Miss Frost's eyes glazed over briefly before she blinked to resume her normal stern school mistress expression. "So, Kevin Fife, if you are determined to go to sea, I will pray for you, and that you will return safely to the arms of your mother."

Kevin was slightly taken aback. He had never seen the softer side of Frosty Knickers. He didn't know that her brother had been killed in the war or that she would know anything about how many sailors died at sea.

"Thank you, Miss Frost."

"Right, off you go."

"Thanks, miss." Kevin turned to leave the classroom.

"Oh, Fife. I didn't really want to cane you this afternoon. I had to show the class that I will not tolerate tomfoolery. And I knew that you defended your friend Tommy Daggers, that was brave of you. It saved him a caning too, and getting a beating from his Dad. So off you go, have a good weekend and - keep - out - of - trouble."

"Yes, miss. I will."

Kevin Fife left the classroom pondering on how to get his own back on Stig Marron and how to go about stealing his pigeons.

~ * ~ * ~ * ~

Kevin and Tom examined the fencing around a deserted chicken shed. The timber slats on the lower part of the fence were grey with age. Kevin pulled at one of the boards, it came away easily in his hands. The chicken wire above the boards going rusty in parts.

"Are you sure we can have this timber?" Tom asked.

"Yes, I'm sure. Johnny Clegg has gone off to war. Anyway, he hasn't used this hen-house for years. Look, it's falling apart." He pulled a second board off the fence. "Come on, our need is greater than his. He might get shot in France, then he won't have any use for a fence."

Tom and Kevin started to dismantle the fence, piling up the timber.

"We need that chicken wire too. Just pull it off the fence and roll it up."

Tom pulled the chicken wire off the posts.

"We'll need these posts too." Kevin rocked a fence post back and forth until it became loose. After one hour of toil, the fence surrounding a disused chicken hut had been dismantled and piled up neatly ready for transport to Mr Stansfield's old house. It took the boys the rest of Saturday morning and half of the afternoon to trolley the timber back to their, soon to be, a chicken house. Jane Black and Maureen Dawson were waiting for them in the garden on their final trip.

"Can we help?" asked Jane. "What do you plan to do with all this wood? There's tons of it."

"We're going to use the wood for the windows, and to fix up the floorboards, then we are going to nail the wire to these posts." Kevin touched the posts with his foot, "to make a chicken run outside. It's called free-range. And we're going to put some of the wire on the upstairs window to stop the pigeons flying off."

"What pigeons?"

"We ain't got them yet."

"Where do you get pigeons from?"

Kevin shuffled, wagging his head. "I know a man who has pigeons and says he will give me a few, for free."

"That's good. When do you get them?"

"As soon as we fix up the window."

"What about the white mice you told us about. When do you get them?"

"Hmm," Kevin mumbled, reluctantly, "we've given up on mice breeding for the time being. We'll get the chicks from Thornberry's chickens next week. Come on then, girls, you dig a hole there, there and there." He pointed to where he wanted the posts to go. "About a foot deep."

Jane and Maureen eagerly set about digging holes in the overgrown garden, while Kevin and Tom nailed the timber slats onto the old window frames. After toiling all afternoon, the chicken wire had been tacked to the posts and the ground floor lounge window had been secured.

"Tomorrow, we'll fix the lounge door and finish off the first-floor windows and floorboards."

The four youngsters stood around in the late afternoon light admiring their work.

"What are you doing tonight?" Maureen asked.

"We're going to the flicks."

"Oh, so are we. We want to see, 'Mr. Smith Goes to Washington' with James Stewart at the Hipp. Are you going to the Hippodrome cinema?"

"No, we're going to the Olympia to see Tom Mix in 'Destry Rides Again.' I've seen it before, it's one of my favourite cowboy movies. I'm going to be a cowboy one day."

"A cowboy? How?" Jane asked. "Cowboys are in America."

"Are they? I didn't know that. Well in that case I'll have to go to America."

Jane glanced at Maureen and raised her eyebrow slightly. "Shall we go to the Olympia instead?"

Maureen screwed up her nose, "if you want, but I'm not keen on cowboy and indian films."

"Shall we go to the flicks together?" Jane asked the boys.

Kevin looked at Tom and nodded. "Yes, okay. Tell you what, because you helped us today, we'll go with you to the Hipp to see James Stewart."

"Oh, great. Alright, meet us outside the Hippodrome at seven. See you later."

The girls walked off to their house for tea, giggling and whispering to each other as they went.

Kevin and Tom watched them go.

"I've never been to the flicks with a girl before," Tom said.

"Neither have I," Kevin said. "I'm not sure what to do. I can't pay for them."

~ * ~ * ~ * ~

The January night sky was moonless. The blackout added to the darkness of the streets. Kevin and Tom peered over the allotment boundary wall.

"All clear?"

"Yeah, I think so."

They had been watching the allotment for nearly half an hour.

"Come on then."

They climbed over the wall, bending over, they hurried between the vegetable plots towards Flogger Links' and Stig Marron's pigeon loft. At the door Kevin pulled a small crowbar from a sack. Looking over his shoulder to make sure nobody was watching, he jemmied off the lock. The door creaked open. Inside, the birds were cooing in their boxes, not afraid of the intruders.

"Open the sack," Kevin said to Tom.

Tom opened the sack, holding it out. Kevin carefully lifted the first bird off its perch and placed it in the sack. He repeated the operation shoving a total of 6 birds in the sack, one on top of the other. By this time the pigeons were restless flapping around in the overcrowded sack.

"I'll carry the sack. You get the rifle."

Tom lifted the air rifle off a shelf.

"Come on, let's go."

"I'm scared," Tom breathed.

"So am I."

The two boys retraced their steps across the allotment. At the boundary wall they checked that the coast was clear. All the streetlamps were turned off for the duration of the war; no one moved on the road. They climbed back over the wall. Kevin hurried along the road with the large heavy sack over his shoulder, almost dragging on the road, Tom tagged on behind trying to hide the rifle inside his coat.

"You look like a robber with a bag of swag over your shoulder."

"Yeah," Kevin giggled.

By the time they reached Stansfield's old house Kevin was exhausted. Tommy unlocked the padlock on the front door and they hurried inside, eager to have a look at the pigeons and examine the air rifle.

The newly fixed lounge door was also locked with a padlock. The padlock and hinges, oiled by Jane earlier, opened easily.

"Come on, shut the door behind you."

The room was as black as night. Tommy flashed his torch; Kevin struck a match and lit the candles. Kevin opened the sack to release the birds. They flew everywhere dive bombing the boys who ducked to avoid being hit. Eventually the birds settled on the floorboards cooing.

After checking out the air rifle, Kevin said, "Flogger won't be shooting any more of his pigeons with this... Hide it up the chimney, just in case the coppers come around."

Tom shoved the air rifle up the chimney.

"Tomorrow, after school, we'll cut off the rings so they can't be identified and get some bird food and some pellets for the air rifle. Come on, Tommy, let's lock up. I'll come back here after school and put the chicken wire on the upstairs window, then we can build some nesting boxes and keep our pigeons up there. There's nowt else we can do here, it's getting late. Come on Tommy, let's go home."

The boys locked up the house and started walking down the street.

"Did you like the picture, last night? Mister do-dah goes to Hollywood."

"No, not really."

"I saw you put your arm around Maureen. Did you kiss her?"

"No, I wanted to, but I didn't dare. Did you kiss Jane?"

"No, but I did hold her hand. She asked me if I would take her to the Church Hall dance, next Saturday."

"Will you?"

"Yeah, why not. I can't dance though."

They arrived at Princess Street.

"See you, Kev."

"Yeah, see you, Tommy."

Kevin and Tom parted. Kevin made his way home, thinking about Jane and pigeons.

~ * ~ * ~ * ~

Monday morning Flogger Links and Stig Marron were absent from class. Kevin looked over at the empty seats and grinned. He gave Tom a thumbs up, Tom acknowledged.

Looking up from the register, Mr Parkinson asked, "does anyone know where Links and Marron are?"

"They go and feed their pigeons in the morning, sir," Durkin called.

"That's no excuse for being late." Parkinson annotated the register. "Right, boys, take out your maths book."

By 9.30 the absentees were still absent. Kevin frowned, feeling nervous. 'I'm so dead, if they find out it was me who stole their pigeons', he thought.

At 10am the classroom door literally burst open. Links charged into the classroom, followed closely by Marron. Flogger Links' brutal face was red with rage. Marron's rat-like face screwed up in revulsion.

"Sir! We've been robbed!"

"Hold on, Links, Marron. Don't just burst in here like a couple of angry bulls. Where do you think you are?"

Links was unapologetic. "We've been fuckin' robbed."

There was a gasp around the classroom. The F word was never used in this school.

Tommy hung his head, "Oh my God," he whispered to Fife. "If they ever find out it was us, they'll kill us both. Marron would use his father's fish-filleting knife to skin us alive." Tommy was now having second thoughts about the night raid on the pigeon coop.

Kevin, sensing Tom's apprehension, whispered, "don't worry, Tommy. No one saw us,"

"Calm down, Links. Calm down," Parkinson called again above the hubbub of chatter. "Who has robbed you and what have they taken?"

"Sir, I don't know who, but some bastard broke into our pigeon coop last night and stole all our pigeons. All of them. And Bongo Blue, my prize bird. If I find out who did it, I'll kill the bastard."

"Links, if I hear you swearing again, I'll add insult to injury and cane you. Both of you. So, calm down, and tell me again what happened."

"Sir, when we went to feed the birds this morning, the coop door lock had been smashed off and all our birds, all 10 of them had gone."

Kevin glanced at Tom with a furrowed brow knowing that they had only taken 6 birds. They couldn't fit any more in the sack.

"And my air rifle, too," Marron added. "That's been stolen."

"Also, sir, one of the old geezers on the allotment said someone had stolen his son's fence."

"Fence?"

"Yes, sir. A fence around his son's chicken hut."

"It's the war," Parkinson lamented. "Nothing is sacred nowadays. But stealing a fence, well that's going too far. I've never heard of that before."

"Well, anyway, sir, the police are onto it."

Kevin's head dropped. *'My mum's going to kill me if the police find out it's me,'* he thought.

"Alright, boys, sit down. Take out your arithmetic exercise book."

Links sat down still chuntering about the bastard who had stolen his pigeons. The lesson and school day continued with Flogger and Stig exaggerating to all and sundry what they would do to the thief or thieves who had robbed them of 10 birds.

~ * ~ * ~ * ~

Monday evening was Tommy's turn to babysit his toddler sister while his mum and dad went to the pictures. Kevin worked alone nailing the wire mesh to the front bedroom window. Satisfied that the windows were secure, he captured each pigeon and released it in the bedroom. The six birds cooed and pecked at the floorboards. He glanced out of the window and recoiled in horror when he saw Police Constable Brownley peddling towards Cobden House.

PC Brownley dismounted and peered through the garden gate, he pushed the gate open. Inside the garden he checked the posts holding the wire mesh. He shook one of the posts.

"Hm, na'then," Brownley murmured to himself, nodding his head. "What do we have here?" He checked out the timber slats boarding up the front room window and looked up at the wire mesh covering the upstairs window frame.

Kevin pulled away from the window hoping the Bobby hadn't seen him. Kevin's heart missed a beat when he heard the front door squeak open.

"Anyone there?" called the Bobby.

Fife didn't answer.

"'Ello, 'ello. Anyone there?" Brownley opened the lounge door looking inside.

The policeman then slowly and carefully climbed the stairs. Halfway up, he drew his truncheon just in case there were gypsies trespassing.

"'Ello, anyone there?" he called again.

Kevin froze in terror. He had no choice but to answer.

"Hello, it's only me," he squeaked.

Relieved, Brownley put his truncheon back in his pocket.

"Who's there? Who's me?"

Kevin appeared on the landing.

"Well, well, if it isn't young Fife. What mischief are you up to now, Fife? What are you doing in this house?"

"I've got permission from Mr Stansfield. He said I could use it to keep chickens."

"Chickens? What chickens? Where are these chickens now?"

"I'm getting them next week. We're going to keep them downstairs. Come and look." Kevin pointed down the stairs trying to edge past the policeman.

"Not so fast, my boy. What are you doing upstairs? Why have you put chicken wire on the upstairs window?"

"Err, just in case."

"Just in case, what?"

"Just in case we…we use it for something."

"We, who's 'we'?"

"Me an' Tommy."

"Would that be Tommy Daggers?"

"Hmm…Yes."

"Hmm, two little tearaways. I told you two last year to keep out of trouble or I would lock you up for the night. Breaking greenhouse windows and stealing pears from the vicar's garden is a serious crime, you know, especially in wartime."

"It wasn't war time then."

"Don't be cheeky, young Fife." Brownley hesitated, listening.

"*Coo, coo.*"

The Bobbies eyebrow furrowed; he shoved his helmet further back on his head.

"Na'then. What's that I hear?"

"*Coo, coo.*"

"Cooing! Come on, Mr Fife, let's look what you have been up to upstairs."

Kevin's heart sank as Constable Brownley gently moved him to one side.

"Well, well, well. What have we got here? Pigeons!" Brownley said when he went inside the bedroom. "You didn't tell me you were keeping pigeons, too."

"Err, yes," Kevin stammered. "Err…no."

"Where did you get these birds from?"

"They are wild pigeons, sir."

"Wild pigeons." Brownley repeated. "How long have you had these wild pigeons then?"

"I dunno, a bit, two weeks or so," Kevin lied.

"Two weeks. Then they will now be homing pigeons."

"Homing pigeons, what's homing pigeons?"

"That means, when you let them out, they will come back here to their home coop."

"Oh, yeah, I suppose they will."

"Na'then, young Fife. You know why I'm here, don't you?"

"No, sir." Kevin said innocently.

"Well, there's been some robberies in the village this weekend. Someone has stolen all the pigeons from a coop on the allotments, and… someone has stolen a fence."

"A fence?"

"Yes, a wooden fence and some chicken wire." The policeman tugged at the chicken wire covering the window opening. Where did you buy this mesh?"

"I found it, Constable Brownley."

"You found it. You found it before it was lost, I think."

"No, the wire was just thrown away. I thought it was okay to take it."

"During my investigations into these serious crimes this morning," Brownley said slowly and importantly, "I was told by a man, that he saw two boys with a trolley, loaded up with timber, and wire, making their way towards this house. Would that be you, Fife, and young Daggers?"

"No, only me. I thought the fence was no good, rotten and not wanted." Kevin admitted.

"So, you brought all this wire and wood here on your own, did you?"

"Yes, on my trolley."

"So, Tommy Daggers didn't help you with the fence?"

"He helped me put up the fence, I told him I'd found the wood and stuff over on Tipside. You know, where that old hen hut is. The fence was all broken and lying around. I didn't think anyone would mind."

"Well, Mrs Clegg minds, she said the fence and the hen hut belongs to her son and he'll want it when he gets back from the war. So, my lad, as far as the law is concerned you stole the fence."

"Sorry, I didn't know."

The constable looked around at the cooing pigeons. "If I open this window and let the birds out, they should come back here?"

Kevin wagged his head reluctantly. "Yes, I suppose they will."

"Let's try it then." PC Brownley pulled and tugged at the mesh until it came away in his hands. He cornered one pigeon and picked it up professionally. "I used to keep pigeons when I was a lad." He took the bird to the window and released it. The bird flew directly towards the municipal allotments. "Hmm. Well, lad, it looks like it's not 'homing' back here, does it?"

Kevin shook his head reluctantly and murmured, "no."

One by one, Brownley released all the other birds. They all followed the first bird to the coop on the allotment.

"I think you'd better come with me to the police station, young Fife. I think you have a lot of explaining to do. Your mum and dad are not going to be too pleased that you have been locked up again. A right little tearaway you are becoming."

PC Brownley, pushing his bicycle, escorted the crestfallen Fife through the darkening streets to the police station.

The sergeant behind the desk towered above Fife. Kevin noted his chest full of medals from the Great War.

"Na'then, Mr Fife," the sergeant said, annotating the charge sheet. "We are charging you with, 'stealing a fence.' What do you say about that?"

"I didn't steal it, Sergeant Bullock, I thought it was no good, left to rot. I was going do it up and paint it and breed chickens. You know, for the war effort."

"A likely story. And what about the pigeons? Did you steal them too?

"No, sir. I found them in Mr Stansfield's garden. I thought they were wild so, I kept them… for safe keeping."

"Another likely story, Fife. Who else was involved in this crime?"

"No one else, Sergeant Bullock. I only found them this evening. In the garden. They followed me into the house."

"So now you are the Pied Piper of pigeons, are you?

"Sir, I don't know what you mean."

"Well, little Kevin Fife. We are going to lock you up 'til your mum and dad come to collect you. Then you can explain yourself to the Magistrates on Wednesday morning."

Sergeant Bullock waved Kevin away from the desk. "Lock him up, Constable Brownley."

PC Brownley led the boy away to the cell, gently shoved him inside and slammed the door shut. Kevin Fife, with tears glistening in his eyes sat on the hard bed totally deflated. All his dreams of breeding chickens for the war effort ruined.

Mrs Florrie Fife, wearing a brown overcoat, sat in the waiting room of the Magistrates Court. Her handbag placed on her knees. Sitting beside her, dressed in his Sunday best clothes, his hair plastered down with Vaseline, Kevin swung his legs nervously.

"I never thought it would come to this, Kevin," she whined. "You in court… and your dad sticking up for you. Whatever will the neighbours think?"

"I've done nowt wrong, mum. I was only trying to help the war effort. Why are they taking so long? We've been sitting here for over an hour."

"Your dad and Miss Frost are in there talking to the magistrates."

"Miss Frost! Why is Frosty in there?

"For some reason she is talking on your behalf as a character witness. Miss Frost was a magistrate herself and she knows the Board and she knows the Chairman of the Bench."

"Kevin Fife!" the court usher called.

Kevin held his hand up.

"Follow me, lad."

"Good luck, Kevin," Mrs Fife called after her son. "Don't forget your manners. You are a good boy. Look the magistrates in the eye when you speak and don't mumble."

"Yes, Mum."

The usher led Kevin through a door marked 'Juvenile Court'. Kevin looked around at the oak panelling and then at the three stern looking magistrates. He saw his dad and Miss Frost sitting in the public gallery. Kevin waved to his dad and nodded to Miss Frost.

"Kevin Fife," started the Clerk of the Court. "You are charged with stealing a fence."

"I didn't steal it, sir. I thought…"

The Clerk held up his hand to silence Kevin. The Clerk turned to speak to the chairman. They spoke for almost five minutes.

The chairman of the Juvenile Board Bench looked over his half-moon glasses at Kevin.

"Master Fife, we have examined the charge sheet, I have listened to your father, who is a good working man of good and sound character, and I have listened to your schoolteacher, Miss Frost, who I know personally. They speak highly of you. However, I disagree with them that the offences were just harmless mischiefs and that you didn't knowingly steal the fence. This is not the first time you have been in trouble with the law. First, it was setting fire to Farmer Davies' field."

"Sir. I didn't set fire to his field, my camp fire set…"

"Don't interrupt me, Fife. As I was saying, you broke into the vicarage grounds to steal pears and vandalised the vicar's greenhouse. And now you have stolen a fence."

Kevin shook his head. "Ah…"

"I said, don't interrupt me," the chairman of the bench said irritably. "You say the fence was broken down and just rubbish. Well Mrs Clegg says differently, she says there was nothing wrong with her son's fence. Her son, by the way, is in France fighting the Germans. Indeed, my colleague Miss Webster here," he indicated the sour faced matronly woman sitting on his right, "who walks her dogs passed the hen houses every day, also said, there was nothing wrong with the fence."

He paused, wagging his finger at Kevin. "As you can see, young Fife, these petty crimes are getting ever more serious, arson, malicious ignition of a field, stealing pears, vandalism and now vandalising and stealing a fence. And we," the magistrate indicated his colleagues on each side of him. "We believe that you are on the road to crime and we need to stop it now before you commit a more serious crime in the future. We have carefully examined your case, Fife. You are clearly not in need of care or protection; however, we feel that you are becoming beyond parental control…"

"That's not true," shouted Kevin's father from the gallery, looking furious. "Kevin is…"

"Silence in court," called the Clerk. "Sit down, Mr Fife."

The magistrate waited until Kevin's father sat back down. "There are ways we can deal with you. One, we can have you taken down to the cells below and have the court's constable give you six strokes of the birch."

Kevin winced at that suggestion.

The magistrate continued, "We can send you off to a correction house or send you for Borstal training." The magistrate let the suggestions sink in before continuing. "There is a fourth option…we can put you in the care of a 'Fit Person'. As you are now 14 years of age, you are old enough for full time employment. We understand from your father and Miss Frost you wish to join the Merchant Navy when you leave school this summer. Therefore, under the terms of the Children and Young Persons Act 1933 we have determined that the Fit Person in your case is the Merchant Navy. We are going to send you tó the Merchant Navy's training ship as a boy seaman. You will go to sea as a deck-boy for a year. Then, it will be up to you should you wish to continue at sea as a career. Therefore, Master Fife," the chairman looked down and read from his notes, "it is the decision of the juvenile board that in your best interest, you report to the Merchant Navy Federation at

Mann Island Liverpool, on Wednesday 31st January, for a medical examination. You will be given railway warrant for you to travel down to Arcaster to begin training on the approved school training ship *Cromwell*. That is the final decision of this board. Good luck, Fife. Keep out of trouble. I don't want to see you back here in one year's time. If you ever come before me again, I will not hesitate in sending you to Borstal."

The magistrate nodded to the Clerk. "Thank you, Mr Thomas. Case closed."

With his future determined, Kevin thanked the bench and returned to his mum and dad waiting for him in the waiting room.

~ * ~ * ~ * ~

Sitting in the back pew of Christ the King church, Kevin and Tommy waited for the choir entrance procession. Tommy leant over and whispered, "we don't see you in here so often, Kev, it's a wonder the roof doesn't fall in on us."

"What you mean, not so often? I come at Christmas, Easter and I came to my aunty Maud's funeral, what more do you want? Anyway, my mum said I better get on friendlier terms with the Lord, before I go off to sea."

"Oh, I thought it might be something to do with seeing Jane Black again."

Tommy was interrupted as the organist struck up, '*Praise to the Lord, the Almighty*', as the entrance procession began. The choir was being led by a young girl carrying a cross and another girl carrying the heavy bible. As Jane passed Kevin's pew, she looked up from her hymn sheet and gave him a smile. Likewise, Maureen gave Tommy a friendly glance too as she passed by, both girls singing lustily. Kevin and Tommy, both looking embarrassed, smiled back at the blue and white robed choristers.

The service dragged on for Kevin, he had promised Jane he would attend the service and meet up with her afterwards. They had arranged to meet in the bell ringing chamber, just above the church porch entrance. After the vicar's blessing, the congregation filed out of the church. Kevin and Tommy hung back, waiting until the last of the parishioners, old Mrs Wills, had shuffled out to chat with the vicar. As soon as they were alone in the porch, Kevin and Tommy nipped through the arched doorway and up the tight spiral stone staircase to the bell-ringing chamber above.

Kevin looked up at the bell ropes disappearing through the ceiling up to the belfry, high above in the clock tower. "I'd have been a bell ringer too, but I couldn't reach the bell rope," Kevin lamented.

"That's what them boxes are for, to stand on," Tommy said, pointing to the wooden boxes. "I miss ringing the changes. It's a pity the war has put a stop to that. We can now only ring the bells if there is an invasion."

"Um, yes, that's right. Have you ever been up there?" Kevin pointed upwards.

"No, never, it's strictly out of bounds."

"Shush, I think the girls are coming."

Jane and Maureen climbed the spiral staircase to join the boys. They had changed out of their cotta and cassocks to black gabardines, woolly hats, scarves and gas mask boxes slung around their shoulders with string.

"I'm glad you came to church today," Jane said to Kevin. "I said a prayer for you that you will be safe when you go off to sea. What time do you leave on Wednesday?"

"Six-o-clock train to Liverpool."

"Can I come and see you off?"

"Yes, sure if you want to." Kevin looked up at the ceiling hatch. "I was just asking Tommy, if he'd ever been up the bell tower. Have you ever been up there?"

"No, you are joking. Dad would never allow me up there, it's too dangerous. The timber ladders are over 200 years old and not safe. It's only the verger and a few others allowed up there."

"I fancy climbing up to look at the bells."

"Me too, I've always wanted to see the bells I've been ringing," Tommy said enthusiastically.

"I don't know, it's out of bounds."

"Aw, come on, let's climb up."

"You'll get me in trouble."

"No, I won't. How about you, Maureen?"

Maureen looked nervously at the wooden raking ladder leading 15 feet up to a hatch in the ceiling. "It's too high, I'm scared of heights. Do you want to climb up there, Jane?"

Jane hesitated, "I wouldn't mind. I'd like to see the bells."

"Come on then, I'll climb up and open the hatch," offered Kevin.

Kevin carefully climbed up the steep raking ladder. He pushed open the trap-door and climbed into the tower. Looking down, he called to the girls, "come on, it's easy."

"Go on, you go first," Tommy said to the girls.

"No! You'll look up my dress at my knickers." Maureen said coyly.

Tommy blushed. "No, I won't. I don't want to see your knickers. Come on then, I'll go first."

Tommy climbed the ladder and joined Kevin through the hatch. Jane climbed up next closely followed by Maureen. The four youngsters stared up at the ropes leading up to the belfry.

Kevin began to climb the old staircase. He tested the handrail. "Be careful, the handrail is a bit rickety."

The three carefully followed Kevin until all four were standing on the belfry platform looking at the circle of bells.

"Wow," Kevin counted the bells. "There are ten bells. Why are they all upside down?"

"It's called the 'up position'," Tommy said. "Makes it easier to start the peal, I suppose."

"Why ten bells?" Kevin lowered his voice and whispered to Tommy, "is that where the expression, 'Knocking ten bells of shit out of someone' comes from?"

Tommy giggled, "no, anyway I think it's seven bells." He then asked Jane, "why are there ten bells, Jane?"

"My dad has told me all about bells," Jane said importantly. "Bell ringing is a Christian tradition. One, to summons the faithful to prayer, you know, like for the Angelis, but another reason is to scare away evil spirits."

"Evil spirits?"

"Yes, like the devil and witches. The more bells, the louder and wider afield the sound. You can hear our ten bells all over the village, keeping us all safe from evil spirits."

"Yes, my mum told me about witches," Maureen added. "Many years ago, some villages in Germany would have church bells rung all night to keep witches away."

"All night long!? Crikey, that would drive me nuts listening to church bells all night long." Kevin pointed up at the hatch opening onto the tower roof. "I'm going on the roof to look around."

"There's nothing up there except the flag pole."

"I'm going up anyway, I bet you can see for miles."

Without waiting for the others, Kevin climbed the wood ladder leading up to the tower roof. Pushing open the trap door, he climbed out onto the tower roof. Standing by the parapet, Kevin could see for miles. He was shortly joined by the other three. The four looked out over the town and the snow-covered moors in the distance, pointing out various landmarks.

"There's the Hippodrome; over there is my house." Kevin walked around the tower.

"Be careful, Kevin. Don't fall over."

Kevin looked down at the graveyard. "My aunty Maud's grave is down there."

Jane came up to his side, they both looked down on the graves. They could see Reverend Black talking to two of his parishioners by the lychgate.

"Don't let my father see us up here, he'd go mad."

Kevin was pleasantly surprised when Jane took hold of his hand. They said nothing, both lost in their own thoughts.

Eventually, Jane said, "I'm going to miss you, Kevin. Please stay safe at sea, I don't want you to get washed overboard."

"I'll be alright. The war will be over soon."

"Erm, I hope so. Come on, let's go down before the verger locks up the church."

Kevin took a final look around the village. "Okay, let's go."

The four climbed down the raking ladder to the belfry.

"Shall I tip the bell over," Kevin joked as he passed the pivotal beam.

"Don't you dare, the village will think the Germans have invaded."

"Just watch this bannister, it's wonky." Kevin said, pushing on the handrail. Suddenly the timber gave way and Kevin crashed through over a 60-foot drop to the floor below. All four screamed as the bannister gave way. Kevin yelled out, grasping for one of the bell ropes. He caught hold of the rope, swinging to and fro. The bell above tipped over clanging loudly, the bell rope lifting him up and then dropping him down then lifting him up again, the bell clanged again; Kevin clung on for dear life.

"Help me," Kevin cried.

"Grab hold of that rope, Kev," Tommy called. "Then swing towards me.

Kevin reached out for the bell rope nearest the gantry. He took hold of one rope letting go of the other. The second bell rope dropped six feet tipping a second bell from the up-position. The bell resounded deafeningly, Kevin still swinging around in circles unable to reach Tommy's hand.

"Help, I can't hang on here much longer."

"Maureen! Run down and pull the rope across so I can reach Kevin," Tommy called.

Maureen ran down the steps to the bottom. Looking at the ten bell ropes, she hesitated, wondering which one to pull. Taking hold of the nearest rope, she pulled it over to the left, this turned out to be the wrong rope. This rope tipped the third bell over, the bell above rang out loudly. On the second attempt she found the rope that Kevin was swinging on and pulled it to the side. Tommy caught hold of the rope pulling Kevin towards the gantry. Kevin climbed back onto the landing.

"Oh my god! The whole town must have heard the bells. They will think the German army have landed."

"Sorry. The rail gave way. I thought I was gunna get killed."

"You would have been if you didn't catch the rope. How did you manage that?"

"I don't know, if I was as fat as Durkin I would have dropped like a stone. Look at my hands, rope burns."

Jane looked sympathetically at the rope burns. "Come on, let's get out of here, quickly."

As they reached the floor above the ringing chamber, they heard voices below.

"Oh no, it's my father and the verger."

"Shush, keep quiet. They may not come up here."

The four youngsters lay flat on the floorboards, Kevin peeping through the rope holes in the floor.

The vicar and verger looked up at the ceiling. "There's no one here."

Kevin's heart missed a beat when he heard the vicar say, "go up top and check it out, see what's happened."

"Must I? My hips are giving me jip this morning," moaned the verger. "It's the cold you know, plays havoc with my arthritis."

Kevin, in a panic, pointed upwards, whispering, "they are coming up, I think. Let's go back up to the roof."

Jane and Maureen nodded and started back up the steps. The four sprinted quickly on tiptoes hardly making a sound. No sooner had they all climbed through the hatch onto the roof, the ringing chamber trap-door opened. Kevin watched the fat verger struggle to squeeze through the hatch.

"The verger is jammed in the hatch." Kevin peeped down again.

He heard the verger calling, "pull me down, pull me down. Aarghh, mind my legs."

"I don't think they'll climb up here now," Kevin said with relief. He closed the roof hatch and sat on it.

Jane began to giggle.

"What's so funny?" Kevin asked, looking up at Jane and raising his eyebrow.

"You, swinging on the bell rope like Tarzan of the Apes."

"I didn't think it was funny, I could have been killed. Shush, listen."

Excited voices could be heard coming from the churchyard below. Kevin and Jane crept to the parapet and peeped over.

"Oh, my goodness," Jane spluttered. "It looks like the LDV have turned out."

"That's Mr Cunliffe… He's in charge of the 'Look, Duck and Vanish' brigade."

"Yes, I've never seen him looking so excited. He's going to have a heart attack."

Cunliffe was joined outside by the vicar, who had left the church to calm down the agitated leader of the Local Defence Volunteers.

"No, Mr Cunliffe it's a false alarm."

The trespassers up on the church tower could hear the vicar assuring Cunliffe that the Germans had not invaded and the bells must have turned over accidentally.

The vicar, the verger and Cunliffe walked down the path towards the lychgate. A small crowd of children had gathered by the church hall waiting for Sunday School.

"I think they are leaving," Jane said. "My mum is running the Sunday School this morning… dad will be helping her. Come on, the church door will be locked. We can leave by the vestry; they won't see us leave through the back door."

Kevin, Tommy and Maureen followed Jane back down the stairs, through the nave to the vestry back door.

"It's a good job they didn't climb up to the belfry they'd have seen the broken bannister and caught us on the roof."

The four began laughing with relief, just in time to see two more LDV men hurrying to join their leader at the church gate.

~ * ~ * ~ * ~

At the Blackstone railway station, Kevin, standing with a small brown cardboard suitcase in his hand, was waiting for the train to take him to Liverpool. He still wore short pants, a tight-fitting jacket fastened with a single button, a schoolboy's cap, and a wool scarf wrapped several times around his neck. His gas mask box was slung around his shoulder. A small group of people stood around him. His mum and dad, Tommy Daggers, Maureen Dawson and Jane Black, the vicar's daughter.

Tommy, in a rare display of affection, gave Kevin a quick hug.

"Thanks, Kev. Thanks for keeping me out of trouble, you're a real pal. You know how my dad is, he'd have given me a real belting if I had gone to court. I wish my dad was like your dad; he never seems to get mad at you."

"That's okay, Tommy, I know how your dad gets mad. My dad says he wasn't like that before the last war. When he came back from the trenches, my dad said he'd changed. Shell shock is terrible; don't be too angry at your dad. Anyway, I think I got away lightly, I've always wanted to join the Merchant Navy and now I am doing."

The train to Liverpool came steaming into the station covering everyone in steam and smoke as the train squealed to a halt.

Jane rushed to embrace Kevin. "I'm going to miss you, Kevin. Thanks for taking me to the pictures and to the dance. I'll teach you dancing next time your home. Will you take me again when you get back home?"

Kevin's face lit up in a smile. "Yes, sure, if you want me to."

To Kevin's astonishment, Jane kissed him on the lips. "Bye, Kevin, be safe at sea. I'm going to say a prayer for you every single day."

"Come on, Kevin," said his dad. "Say goodbye to your mother."

Mrs Fife opened her arms wide to embrace her son. "Farewell, my boy. Be safe. Write to me every week. We shall all miss you," Florrie Fife sobbed. "My boy is too young to be going off to war. He's only 14." Tears streamed down her face.

"Bye, Kev," Maureen called. "When you get back, we will all get together for a party. Summer 1941 is going to be the best summer ever."

"So long, pal," said Tommy. "Here, take this, a present for you." He pressed a gift into Kevin's hand. "Keep this for good luck."

Kevin looked at his hand, there was a silver star with the word SHERIFF embossed across it. Kevin knew it was one of Tommy's favourite items.

"Oh, thanks, Tommy." Kevin looked again at the tin star. "Yeah, thanks, I'll keep it for good luck, it'll remind me of the times we played cowboys and indians down on the Tipside. Happy days…"

The steam train let out a scream of steam and smoke.

"All aboard," the porter called.

Kevin slipped the imitation sheriff's badge into his pocket and climbed up into the carriage.

Jimmy Fife turned to his wife. "I'll sign the agreement in the shipping federation on his behalf and see him off safely to Arcaster, I should be home tomorrow dinner time." He followed Kevin into the carriage.

The carriage door slammed shut and the train pulled out of the station. Kevin hung out of the open carriage window waving to his mum and his friends. The platform disappeared out of sight, leaving two crying girls, a heartbroken mother and a sad cowboy waving goodbye.

CHAPTER 2

HAVING SPENT THE NIGHT IN the Gordon Smith Institute for Seamen accommodation for sailors, not much better than a doss house, Kevin and his father stood amongst the throng of soldiers, sailors and airmen crowded on the platform of Liverpool's Exchange Station. The early morning train to Crewe belched out steam and smoke.

"I'm glad I passed my medical to be on deck, Dad. I didn't want to be a cabin boy."

"Well, if that's what you want, Kevin, just don't fall overboard. I don't want you to be swept off the deck in rough weather."

"I won't."

"All aboard," called the red flag carrying porter interrupting Kevin.

Kevin's dad looked down the platform at the engine, fighting back tears.

"Take good care of yourself, son. Write to your mum, let us know how you are doing. Your mum loves you, you know. She says you are too young to be going off to sea in wartime."

Kevin, noticing the tears in his father's eyes, gave his father a hug. "Thanks for everything, Dad. I'll be alright; the radio said the war will soon be over. Then it will be good at sea. Just like granddad used to say."

"Alright, boy. Get yourself aboard and we'll see you soon."

Kevin boarded the train, leaving his sad father on the platform. He waved at him through the carriage window. Fighting back his own tears, he found himself a seat in the overcrowded train. The train chuffed slowly out of the station.

"Excuse me, can I sit there?" A gangling youth asked.

"Yeah, sure." Kevin budged along the bench seat to allow the boy to sit down."

"Thanks, I saw you at the Federation. Was that your grandfather with you?"

Kevin wasn't bothered about people mistaking his fifty-five-year-old father for his grandfather. "No, he's my dad."

"Oh, I'm sorry. I didn't mean to be rude."

"That's alright."

"I'm going to the *TS Cromwell*. Are you going to the *Crommie*?"

"Yeah, I wonder how long it will take us to get there."

"All day I expect." The boy checked his itinerary. "Change at Crewe for Norwich, then another train to Arcaster Harbour. What's your name?"

"Kevin."

"Hello, Kevin, I'm Hector." He held his hand out to shake.

Kevin didn't know anyone at home called Hector nor had he ever met a boy who wanted to shake his hand before. Kevin got the impression that Hector was a 'posh boy'.

"What department are you joining?" Hector asked. "I'm going to be a cabin boy, or maybe a galley boy. My father is at sea; he told me all about ships and whatnot. What do you know about the *Cromwell*?"

"Nothing really, it's a training ship, that's all I know. I'm going to be a deck boy. I just about managed to pass my eyesight and colour vision test, I thought I'd fail cos I sometimes wear specs for reading." Kevin looked Hector over. He guessed he was the same age, about 14 or 15. 5 foot 9 inches tall with a poor complexion. His clothes looked good quality but getting threadbare. Hector wore thick lens glasses. "The magistrates told me the ship had been moved from the Thames to Arcaster to avoid the bombing. That's all I know."

"The magistrates! Oh, I say. Have you been a naughty boy? Have they sent you off to sea for punishment?

'*Oh, I say!*' The lads I know never say, '*Oh, I say*' or '*naughty boy*', Kevin thought. He said quietly, "I got into a spot of bother," not wanting to articulate his thoughts.

"Well, I do know a bit of the ship's history," Hector said. "The Marine Superintendent at Mann Island, who knows my father, told me that it's an old sailing ship, that's been converted for training seamen. The boys on it are aged between 14 and 16. Also, do you know the *Crommie, Cromwell*, was a training ship for German submariners during the last war? It wasn't called *Cromwell* then; it had a German name, *Bremen Harben*, I think."

"Wow, no, I didn't know that. I hope they didn't train them too well. The men on the U-boats at sea now will have been trained on our training ship."

"Yes, ironic, isn't it?"

Kevin's brows furrowed; he didn't understand what 'ironic' meant. He got the feeling that Hector was educated to a much higher standard than himself. Hector spoke well, with just a trace of the Manchester accent.

"You will be shipping out of Liverpool, I guess.

So will I. I don't want to ship out of Manchester. My father is a captain on the Manchester boats and I don't want to be sailing with him."

"A captain! Why do you want to be a steward?"

"Steward, seaman, officer cadet, they are all the same to me. I just wanted to get away from Rossall. Anyway, my eyesight isn't good. I'm not A1 for the forces."

"Who's Ross Hall?"

"Rossall, It's a school in Lancashire. A public school. I'll be at the *Crommie* 12 weeks like you. Apparently, before the war, steward's training was only 8 weeks but because of the war, we also get extra training. The superintendent at Liverpool said we will be doing extra lifeboat drills; firefighting, damage control and we'll have a spell on the Oerlikon gun."

"Oerlikon gun, what's that?"

"I think it's an anti-aircraft gun. We might be called upon to use one. My father is a trained gunner from the last war. He trained at *HMS Drake* at Devonport. Dad says we will be arming merchant ships with AA and 4-inch naval guns. That's the nearest I'll ever get to shooting at the enemy with my poor eyesight."

Kevin sat back pondering on having to shoot at the enemy, that had never crossed his mind.

~ * ~ * ~ * ~

At Norwich, the boys changed trains again, taking the train to Arcaster.

"I'm starving," Hector said as he settled down in the carriage. "I missed my breakfast this morning and there was no food at Crewe."

Kevin snapped open his suitcase. "My mum put me up some butties if you want to share them with me?"

"Oh, yes please."

Kevin took out a small tin box and opened it, taking out a cheese sandwich and a piece of fruit cake wrapped up in greaseproof paper.

"They should still be fresh," Kevin said as he gave half the sandwich and half the fruit cake to Hector.

"Oh, thanks very much, Kevin." Hector bit into the sandwich, watching Kevin putting items into the tin. "That's a nice box. Where did you get it?"

"This Christmas. I think my mum and dad bought the toffees before rationing started." Kevin showed the tin to Hector. A picture of King George VI and Queen Elizabeth on the lid. "It's a souvenir of the King's coronation. My Dad said I should keep souvenirs of the places I visit, like a post card or a shell off the beach. I'm going to keep my bits and pieces in it."

Kevin looked into the tin, now empty except for his mother's St Christopher medal, the small silver cross that Jane had given him, Tommy's sheriff silver star and his National Identity Card. He snapped the tin shut and put it back in his suitcase.

On the long journey from Liverpool to Arcaster, Kevin got to know and like Hector. He was more knowledgeable about almost everything than himself; Hector knew a lot more about ships and about the rest of the world than he did, but Hector was not cocky or boastful about his knowledge. Kevin thought Hector was a modest, down to earth person. There appeared to be no airs and graces about this Public Schoolboy.

~ * ~ * ~ * ~

Late in the afternoon, the ancient steam train pulled into Arcaster station.

"Arcaster Harbour… Arcaster Harbour," called the porter.

The carriage doors opened and 24 young boys piled out with their suitcases, bags and army surplus kitbags. Kevin and Hector climbed down from the carriage. The boys mingling on the platform wore a variety of clothing and headwear. The bigger boys wearing long trousers, overcoats, scarves, balaclavas or leather flying helmets; one boy wearing a Scottish kilt with a leather Celtic sporran. Kevin, despite the freezing weather, wore shorts, a jacket with his shirt collar over the jacket collar and a schoolboy's cap. Most of them carried gas mask boxes slung over their shoulders.

An officer from the camp met them at the station.

"All boys going to the training ship *Cromwell* line up here."

The Merchant Navy officer dressed in a naval officer's greatcoat with three faded gold rings on the shoulder and a black peaked cap and a white silk scarf wound twice around his neck.

"Come on, sort yourselves out. Line up here, three-deep. We're going to march to the camp."

None of the boys had any military training, 'three-deep,' meant nothing to them. The officer spent ten minutes sorting them into three ranks.

"When I order, '*Right turn*' everyone will turn to the right. Then, when I call, '*Quick March*' everyone will step off with your left foot... in that direction." He pointed down the road.

Kevin Fife found himself in the middle of some big lads, they all looked well over sixteen or seventeen. Some even looked like men. Kevin had to lean to one side to see the officer.

The officer addressed the boys. "My name is 'Wright-Bussard' and as the name implies, I can be a right bastard. I am the chief mate here at Arcaster. If I shout, 'shit' you all start looking for a shovel. You understand?"

"What the fuck is he on about?" whispered one of the boys at the back, out of Wright-Bussard's hearing.

"Yes, sir," some of the other boys mumbled

"At sea," the officer continued, "especially in wartime, when you are given an order you will obey without question or you might find yourself freezing to death in the North Atlantic without a boat or lifejacket to save you. At the *TS Cromwell,* you will act in a 'seaman like manner' at all times. If you fail to come up to my standards, you will be given a rail warrant and sent packing to where you came from. That will mean Borstal training for some of you, or the army for others. Tomorrow morning, if you are still with us, you will have your photograph taken, you will sign articles of agreement and will be given a Seaman's Discharge Book. That means you will subject to the rules and regulations of the Merchant Navy. Although the *Cromwell*, is an approved school, it is not like the *TS Cornwall* which is a reformatory school ship, here we train you to be a seaman. Nevertheless, the captain here has the power to send any one of you to Borstal or even prison should you break the regulations or commit a civilian crime. Do you all understand?"

"Yes, sir."

"Alright then, lads. Right turn."

Three boys turned to the left; the remainder turned right. The officer waited until everyone faced the same direction.

"By the left, quick, march."

The columns of recruits set off marching in the direction of the training camp. On route they passed a faded sign, '*Arcaster Holiday Park*'.

"Arcaster holiday park?" a boy with a Scottish accent called. "I didna know the sheriffs were sending mi to a holiday camp."

"From what I've 'eard, the *Cromwell* ain't a 'oliday park," another boy with a Cockney accent said.

The first structure Kevin noticed behind the camp fence was an 80-foot-high mast. A massive Red Ensign flying off the yard arm. The column marched, mostly out of step, through the entrance gate, passing the guard house and onto the parade ground.

Kevin looked around at the camp. Although it was getting dark, he could make out some of the old holiday camp buildings. The camp's car park was now the parade ground and the camp reception office had been renamed 'Guard Room'. The line of long timber huts looked fairly new. The holiday chalets were now being used as staff accommodation.

"Right," Wright-Bussard called. "All catering boys fall in over there. All deck boys fall in over here."

Kevin joined the other 11 deck boys. Hector Davis-Davidson joined the catering boys. Once again, Kevin noticed how big some of the boys were. The boy with the Cockney accent, gave Kevin a poke.

"You, you little fucker will get blown over the side in a light breeze." He pointed to Kevin's short trousers. "Still wearing your school pants. Why aren't you in long trousers?"

Kevin, who didn't own a pair of long trousers, ignored him. Instead, he looked over towards the guard room. An elderly man dressed in a different battle-dress style uniform came out of the guard room over to the deck boys. Kevin guessed he'd be well over 60 years old.

Holding a clipboard, the man addressed the boys. "Right, lads, my name is Heygate, I will be your training officer for the next 12 weeks. You will address me as 'Bosun'. Or, Bosun Heygate. Understand?"

"Yes, Bosun," the boys answered.

"Over there is the air raid shelter."

The twelve recruits looked at the shelter.

"In case of a raid, the bugler will sound off, '*Action Stations*' and then the '*Carry on*' for the '*All clear*' signal. You will learn to recognise bugle calls." The bosun looked at his clip board. "Alrighty, tell me your names and where you come from." The bosun pointed to the first boy. The Cockney. "You, loudmouth, what's your name and where you from?"

"Crocker, from 'ackney, 'ackney, London."

"Hackney, a right shit hole, isn't it? You." He pointed to the next boy. "What's your name?"

"Colin, Bosun."

"Colin!" Frowning, the bosun checked his clipboard, "Is that your last name?"

"No, bosun. I'm called Colin Emmitt."

"Surnames only. I'm not your mother," Heygate said sarcastically. "Where you from Emmitt?"

"Well, I'm from Donny."

"Donny? Where's that?"

"Doncaster, bosun, in Yorkshire."

Heygate lifted his eyebrow, pointing at the next boy.

"Riley, frey Glasgie."

"Is that Scottish for 'from Glasgow'?"

Riley nodded, "aye, that's right."

"McGinn, frey Paisley. Scotland."

"Fife from Blackstone, England." Kevin said, when it was his turn.

"Blackstone. Where's that?

"Lancashire, Bosun. Near Manchester."

"How old are you, sunshine?"

"14 and nearly three months, Bosun."

The bosun shook his head slightly, annotating his clipboard.

"We'll be taking 'em from junior school next," he muttered under his breath. He pointed his pencil at the next boy.

"Sutcliffe from Brum, Bosun."

"Brum, where's Brum?" said the bosun, knowing quite well where Brum was.

"Birmingham, Bosun."

"Well then, say Birmingham."

"Jones from Cardiff."

"MacBride from Belfast."

"Belling, I come from Plymouth."

"Griffith from Newport, Wales.

"Millward from Manchester."

"I'm called McGowan and I come from Hull. That's also in England."

"I know where Hull is. I shipped out of Hull for more than 30 years." Bosun Heygate ticked his sheet. "All present and correct. First job, before it gets dark, is to fill your palliasses with straw."

"Sir, Bosun, what's a palli arse?" asked Griffith.

"It's what you sleep on. Better known as a 'Donkeys' Breakfast'."

"Sleeping on a straw mattress, you must be joking?" McGowan complained.

Bosun Heygate said, "alright, chaps, leave your bags here and follow me. No need to march down the slope." He escorted them down to a barn on the dock side. The barn was full of dry straw. Each boy was given a new paillasse. "The more you get in the palliasses the comfier you will be."

Kevin delved into the pile of straw, packing his mattress with as much straw as he could get in.

Carrying the beds above their heads the 12 recruits struggled back to the huts.

"Right, this is your billet," Heygate said. "Take your mattresses inside and find yourself a bunk, there's a pillow and blanket on the bed. You boys will be sleeping here in the camp. Nobody sleeps on the ship. All training will be carried out on the *Cromwell* and in the dock, and later, sailing the cutters in the river. However, everyone eats on the ship. Are you hungry?

"Yeah, I could eat a fuckín' 'orse," Crocker called, grinning at the other boys.

"Cut out that swearing, Crocker. You're not down the Eastend slums now, you blooming Cockney Thames mud digger. It's only me that's allowed to swear. Follow me."

The 12 boys followed the bosun into the hut. Inside the long wooden hut there were two tier bunks on each side. A large potbellied stove already burning was located in centre of the hut. The hut was warm and smelled of floor polish. The windows had been painted black for the blackout.

"I have made a list of who does what to keep this place and the bathroom spotless and who polishes the deck and who keeps the fire lit and so on. This billet is the cleanest on the camp and I expect you to keep it so. Captain's inspection every Sunday after church parade. Right, pick a bunk and put your paillasse on it."

The boys obeyed, scrambling to find the best bed. Kevin decided he'd be better off with the top bunk near the potbellied stove and he made a b-line for it, throwing his straw filled mattress onto the springs.

"I want that top bunk," Harry Millward said to Kevin. "You take the bottom bunk."

"No, I saw it first, *you* take the bottom bunk." he said forcefully, half expecting a clout or an argument from the bigger boy.

Instead, Millward, pursed his lips, furrowed his brow, shrugged and said, "okay, mate, you have it. I'll have the bottom bunk, just don't pee in bed or it will drop through onto me."

"I haven't peed in bed since I was 2 years old."

"Alright... Just don't." Millward walked away to warm his hands on the stove.

McGinn, watching the minor confrontation said, "you know how to stand up fer yoursen, he's twice your size. What's ya name?"

"Kevin, Kevin Fife." Kevin noted the boy was even shorter in height that he was.

"Hello, Kevin. I'm Alex. Alex McGinn. Some folk at home call me 'Wee Jock' cos of me size. Some folk try pushing me around too, but I dinna let them. You've gotta stand up fer yoursen or they will make ya life a misery."

"Yeah, I know what you mean. I got bullied all the time at school, that was until I started standing up for myself. My dad say's the bigger the boy the bigger the baby."

Wee Jock laughed, "aye, the bigger they are the harder they fall."

"I wish I was a bit taller. Some kids back home started calling me Five-foot-Fife, and I'm five foot two and a half."

"Where's haim? Fife's a place in Scotland." Alex had a strong Scottish accent.

"I'm from a place called Blackstone, you won't know it. It's a small town in Lancashire, near the Manchester ship canal. Where you from, are you Irish?"

"Irish? Don't insult me, I'm Scottish. I'm frey Paisley, near Glasgow. On the River Clyde."

"Scotland. Do you know the boy in the kilt?"

"No, he travelled down with us frey Glasgow, he's frey Stornoway up in the Outer Hebrides. I canna understand a word he says. He's got a very strong accent. He's joining the catering department."

"What made you come here?"

"The sheriffs sent me."

"Me too! Well, not the sheriff, the magistrates sent me here. What did you do wrong?"

"Not a lot, playing and messing about on the railway lines, putting a halfpenny on the line to make a penny. I was done for setting fire to a workman's hut. I didna mean to, I overloaded the hut's stove, it got red hot and set fire to the wood walls. It was either join the Merchant Navy or get a birching. My elder brother got birched, he still has 6 white scars on his arse, so I didna fancy that." Alex looked around at the boys settling into the accommodation. "There's some big laddies in here, aye. Rough lookers too. I bet some of them have scars on their arses too…Why were you sent here?"

"The coppers said I stole a fence."

"Stole a fence?"

"Yeah, an old broken-down fence."

"Right, lads," shouted the bosun, interrupting Kevin. "Follow me." He led them across to the ablution block adjoining the sleeping accommodation hut. Inside there were doorless WCs and a long, galvanized iron trough. The place smelled strongly of carbolic soap. "There's no hot water in here. You all better get used to washing in cold water."

"My God, sleeping on straw and washing in cold water," complained Alex

"What's new, I sleep on straw and wash in cold water back home, back in Belfast," said Paddy McBride.

It was clear to Kevin that the new intake was drawn from all parts of the Kingdom. From the far north of Scotland to the south coast of England, Wales and Northern Ireland. Already he had heard a dozen different accents, none he had heard before.

"Make sure you wash and keep yourselves clean," said the bosun. "Dirty smelly boys at sea will soon be thrown in the shower and scrubbed down with a deck brush."

"What's a shower?" Riley asked.

"Don't know," answered Crocker.

"Right, now that you know where you sleep and where you wash, I'll take you down to the ship for your supper. We eat on the ship in two shifts. The older intake eats first, then they clear the mess deck and go on the upper deck. Then it will be your turn to eat, tonight's supper is everyone's favourite... Sea pie. Take no notice of the boys on the upper deck, they may try and taunt you. Just ignore them. Are you all ready to eat?"

"Yes, Bosun," the boys called.

The 12 new recruits for the deck department trooped down the slope from the camp to where the *TS Cromwell* was moored alongside a dock wall.

Kevin looked up at the ship with apprehension. The once proud clipper was now a black hulk, devoid of its masts and riggings. An extra deck had been built over the original main deck. Lining the upper deck were a crowd of lads hanging over the handrails and hurling abuse down at the new entries lining up on the dockside below. The howling mob on the upper deck, all dressed in navy battle-dress, looked more like rioting convicts on a prison ship than trainee sailors. The offensive noise of the chanting boys above, the blasphemous response from the bigger loutish boys crushing around him and the freezing easterly wind blowing off the Wash and North Sea, made Kevin shiver, thinking he had landed in a frozen hell.

"You ain't never going home, new boy," the cadets yelled down and showered those below with spit, green snot and insults.

The boys on the bank were as big and as rough as the boys on the ship. One scruffy boy with a strong Cockney accent, yelled back, shaking his fist at a chanting youth, "I'll effin rip yer effin 'ead off and stick it up yer effin arse."

"I'll tell you what, Jock, life here at the *Crommie* training camp isn't going to be a holiday, is it?"

"I don't think I'm going to like it here," said Hector Davies-Davidson, who had latched onto Kevin and Wee Jock. "It's worse even than a public school, and they are bad enough."

Jock shook his head and flicked some spittle off his coat. "Dirty bastards," he called up to the ranting boys shaking his fist at them. "I'll do ya over if I catch hold of ya who spit on me jacket."

"Okay, lads, up the gangway," called the bosun, "line up at the gallery hatch and then find a table. When you finish eating, clear away your plates and go up on the upper deck with the other trainees."

The gangway led to a door in the ship's port side. The dining mess hall stunk of cabbage water, tea and sweaty youths. A spotty faced catering boy in the galley handed Kevin a plate loaded up with what looked like shepherd's pie and red cabbage.

"What's in it?" he asked the steward.

"Don't ask. Move on."

Wee Jock and Hector followed Kevin to a table. The scrubbed wooden tabletops were bare. No tablecloth, no salt or pepper.

Hector poked around in his potatoes. "What kind of meat is this? Are these peas or what?" He tasted the sea pie and grimaced. "Erg, it's awful."

Kevin tasted his sea pie. "It's alright, salty beef, I think. Or maybe it's fish. In fact, it's quite tasty. Doesn't need any more salt for sure."

"Do you want mine, Kev?" Hector offered Kevin his plate.

"Thanks, Hector, I'm starving. I'll share my food with you tomorrow."

After they had finished supper the mess deck was cleared, and the new entries shoved outside onto the open upper deck. The wind blew freezing off the Fens. One hundred boys shuffling around like groups of penguins, hands in pockets, chuntering, waiting for their instructors to take them off the ship and back to their billets. Kevin, Jock and Hector huddled together by the vents above the galley for warmth, all three looking at the grey sky, wondering if there would be an air raid on the docks and wondering what the next three months would bring.

The first day's training at the *Training Ship Cromwell* began at 0600 with a bugler sounding off the naval reveille. The bugle call resounded over the frosty camp. Another boy hoisted the red ensign up on the mast's yardarm. A light mist covered the top gallant of the mast.

Bosun Heygate, already washed and shaved, marched up and down the dormitory calling, "wakey, wakey, rise and shine, the morning's bright, the morning's fine. Come on, get up. Hands off your cocks, on with your socks. Come on, lads, get up, the sun will burn your eyes out this warm sunny morning."

Kevin, moaning, tumbled off the top bunk and grabbed his towel, soap and toothbrush and dashed across to the toilet block. It was freezing in the ablutions. The long communal washing trough was filling up with cold water, the wash house smelled of carbolic soap and urine. Kevin washed himself all over with a face flannel in double quick time eager to get dressed.

Fifteen minutes later the 12 recruits lined up outside the billet waiting for Bosun Heygate to sort them out. A heavy frost lay on the ground, clouds of breath hung around the boy's faces; Kevin flapped his arms and blew into his hands to warm them up.

Bosun Heygate reappeared out of the nearby staff chalet. "Has everyone washed themselves this morning?"

"Yes, Bosun,"

"Okay, lads, let's see your feet. Off with your shoes and socks."

"Oh, come on, Bosun, it's freezing," Crocker complained.

"Come on. Get 'em, off. You won't die."

Reluctantly the boys removed their shoes and socks and stood in a line for foot inspection.

Heygate checked each boy. When he saw the Cockney's feet, he scowled, "what's your name, sunshine?"

"Crocker, Bosun."

"Step out here, Crocker. You too, mi lad." He singled out the boy from Newcastle. "What's your name?"

"Murrey,"

"Right then, Crocker and Murrey. Stand out here and show everyone your feet."

Crocker and Murrey shuffled in their bare feet out of the ranks and stood facing the rest.

"Take a look at these feet," the bosun said. "Filthy."

All the boys looked down at Murrey and Crocker's feet. They were dirty black, looking like they hadn't been washed in weeks.

"When did you last wash your plates of meat?" he asked Crocker.

"Yesterday, Bosun."

"Yesterday, my arse. Them feet haven't seen soap and water for months. Get back in there and get them scrubbed clean." He looked at Murrey. "When did you last wash your feet?"

Murrey shrugged, "don't know, I nebber wash mi feet. Nobody ever sees mi feet."

"I can see that, Murrey, you can grow tatties in the dirt between your toes. Open your mouth, Murrey, let's take a look at your teeth."

Murrey showed his teeth.

"Oh, my God, Murrey. When did you last brush your pearly whites?"

Murrey frowned. "I nebber brush mi teeth. Ain't got a brush."

"Alright, Murrey. Get back in there and scrub your feet clean. I'll find you a toothbrush later."

Murrey followed Crocker back into the ablution block.

Heygate addressed the remainder. "At sea, when you are in close contact with your fellow shipmates, it's essential you keep yourselves clean and smelling fresh…including your breath, otherwise you will find yourself thrown in the shower and scrubbed off with a hard deck brush."

Murrey and Crocker returned to the squad.

Bosun Heygate pointed his swagger stick towards the dock. "A little bit of history for you. This dock, Arcaster, is now virtually unused. It used to be a busy port back in the day. Roman. The river has silted, therefore only small timber carrying coasters discharge here now."

"Sir, Bosun." Griffith interrupted. "Is that boom to stop torpedoes from hitting our ship?"

Heygate laughed, "I don't think a German submarine would waste a torpedo trying to sink the *Cromwell,* lad. Besides a sub couldn't get up the river."

"I meant a torpedo carrying aeroplane, Bosun."

"If a torpedo carrying aeroplane should come up the river it would be shot down by our gallant heroes from the Royal Artillery." Heygate sounded slightly sarcastic. "No, that boom is simply there to stop rubbish floating into the sea-lock."

The early February watery sun was beginning to burn off the mist. From where Kevin stood, he could see the dock below and the sea-lock that would take ships down to river level at high tide. A small canal fed into the dock. Two anti-aircraft gun posts, surrounded by sandbags, protected the docks. Beyond the dock the flat Fens stretched out towards the North Sea; the River Welland looking like a silver snake in the early morning dawn. The training ship itself could be seen tied up alongside the dock. There was only one other small ship in the harbour, a coaster discharging timber.

"Right then," Heygate called. "To warm you up and give you an appetite for breakfast we're going to march at the double around the parade ground a few times. Then it's breakfast. After breakfast, you will get fitted up with your uniforms, then the barbers for short back and sides and then photos for your Seaman's Discharge Books."

Bosun Heygate double-marched the boys around the drill square and then down the hill to the ship for breakfast. Heygate left the boys waiting on the dock side while he went aboard for his own breakfast.

Kevin, Wee Jock, and Hector stood together on the dock waiting for the second sitting. The boys around Kevin and Jock towered above them by six or seven inches. The bigger boys looked more like 18-year-olds than 14, 15 or 16-year-olds.

Wee Jock pointed out a fellow Scotsman. "He's frey Glasgow. The Gorbals. I travelled down with him. He's a proper bampot."

"Bampot?"

"Yeah, an eegit, he should be in prison for slashing a boy's face wi' a cut - throat razor. Sheriff sent him here instead."

The scruffy Glaswegian noticed Wee Jock talking to Kevin.

"Haw you! Twat face!" The Glaswegian called.

"Who me?" answered Kevin.

"Aye you, Jimmy. Howsa wee tumshie like yo' gonna survive at sea?"

"What you mean, survive?" Kevin replied, not knowing what a tumshie was and not quite understanding his Scottish accent.

"He means, 'ow's a little fucker like you gonna stand up for yer self. You gonna get pushed around." Cockney Crocker added.

"No, I'm not," Kevin said, trying not to look as intimidated as he felt. "I can take care of myself, and ... I've been having self-defence lessons."

"Ooo, self-defence lessons!" they skittered him. "What kinda self-defence lessons?"

"Well," Kevin said, remembering what his dad had taught him. "If you come at me with a knife, I can disarm you, or if you tried to strangle me, I can get out of the strangle hold."

In a flash the cockney grabbed Kevin by the throat and hoisted him off his feet. His huge hands clamped around Kevin's skinny neck, Kevin's feet dangling a foot off the floor, his glasses hanging off his nose.

"Get out of a strangle hold, can you? Well, get outta that then!" he roared with laughter, shaking Kevin like a dog with a rat before dropping him on the ground in a heap.

The Cockney, the Geordie and the Glaswegian, all fell about laughing.

Once again Cockney Crocker turned his unwanted attention on Kevin and Wee Jock.

"Little squirts like you two will have a 'ard time at sea, getting pushed around. If I was you, I'd go 'ome now and come back when you've grown a bit."

"If I was you," Kevin retaliated, still rubbing his sore throat and still flat on his backside looking up, said, "I'd go home and ask your mum how to wash your feet."

"Oh, a fly boy, are you? Shut yer trap or I'll sling you in the dock."

"Why don't you pick on someone your own size," intervened Harry Millward, the boy from Manchester.

Crocker scowled at the Manchurian. "Like who?"

"Like me."

Crocker weighing up the boy, decided not to pick a fight with him. Instead, he turned to his Glaswegian friend for support. The boy from the Gorbals had lost interest in the fight and was trying unsuccessfully to light a cigarette in the wind.

Hector and Jock helped Kevin to his feet.

Kevin, dusting himself off, said to the Manchester boy, "thanks, mate."

"That's okay, like all loudmouth bullies, if you stand up to them, they turn into cowards."

"That's what my dad told me, thanks anyway."

"Harry."

"Anyway, thanks, Harry. I'm not really a coward but sometimes you can't always fight back, he's too big and hard for me."

"Discretion is the better part of valour," said Hector.

"True," agreed Harry, "but I don't think you are a coward. You stood up to me yesterday. I bet you could be a *Crommie Boy* before them ratty buggers from London and Glasgow. You're a Northerner like me."

"What's a *Crommie Boy*?"

"My brother was here last year. He's at sea now with British Continental Shipping. He said, to become a proper *Crommie Boy* you have to do three tasks. You see that mast?" Harry pointed to a stanchion post and derrick.

"One task is to climb up the rope to the top, hand over hand and then down the other side. The next task is to climb onto the bowsprit. You've got to crawl along the bowsprit and fondle Mrs Cromwell's titties. With both hands."

"Mrs Cromwell? Who's Mrs Cromwell?"

"Mrs Cromwell is Oliver Cromwell's wife; the figure head. It's not really Cromwell's wife. My brother thinks it's the wife of the man who built the ship. She's got a big bosom."

Kevin and the others gawped up at the figure head. The lady boasted huge, semi naked breasts.

"Anyway, the final task is to run across that boom." Harry pointed to a boom floating across the dock. The boom consisted of a line of timber railway sleepers chained together. "Can you see that boom down there across the dock?"

"Yes, bosun said it's for stopping rubbish floating into the lock."

"Yeah, that's right. When a ship is moving from the dock to the river, the lock master opens the boom for ships to pass into the sea-lock."

"Sea-lock?" asked Jock.

"Yeah, that lock down there, takes ships from the harbour down to river level when the tide is high enough."

The four boys looked towards the sea-lock.

"As I said, the third task is to run across the boom. It's not as easy as it looks. Once you step on the boom you've gotta keep moving quickly across it otherwise the boom will rock about and turn over and pitch you into the water."

"I reckon I could do all three," said Jock

"Me too," Kevin said

"Yes, me too," Harry added

Hector looked up at the mast. "I don't think I could do any of the tasks. I'm scared of heights."

"So, that's what we'll do then. We'll do all three before Crocker and Razor Riley and make sure they know it."

Kevin looked at Crocker and Riley who were both smoking cigarettes and exchanging dirty jokes. Kevin had to fight off a desire to attack Crocker from behind. 'Bastard! Making me look like a fool... but one day, before I leave this place, I'm going to get my own back on him.' He promised himself.

With the first breakfast sitting over, the second sitting trooped aboard for their watery porridge, dripping butties and a pot of tea.

~ * ~ * ~ * ~

On the Monday morning of the second week, seamanship training was well under way. Kevin gathered with his shipmates on the open deck of the training ship. For the first time in his life, he wore long trousers and black boots. He also wore a navy battledress blouse that was miles too big for him. On his shoulder a flash with the words Merchant Navy stitched in red. On his head he wore a navy-blue beret with a red MN badge. He looked over the windswept open deck towards the river and at the army gunners manning the two Oerlikon 20mm machine guns. The soldiers were watching the sky for any war plane planning to attack Arcaster Harbour or the camp above.

Bosun Heygate, standing on the starboard side of the vessel alongside a large heavy timber lifeboat, spoke to the gathered boys.

"It appears that Mr Riley and Mr Belling have decided the Merchant Navy is not for them. Sometime during the night, they went 'Over the Wall' and deserted. Do any of you know why or where they have gone?"

"No, sir," piped up Crocker. "Except Hoggy Bellings cried for his mum most nights and wanted to go home. I think Razor Riley has gone up to London. Riley sez cold baths and marching up and down are not for him. He sez if he wanted to march around with bloody great big boots on, he'd have joined the army."

"Alright, Crocker. If the police catch up with him, he'll be sent back to Glasgow, to the correction house or for Borstal training."

"Well, that's the point, Bosun, Razor Riley sez it's worse 'ere than in Borstal. He sez 'e's bin in the correction 'arse, the work 'arse and Borstal. He sez *Cromwell* is 'arder than all of them. He sez he'd sooner be in prison than 'ere."

By this time, most of the recruits had been given nicknames. Kevin was glad to see the back of 'Razor' Riley. The 12 new boys were now down to ten.

"Alright, lads. It is hard here, that's deliberate, we got to sort the men from the boys. Life at sea is hard, not a place for cry-babies or men like Riley. So, let's get on. Today's training is basic lifeboat drill. Very important; if this war continues some of you might have to launch a lifeboat. When I order, 'Boat's Crew, Fall In,' I want you to fall in, in a straight line facing the lifeboat." Heygate waited for a few seconds, then ordered, "Crew, Fall in."

Nine boys formed a crooked line facing the lifeboat. Geordie Murrey faced the wrong way.

"What is it about you, Murrey? You don't know your left from your right, and when I say face the lifeboat you have your back to it."

"Sorry, Bosun," Murrey said sheepishly, turning to face the boat.

"Come on then, dress off in a straight line."

The boys shuffled into a straight line.

"Right, lads, listen up," the bosun started. "Normally in peacetime, before you start lifeboat training, and, before you can go for your lifeboat ticket, you have to have served at least 12 months at sea, be at least 18 years old and be physically fit. However, gentlemen, it's no longer peacetime, we are at war! Therefore, we are going to train on this boat until you can launch it with your eyes shut."

"It's an auld boat, Bosun. Do ships still have these types of lifeboats anymore?" Wee Jock asked. "The ships we build in Paisley have different types of lifeboats."

"Yes, you are right, McGinn, there are different types of davits. These davits are what's known as Radial Davits. It matters not, what davits we are using, the purpose of this boat drill is to get you working as a team. To know all parts of the boat and launching mechanism. I'm telling you, if your ship gets torpedoed, you better get your boats away pretty damn quick or you will finish up freezing to death in the sea or drowning in heavy fuel oil."

Kevin pictured seamen spluttering and glugging on thick heavy oil. "Have you ever been torpedoed, Bosun?" he asked.

The bosun nodded, "yes, I have. Twice. Once in the North Sea sailing out of Hull, that time by a surface raider, and in 1917 my ship was torpedoed by a submarine off Dogger Bank. Wright-Bussard, the chief mate here, he has been shipwrecked three times."

"Remind me not to sail with him," joked Alex McGinn. "He's a Jonah!"

The boys laughed.

"It's not a laughing matter seeing your shipmates drowning, covered in oil or freezing to death in an open lifeboat. So, pay attention here. When I call, *'From the right, number',* I want you to number off from the right. You, Crocker, will be number one."

"Aye, aye, Bosun."

"Alright, from the right…number!"

"One," Crocker shouted.

"One," Jones called.

"One," McGinn repeated.

"Rest, rest," called the bosun. "No, you are not all number one. You, Crocker," he pointed at Crocker, "you are number one. You, Jones are number two. And you, McGinn, are number three and so on. Right let's try again. Are you ready?"

"Yes, Bosun."

"Crew. From the right…number!"

"One," called Crocker.

"Two," shouted Jones.

"Three and so on," shouted McGinn confidently.

"No, no, no," cried the bosun. "You don't say 'three and so on,' you just call 'three'."

"I thought you said fer mi to say 'three and so on'."

The bosun shook his head in resignation. "Right for the final time, when I call from the right number, you," he pointed to each boy in turn "you are number one, you are number two, you are three and you, Fife, are number four." He looked at the diminutive Fife and the bigger Crocker. "Fife, you swap with Crocker, you, Crocker, change places with Fife." The bosun then resumed numbering the boys off from right to left from one to ten.

On the third attempt the boats crew numbered off from one to ten.

"That's it. Okay, lads, it will take ten men to launch this heavy boat. Each one of you will have a specific task to do."

"Sir, Bosun, sir. What does Spu…specific mean?" asked Murrey

"Oh my god, don't you know anything, Murrey?"

Murrey shrugged and hung his head.

"Number one, that's you, Fife. You will get into the bow of the boat and pass the painter to number 2 who will take the painter forward, clear?"

"Sir, who is the painter?"

"Peter the Painter," Crocker laughed.

"Pipe down, Crocker. The painter is not a person," said the exasperated bosun. "It's the bow line. Fife, you take the painter and pass it to Jones. Three and four, you two will stand by the forward falls." The bosun pointed to the falls. "Number five, you will let go the forward gripes and chocks. Six and seven stand-by the after falls. Number eight, you will let go the after gripes...outboard first. Right, this is important." The bosun paused. "Are you listening, Crocker? The reason number five and number 8 have to let go of the outboard gripes first is that if you let go of the inner ones first then went to the outboard ones and the boat cantered you would be knocked overboard and may be killed."

Crocker stopped his joking and muttered, "yes, Bosun."

Heygate continued. "Number nine, that's you, McBride, tends the after guy."

"Which man is the after guy?" McBride said in his broad Belfast accent. "Do I tend to Griffith?"

"No, no, no. The 'guy' is that line there that controls the after arm of the davit." The bosun, shaking his head, pressed on. "And number ten, you will get in the stern of the boat, and, for your information, Murrey, that's the blunt end. Your first job is to ship the plug. And when the boat is swung out, ship the rudder. Do you all know what job you will do to launch this boat?"

One or two of the crew mumbled, "Yes, Bosun."

"The golden rule to observe during boat exercises is, *'Don't talk unless you have to.'* The only person talking is the coxswain, that's me. I will give you orders. Shouting and conversation between individual crew members, both, will have a disturbing effect and must not occur. Do you all understand?"

"Yes, Bosun."

"When I call, *'Stations'*, each member will go smartly to his station. Next order will be *'Slack away forward guy'*. The next order will be *'Haul away after guy'* and *'launch boat aft'*. Are you all ready?"

"Yes, Bosun," the crew answered.

"Stations."

The boys moved to their allotted stations.

Bosun Heygate checked that the crew were at their correct positions. He ordered, "slack away forward guy, haul away after guy. Launch boat aft."

The crew shuffled around, not too sure what to do.

"No, you fuckin' numbskull," Crocker yelled at Jones, pointing to the guy line. "You 'aul way that rope there."

"Bollocks, Crocker! You do that. I'm on this thing here," Taffy Jones shouted back. "Fife, don't just stand there, get in the boat and pass me Peter the Painter."

Fife looked up at the boat still sitting on its blocks. "It's too high, give us a hand up."

"Somebody give Fife a hand-up, he's too short to climb into the boat!"

The maxim, don't talk unless you have to, had already been forgotten. The lifeboat, now two-foot higher forward than it was aft, swung on the blocks.

"Swing the boat aft," called the coxswain. "No…not like that. Swing the stem clear of the davit. Oh my God. Rest, rest. Hold it there."

The ten boys stood looking at the bosun. "Right, let's get the boat swung outboard." The bosun then proceeded to guide the trainees through the basic manoeuvres to get the boat lifted from the blocks and swung clear of the davits until the lifeboat hung over the starboard side of the ship ready for lowering.

"Right, lads, trim guys and make fast."

The boat was levelled.

"Stand by to lower." The bosun watched as the turns were taken off the bollards. "That's it. Lower away smartly and smoothly."

The boat lowered until it reached the water.

The bosun then ordered, "make fast."

"Sir, sir, Bosun. We're leaking!" Murrey cried from the stern of the boat.

The bosun looked over the side, a fountain of water spurting from the boat's drain hole. "Murrey, what did I tell you? Put the bung in the hole *before* we lower the boat. Alright, lads, lift the boat so Murrey can ship the plug before it sinks."

Ten minutes later the drained lifeboat sat riding on the water with all the young crew sat on the thwart seats looking at the coxswain.

"Well done, lads, have a rest while I have a little smoko." Relaxing in the stern, the bosun pulled out his pipe. He lit the tobacco that was already in the bowl. Blowing out a long sigh with the smoke he said, "I'm telling you, boys. Launching a boat here on a millpond on a cold and frosty morning is a lot different to launching at night in a howling gale, with the ship listing and sinking fast - and the sea is on fire - But, for a first attempt, not bad. We'll lift the boat back onto the deck then you can knock off for smoko. But, before that, I'll tell you what I did during the last war in case my ship was torpedoed and we had to abandon ship. I made myself a grab-bag."

"A grab bag, what's that?"

"It's a bag containing my valuables, you know, like my wallet, my ID card and Seaman's Book, some sweets, a torch and so on. I kept it close at hand with my lifejacket, so that I could grab the bag and go to the lifeboat."

"That's a good idea."

"Yes, I also used to wrap my wallet in a Board of Trade prophylactics."

"Prophylactic?" Kevin asked.

"Yes, better known as rubber Jonnies, or condoms. The Board of Trade Jonnies, issued to all merchant ships, are waterproof and will keep out seawater for two years or more. You can wrap your wallet and things you need to keep dry in these super strong condoms."

A toot from a ship's horn made the lifeboat crew look towards the sea-lock.

"Hey, Bosun. Look over there!" called Murrey.

Bosun Heygate looked towards the lock and stared at the ship entering the harbour. "Oh my goodness, it looks like she has been in the wars alright. The holes in the superstructure and funnel look like cannon shell holes to me."

The small coaster was peppered with bullet holes and structural damage. The top half of the foremast had been shot away. The young lifeboat crew watched open-mouthed as the ship limped to the harbour wall. Two fire pumps on the coaster, working at full revs, emptying gallons of water out of the damaged ship's hull.

"Crikey, it's listing too." Kevin said.

The ship listed over to starboard.

"Too much water inside a ship can cause the ship to turn over. But we'll cover that subject when we do firefighting and damage control. Alright lads," said the bosun. "Nothing we can do. Let's get this boat back up on deck."

After a lot of heaving and cursing the young crew lifted and secured the boat ready for the next drill. The boys trooped down to the messdeck for tea and a slice of bread and butter.

~ * ~ * ~ * ~

During stand-down the following day, Kevin, with Horace, Jock and Harry, now inseparable friends, made their way around the harbour to have a closer look at the damaged coaster that had limped into port the previous morning.

The gangway had been lowered. A couple of dock yard workers were inspecting the damaged superstructure and mast, making notes on a clipboard. The fire pumps still working flat out pumping water overboard.

Kevin looked up at the ship's name painted on the stern. "*Fiddler's Green*! That's a funny name for a ship."

An old sailor sat on the bollard smoking his pipe.

"What happened?" Horace called up to the sailor, indicating the damage to the ship's superstructure, bridge and mast.

"We were attacked by an S-boat."

"Can we come aboard for a look around at the damage?"

The man nodded. "Yes, sure, boys. Come up, just keep clear of the surveyors."

The four boys climbed aboard the coaster.

"How's the training going?" the sailor asked, pointing the stem of his pipe towards the training ship *Cromwell*.

"We only just started here a couple of weeks back. But we should be on ships of our own by the end of April."

"Well, I wish you all the best of luck, lads. Let's hope this war is over before you do go out to sea."

"You say you were attacked by S-boats? What's an S-boat?"

"It's a fast German gun-boat, they will do about 45 knots. They were in amongst us in the middle of the night. They sank two coasters and badly damaged about six more ships and then fled before our navy could respond. Our fastest warship will only do about 20 knots so the Jerries' were back in Germany before our navy got out of bed. We were sailing in a coastal convoy from the Tyne to the Thames, about sixty ships in all, mainly colliers. We had to break away from the convoy for repairs here, before we sunk." The sailor cut a slice of tobacco from the rope twist, rolled it around in his hand before stuffing the tobacco in his pipe.

"What's that you're smoking?" asked Harry.

"Black Irish Twist," he said. "Managed to get some in Newcastle. Do you want to try some?"

"No, not me thanks. I don't smoke."

Kevin looked at the damaged mast and dangling radio aerials.

"Was anyone hurt when Jerry attacked?"

"Luckily not on this ship. Everyone dived down onto the deck for cover when the shooting started. Bullets flying everywhere over our heads. But I believe some sailors were killed on the ships that were sunk. If the Germans keep on sinking us at this rate, you'll be able to walk from the Tyne to the Thames on the shipwrecks along the coast."

"Why is this ship called *Fiddler's Green*? What's a fiddler's green?"

The old sailor pointed his pipe to the forecastle. "In the old days of sailing ships, to weight the anchor, men had to turn a capstan manually. It was hard physical work, pushing on the spars to turn the capstan. To make the work easier, a fiddler used to sit on top of the capstan and play a sea shanty. The sailors would sing as they pushed. The top of the capstan was called the '*Fiddler's Green*'. Because sailors thought sitting on the green was a good place to be, they called paradise Fiddler's Green, a sailor's heaven. A sailor's Valhalla."

"Oh, thanks," Hector said. "When I die, I want to go to Fiddler's Green."

Harry, Jock and Kevin agreed. After inspecting the damage, the four boys thanked the old sailor and bid him farewell. They returned to their billet.

~ * ~ * ~ * ~

The boson came into the hut holding a handful of letters.

"Fife," called Heygate.

Kevin put his hand up. "Here, Bosun."

"Letter from home." Heygate sniffed at the envelope. "Smells like lavender, young Fife. From your girlfriend, is it?"

Kevin blushed and said awkwardly, "I don't have a girlfriend."

Kevin took the letter and recognised Jane Black's handwriting. Jane had written to him already, but this was the first letter to have a scent of lavender. He put the envelope to his nose and breathed in the fragrance. *'The fragrance of a young girl is so much better than the smell of carbolic soap, cabbage water and sweaty socks,'* he thought. He read the letter.

'Dearest Kevin. I hope this letter finds you well and happy. Thank you for your letter that I got on Monday. I was so pleased to hear from you and that you have settled into your new life as a sailor. I hope you don't mind me writing again. You know, I don't have a boyfriend and I would love it if you would be my boyfriend, my sweetheart. I have only known you for a few

weeks and we only went to the pictures once and to the dance once, but even so, I feel I have known you for ages and ages. I hope you feel the same way about me.'

Kevin's lips curled into a smile when he read that Jane wanted to be his sweetheart. He had secretly admired Jane Black, the vicar's daughter, from a distance, as she played in the vicarage garden. He continued reading the rest of the letter. He read it again for a second time. The letter ended with '*Love and kisses from Jane XXXXXXXXXXXX.'* He counted the twelve kisses, pressing the letter to his own lips. He carefully folded the letter and placed it in his toffee tin, along with Jane's first letter and silver cross, Tommy's tin star and the St Christopher medal his mother had given him. He lay back on his 'donkeys' breakfast bed', smiling and daydreaming about going home and seeing Jane again.

~ * ~ * ~ * ~

In the early spring evening sunshine, Kevin, Wee Jock, Hector and Harry examined the boom across the dock. The ice around the edges had melted and dashing across the boom seemed less daunting now the weather had warmed up a bit. The three-month training course was nearing its end.

"Who's going first?"

"Me," volunteered Kevin. "I'll go first."

Sitting on the bank, Kevin gingerly lowered himself down putting one foot on the sleeper. He gave it a push. The boom waved slightly; the linking chains clinked.

"Go on then, Fife, I dare you," called Crocker, who was watching.

"If I do it, will you try?"

Crocker shrugged uncertainly.

"Crocker won't try; he's a coward," mocked Harry Millward.

"Who you calling a coward? I...I can do it...no problem. I just don't want to do it now. I'll do it later."

"Later? We'll have finished training by then. That's what you said when you couldn't climb up the rope. You fat bugger, can't lift your own weight."

Crocker shrugged. "Go on, Fife. I hope you fall in."

Kevin ignored Crocker. He carefully stepped down onto the boom. The first sleeper holding his weight sank an inch. With his arms held out horizontal to the water for balance, he set off at a trot stepping from one sleeper to the next. The boom swayed from left to right and dipped up and down ahead and behind him. Keeping his eyes on the bank and the boom ahead, he crossed safely to the opposite dock wall. Kevin's three friends cheered. Kevin raised his arms in triumph before retracing his steps back over the boom.

"It's only because he's so small. I'm too heavy to do it."

"I'm heavier than you; so, if I can do it, so can you," Harry challenged.

With no further ado, Harry stepped down onto the boom, got his balance and set off stepping quickly from sleeper to sleeper safely reaching the other side of the dock.

Lifting his arms, he called across the dock, "come on then, Crocker, let's see you do it."

Cockney Crocker screwed his mouth. "I can do it, easy, but I've got better things to do than play silly games. Get out of the way, Fife." He pushed past the grinning Kevin.

"You're all mouth, Crocker." Kevin scoffed.

"You're a little gobshite, Fife. One day I'm gonna toss you 'ead first into the 'arbour."

"At least I've passed all the *Crommie Boy* tests. You haven't done one."

Crocker turned and looked at the boom. "I... I can do that easy."

"Come on then, seeing is believing."

Crocker had a second good look at the boom. Ape-like, he ambled to the dock side. Reaching down, he put his foot on the boom. He gave the boom a good push down. Kevin sat down on the bank his dangling feet, 18 inches above the water, and about a yard away from the boom. Crocker nervously waited until the boom stopped moving before he stood up on the timber sleeper. Balancing with his arms outstretched, he carefully stepped out onto the next sleeper. Kevin shuffled his bottom inch by inch closer to the boom. Crocker was nearly half way across when Fife put his foot on the boom pushing downwards, twice. This set off an oscillating motion that caught up with Crocker with a further five sleepers to go to the opposite bank. Crocker wobbled uncertainly, trying desperately to regain his balance. It was in vain. The boom twisted throwing Crocker, shrieking as he fell, backwards into the cold harbour water. A loud cheer went up from the watching boys.

Crocker surfaced spluttering, thrashing around in the water, desperately trying to reach out to the boom calling. "I can't swim...help."

"Oh, heck! I didn't know he couldn't swim." Kevin sprung up, looking around for the life-ring. Seeing the red box by the sea-lock, he ran over to it. Grabbing the life-ring and life-line rope, he sprinted back to the boom. Harry Millward took the ring off Kevin and threw it to the drowning Crocker. Crocker managed to catch hold of the lifesaver. Kevin tugged the rope and pulled the panic-stricken Londoner to the bank. The four boys pulled the saturated Cockney out of the water onto the dock side.

"I lost me balance," he panted, nearly crying. "I thought I was gonna drown."

"You would have done if Kevin hadn't run so fast to the lock and got the life ring," said Hector. "He saved your life, you were going down for the third time."

Crocker looked up at Kevin. Wagging his head, he said reluctantly, "Thanks, Fife. I owe you one."

Kevin breathed a massive sigh of relief. '*If he finds out I pushed the boom, he'll kill me,*' he thought.

Crocker, with his heavy battledress uniform dripping water, made his way back up the slope to the billet.

Hector, watching Crocker leave, turned to Kevin. "Naughty boy, Kev, I saw you pushing the boom."

"Erm, yeah," said Kevin, "that'll teach him not to strangle me and make me look like a fool."

"Revenge is a potent source of satisfaction and pleasure," said Hector, quoting something he had picked up at the boarding school.

Kevin, Wee Jock, Hector and Harry laughed. The four boys, laughing and pushing each other, followed Crocker back to the billet.

On a warm and sunny Sunday morning in Norfolk, the entire ship's company of 100 boys fell in on the parade ground for the captain's address and church parade. This was the final parade for the February 1940 intake. 12 weeks of hard training had been completed. A table had been set up at the edge of the parade square, with a white table cloth. Sitting on the table were two silver cups and two tiny boxes. The gentle breeze lifted the edge of the tablecloth, the vicar's stole also lifted in the breeze. The vicar's medals hanging on his garments glinted in the sun. With the vicar were Captain Hollows and the Chief Officer along with the establishment's instructors, bosuns and stewards. They were dressed in full uniforms of officers of the Merchant Navy, their medals too, shone in the sun.

"Let us pray," intoned the vicar, reading from a prayer book. "*Oh eternal Lord God who alone rulest the raging of the sea, who has compassed the waters with bounds until day and night come to an end, be pleased to receive into Thy almighty and gracious protection the persons of us, Thy servants, and the Fleet in which we serve. Preserve us from the dangers of the sea, and from the violence of the enemy; that we may be a safeguard unto our most gracious Sovereign Lord, King George the Sixth and his dominions and a security for such as pass upon the seas upon their lawful occasions; that the inhabitants of our Empire may in peace and quietness serve Thee our God; and that we may return in safety to enjoy the blessings of the land, with the fruits of our labour and with thankful remembrance of Thy mercy to praise and glorify Thy name. Amen.*"

"Amen," repeated the ship's company.

The captain of *TS Cromwell* addressed the parade. "Today we see the graduation day for 20 young men who have completed their pre-sea training. Over the past 12 weeks you have been taught many things, including, basic navigation, seamanship, boat knowledge, sailing, cooking and catering. But most importantly you have shown us here at *TS Cromwell* that you are fit and able to stand the rigors of life at sea and the rigors that seafaring in wartime may bring. Many of us thought this conflict would be over by Easter. Well, that was not to be. The war at sea continues. You will face many dangers. You will not be well rewarded for facing the dangers of the sea and the violence of the enemy. In the event of your ship being torpedoed, bombed or strafed and goes to the bottom, your pay will stop the minute your ship sinks. You may face abuse in the pubs of Liverpool, Glasgow and London for not being in uniform. Little do they know. I can tell you this, men, and you are now men, that without the sailors of the British Merchant Navy, this island of ours will not survive this war. By this time next year, or even sooner, Great Britain will be starved into submission. So those of you who are off to sea this week, I say, God speed. Bon voyage and return to your home ports safely. Thank you."

The chief officer spoke next. "The bosuns and chief stewards have voted who are the top cadets, the boy who has improved the most, who has shown the most enthusiasm and excelled in all subjects. The senior catering boy is...Hector Davis-Davidson."

The gathered students clapped.

Hector turned to the right and doubled up to the table.

"Following in your father's footsteps, eh, Davis-Davidson? Well done."

"Yes, sir. Thank you."

The captain handed Hector the silver cup. Hector held it aloft. The boys cheered. The captain then presented Hector with the small box. Hector left the cup on the table and doubled back to the squad.

The chief mate continued. "The top deck boy is...Kevin Fife."

An unexpected cheer went up from the entire ship's company. Fife blushed as he doubled up to the captain's table.

"Well done, Fife. It looks like your trousers have shrunk a bit or have you grown since you came here?"

"I've grown a bit, sir, nearly two inches."

"When I first saw you climb off the train with your little brown suitcase, I didn't think you would last two minutes down here. I was mistaken. Not only have you survived *TS Cromwell*, you are clearly one of the best and well-liked cadets we've ever had. I wish you good fortune at sea. You may not believe this but I wish I was in your shoes, starting life again at sea. I'm sure you will do well."

The captain handed Kevin the second cup.

"Can I keep it?" Kevin asked hopefully.

"No, sorry, lad. The cup stays here at *Cromwell*, however your name will be engraved on the cup and your Discharge Book has been annotated to say you were top deck-boy here at *TS Cromwell*."

The captain then gave Kevin the small box. Kevin opened it to reveal a silver reef-knot encompassing the letters MN in the centre.

"You can keep that, Fife. Wear it with pride. I hear that you have to report to Liverpool first thing tomorrow. Maybe you'll get a spot of leave before your ship sails."

"I hope so, sir. I'm missing my mum's cooking. I'm missing my dad and I'm looking forward to seeing my friends again soon. But, yes sir, I've been ordered to report to the Federation in Liverpool tomorrow morning."

"You may get a couple of days off before you sail. Good luck, Fife. I'm sure you'll see your family soon and that you will do well at sea."

"Thank you, sir." Kevin turned to face the parade. He held the silver cup aloft to show the boys. The parade cheered for the second time. He saluted the captain and returned to his squad.

With the formalities over, the boys marched off the parade ground to their respective billets.

Kevin stuffed the final pair of socks in his canvas kitbag, a kitbag provided for all cadets on graduation. He opened his toffee tin and placed the MN badge inside with his other treasures, letters from his mum and Jane Black.

Wee Jock, sitting on the next bunk was watching him. "What's that silver star."

Kevin grinned. "It's a toy sheriffs' badge. My mate gave it to me for good luck. He wants to be a cowboy."

"Nothing wrong with that, I wanted to be a spaceman."

Kevin handed the badge to Alex.

Alex turned the star over, examining both sides before handing it back.

"I hope it does bring you good luck. Keep in touch, Kev. I'll give you my mum's address, she will forward your mail to me."

"Yeah, okay, Jock. I'll do that. I hope you'll keep safe too. Bosun said there are German subs lurking just outside the Clyde, waiting for ships from Glasgow to come out."

"Aye, I heard. The war may be over soon. Poland has gone. We won't be able to get it back off the Jerries or Soviets, might as well make peace with Hitler now while the goings good."

"My dad said Churchill won't make peace. He's hell bent on a war."

"Aye, maybe."

Kevin pulled the drawstring on his kitbag. "Well, that's it, Alex. Let's go and see Bosun Heygate." He looked around the billet for the last time. "I'm not sorry to be leaving this place and I'm looking forward to having a hot bath."

Outside the billet the deck boys of the 1940 February intake milled about waiting for their instructor Bosun Heygate.

Heygate came out of his chalet. "Alright, lads, fall in. Let's march out of the camp, a bit smarter that you trooped through the gates 12 weeks ago. You've a train to catch."

The boys of the catering intake were waiting with their instructor, Steward Hatley. The two intakes joined together for the march to the station.

The 10 deck boys, and 10 catering boys, escorted by Bosun Heygate, and the steward, marched out of the camp singing the camp's song.

"We're going to join, we're going to join, we're gonna join old Heygates Navy. Up at 6 o'clock, twice around the block, dirty great big icicles hanging off our cocks..."

Heygate laughed.

The boys continued singing as they marched through the camp gates, *"We're going to join, we're going to join, we're gonna join old Heygates Navy. Sitting on the grass, polishing the brass, dirty great big spiders crawling up your arse."*

Now, the boys clear of the camp, continued singing even louder.

"We're going to join, we're going to join, we're gonna join old Heygates Navy. 2 bob a week, nothing to eat, dirty great big Crommie boots hanging off our feet."

The train for Norwich stood in the station; steam hissing out of the pistons, smoke belching out of the chimney. The marching column halted outside the station entrance and turned inboard to face the bosun.

"Well, lads. This is it. Have a safe journey home."

"I'm not going home, Bosun," moaned Crocker. "I'm sailing this week. Gotta ship waitin' just for me in KG five docks. The captain won't sail without me."

"Neither am I," said Griffith. "I'm shipping out tomorrow."

"Nor me, I'm not going home yet," Kevin said, "I have to report to the federation first thing in the morning." He fished around in the top of his kit bag and brought out a small tin. "Err, Bosun...," he said nervously, not used to being nominated as a spokesperson. "We, the deck boys, have clubbed together and bought you this small present to say thank you."

Kevin handed over a tin of Black Irish rope twist tobacco.

"The lads have asked me to say, 'Thank you, Bosun, for your patience with us. For passing on your wealth of knowledge about the sea and seafaring. What you have taught us this year will be with us all forever."

Heygate looked at the tobacco tin with amazement. "Goodness me! Where did you get this from? Black twist is so hard to get nowadays, and my favourite baccy too. Thanks very much, lads."

"We got it off an old sailor, off one of the coasters that come into the harbour. We all chipped in, even Crocker."

"Well, many thanks. I'll remember you lot for a long time. Especially you, Murrey. I'm glad you now know your left from your right, and that you passed out successfully and not back-classed. Come on then, get aboard the train, and if you are ever down this neck of the woods come and see me. In the meantime, keep safe, lads. God bless you all."

The boys climbed aboard the train. As the steam train chuffed out of the station, the boys hung out the window waving and shouting farewell to Bosun Heygate and Steward Hartley. 10 deck boys 10 catering boys, all under the age of 16 years, were heading off for war at sea.

CHAPTER 3

THE SS ALICE MORGAN – MAY 1940

KEVIN AND HECTOR MADE THEIR way down Tithebarn Street towards the Seaman's Mission on the Liverpool waterfront. The streets were darkened, weirdly quiet and deserted; except for a patrolling ARP warden. Occasionally a ship's horn tooted from the unseen Mersey River. The journey from Arcaster to Liverpool had been long. Kevin was tired and looking forward to a good night's sleep in the Flying Angel mission.

Although no lights showed from the building windows, Kevin could hear people talking, laughing and occasional bursts of a song coming out of the mission's door. Hector pushed open the door; tobacco smoke poured out. Inside the building, seamen were sat around wood tables, drinking beer, smoking and chatting to some women. Kevin was surprised, he thought a mission was the same as a church hall, not like a pub tap-room. Nobody took any notice of the two boys as they made their way to the reception desk.

The padre looked up from the desk, frowned at the boys and asked, "Yes, lads, what can I do for you?"

"We'd like a room for the night, please."

"Sorry, son, no children allowed in the mission. What you doing wandering around Liverpool at this time of night in the blackout?"

"We aren't children, we are seamen now." Hector said, taking his Seaman's Discharge Book out of his kitbag.

Kevin took his book out, handing it over to the vicar.

The padre looked at the photograph of Kevin and shook his head.

"Date of birth - November 1926. Heavens above, you are still a child. 14

is too young to leave school. Oh well, I'll sign you both in. There's a twin berth available. How long are you staying?"

"One night. We are signing on in the morning."

"Alright then. You keep out of the bar, no drinking. And be careful who you talk to. Not everyone using the mission are good Christian men. Keep your room door locked, don't let anyone in. Even women. Understand?"

"Yes, vicar. Any chance of some supper?"

The padre turned to look at the clock. "Sorry, lads, kitchen closed at 10. Breakfast starts at 6am."

Tired and hungry the boys turned in for the night.

Kevin lay on the bed pondering. "Hector, what did the padre mean about not letting women in our room?"

"I expect he was referring to 'Ladies of the Night'."

"Ladies of the night, who are they?"

"Prostitutes."

"Prostitutes, what's a prostitute?"

"Well, I've never met one myself, but as far as I can gather, they sell themselves for sex."

"Sex?"

"Yes, sexual intercourse."

"Intercourse…what's that?

"Oh my God. Don't you know anything? Go to sleep, Kev. Good night."

"Good night." A minute later Kevin asked, "Hector, is sexual intercourse the same as shagging?"

"Tut, go to sleep, Kevin."

~ * ~ * ~ * ~

Early the following morning Kevin and Hector made their way down to the shipping federation offices.

"I wonder what kind of ship we'll get and where she will be sailing to?" Kevin queried.

"I wouldn't mind a luxury passenger liner, sailing to the Caribbean or New York."

"I want to go to the Pacific or the Far East, like my granddad. He told me stories of the South Sea Islands, crystal clear blue seas. Japan, and the Geisha

Girls. He said the beds of the orient are the softest. I don't know what he meant by that."

"Any bed is better than the donkey's breakfast."

"I hope I get a passenger-cargo liner, maybe Blue Funnel Line or Cunard."

"Yes, me too. I'll settle for a prestigious shipping company and a good feeder."

"A good feeder?"

"Yeah, there's good feeder ships and hungry ships. My father says some ships are good feeders, good food and plenty of it, and some ships are not so good, with poor food and meagre rations, they are called hungry ships. It all depends on the Chief Steward and the Chief Cook, I suppose."

"Um, I never thought of that. Will we need our ration books for food?"

"No, I don't think so. Anyway, if we get a luxury liner, we will be eating 'posh nosh', beef tenderloin and lobster ravioli, yum." Hector smacked his lips.

"Lobster ravioli. I've never heard of that. My mum makes great meat and potato pie."

At the brick-built federation offices, they pushed their way through the doors. The waiting area of the shipping office was crowded with men. Most of the men wore civilian clothing, three-piece-suits or jackets. Flat caps, bowler hats or trilbies. Some wore parts of naval apparel, peak caps and naval jumpers. Kevin and Hector were still dressed in their sea-school battledress and berets.

After waiting his turn, Kevin was called over to the vacant desk.

"I'll see you outside, Hector."

"Yes, good luck, Kevin. I hope you get a ship going to the Pacific."

The attendant examined Kevin's documents, seaman's book, his ration book and his National ID Card.

"Right, young man, he said, handing the documents back. "I want you to go get the ferry across to Birkenhead, West Float Dock, and sign on the SS *Alice Morgan*. She belongs to South Wales Coal and Coke Shipping Company. She's been in dry dock, but is now ready for sea and is signing on the crew this morning."

"I was told we had the choice of three ships."

"Not in wartime, sonny Jim, and not for a first-tripper. You take what ship you are given."

Kevin didn't argue. He put the documents back in his kit bag and waited outside the offices for Hector.

"What ship did you get?"

Looking glum, Hector said, "*SS Alice Morgan*, over in Birkenhead."

"Oh, wow. Me too! We'll be sailing together, that's great."

"Hmm, yes, I'm glad about that," Hector said excitedly. "But I think she's a collier."

"A collier, what's that?"

"A ship carrying coal."

"Do you know where to?

"No, the 'Super' wouldn't tell me. He said it's classified information. He said he didn't want people to know ship movements in case there are spies about, who could relay the information to the U-boats. Colliers are usually coastal ships taking coal from the mines to the power stations. Not very glamourous."

"So much for sailing to the Caribbean and South Seas."

"At least sailing through the Irish Sea and English Channel will be safer than crossing the Atlantic."

The boys boarded the ferry at the Pier Head. The River Mersey was choppy with a wind blowing up from the sea. The sky above was clear blue with gulls swooping overhead. Kevin, feeling the fresh spring wind on his face, had a feeling of excitement as the ferry let go her moorings and headed towards Birkenhead. He looked up and down the river and at the Liver Buildings and Cunard Buildings on the Liverpool waterfront. He felt that this was the first voyage to a life of adventure at sea, albeit just crossing a river. On this Monday morning, apart from the sight of barrage balloons flying high over the docks, and spotting the occasional anti-aircraft battery on the shore, the world looked at peace.

From the ferry terminal on the Birkenhead side of the Mersey, they walked along Dock Road with their little brown cardboard suitcases in one hand, a canvas kitbag slung over their shoulder and the gas mask slung over the other shoulder. Making their way past East Float Dock, over railway lines, around coils of wire and packing cases they found the West Float Dock. At the wharf edge, they stood with their mouths open staring at the *Alice Morgan*

"Oh my God!" exclaimed Hector. "What a dirty old tramp."

The collier's superstructure painted a drab grey, the hull painted black. Black smoke poured out of the tall funnel. Although just out of dry-dock, coal dust still clung to the upperparts and bridge.

Kevin's heart sank. His dreams of a sleek 10,000-ton passenger cargo liner gone.

"You two!" An officer on the deck shouted down to the boys. "Are you signing on the *Alice Morgan*."

"Yes, sir."

"Well get aboard then, we are sailing on the tide."

Kevin and Hector made their way up the gangway, Kevin grumbling. "Sailing today. No home leave then."

"No, 'fraid not. You know my father was away at sea from 1914 to 1918 with no leave. I think my mum suspected him of having another wife somewhere."

"Follow me," the officer called. "The crew are signing on in the officers' mess room."

They followed the officer up a ladder to the deck above the main deck and into the officers' dining room. The space was small and crowded with men signing on. The captain sat at the head of a small table with the Articles of Agreement book open in front of him. A stamp and inkpad lay by the book.

Kevin was the second to last to be called to the table.

"Deck boy, Fife," the captain called.

"Here, sir."

"Come on then, son. Sign here, please."

The captain pointed to a space on the Articles of Agreement. Kevin signed his name in the register. The captain opened Kevin's Seaman's Discharge Book. "This is your first entry stamp, Fife. There will be many more before you retire in 40 years' time, I would think, but you will always remember signing on your first ship." He pressed the stamp into the first space on the first page of his book. "Welcome on board," the captain said pleasantly. "My name is Abraham. Captain Issac Abraham."

"Pleased to meet you, sir," said Kevin, remembering his mother's advice about manners.

Captain Abraham indicated the other officer. "The Chief Officer is Mr Chapman."

"Hello, son," said Chapman, also in a friendly tone.

"Hello, Mr Chapman."

"You'll be on Freddy Todd's watch. Mr Todd is the second mate."

Freddy Todd gave Kevin a brief wave.

Kevin glanced at the first stamp in his discharge book, SS Alice Morgan – POR Cardiff - Gross Ton; 2490 – Engagement; Birkenhead 29 April 1940 – Rating; Dk Boy.'

Hector was the last person to be signed on

"Cabin boy, Davies-Davidson."

"Here, sir."

"Sign here, son."

Hector signed the Articles.

Captain Abraham, lit a pipe, sat back in his chair and addressed the crew, "Well, gentlemen, I don't know what you know about this ship and why there are so many of us making up the crew. For those of you who have sailed on colliers before, you'll know the system. Normally a crew of around six or seven, two watch system, no cook, all hands helping out with cooking and so on. Two officers on deck, two engineers below, a couple of deck hands and a couple of stokers. The colliers are usually confined to the UK coastal waters, however, we, gentlemen, are sailing south to Freetown in Sierra Leone."

There was a brief chuntering and comments amongst the crew.

The captain continued. "That's why we have a full crew of 20 men. We are taking coal from the Cardiff staithes. Coal from the South Wales coalfields to Freetown. Coal is still required for ship's fuel bunkers. Some ships, as you know, are still coal-burners, like the *Alice Morgan*. So that's where we're off to, West Africa. We have a cook - Mr Cameron."

Cameron lifted his hand in acknowledgement.

"We also have two deck officers, two engineers, a bosun, 4 AB's, 4 stokers in the black gang, and a radio operator and chief steward, myself and Mr Hollander our Chief Engineer. Also, we have two young men here making their first voyage. You two," the captain indicated Kevin and Hector, "will learn from us older and wiser men all about seafaring. You, Davis-Davidson will be galley boy, cabin boy and general dog's body, and you, Fife, will be deck boy, sailors mess boy and general dog's body better known as the '*peggie*'."

Both Kevin and Hector smiled, pleased that the captain and chief mate were friendly and apparently easy going, not like some crusty old sea-dogs they'd heard about while at the *Cromwell*.

"When we have loaded the coal, we will sail independent of the convoy system to Freetown."

"Why's that, Captain?" asked one of the sailors.

"Well, we can only make 6 knots top speed and maintaining position in convoy is difficult. But, secondly, I'm not sailing under the command of some snotty-nosed RNVR officer who knows next to nothing about the sea. I like sea-room and room to manoeuvre. Not confined in a convoy like a sitting duck."

There was a muted cheer from the sailors, who appeared to have some contempt of the Royal Navy when it came to escorting merchant vessels.

"As yet we are unarmed, although the Admiralty have promised they will fit us with two machine guns in Cardiff, but don't hold your breath on that."

"Effin' useless, pre 1914 guns they are fitting to merchant ships," complained Chapman. "Always jamming up or misfiring, anyway, what good is a machine gun against U-boats and dive-bombers."

"Yes, you are right, chief," the captain spoke to the chief engineer, "Are the engines all fired up, Mr Hollander?"

"Yeap, Cap'. Steams up. All ready below."

The captain glanced at the clock. He looked around the gathered crew. "Any questions?"

Kevin timidly held up his hand.

"Yes, Peggie."

"Sir, why are you calling me Peggie, a girl's name?"

Captain Abraham grinned. "Peggie is not a girl's name; it refers to a peg-leg sailor. In the days of sailing ships, if a sailor lost his leg in battle, he couldn't climb up the rigging. So, he got a job as cook or messman, hence the name Peggie."

"Oh, right, thanks."

"Right, men. I've been informed by the Admiralty that U-boats have been laying mines in the Mersey Estuary and the Bristol Channel. So, lookouts, and everybody else, keep a good lookout at all times. Keep your eyes peeled for subs and mines, and yell out if you see one. Report red or green, near or far and the points where the sub or mine... or aircraft, was seen. Any questions?"

No one had any further questions.

"Right, lads, it's nearly high water, we'll catch the ebb. Let's get this little ship to sea and down to Welsh Wales."

Talking amongst themselves, the crew dispersed to their leaving harbour stations.

~ * ~ * ~ * ~

Kevin, standing at the stern end of the collier with Mr Todd the second mate and an aging sailor named Froggy Jackson, had butterflies in his stomach, excited at his first day as a sailor and at the very beginning of his first voyage to sea. Todd looked towards the bridge waiting for the order to cast off the aft mooring lines.

The river pilot gave the order to let go. The ship's horn gave out a single toot and the ship's head moved off the dock side the stern lines acting as a fulcrum.

"Let go aft," called the captain.

Freddy Todd signalled to the dockers to cast off. The line was taken off the bollards and wound in, Kevin coiled it neatly on the deck.

"Well done, Peggie, where did you learn to do that."

"Bosun Heygate, showed me, sir."

"Good, when we are clear of the dock, we'll stow away the lines in the rope locker."

The ship, with the aid of a tug, moved from the berth through the locks, into the River Mersey and headed towards the sea.

"You see that large building on the Liverpool side?" Todd asked, pointing to the Liver Building. "The one with the big stone birds on the roof?"

Kevin looked across at the Liver Building on the Liverpool waterfront "Yeah."

"Those birds are called the Liver Birds. Well, every time a 16 -year-old virgin passes by, the Liver Birds flap their wings."

Kevin looked up at the stone birds. "Really? I didn't know that." Thinking, '*I wonder how stone birds can flap their wings.*' Until the penny dropped. He smiled at the joke.

The *Alice Morgan* was now steaming full speed ahead down river, leaving a long trail of black smoke in its wake. At the mouth of the River Mersey, the

Lynas pilot station boat came alongside to take off the river pilot. Captain Abraham rang the telegraph several times back and forth to tell the engine room that the voyage south was underway with no more stopping and starting the engine. Two naval mine sweepers were working in the estuary, clearing a channel for ships leaving and entering the docks of Liverpool and Manchester, reminding all the mariners they were now in a dangerous war zone.

Kevin stood next to Hector by the handrails looking back at the shoreline.

"Just think, Hector, this time yesterday we were at Church Parade in Arcaster."

"Yes, that's right. Are you excited?"

Kevin nodded, "Erm, yes, I think I'm going to like life at sea. I can't get over how friendly the captain is, and all the crew, Mr Chapman and Freddy Todd are also really nice and helpful. Not once have they commented on me being small. Yeah, I like this ship." He showed Hector the short length of canvas he was holding. "The bosun gave me this canvas, I'm going to make myself a grab-bag. Old Willie Wilde leant me his palm and needle and yarn and showed me how to stich canvas."

"How old do you reckon Willie is?"

"I don't know, but I do know he sailed on tea-clippers. He must be over a hundred."

Hector smiled, "I think he is 70-years-old. The Chief Steward is over 65. Mr Cameron says there is around 400 years of sea-going experience between the crew."

Kevin thought about the crew of the *Alice Morgan*. "Yeah, I bet he's right. Mr Hollander is as old as God, Murgatroyd the chief steward is ancient. Froggy is at least 65 … Captain Abraham isn't a spring chicken, is he?"

"No, apart from us two there's no one aged under fifty!"

"I don't care how old they are, I learned so much from Bosun Heygate at the *Cromwell*." Kevin glanced up at the smoke belching out of the funnel, at the gulls flying above the wake and the green-grey sea all around him. "Yes. This is a good ship and a good crew; I really do like being at sea. See you later, Hector."

Kevin left the deck to prepare a pot of tea for the off coming watch.

~ * ~ * ~ * ~

The passage from Birkenhead to Cardiff had been uneventful. Unfortunately for the crew, the coaling Staithes of Cardiff, the busiest in the world, were booked solid with other colliers; The *Alice Morgan* being forced to anchor off the Cardiff docks to await a slot. They had been swinging around their anchor for nearly five weeks.

"What do you think, Froggy?" Kevin, sitting at the crews messroom table, handed his newly completed canvas grab bag to Able Seaman Froggy Jackson.

"Yeah, Peggie." Jackson examined the stitching. "You done a good job there, you could get a job as a sailmaker. What you going to keep in it?"

"A bottle of water, my torch that my dad gave me, a fishing line, some barley sugar sweets and my toffee tin with my…"

"Shush, listen," called Able Seaman Alfredson. "The British army are being evacuated out of France."

The sailors stopped chattering to listen to the radio. The BBC light programme being relayed from the wireless room. The sailors' faces were solemn as they listened to the news from France and the sombre tone of Bernard Stubbs reporting from Dover on the evacuation of Dunkirk.

"My boy is in France with the HLI," Able Seaman Frazer said.

"Let's hope he's with the evacuated soldiers, Duncan."

"I hope so, but someone has to fight the rear guard and it's usually the Highlanders who have to do that."

"Alright, lads, let's get back to work." The bosun called, popping his head through the mess room door. "We're going alongside."

The sailors and stokers left the messroom to go to work. Kevin was left to wash up the tea cups.

"Peggie, when you have finished in here go aft and help the second mate."

"Okay, Bosun." Kevin quickly finished washing up, he would much prefer to be out on deck than washing dishes. He glanced around the seaman's mess room, at the bunks, the oilskins hung on hooks, the bare table and the coal burning stove. Satisfied the compartment was clean and tidy he left to go up to the main deck.

~ * ~ * ~ * ~

At long last a berth had become available and the loading of the coal had begun; the coal dust settling over the decks and superstructure. A gang of dockyard workers came on board to fit the rotating base of a Holman Projector. The base of the anti-aircraft weapon was welded to the deck above the wheelhouse and the steam pipe fitted. With the work completed, the foreman of the gang asked Captain Abraham to assemble the crew for training.

All the crew including the two boy ratings were expected to be shown how to fire the Holman. Kevin sat cross-legged in front of the sailors, watching and listening to the foreman.

"Right, gents," said the foreman. "Here we have the Mk2 Holman Projector. This is an anti-aircraft weapon. Mk2 is an improvement on the Mk1 as this one is powered by high-pressure steam and is fitted with a trigger. Here." The foreman pointed to the trigger. "This weapon fires HE…high explosive rounds kept in this ammo ready box." He pointed to the metal box containing 20 Mills bombs. "The Holman can fire a projectile 600 feet into the air. The Mills will explode on contact or it will explode after 3.5 seconds. This barrel is unrifled, smooth bore, it will fire anything from beer bottles to potatoes. As well as an anti-aircraft weapon it can fire an illuminating projectile, but your main use will be anti-aircraft. The Mills bomb makes some smoke when it explodes; that's good as German pilots think it's ack-ack and will keep higher, thus less accurate bombing. Line up this sight with the aircraft,' and fire."

The Holman was fitted with a crude anti-aircraft sight fitted to the mortar barrel.

"Happy so far?"

"Yes, carry on," answered the captain.

"Right." The foreman took a round from the ammunition box. "This is how you prime the mortar. Remove the safety pin; remove the cap, here; turn this, then quickly drop the mortar into the tube, aim, and fire." The foreman demonstrated how to prime and load the projectile.

One by one, each member of the crew had a dummy run on how to prime, load, aim and fire the weapon. With the training over the men returned to their duties, satisfied that in the event of an air attack they would at least be able to fire at the planes.

~ * ~ * ~ * ~

Kevin finished mopping out the sailors messroom. Checking everything was neat and tidy he strolled to the deck for a breath of air, the sun now setting over the Irish Sea. Hector, having finished cleaning the galley, joined him.

"Come on, Hector, let's have a closer look at the Holman, you never know we might get to use it one day."

"I wouldn't mess around with it if I was you."

"I'm not going to mess around with it, just have a closer look."

The two boys climbed up onto the monkey island, the small deck above the wheelhouse. Kevin removed the canvas cover. He swung the barrel one way, then the other way, elevating and depressing the barrel. Taking aim at an imaginary aircraft, "Boom," he mouthed, mimicking the sound of an exploding Mills bomb. "The man who fitted the gun said it will fire anything that will fit in the barrel."

"Hmm, potatoes even."

"Yeah, spuds. Go and get one, from the galley."

"You're not planning on firing it, are you?"

"Why not, just a spud. Come on, Hector, no one will know."

Hector examined the weapon. "Alright then, just one spud."

"Get a big one."

Hector disappeared off the monkey island returning two minutes later holding a large potato.

Kevin turned on the steam. A hiss and popping noise emitted from the barrel. "What shall I aim at?"

Hector looked around the coaling staithe. "See if you can clear the roof of that building." He pointed to the two-storey dock office building 300 yards away from the staithes.

"Alright then. Watch this."

Kevin took aim over the roof. He pulled the trigger.

'Whoosh' the steam blasted the potato out of the barrel at high speed.

The two boys watched, open mouthed, as the projectile flew at high speed, arching through the sky.

"Wow! Look…at…that…"

Their expression changed as the potato began to fall short of the roof. Instead of clearing the roof the potato smashed through the window of the dock-architect's office, hitting and splattering over the drawing board. Almost knocking the draftsman off his chair.

Kevin coughed, "err, I think we'd better disappear."

"Oh, bugger! Turn off the steam, turn off the steam."

Kevin shut down the valve while glancing nervously towards the broken window. The two boys scurried off the bridge and disappeared inside the accommodation.

~ * ~ * ~ * ~

Swilling coal dust off the bridge wing with a hosepipe, Kevin listened to the architect speaking angrily to Captain Abraham.

"It came from the direction of your ship, Captain. It was flying so bloody fast it could have only come from your Holman. Nobody could throw a potato like that. I thought there was an air raid on; nearly gave me a heart attack."

Captain Abraham listened patiently to the architect. "Alright, I will investigate, however, there is no proof that it came from my ship. I'm sorry, but there is not much more I can do. No-one saw anything untoward and at the time you said the potato crashed through your window, all my crew were stood down and no training taking place. You say you saw no-one outside the offices," the captain shrugged. "So, Mr Roberts, there is nothing more I can say. I promise I will look into it. So, then. Good day to you."

Kevin breathed a sigh of relief as he moved out of the way of Roberts as he stormed off the deck.

Kevin and the captain watched the architect leave the ship.

"Do you know anything about this, Peggie?"

"Err, no, sir," he said innocently.

"Erm, well, if I find out that the Holman was used for firing potatoes, there will be trouble… Potatoes are hard to come by in wartime." Captain Abraham, looking up at the dock office window, could not hide the smile on his face.

As the architect walked off the staithe, an army waggon approached the coaling berth. The waggon pulled up at the gangway. Four soldiers jumped down from the tailgate; another soldier handed the men two heavy machine guns, two ammunition boxes, gas masks and four British Army backpacks.

"Right lads," the chief mate called to Kevin and Hector. "Go and help the Pongos with their kit. They are sailing with us."

"Pongos?" Kevin asked Hector

Hector shrugged, "don't know, come on."

The soldier's shoulder flashes said 'Royal Artillery'. They wore army battledress, black hob-nail boots with army gaiters.

"Carry the ammo boxes between you," said a corporal, who appeared to be the man in charge of the soldiers. "We'll bring up the rest."

On the main deck, the mate greeted the soldiers. "You are sleeping in the fo'c'sle. That's up the front."

The two boys struggled with the heavy ammunition boxes lumping them up the gangway to the main deck.

"Take them up to the monkey island," ordered the mate. "And put them next to the Mills bomb boxes. That's where the pongos will mount their machine guns."

"Machine guns and Mills bombs," Hector said to Kevin as they heaved the heavy boxes up the ladder to the monkey island. "It's getting quite exciting, don't you think?"

"Exciting? I'm getting a bit nervous now. This is more serious than scrumping pears from the vicarage garden."

Later in the afternoon Captain Abraham called all the crew to the officers' dining room. Holding his sailing orders, he spoke to the assembled crew.

"Since we left Liverpool, the war has taken a turn for the worse. France is more or less in German hands. At this very moment the BEF is being evacuated from Dunkirk. If the Germans take the French Atlantic ports, life at sea for us will become more dangerous, with U-boats refuelling and sailing out of Brest and La Rochelle." He waved the orders. "The admiralty, in their wisdom, because of the dangers of mines, have ordered us to sail with a coastal convoy as far as Land's End. After that we will be on our own to Freetown. Therefore gentlemen, I intend sailing well clear of the coast and we will be zig-zagging during daylight hours. It may take us longer to get to Freetown, but less chance of attacks from aircraft, from the mainland, and by zig-zagging, less chance of being attacked by U-boats...I hope. The unfortunate thing is, we have to return to the anchorage to wait for the convoy to assemble."

Groans of disappointment came from the crew. "Nothin' worse than swinging round the pick," moaned Froggy Jackson.

At 2100, the *Alice Morgan* left Cardiff for the short trip down the Bristol Channel to an anchorage off the Mumbles to await the convoy to assemble.

~ * ~ * ~ * ~

With a cacophony of foghorn signals and code flags flying, the SS *Alice Morgan* carrying 3000 tons of coal weighed anchor. Kevin, working with Willie Wilde washing coal dust off the bulkheads, looked around at the 30 or more merchant ships weighing anchor or manoeuvring back and forth trying to take up their allotted positions in the convoy. A couple of naval corvettes plied up and down the fleet signalling orders to the merchantmen. Captain Abraham held back waiting for the other ships to move off.

"Let them sort themselves out. Let the part time, hostilities only, royal naval reserve officers have their day, strutting up and down the convoy like some latter-day Admiral Benbow."

Kevin whispered to Willie Wilde, "why is the captain so cross with the navy?"

"I think it's something to do with the convoy cockups from the last war and the arrogance of some of the RN officers thinking us merchant seamen are ill-disciplined scruffy seadogs."

"Alright, Mr Chapman. Half speed ahead if you please," called the captain to his chief officer.

The mate rang the telegraph to the engine room to fire up the main engine. A few minutes later, satisfied that the way ahead was clear, the captain gave the order. "Ring her away, Mr Chapman."

Once again, the chief mate rang the telegraph to indicate the voyage proper had started and there would be no more stopping and starting the engine. With the convoy formed up and underway, the *Alice Morgan* tagged on behind the slow-moving convoy. All the ships, except the *Alice Morgan* were heading for the English Channel bound for the Isle of Sheppey in the River Thames. The old collier began to fall astern of the convoy.

"Here come our gallant heroes," Willie Wilde said to Kevin as a corvette rove up on the port side. The grey corvette came up alongside like a shepherd rounding up his sheep. The corvette's captain called across using a megaphone. "*Alice Morgan*. Maintain your best speed. Take up your position astern on the starboard outer line."

"Tell him to fuck off," Captain Abraham said to no one in particular. Instead, the captain shouted back, "will endeavour to maintain good speed and position with the convoy."

The corvette opened his throttle and steamed away doing around 20 knots. The *Alice Morgan* fell further astern. Kevin glanced around at the Atlantic Ocean to the right. He gave a momentary shudder, thinking about the dangers lurking under the waves. He then looked up at the sky thinking, a German dive-bomber could pounce out of the blue at any time they were near the coast. He continued swilling the bulkheads and decks with a hosepipe; getting rid of the invasive coal dust.

Scarcely eight hours after leaving the anchorage, just off the coast of St Ives in Cornwall, the *Alice Morgan* slowed down to a stop, waiting for a motor launch to pull up alongside. The four soldiers, their guns and their equipment, who had joined the ship in Cardiff, were waiting to be taken off the ship.

"Are they leaving already?" a surprised Kevin asked Freddy Todd the second mate. "They've only just joined us."

"Yes, they only escort ships on the coast. We will be sailing south with only the Holman for protection."

Freddy and Kevin lowered a Jacobs ladder over the handrails and helped the soldiers over the side. Using a rope, they lowered the machine guns and ammo boxes down to the launch. The corporal was the last soldier to leave the ship.

"So long, lads. Have a safe trip. I wish we could stay with you, but you know, orders are orders." He climbed over the handrail and down the Jacobs ladder; standing in the stern of the boat the corporal and the other soldiers waved.

Kevin waved back and watched as the launch headed towards the Cornish coast.

"Do you wish you were leaving too?" asked Hector who had joined Kevin at the handrails.

"Kind of. I'm missing my mum, and I'm a bit scared of what's out there." Kevin pointed to the Atlantic. "I'm sleeping in my lifejacket, what about you?"

"Too true. I'm not the best swimmer in the world."

The coastal convoy altered course towards the English Channel while the

Alice Morgan, breaking away from the protection of the corvettes, altered her course heading for the Bay of Biscay alone and unprotected.

~ * ~ * ~ * ~

Out in the open sea with no convoy station to maintain, Kevin, for only the second time, was allowed to steer the ship. He took hold of the ship's wheel.

"The ship is taking starboard helm," advised his mentor, Willie, an old sailor who should have retired long ago. Kevin had found out that old Willie Wilde was over 70 years old. "The Atlantic swell is pushing us to port. That's it, Peggie. Don't chase the compass."

Kevin was determined to master the art of maintaining a straight course. After 15 minutes he was left alone. The reassuring sound of Morse code *dit-dahs* coming from the radio room located just behind the wheelhouse. The collier rolled gently on the long swell of the North Atlantic. Occasionally, when Kevin drifted off course the ship dipped its bows into a wave sending sea spray over the wheelhouse reminding him to get back on course. By this time both Hector and Kevin had got their sea legs and had gotten over their bouts of seasickness. Captain Abraham strolled around the wheelhouse and out onto the bridge wings. A pair of binoculars hanging around his neck, Willie Wilde stood out on the starboard wing keeping lookout. A gentle breeze blowing through the open wheelhouse doors. Every half hour the captain ordered a change of course, trying to frustrate any prowling U-boat from taking aim at his ship and firing off a torpedo. After one hour on the wheel, Kevin was relieved by Froggy Jackson, the second of the sailors on Toddy's watch.

"She's still taking starboard wheel," Kevin reported to Jackson.

"Thanks, Peggie," he said, taking over the helm.

Kevin strolled out onto the bridge wing to take his turn at lookout. Half of his time he spent in the mess, looking after the sailors, making brews of tea and washing up and scrubbing out the messdeck. The other half of his time he spent learning the job of a deck hand; this he enjoyed most of all. Willie Wilde had given him a battered copy of 'The Seaman's Manual'. He read it every spare moment.

Kevin, daydreaming of home, heard what he thought was an airplane engine. He scanned the sky over the port side of the ship.

"I think I can hear a plane, Captain," he called.

Captain Abraham came over to the port wing. He listened intently, scanning the clouds.

"Your ears must be better than mine, Peggie. I can't hear a thing."

"I can still hear it, sir." He pointed to the northeast.

The engine revs grew louder. "I can hear it now."

"I can see it. Look!"

A twin-engine plane appeared out of the misty clouds. The aircraft was still too far away for identification.

"Let's hope it hasn't seen us and goes on its way."

The aircraft suddenly changed course, heading for the *Alice Morgan*.

As it drew closer, the captain identified the aircraft. "Heinkel!" he shouted before rushing over to the alarm. He pressed the Klaxon. The alarm bells resounding throughout the ship sent sailors tumbling out onto the deck.

"German warplane!" The captain pointed to the plane that was taking up a position to attack. "Hard a starboard, helmsman."

Jackson swung the ship's wheel hard to the right.

"Get up here, lads, man this bloody Holman." Abraham shouted down to the men standing by the handrails looking up at the aircraft.

The radio officer came out of the radio cabin to see what the commotion was about.

"Sparks, send off the AAAA signal. Being attacked by an aircraft."

"Right…right. Will do, Captain." The radio operator rushed back into the radio cabin to send off a coded message to the admiralty and other ships warning them of enemy aircraft in the area.

"Peggie, get up there and pass the Mills rockets to the gunners. Helmsman keep zigzagging."

"Aye, aye, sir." Froggy Jackson spun the wheel again.

Kevin sprang into action, climbing quickly up the raking ladder onto the monkey island. He removed the canvas covering the Holman Projector and opened the steam valve. Within one minute, two able seamen from the chief mate's watch joined him on the island; now a gun deck. Kevin pulled a projectile out of the ready-use ammo locker, waiting for orders.

"Okay, Peggie, do you remember how to prime it?" asked gunner Able Seaman Habbard.

"Yeah, sure. I think."

"Okay, as soon as we fire off a rocket take another out and prime it."

The attacking aircraft's engine now became a roar. The black cross on the fuselage and the swastika on the tail plane clearly visible. The roar changing to a scream as the Heinkel bomber lined up to drop its bombs.

The captain shouted from the bridge wing, "now, now. Put up a barrage. As many as you can fire off." He glanced up at the plane. "Now, fire off now, put the pilot off."

Kevin pulled out the safety pin and primed the rocket, handing it to the loader. Habbard dropped the bomb down the barrel. Seaman Alfredson took aim and pulled the trigger. 'Pop!' The Mills bomb flew skywards. At 600 feet it exploded in a puff of fire and smoke. Kevin handed over the next rocket, working flat out to keep up the rate of fire. The puffs of smoke, looking like ack-ack fire, seemed to have the desired effect. The bomber pilot veered away flying round in a large circle. The Heinkel lined up again for a second attack. This time the pilot keeping his aircraft higher than the first attack. The puffs of smoke, looking like ack-ack, again, did have the desired effect; the pilot dropped his bombs too early. Kevin could see the two bombs clearly as they fell; they hit the sea and detonated less than twenty yards astern but near enough to send seawater flying over the stern of the *Alice Morgan*. The entire ship shuddered. Kevin handed another rocket to the Holman loader. The fifth rocket only reached 200 feet before curving gracefully dropping into the sea exploding on impact. The steam pressure firing the Holman dropped dramatically. The sixth rocket barely popped out of the barrel. The projectile reached 40 feet, not much higher than the ship's foremast. It then fell out of the sky onto the *Alice Morgan's* foredeck.

"Oh, no!" cried Kevin.

"Take cover!" screamed the captain.

Everyone dropped down flat on the deck as the rocket exploded on hitting the ship's deck. The explosion blew a hole in the steel deck. Lumps of coal shot out of the hole bouncing and clattering over the deck. The aircraft minus its two bombs, veered away again on its way back to an airfield in France. The helmsman resumed a steady course south.

"Bloody hell, that was close," said Alfredson. "We lost steam pressure."

Kevin looked over the damaged foredeck. "It's blown a flipping great hole in the deck."

The captain called, "anyone hurt up there?"

"No, sir," answered Habbard. Lucky for us the projectile didn't drop on us or we'd be blown to kingdom come."

"Someone, you, Peggie, you, get onto the foredeck and make sure the coal is not on fire."

Kevin hurried down the ladder and onto the foredeck. Pieces of coal littered the deck. He looked down into the hold. No sign that the exploding projectile had set fire to the coal.

"No fire, Captain."

"Okay, Peggie. Good work. Pick up the coal and drop it back in the hold; we don't want to waste any of it." The captain's voice calm and relaxing as if the local coalman had spilt a bit of coal outside the coal grate, instead of a wayward Mills bomb blowing a great big hole in the deck of his ship.

Hector joined Kevin helping him pick up the lumps of coal scattered around the deck.

"Crikey, that was exciting," Kevin said.

"You think so? I was shit scared. If those bombs had been a bit closer, they could have broken the ship's back."

"It's a good job the Mills rocket didn't drop down the engine room lantern light, the old chief engineer Hollander would have had the shock of his life."

"A bit like the port-architect when that spud hit his drawing board."

The two boys started giggling, mainly out of relief that the bomber had missed its target, but partly at remembering the potato crashing through the dock office window.

The *SS Alice Morgan* resumed its southerly course towards Sierra Leone.

The *Alice Morgan* navigated safely through the Bay of Biscay, passing Cape Finisterre and passing well clear of the normal shipping routes between Europe and Africa, trying to avoid any lurking U-boats. The weather had turned hot, the butter melted in the butter dish.

"Keep your shirt on, Peggie, sunburn is a self-inflicted wound, you know. Also, if we must abandon ship in the tropics, you'll need protection from the sun." The captain gave the practical advice to Kevin.

Hungry for knowledge, Kevin took on-board all the advice he could. From the captain, from the chief mate and from the experienced sailors. Checking through his Boatswain's Manual he ticked off things he had learned so far. Liverpool salvaging splice, rigging a bosun's chair and painting stage and how to steer a ship; things he needed to know to become an able-bodied seaman. His schoolboy shorts that he'd had since joining the *TS Cromwell* now came in handy in the warm weather, although they were getting too tight for him. He had grown nearly two inches since February. He now stood at five foot four and a half inches tall. The half inch very important to Kevin.

Looking out at the calm blue sea, the world looked at peace. The war, the blackouts, the rationing that started in January all seemed a thing of the past.

'We've been attacked by an aircraft,' he thought, *'surely lightning doesn't strike the same place twice.'*

~ * ~ * ~ * ~

Captain Abraham called all the crew to the officers' dining room for his regular updates on the war.

"As promised, I will endeavour to keep you up to date with the war." The captain looked down at the notes typed by the radio officer. "France has surrendered. French overseas territories are now under Vichy rule. The Germans are in charge in Tunisia, Morocco and Algeria and French West Africa. Britain has been bombed by the Luftwaffe. More dangerously for us, the Nazis are using French ports to harbour and service their U-boats. Winston Churchill has won a vote in Parliament to continue with the war and not to sue for peace with Hitler. That's not good news for us seafarers. The war at sea continues."

The gathered sailors gave a collective groan.

"What's it got to do with Churchill?"

"Don't you know? He's now the Prime Minister."

"God, help us."

"My dad served with Winston Churchill in France in 1917, after his cockup in Gallipoli," Cameron the cook said. "He was an officer with the Royal Scots Fusiliers. My dad said he's a fighter and won't surrender to the Jerries."

The crew chattered between themselves, talking about the war until Captain Abraham called, "alright, gents, get back to work and keep your eyes peeled for U-boats."

"Thanks, Captain," the men said as they left the room.

On his way back to work, Kevin asked, "what's Vichy rule, Willie? Who is Vichy?"

"I don't rightly know, Peggie," replied Willie Wilde. "I think it's a place. A place in France."

"Erm, it's complicated."

~ * ~ * ~ * ~

A lull fell over the ship. An anti-climax following the Heinkel attack. The engines thumped, thumped, without missing a beat. Grey-black smoke issued from the funnel darkening the otherwise clear blue sky. The sea in front flat calm and another ten days of boredom before they reached Freetown. Freddy Todd, the navigator, studied the chart in the chart room. John Burch, the radio officer, dozed in the radio room struggling to stay awake in the mid-day heat.

Kevin turned the wheel. Glancing from time to time at the compass repeater. Thinking all the time of Jane Black his girlfriend back home but trying at the same time on keeping a straight course. He looked up at the ship's clock for the umpteenth time wishing it was change of watch time. He snapped out of his daydream when Froggy Jackson screamed from the port bridge wing.

"Torpedo!" Jackson pointed to the port bow.

Kevin just caught the sight of a torpedo wake flash past the bows of the *Alice Morgan*.

"Where? Are you sure it was a torpedo?" Freddy Todd called, rushing out onto the bridge port wing.

"I'm sure. It passed from port to starboard."

"I saw it too, Mr Todd," Kevin shouted from the wheelhouse. "I saw the wake disappear over there." He pointed to the starboard bow.

The captain came out of his sea cabin to investigate the commotion.

"A torpedo, Captain. Came at us from forward of the port beam."

Captain Abraham looked aft, trying to guess the place where the U-Boat must have fired from. "Hard a starboard!" he shouted. Trying to put his stern aspect to the attacking submarine, making a smaller target.

Kevin spun the wheel hard right.

"Torpedo! Coming up from the port quarter," the lookout shouted again.

A second torpedo fizzed along the port side from aft to forward speeding harmlessly off into the distance. This time the captain saw it. No doubt now they were under attack from a U-boat he pressed the action stations alarm for the second time in a week. The crew of the *Alice Morgan,* donning their lifejackets, hastened out of the accommodation, scrambled to boat deck, and awaited instructions from the captain. Within two minutes most of the crew were out on the main deck scanning the sea for the U-Boat.

"Sparky," Captain Abraham called to the radio officer. "Send the signal SSSS - being attacked by submarine. Send our position."

"Roger. Will do, Captain," replied the radio officer picking up the noon position chitty. He rushed back into the radio room to send off the wartime distress call.

Willie Wilde, a more experienced helmsman, took the wheel off Kevin.

"Go and assist the skipper."

"Okay, Willie." Kevin, not knowing what to do next, wandered outside to stand with the captain and Jackson.

"Steer a ziz, zag course, Mr Wilde."

"Bugger me," the captain said to no one in particular. "The Jerries are determined to sink us. God knows why, we are only carrying coal. Not exactly a prime target for the Kriegsmarine."

"Torpedo," Jackson screamed again, pointing to a rapidly approaching wake. The torpedo could be seen clearly in front of the bubbling wake. At the same moment, as the men on the bridge braced themselves for a torpedo strike, the ship veered. Instead of detonating, the torpedo scraped alongside the hull before overtaking the collier and heading harmlessly out towards the empty sea.

"Bloody hell, that was close. Three torpedoes. I don't believe it. Do you know how much them bloody things cost? I've been told they cost around 30,000 Reichsmarks each!" The captain shook his head, "the skipper won't quit now. He'll be as mad as hell, wasting three torpedoes."

No sooner had the captain spoke, a U-boat began to surface.

"U-boat. Red 45, near!" Jackson pointed to the submarine.

Everyone stared in the direction given. The U-boat emerged from the sea, seawater draining off its decks. Almost immediately the conning tower hatch opened, and German sailors poured onto the deck, heading for the deck gun.

"Keep zig zagging, Mr Jackson. They are going to shoot at us. Sparks, have you sent off that coded message?"

"I have, I have, but I haven't got any reply yet. Except a signal from that U-Boat ordering me to stop transmitting." Radio Officer John Burch called from the radio room. "He said he'd fire at the bridge if I didn't stop sending out the SSSS signal."

"Never mind that. Keep trying, Sparky. The sub is going to sink us with gun fire. We've no chance now."

Captain Abraham spoke to the chief mate who had joined them on the bridge. "Mr Chapman, go and organise the starboard lifeboat. Swing it outboard. Get ready to abandon ship." He handed the chief mate the sink-bag containing the ship's confidential papers. "On the order abandon ship, drop this bag overboard. Make sure it sinks; we don't want to give the enemy the Admiralties pre-arranged routes, secret codes and signals."

"Right, Captain," Chapman said, taking the bag. "Come with me, Peggie, help us get the boat ready."

Kevin followed the mate towards the starboard lifeboat. "My grab bag...I need my bag."

Before Chapman could stop him, Kevin ran off towards the sailors messdeck.

"Where the hell are you off to!?"

"I've got to get my grab bag," he called over his shoulder. "It's got my tin in it."

"Tin in it? What fuckin' tin in it?"

Kevin didn't answer. He disappeared inside the ship. 90 seconds later he emerged carrying his grab bag.

Chapman looked at the bag. "Don't do that again. Don't you risk your life for a tin of sweets."

"There's no sweets in the tin. Just my mum's St Christopher."

The mate shook his head incredulously. "Come on..."

The submarine's 88mm cannon opened fire interrupting the chief mate. The first salvo aimed at the masts and radio aerial. All five shells screamed through the rigging without affect. The radio officer continued tapping out the distress signals. The U-boat skipper then carried out his threat. The submarines gun crew began to shell the bridge. The second salvo pumping two shells into the bridge and radio room. The radio room exploded; smoke began to pour out of the shell hole. Following a brief pause, the cannon opened up again, this time firing at the lifeboats. The first of the shells hit the portside lifeboat blowing the timber boat to pieces sending shards of timber flying across the deck. The timber spears hitting Cameron the cook and Hector who were crossing the open deck making their way to the boat station. They both fell down. Another shell hit the funnel. A cloud of smoke and soot mushroomed over the ship covering everything and everyone in black oily soot.

Kevin blinked in horror at the sight of Captain Abraham staggering out of the wheelhouse onto the starboard bridge wing. His face black, his brown suit torn and covered in blood.

"Abandon ship," the captain shouted down to the men standing by the starboard boat, before he rushed back into the burning wheelhouse.

Chapman acknowledged, "okay, Skipper."

The mate threw the sink-bag overboard. He watched it sink.

A minute later the captain emerged from the smoke, dragging the body of the radio officer. He dropped Burch's body, shaking his head in despair. Captain Abraham stumbled down the steps to join the men launching the lifeboat.

"The sparky is dead. I told him to keep transmitting. I didn't think they would deliberately target the radio officer transmitting a distress call. They bloody well murdered him," the captain said angrily, looking around at his crew. "Are we all here?"

The mate looked down at a sheet of paper he was holding. "Right, men, answer your name. Captain's here, chief engineer's here, second engineer?"

"I'm here," called Josh White

"Second mate?" He looked at the gathering crew. "Freddy, are you okay?"

Freddy Todd, busily winding out the davits, looked up. "Yeah, I'm okay."

The mate continued with the roll call, "Mr Cameron? Hector? Where's the cook and the boy?"

Kevin looked around for his friend. He then noticed two bodies lying face down on the other side of the boat deck. He recoiled at the sight of Hector lying in a pool of blood.

"Hector!" Kevin ran across to him. Pieces of wood were sticking out of Hector's back like porcupine quills; he was barely conscious and bleeding badly. Kevin looked down at the cook. A large splinter was embedded in

Cameron's skull. Kevin had never seen a dead man before, but he knew the cook was dead.

Captain Abraham joined Kevin. He checked the cook and confirmed the worse, "'fraid he's dead."

"Hector, come on," Kevin sobbed. He grasped hold of Hector's wrist. The captain took hold of his other wrist and between them, bending over double, they dragged Hector towards the lifeboat.

Another shell screamed over the captain's head and exploded into the superstructure. The blast sent shrapnel scything across the deck. The flying metal flew over the captain and Kevin's crouching bodies but hit two of the standing sailors working to wind out the boat. Habbard dropped like a stone with a massive head wound. His brains bubbling out onto the deck. Alfredson pirouetted like a ballet dancer with the force of the hot metal hitting him in the chest. He too fell down dead. Kevin could not believe his eyes at the carnage he was witnessing, wishing he could dig a hole in the deck and hide in it, wishing he was back home in the safety of his dad's house.

Willie Wilde rushed over to help the captain and Kevin with Hector. "Come on, lads, let's get you both in the boat."

Chapman continued calmly reading from a crew list, checking each man as they milled around the lifeboat. At the same time watching the bosun organising the men swinging out the lifeboat.

"The cook's dead, chief," Abraham informed his chief mate.

"So are Able Seaman Habbard and AB Alfredson," the chief engineer said. "I've checked them both. Both killed instantly."

"Fucking murdered, you mean, bastard Jerries."

"Chief steward! Anyone seen the chief steward?" the mate called

"Here I am, Mr Mate." Murgatroyd came hurrying up the deck carrying an armful of loaves. He tossed the bread into the boat.

"Alright, Mr Murgatroyd, get in the boat." Chapman counted the men. "Right, we're all here. Captain, you climb in the boat, I'll stay on deck till you are down in the water."

The chief engineer pointed to the three dead sailors lying out on the boat deck and up at the bridge wing. "Four good lads killed, no need for that. The Germans committed war crimes in the last war, the Geneva Convention clearly states not to shell merchant ships while the crew are abandoning it."

"Alright men, that's it. We're all here." Captain Abraham said, looking around at his ship, blown to bits and on fire. "Lower away."

The boat was lowered to the sea and the falls were disconnected. Four sailors using the boats oars began to pull the lifeboat clear of the ship. The U-boat skipper continued to have the *Alice Morgan* shelled. More than 50 rounds had been pumped into the ship before there were signs that she was sinking.

"Captain, you are Jewish, right?" asked Chapman.

"That's right, I am"

"The Nazis treat the Jews badly."

"Yes, I believe they do."

"In the last war, U-boats took the captain and chief engineers of merchant ships as prisoners of war."

"That's true, they did."

"Well, lads," the chief mate spoke to the boat's crew. "If they ask for the captain or chief engineer, tell the bastards on the U-boat the captain and chief engineer have been killed."

The men in the boat nodded in understanding.

Well clear of the sinking ship, the crew of the old collier watched her go down by the head, slowly at first, then more quickly. The *Alice Morgan* slipped under the waves taking four of its crew with her.

The submarine motored up to the lifeboat. The U-boat skipper and another submariner in the conning towers looked over at the men in the lifeboat.

"*Wo ist dein Kapitan?*"

Able seaman Jackson, shrugging, pretended not to understand.

The second man in the conning tower translated, "where is your captain?"

"He's dead. Murdered when you bastards shelled the bridge," called Jackson resting on his oar. Other men in the lifeboat shouted at the skipper calling him a murderer.

The translator translated Jackson's reply.

"*Wo ist dein Ingenieur?*"

"Where is your Engineer?"

"He's dead too. And our radio officer and two sailors. It's against the Geneva Convention to shell merchant ships while the crew are abandoning ship."

Once again, the translator translated Jackson's comments. The U-boat commander appeared unapologetic.

The submarine captain looked at Kevin. *"Tragen Sie Passagiere?"*

"Do you have passengers?

"No, no passengers"

"Wer ist dieser Junge?"

"Who is that young boy?"

"I'm a sailor." Kevin replied defiantly.

"Die deutsche marine schickt kein kinder sur see."

"The Kriegsmarine do not send children to sea," repeated the translator.

"We don't shoot innocent civilians or at sailors abandoning ships. Attacking unarmed merchant ships without warning is a war crime," shouted Jackson angrily.

The U-boat commander listened to the translation without showing any emotion. He spoke to the translator.

"All British merchant ships are being armed," called down the translator. "Therefore, we consider all British ships to be warships." He then looked directly at Abraham, "who are you?"

"I'm a steward," the captain lied. "Admiral Donitz is not going to be very pleased with you, Captain, wasting three torpedoes and fifty shells to sink an old collier ship carrying coal to Africa, a neutral country."

This response irritated the commander. He gave sharp orders to clear the bridge, saying no more to the men in the lifeboat. The submarine motored towards the west. Within five minutes the U-boat dived below the waves and disappeared, leaving the lifeboat and its crew 300 miles from the African coast.

~ * ~ * ~ * ~

The lifeboat's mast stepped and the main sail and jib were hoisted.

"We can sail on the trades 3000 miles to South America or tack and row our way 300 miles to Morocco, or try for the Canaries. If this wind keeps up, we'll be better off tacking and rowing to Morocco."

"Morocco, is now Vichy French. Not exactly on our side, Captain."

"We'll have to chance it; we are civilians after all. There will be a British Consulate in Rabat. They will have to repatriate us to England."

"I don't trust the Arabs as far as I could chuck a grand piano. The French are as bad. I heard on the radio the French were not too happy about us leaving them in the shit at Dunkirk."

"Alright, gentlemen. This is what we are going to do. We will sail eastwards to the African coast. If we get back to blighty, err, when we get back to blighty, I'm going to tell the family of Mr Cameron the cook, Mr Burch the radio officer, Able Seaman Habbard and AB Alfredson, the position where the *Alice Morgan* sank. Anyone got a pencil?"

The chief engineer handed the captain the stub of a pencil.

Captain Abraham took the crew list sheet. "I'm going to write down the latitude and longitude of where *Alice* sank. What's the date?"

"30th June."

"Sunday 30th June, 1940." The captain said, writing on the paper. "Has anyone got a safe place to keep this note?"

"I've got my tin, captain." Kevin offered his toffee tin as a place to keep the note.

"Right, keep this position safe, just in case I forget it."

Kevin put the sheet of paper, listing all the crew's names, into the tin box along with his seaman's book, ID card, his mother's St Christopher medal, Jane Black's little silver cross, Jane's letters and Tommy's sheriffs tin star.

"If we make it to Morocco, I've got a girlfriend in Casablanca." Josh White, the second engineer, said out of the blue. "Maybe she could help us."

"A girlfriend?"

"Well, she's a cabaret singer. She owns a bar near the harbour, we were pretty good friends. I was on the iron-ore run from Casablanca to Middlesbrough for five years."

"Sir, is there anything we can do for Hector?" Kevin asked. "He's looking pretty bad. How long will it be before we can get some help for him?"

"Don't know the answer to that, Peggie. It could take us a week or more to get to Morocco."

Kevin fussed over Hector who was drifting in and out of consciousness. Hector's wounds had stopped bleeding, the blood congealed. Kevin fed him sips of water from the water bottle he had kept in his grab bag.

Night fell. The sea around the lifeboat became pitch black. The stars above shone like crystal. Kevin, cradling Hector, looked up at the sky.

"Have you ever seen such bright stars, Hector? You can see the whole universe."

Hector gazed upwards, he didn't speak, he just blinked his eyes in acknowledgement.

Captain Abraham pointed to the constellations. "We can't see the compass in this light, but we can navigate by the stars. You see the seven stars there?" Hector and Kevin followed the direct of the captain's finger, both mesmerised by the shimmering galaxy. "That's the Big Dipper, Ursa Major, looks like a butcher's cleaver or a saucepan."

"Erm," murmured Kevin.

"If you draw an imaginary line from the two bottom stars, it will lead you to Polaris, or the north star. That's the brightest star there. On the other side of Polaris is the Little Bear or Ursa Minor. They both point to Polaris. If you sail towards Polaris, you are sailing north. At this time of year, they lie low on the horizon, but because we are at sea, we can still see them clearly."

"Is that how you navigate at night?"

"Well, not exactly. I use my sextant and charts, but because of the fire in the chartroom I couldn't get to the charts. We are sailing east so, there's the north, that way is the south, over there is the west and the way we are going is east."

"Thanks, Captain." Kevin fell asleep huddled close to Hector.

As dawn broke the following morning, Kevin checked on his friend. Hector had been growing weaker as each hour passed.

He whispered to Kevin, "I'm so tired, Kev."

"Go to sleep, Hector. You're going to be alright."

Hector smiled weakly. "Maybe. You know, Kev, I've never kissed a girl...," his voice trailed off. A few minutes later, hardly perceptible, he said to Kevin, "if I don't make it back home, Kev, will you give this to my mother?"

Hector opened his hand. Kevin took the little MN badge given to Hector at the training ship for being top-boy.

Kevin pressed the badge back into Hector's palm. "No, you keep it, Hector. You give it to your mother yourself. I'm telling you; you are going to be alright. Go to sleep and get your strength back."

Hector nodded weakly and fell asleep again huddled up under the thwart.

The boat sailed slowly towards the African coast. The crew taking turns at keeping lookout, steering the boat, taking turns on the oars and adjusting the sails whenever the wind changed.

On the third night after the *Alice Morgan* sank, Hector Davies - Davidson died.

Kevin shook Hector's shoulder. "Wake up, Hector, wake up... Captain, Hector isn't moving."

"Move over, sunshine, let me look," the captain said gently. The captain examined the boy and shook his head. "Sorry, lad, he's gone."

"Oh, no." Kevin sobbed. He wept openly. He tried shaking Hector again. "Wake up, Hector, please, wake up."

The sailors looked on sympathetically. Kevin stroked the hair of his dead friend, holding onto Hector's body, not wanting to believe his friend had died.

After an hour had passed the captain asked, "are you alright, Peggie? We're going to have to put him over the side now."

Kevin sniffed and nodded. "Yeah, I'm okay, thanks...just a minute though." He opened the tightly clasped fingers of Hector and took the badge out of his hand. "I'm alright now, thanks."

"Would anyone like to say a Christian prayer, before we commit Hector's body to the deep?"

"I know a prayer," said old Willie Wilde. "Well, maybe not a prayer, a poem."

The crew bowed their heads.

After a short pause, Willie Wilde started. "*No cross marks the place where he now lies. What happened is known but to us. You asked, and he gave his life to protect our land from the enemy's curse. No Flanders Field where poppies blow, no gleaming crosses, row on row. No unnamed tomb for all to see... and pause... and wonder who he may be. The sailors Valhalla is where he lies, on the ocean bed, watching ships pass by. Sailing in safety now through the waves, often right over his sea locked grave. We ask you, just to remember him. Amen.*"

"Amen," repeated the sailors.

Willie Wilde and Froggy Jackson carefully lifted Hector's body and looked towards the chief mate, waiting for the order to proceed with the burial.

The chief mate removed his cap. "*Into thy hands, oh Lord, we commend the soul of thy servant departed, now called into eternal rest, and we commit his body to the deep.*"

The mate gave a single nod to carry on. The two able seamen slid the body of Hector over the boat's side.

With tears streaming down his face, Kevin watched Hector slowly sink below the waves.

"How old was young Hector?" Josh White asked.

"Just 15," replied the captain. "He was just 15 years old."

The lifeboat made slow progress towards the African Coast. Captain Abraham and the chief mate, with only the boats compass, the sun during the day and the stars at night to navigate by, could only guess at their progress. Captain Abraham dipped the dipper in the water keg.

He handed the thimbleful of water to Kevin. "Just a sip, Peggie, make it last."

Kevin's lips, now cracked and swollen by the sun, wetted his tongue. He smiled weakly. "Thanks, Captain. I could just drink a pint of hop-bitters."

"Never heard of hop-bitters, is it beer?" asked the captain, trying to encourage Kevin to talk instead of moping quietly in the corner of the boat.

"No, not real beer. Someone said it's made from dandelions, like a herbal drink. It looks like beer with a frothy head, but there's no alcohol in it. They sell it at the 'Hop Bitter Shop' next to the school at home. Sixpence a pint. I was dreaming about sitting in the shop with my pal, Tommy Daggers and…"

"Land oh!" the lookout called out, interrupting Kevin.

The call aroused the listless crew; everyone scrambling to look over to the east.

Kevin stood up on the gunnel, gripping the forestay. "There, there's land. I can see it."

The low-lying land shimmered in the heat of the day. A freshening onshore breeze sprung up from nowhere. The coxswain tightened the foresheets and pulled in the main sheets. The cumbersome heavy lifeboat heeled slightly before picking up speed. The coastline getting more prominent each hour.

"I've no idea where we are," Captain Abraham admitted. "We'll get as close to the coast and try and find a safe place to land. I think we are well south of Casablanca."

The *SS Alice Morgan's* survivors scanned the shore for a place to land.

"The last thing we want," the captain said, "is to get overturned on the breaking surf after enduring seven days in this boat."

Kevin looked around at the crew. All were sunburned, all were thirsty, but they all remained positively upbeat.

"There's a fishing boat, Captain," Kevin called.

Captain Abraham stood up to look at the fishing boat. Between them and the coast he could see a boat with two men onboard, dragging in their nets. The fishing boat bobbed up and down but was not otherwise moving.

"Get alongside the boat, they will give us directions to their port. A fishing village, maybe?"

With a renewed enthusiasm the sailors shipped the oars, pulling and tacking towards the small open-decked fishing boat. As they drew near, Kevin waved to the boat. The two fishermen returned his wave. They stopped working with their nets and waited until the lifeboat reached alongside.

"Do you speak English?" the captain called.

The fisherman shrugged, indicating with his hands he didn't understand the captain's question.

"*Parle francais?*

"*Non, no parle Francais, pas si bon,*" replied the fisherman. "*Parle Darija, darija. Arab, Arab. Non parle francais bon.*"

"He says he speaks Darija. My girlfriend in Casablanca speaks Darija," said Josh White. "I think it's a local derivation of Arabic."

"Can you speak Darija, Mr White?"

"No. The only words I know is, '*iinaa aab*; 'I love you.' Better not say that to these two fishermen, they may get the wrong idea."

"Anyone speak Arabic?"

"No." Everyone shook their heads.

"I know a few words in Japanese," offered White. "I learned them from my girlfriend in Yokohama."

"How many girlfriends do you have?"

"One or two, around the world. I sailed on a Japanese time charter for 12 months trading on the Japanese coast."

"Well, anyway, Japanese isn't much use in Morocco. I only know a bit of French," said the captain. He asked the men in the fishing boat, "*es-tu de Casablanca?*"

"*Non*, Agadir, Agadir." The fisherman pointed towards the coast.

"Agadir must be their home port." The captain asked the fishermen in broken French, "*ou se trouve Agadir?*"

The fisherman pointed towards the land. He counted with his fingers, "*un, deux, trois kilometres, trois kilometres.*"

"Three kilometres. Come on then lads, three more miles. We'll land in Agadir port and report to the local police station."

The other fisherman held up a large flagon wrapped in straw mesh, indicating for the men to take a drink. The water flask was passed from sailor to sailor, they drank their fill. Each man thanking the fishermen. Next, the Moroccan fisherman handed over box of dates making an eating motion with his fingers.

"Thank you very much," the sailors said gratefully.

Kevin, licking his fingers, said, "I've never tasted anything so delicious in my life."

The others agreed.

"*Merci beaucoup*," some of the lifeboat crew called to the fishermen, the only French words they knew. As they were about to set off towards the port, the fisherman passed a manila line across to them, beckoning them to follow. The fishing boat's engine fired up and began to tow the lifeboat towards their fishing village. The mainsail and foresail were dropped, and the oars were shipped inboard. The sailors in the lifeboat could now sit back and relax as the fishermen towed and navigated them to the mainland. An hour later the SS *Alice Morgan's* survivors were safely tied up alongside the fish dock in Agadir.

CHAPTER 4

MOROCCO – JULY 1940

FOLLOWED BY MORE THAN 30 locals, the 15 sailors made their way along the dusty unpaved road to the police station. The station by the harbour was little more than a cinderblock single-storey building with a corrugated tin roof. A faded sign over the entrance read, POLIZEISTATION.

The police officer behind the desk looked up at the seamen, surprised at the sight of 14 unshaven sailors and a boy lining up at his desk.

The puzzled gendarme asked, "*Oui, qui es-tu et d'ou veins-tu?*"

"Do you speak English?

"*Non.* You English?" he asked in English.

"Yes. We are British sailors."

"Ah, English *matelot*," he said, looking carefully at each one of the survivors in turn, nodding all the time. He then beckoned, "*Suis moi,*"

"I think he said, 'follow me'," the captain said.

The gendarme, short in stature, pot-bellied, sporting a heavy moustache, looking more like a Mexican bandit than a French police officer, led them to a small room, indicating for them to go inside. The 15 men squeezed into the room at the far end of the police station. When they were all inside, the police officer slammed door shut and locked it.

"Hey, what you doing?" the captain called, pressing his face up to the small barred window in the door. "Why have you locked us up? We are British seamen; we are asking for help from a neutral country."

The police officer ignored their pleas for help, shouting back at the cell, "*Vous entrez Dan's le pays sans visa.*"

Captain Abraham couldn't believe his ears. "I think he said we entered the country without a visa! Where the hell would we get a visa!? ...Hey *policier*...We are merchant seamen..."

"It's no use, he's not listening."

Kevin looked around the cell. The cell door was steel lined with a tiny barred window, the only other window was a small barred quarter light at ceiling level. The only furniture in the room, a wooden bench and an empty bucket. The fly spotted, cockroach infested room was overbearingly hot and stuffy and stank of urine. The men sat down on the bench and squatted on the floor.

"He can't leave us in here for long, we'll suffocate."

Both the captain and chief mate took turns banging on the cell door and calling for the policeman, who appeared to be the only gendarme on duty. It was all in vain. The policeman refused to answer their shouts.

"What the hell is he up to?"

The survivors of the *Alice Morgan* sat languishing in the cell for eight hours, with no food or water. The sun had set. Inside the cell, flies, giant moths and mosquitos buzzed around the single lamp. Outside the cicadas chirped incessantly. Captain Abraham looked at his wristwatch. 8pm.

The sound of a waggon outside aroused the men.

"Peggie, have a look outside, see what's going on."

Two sailors lifted Kevin up to the small window.

"I can see a lorry. It looks like an army waggon."

A canvas covered army waggon parked outside the front of the police station. The headlights lighting up hundreds of flying insects.

The cell door lock rattled open. Outside the cell, four soldiers wearing French Foreign Legion kepis and armed with sub machine guns ordered the men out of the cells. They were taken outside to the truck.

Kevin was dancing and holding his groin. "Captain, captain, I need the toilet. I couldn't do it on the bucket."

Abraham looked around. "Go behind that bush. But be quick."

"Have you got any paper?" Kevin asked hopefully.

"No. Wipe your backside on a leaf."

Kevin looked towards the bush. "I wish I was home using our lav."

Abraham smiled. "Don't be long."

Kevin disappeared and crouched behind the bush. He could see his shipmates being lined up and counted. After he had finished, Kevin re-joined the others.

The French Foreign Legion Lieutenant in charge said in English. "You are to be taken to Casablanca, for internment."

"Internment? Why? We are British merchant seamen. We are survivors from a ship sunk by a German U-boat."

"You will have access to British Consul in Casablanca."

"My men have been locked up for 8 hours with no food or water. That is no way to treat us."

"You are now prisoners of war."

"What do you mean, prisoners of war? We are not at war with Morocco... Or France. It's against the Geneva Convention to take civilian seamen as prisoners of war."

"You will have the opportunity to tell that to our commander in Casablanca."

The Legionnaire officer spoke to his corporal, a 6 feet 6 inches giant of a man, with his rolled-up shirt sleeve fitting tightly around his bulging biceps, his forearms as big as hams and massive balled fists. The corporal disappeared inside the police station. Shouting, banging and painful cries could be heard coming out of the police station entrance. After five minutes the corporal emerged from the station with two bottles of water. The water bottles were passed up to Captain Abraham.

"The gendarme there is not a true Frenchman, he's an Algerian peasant. My corporal has taught him a lesson he won't forget in a hurry. We French are civilized; we treat our prisoners with respect."

"Thank you, for that, but why are you taking us as prisoners of war?"

"Orders are orders. My orders are to transport you to custody in Casablanca. Morocco is now Vichy and we..." he hesitated briefly, "Vichy France is now allied to Nazi Germany." The lieutenant sounded less than enthusiastic about the alliance.

With all the men loaded aboard the waggon, the tailgate was slammed shut and the waggon drove off into the night.

~ * ~ * ~ * ~

Driving for six hours the waggon eventually passed through the gates of a military compound guarded by armed soldiers. Dawn was breaking when Kevin, following the others, jumped down from the waggon. A high wire fence surrounded the camp; there were several long huts in a line. Guarding the compound there were sentry towers with searchlights and machine guns. Kevin looked at the soldiers guarding the compound. They were all black men, wearing scarlet hats. They also wore a scarlet sash around their midriff, with a dangerous looking machete hanging from their belts. Kevin guessed they were not Frenchmen. The crew were taken to a hut with a sign over the door. PERSONNEL NON MILITAIRE.

"*quatorze prisonniers. Marins Marchand,*" the French Legionnaire officer said as he handed over his charges to the soldier in charge of the hut. The guard opened the door bidding, by the lifting of his chin, for the sailors to go inside. Inside the hut they were greeted by four dozen other seamen.

"Hello, lads, welcome to Stalag Casablanca," said a friendly seaman with a Yorkshire accent. "What ship?"

"Hello, I'm the captain of the *SS Alice Morgan*, out of Cardiff, shelled by a U-boat a week ago. We spent a week in an open boat and a day in a Moroccan shit hole police cell. What's the score here? Where is this camp. Why are we prisoners?"

"Hello, Skipper," said the Yorkshireman. "I'm Danny Scotton, Master of the *SS Markham Point*. We were torpedoed two weeks ago. This is a prison camp. It's located just a couple of miles south of Casablanca. We don't know why we are being held prisoners. Nobody tells us anything."

Another seaman wearing Merchant Navy captain's rank marking on his shoulder epaulets, said, "We are prisoners of war. This place is a Vichy internment camp. Anyone not on the side of Petain's Vichy France are being held here." The captain shook hands with Abraham. "I'm John Glover, skipper of the *SS Devon Star*. We were taken off our ship in Port Larache a month ago now. That's up north of here. We were loading wheat, barley and dates when France capitulated and Phillippe Petain aligned with the Nazis, they interned our ship and locked us up here."

Kevin looked around the hut. Rough cut timber double-layer bunk beds, not much wider than orange boxes, lined each side of the hut. There were now more than sixty sailors packed inside the hut. The sailors from the *SS Devon Star* and *SS Markham Point* gathered around the newcomers, eager to ask questions about what was the latest news from the outside world. Kevin noted two boys not much older than himself squatting on the floor. One of the boys held a billycan over a tiny paraffin cooker. The other boy beckoned Kevin over.

"Hi mate," the smaller of the two boys said. "Pull up an armchair."

Kevin sat down on the floorboards.

"What's brought you to the Ritz? Must be our High Teas."

"My ship got sunk about a week ago. My mate got killed."

"That's sad. My ship has been impounded by the Vichy. I'm off the *Devon Star.*"

"What's that you're boiling?"

"Tea," the boy holding the billy said. "Well, something like tea. Sorry no milk or sugar." He poured out a measure into a tin mug, handing it to Kevin. "Here."

Kevin sniffed at the tea then had a sip. "It's good, thanks. What's your name?"

"I'm Stan and he's Des." Stan said. "I'm a junior seaman, off the *SS Markham Point.* We got torpedoed about three weeks ago. Des has been in this camp over a month now…."

"Hey, Peggie, come over here." Captain Abraham called Kevin over to join him and the two other captains. "Listen, when we were handed over to the soldier in charge of this hut, the French officer said, *quatorze prisonniers* – 14 prisoners. They didn't count the Peggie here."

"Why was that?" Scotton asked.

"Because he was having a crap behind a bush when they carried out the count. I'm wondering if we can use that, him not being counted, to our advantage somehow."

"How?"

"Don't know yet. Do they carry out a daily count? Also, what about rations? I'm wondering if we should report him to be counted or keep it a secret from the guards."

"Well, I tell you what, an extra man might come in handy if we could get a man over the fence. We have been planning for one of us to get over the fence and get to the consulates' office. Find out why we are prisoners and why no one has come to see us," Scotton said. "The guards here are Senegalese soldiers. They are well known throughout French West Africa as fierce fighters, loyal to France, but I gather they don't like being relegated to guarding prisoners. They are not the most conscientious turnkeys, sometimes they do a roll call, other days they don't bother. They are not as disciplined as the French Legionnaires, but don't let that fool you, they will shoot anyone trying to escape. They count us in last thing before they lock us up for the night. The food, if you can call it food, isn't a problem, we just line up with our plates and the cooks just dish out the slop. We aren't counted at mealtimes. I think we should keep it quiet for the time being. When we first came here, the guards were friendly, but suddenly, last week, they have become less friendly. Don't know why."

"The British consul should come and see us. We are not at war with Morocco. It's their job to look after British nationals," Abraham said.

"You must be joking. They are not interested in Merchant Seamen. We are second class citizens as far as they are concerned. It's too much bother for them to waste diplomacy on us. If we were the military, the consulate would be banging the table demanding our release."

"What about the Red Cross? We need to let our families know we are safe and let the family of the four, five of our lads who were killed."

"No Red Cross as yet."

"What about the camp commandant. Will he help?"

"No. He is French. At first, he too was friendly and promised to get the consulate to come and see us, but, then for some reason he changed. He became less friendly and refused to see us. Don't know why. When we first came here the Senegalese guards were friendly towards us, they too, have changed. I was told by one guard that other merchant seamen, British, Dutch and Norwegians, have been taken to a labour camp at Qued Zem, inland from here. He said it's a hell hole, working 10-hour shifts, rancid water, disease. He said we'll be taken there sooner or later."

"Labour camps! Can they do that?"'

"You better believe it."

"It's essential that we let our families know we are safe. How can we do that if the consulate, Red Cross and the camp commandant won't visit us? I think we should try and escape while we're near the coast. Escaping from Qued Zem will be nigh impossible."

"If we could get a message to my friend Jacqueline," Josh White said, "she could make the call to the Cardiff office and they will let all the families of survivors of our three ships know we are safe. They must all think we're dead, lost at sea."

"Your friend?" Captain Abraham looked up at the engineer. "And how do you suppose we do that!?"

White shrugged. "Just a suggestion."

Abraham then spoke to his crew. "Alright, men. Let's have a rest, then we'll plan how to get a message home."

The *Alice Morgan's* exhausted crew settled down for some sleep. The unbearable mid-day heat kept Kevin awake.

He called across to Des. "I've never been so hot in my life. It must be 100 degrees in here."

"Let's have a wander outside," Des said. "It might be cooler in the shade outside."

Kevin looked around at the overcrowded hut. Sailors were lying on their bunks sleeping, others were sitting around a makeshift table moaning about their situation. Kevin, Des and Stan strolled outside to look around the compound. There were many negro prisoners, some Arabs and a few civilians. None of the other prisoners were British.

"Who are these black men?" Kevin asked, watching the sullen prisoners shuffling around aimlessly in the dust.

"They are what they call undesirables. Soldiers who have shown bad behaviour," Des said.

The three boys walked around the entire periphery of the fence. Kevin checking out each foot of the fence. The ten-foot-high fence was constructed of chain links with coiled razor wire on the top. At each corner and in the middle of three sides there were manned watchtowers.

The boys stood to one side, waiting for the dog-patrol to pass.

"That's a fierce looking dog."

"Yeah, it is and it's always barking."

Kevin said, "have you seen that hole in the fence?" He pointed to a small gap between the concrete post and the bottom of the chain linked fence. "I could get through that hole easily."

Des looked down at the hole. "No, it's too small, you'd never get through that."

"Des's right, the hole is too small, a rabbit would struggle to get through."

"I reckon I could get through there."

"Where would you go if you could get through the hole?"

"I'd go down to the beach for a swim."

Des and Stan laughed.

Stan looked towards the sea. "Yeah, the sea does look inviting, blue, not brown and shitty like back home in Southsea."

Beyond the fence the Atlantic Ocean shimmered in the mid-day sun. The golden sandy beach deserted. A smell of frying fish wafted on the breeze.

"Oh, smell that, fish and chips. It reminds me of home, fish and chips at the seaside."

"Yeah, cockles and prawns in a paper bag with salt and vinegar, yum."

The boys drooled over imaginary sea-food back home in the United Kingdom.

"Where's the smell coming from?"

"I noticed a small bar up the road when we passed it last week. It was full of French soldiers.

"The French don't do fish and chips. They eat snails and frogs."

"Urg."

"No, they don't."

"Yes, they do, my dad told me."

"Come on, let's get back inside out of this hot sun."

To get out of the blazing sunshine they returned to the stifling heat of the hut. The three boys flopped down on the floorboards, bored stiff.

"Tonight," Kevin announced suddenly, "I'm going to sneak through that hole and have a swim in the sea,"

"And have an ice-cream afterwards," Stan joked. "And candy floss. I used to hire out deckchairs on the Southend beach."

"I mean it, I'm going for a swim."

"Don't be daft, you'll get caught...or shot. Anyway, you ain't got a cossie," Des said.

"I don't need a cossie, I'll go skinny-dippin'. We used to go skinny-dippin' in the cut back home in summer."

"I'd like a swim too, 'cept I couldn't get through the hole in the fence."

"My dad said, if you can get your head through a hole, then you can get your whole body through," Kevin said.

"Your dad tells you lots of things."

"Yeap, he does." Kevin said sadly. "I miss my dad. Come on let's try, when it gets dark."

"I don't know, what if they catch us? What about the war dogs? The guards in the watchtowers will shoot anyone trying to escape. It's not worth the risk, just to go swimming in the sea."

The boys lay on the floorboards gazing up at the ceiling.

Des said, "I do know there is a loose floorboard under Captain Scotton's bunk. I found it last week. There's a 12-inch gap between the floorboards and the ground. Getting out of this hut is no problem," he added nervously, "If you really want to try."

"Erm, well, in that case, we could get out of the hut and sneak over to the fence," said Stan, "so, if you are serious, I'll try if you try."

"Alright then, let's do it. Don't tell Captain Scotton though, he'll stop us."

The three boys agreed, come nightfall they would sneak out of the hut and try to squeeze through the gap in the fence.

After roll call that evening, and with the prisoners locked up for the night, Kevin whispered to Des and Stan, "come on then, let's go for a dip."

The three boys waited until the older men gathered around the table to discuss an escape plan.

"Wait until the dog patrol has passed," Des whispered. "It takes them a good hour to patrol the fence."

Un-noticed by the other men, the three boys crept towards the bed concealing the loose-fitting floorboard. One by one they dropped through the hole onto the ground. Kevin leading, they crawled under the floorboards. Popping his head into the open, Kevin checked left and right then scampered over to the fence. He waited until Stan and Des had joined him.

"Are you ready?"

Stan nodded.

Kevin put his right arm through the hole, then his head and shoulder, next his left shoulder and his left arm. Finally squeezing his chest, hips and legs through the hole, he was safely through on the outside.

Kevin whispered to Stan, "put your arm and shoulder through. That's it... now your head."

Stan followed the instructions.

"That's it, now squeeze your chest through."

Stan wriggled and rocked his body until he too was out on the other side of the compound. With a lot of tugging and pulling Des managed to get his heavier body through the hole.

"Come on, this way."

The three boys scampered down a banking, over a length of scrubby ground and down into a dry monsoon ditch. They waited until the road was free of traffic before dashing across to the beach on the other side. The sound of crashing waves spurred them on.

Stripping off their clothes, the three boys ran full tilt into the sea. Well clear of the camp they splashed and laughed and dived under the waves. They swam around for a full hour before lying on the beach to dry out. The smell of frying food wafting down the coast roused their interest.

"Come on, lads," Kevin said, "let's investigate."

Concealed by the darkness of the beach, the boys made their way towards the bar. The beachside bar backed onto the sands. The boys sneaked up to the back yard, hiding behind beer crates and bins. Through the open back door, they could see into the kitchen. On the counter there was a selection of pies, pastries and seeded bread rolls. A chef worked over a stove.

"Whoa, look at them pies," Stan whispered. "I wish the cook would bugger off."

"He must need a break sooner or later, to go to the toilet or whatever."

A waitress came into the kitchen, had a chat with the cook then returned to the bar with a tray full of food. Loud chattering and singing could be heard coming from the bar area. Now and then a soldier would stagger out of the bar to use the lavatory at the back.

Kevin waited until the coast was clear, creeping closer to the open kitchen door. "I'm starving. I'm going to have them pies." He indicated to his pals to stay low. He waited patiently, waiting for an opportunity to raid the kitchen. A shout came from front of house. The cook wiped his hands on his apron and made his way into the bar leaving the kitchen unattended. Like a shot, Kevin tiptoed into the kitchen and helped himself to the pies, stuffing them into his shirt. A few seconds later he was back outside with Des and Stan.

"Come on," he said, handing out the pies. "Let's get out of here."

The three hurried back down the beach, munching on the pies as they went.

Well clear of the bar they flopped down on the sand laughing and giggling.

"How many pies did you get, Kevin?

Kevin pulled the pies from his bulging shirt. "One, two, three." He handed three pies to Stan. "Four, five, six." He handed Des three pies. "seven, eight, nine, ten."

"13 pies," Stan said as he hid the three pies in his own shirt. "They're delicious, chicken, I think."

Des poked around in his pie. "Chicken and veg. You, know, I think it's pigeon, pigeon pie. I had pigeon pie at home once."

Kevin's pie halted at his mouth as he remembered stealing Flogger's pigeons. His head sank as he thought about what he'd seen and been through since that evening back in January. The reflective thoughts didn't last long before he got stuck into finishing his pie.

"I'm taking mine back to share with the lads," Stan said.

"So will I."

"Me an all," Des added. "If we eat too many pies we won't fit back through the fence."

The boys fell about laughing again. They lay on the sand staring up at the stars, reluctant to return to the stuffy hut.

"You know what, Kev," Stan said laughing, "you're bloody mad!"

Kevin didn't answer, he just laid there, looking up at Ursa Major, thinking about the starry night Hector died.

"I wish I was back home," lamented Stan. "I miss my mum and dad."

"Me too."

When they heard shouting coming from the direction of the bar, and the sight of the cook outside in the backyard rummaging around the beer crates, they decided to get off the beach and back to the safety of the prisoner of war camp.

~ * ~ * ~ * ~

Safely navigating their way back to the compound fence, they waited for the dog patrol to pass. One by one they squeezed back through the hole in the fence. Dodging the sweeping searchlight, they scurried over the open ground before scrambling back under their hut. The three boys emerged from under Captain Scotton's bed making their way to the table. The men in the hut looked on in bewilderment at the ten meat pies lined up on the table.

"You sneaked out of the camp to swim in the sea?" Captain Abraham said in astonishment, looking at the pies. "Do you know you could have been shot? We didn't even miss you."

"We've had our share," said Kevin, ignoring the captain's reprimand

Josh White lifted one of the pies. "I've had these pies before. I can't remember the name, something that sounds like Bisteeya, they are Moroccan pigeon pies."

"There, I told you they are pigeon pies," Des said gleefully.

"I tell you what, lads, the redheads look dozy, but they won't hesitate shooting you like dogs if they catch you trying to escape…" Captain Scotton chastised them. He drew in a deep breath. "Alright, as long as you are all safe. But do not, I repeat, do not do it again."

Captain Abraham muttered under his breath, "skinny dipping, I just don't believe it. What next!"

Captain Glover chopped the pies into equal pieces and dished them out to the flabbergasted sailors; and the men enjoyed their unexpected supper.

The seamen in the civilian's hut gathered around the table. Kevin sat on the floor listening intently to the men discussing an escape plan.

"Well, men, what are we going do? Sit here rotting 'til the war is over? If we get moved to the camp in Timbuktu or Qued Zen, we'll never get home. Or, do we help ourselves and escape back to England?"

"If we could get out of here, we could make our way to Melilla and claim asylum."

"Melilla, where's that?"

"Melilla is a Spanish port on the north African coast, on the Mediterranean. Spain is a neutral country. Once we are in Melilla, we can claim distressed British seaman status."

"We could do with a bit of outside help."

"Like the British consulate?"

"Forget them. What about the girl you know in Casablanca, Josh? Tell us about her."

"I'm sure she will help us," Josh said. "She will know who's on our side and who is on Petain's side. I know she hates the Germans; her father was killed at the battle of the Ardennes in 1914 when she was a toddler. She regrets her father never saw her."

"Well, if we could get a message to her, but there's not much chance of that. Anyway, she may not be in Casablanca anymore."

"I'm sure she will still be there; she owns a nightclub. She'll be around 27, 28 years old now. She told me she'd like to retire to the South of France, where the weather is not as hot as Morocco. The question is, how do we contact her?"

"I could contact her," piped up Kevin, holding up his hand.

The men looked down at the boy sitting cross legged on the floor.

"I mean, I could get through the fence and go and see her."

"Forget it, Peggie," Willie Wilde said. "It'll be too dangerous for a young lad. There are all kinds of queer folk in Casablanca, refugees from Europe, Arabs from Algeria and Tunisia. A Young English boy wandering around the Casbah will stand out like a sore thumb."

"I don't mind."

The men around the table stopped talking, thinking over what Kevin had said.

"Well, if you could get a message to Jacqueline, she will definitely know someone who could help us escape and get to Spain," Josh said.

"I could get out and back in, no problem. None of you men will fit through the hole in the fence."

"They won't miss Peggie at roll call."

Captain Abraham thought about it. "I'm not happy. Trying to escape from a prisoner of war camp is so dangerous, the guards have been told to shoot anyone trying to escape. But, as I see it, there's no other way to contact the outside world." Abraham pondered over the situation. Eventually he said, "if you could get her to send a message to our company in Cardiff, at least our families will know we are safe."

"What have we got to lose?" Scotton asked.

"Apart from Peggie getting shot or picked up by the police and being locked up in some Moroccan shit-hole prison," Abraham answered.

"Or worse," added Willie.

"What do you think, Peggie?"

"I don't mind. I know I can squeeze through the hole in the fence. No problem."

"Alright then. It seems to me the only way to contact the outside world. Josh, tell Fifie all about this girlfriend of yours."

"Alright then, listen up, Peggie. The bar is called *Café la Belle France*. It's down by the docks. The café owner is called Jacqueline, Jacqueline Babineaux."

"Bab-in-nore," repeated Kevin.

"Yes, Babineaux. She knows me by the name 'Stoker White'. 'Stoker' is my nickname. Jacqui and I were good friends, if you know what I mean?"

Kevin didn't know what he meant, but what he did know, was that Josh White was a good-looking man who had a reputation of being a 'ladies' man', who supposedly had a girl in every port.

"Ask her if she can get us any help to get out of this place. If not, ask her if she can get the consul to contact our office in Cardiff. Then you get back to us here. Can you do that?"

"Yeah, I'm sure I can."

"Is there a curfew?" Captain Abraham asked.

"No, not as far as I know," Glover said. "I know the Gestapo have an office in Casablanca, and there are some German soldiers knocking about. They are there to make sure French Morocco is sticking to the terms of the Armistice."

"So, if Kevin gets picked up by the Gestapo he could be in deep trouble."

"Hmm, yes, he would be."

"I won't be picked up. I'd still like to try."

"Alright, Peggie, come outside with me."

Josh and Kevin wandered outside and over to the boundary fence.

White pointed to the ocean. "There is the Atlantic to the west."

"Yeah, I know. I had a swim in it, last night."

"Hmm, yeah, well. That way is north. Follow the road north. The road is called *Boulevard de l'ocean Atlantique*. Captain Glover says we are about 3 miles out of the city. You will pass Café de Paris, don't go in there, it's too expensive for a deck boy." White grinned at his own joke. "You will see the port office building on the left. Directly opposite, on the right side of the road, there is a street called, *Rue de Rouen*, on that street you will find *Café La Belle France*. Jacqueline Babineaux is the owner. Tell her where we are, and ask her if she can get us some help. Help to get a message to our families in England or help to get us out of here and repatriated."

Kevin looked towards Casablanca and nodded. "I'll find my way to the café."

White continued, "get back to us with what she has to say. If it's past daybreak, don't risk getting caught on your way back. Keep low 'til night-time."

As they walked back to their hut, Kevin looked up at the watchtowers guarding the fence and the evil looking machine gun covering the compound. They returned to the hut to wait for nightfall.

"To be on the safe side, Peggie, I recommend you stay out of sight at supper just in case the guards do a spot check," Scotton advised Kevin. "If they discover there are 60 of us in the hut instead of 59, they will expect 60 at the next roll call. The guards here are lax, but sometimes they do spring a roll call without warning."

Kevin agreed not to take the chance of being counted and decided to stay hidden inside the hut.

At 8pm a guard opened the door. He called loudly, *"Tours a l'exterieur, alignement pour inspection!"*

Kevin rolled under a bed while the others paraded outside for roll call. The guard walked up and down the billet checking everyone had gone outside. Kevin could see the guard's boots, his heart pounding, in case the guard looked under the beds. He stayed under the bed while evening roll call was taken. After each man had been counted, they were shoved back into the hut and the door locked.

The grounds outside were occasionally illuminated by a watchtower searchlight sweeping the fences and the huts, otherwise there was total darkness on this moonless night. Kevin was eager to move. He wanted to get into town before the café closed for the night. He had committed to memory the route to Jacqueline's café, her surname and the messages to give her.

At just after 8.30 Captain Scotton lifted the floorboard. "Good luck, Kevin."

"Yeah, good luck, Peggie. Just be careful," Captain Abraham whispered.

Kevin nodded, "I'm okay. See you later." He waited until the dog patrol had passed before he slipped through the hole, dropping to the ground under the hut. Crawling on his belly, he emerged on the side of the hut nearest to the hole in the fence. He carefully emerged from under the hut into the open, looking left and right and up at the nearest watchtower.

"All clear," he muttered under his breath. He then scampered on all-fours across to the fence, looking over his shoulder checking the coast was still clear. Without wasting time, he squeezed through the hole and was free. Checking left and right, in front and behind him, he darted across open ground to a group of palm trees. From the grove he could see traffic driving up and down the coastal road with their headlights on.

"No blackout here," Kevin said to himself. Looking to the north he could see the lights of Casablanca. "Never mind, here goes." He set off walking quickly the three miles into Casablanca. The night was warm, cicadas chirped loudly. Over to his left, the Atlantic waves crashed onto the beach. Lamps from houses on the way into town shone dimly, smoke from cooking fires hung around, the smell of Moroccan cooking wafted on the breeze, making him feel hungry. For the first time since his friend Hector had died, he felt happy, more carefree. An hour and a half later, walking down *Boulevard de l'ocean Atlantique*, he found himself mingling with the locals in downtown Casablanca. People sat outside cafes around little tables set on the pavement. The men smoking hookahs and drinking out of tiny coffee cups. Kevin stood for a minute watching a young acrobat leaping about for the enjoyment of the local population. He began to feel the excitement of being in a foreign country; this was the first foreign country he had ever seen. Turning right into *Rue de Rouen* he could now see the coloured neon sign over the entrance, *Café La Belle France*. He heard music coming out of the door.

A large Arab guarding the door stopped him.

"*Que Velux-tu mon garcon? Vous ne pouvez pas ynaller.*"

"Sorry, do you speak English?"

The doorman frowned. "A little. What do you want? You are not allowed in here."

"I've come to speak with Miss Babineaux."

"What does a young boy want with Mademoiselle Babineaux?

"I have a message for her from a friend of hers."

"A friend?"

"Yes, Josh White. Stoker White."

"Ah, Stoker White, my old friend. Where is he now?"

"I can't say, sorry. But it is important that I pass on his message to Miss Babineaux."

The doorman hesitated, looking over Kevin, before saying, "come, follow me."

He led Kevin inside the dimly lit café. The café looked more like a night-club than a café to Kevin. There was a long bar, a small stage, tables and chairs. Kevin looked around at the patrons. French soldiers, police officers, local Arabs and civilians in white tropical suits. A lady walked elegantly through the patrons, chatting to some of them before stepping up onto the stage. There was a polite round of applause. The pianist started playing. The lady began to sing in French. Kevin stood open-mouthed, mesmerised by the song and the beautiful woman singing it.

"Stay here out of sight," the doorman said. "Do not go near the bar or the police chief." He indicated a uniformed officer sat in the shade with a much younger woman. "The police chief will arrest you for being underage and he will shut down the café. I will bring Mademoiselle Babineaux to you when she has finished her cabaret."

"Alright, thank you." Kevin was left alone, he melted into a darkened corner to wait.

When the singer finished her songs, the doorman met her and whispered in her ear. She looked towards where Kevin was waiting. When she saw him, her face broke into a smile, she came across to him.

"Hello, my young friend, what brings you to Café La Belle France? Abdullah says you have a message from my friend Stoker White."

Kevin, overcome with embarrassment at being so close to this beautiful woman stammered, "I…I , we, he, Josh… Stoker White is in a prison camp. We, my ship…"

"Your ship?" she interrupted. "Are you a seaman?"

"Yes, a deck boy."

Her eyebrows lifted slightly, "Tut, you're just a …" She shook her head in dismay. "Go on, *mon cheri*. Tell me how you and my good friend Stoker got yourselves locked up in a prison camp in Morocco."

"Our ship got sunk by a U-boat off the Moroccan coast. We sailed our lifeboat to the coast. When we landed, we were taken by soldiers and locked up. The crew of the *Alice Morgan* were taken to a prisoner of war camp, but the British Consul has forgotten us. Some of the men have been in the camp for over a month now and no one has told our families back in Britain that we are safe. Stoker White wonders if you could contact our office in Cardiff and tell them where we are."

Jacqueline smiled, "Come with me, *mi petit* boy. Are you hungry?"

"Yes, miss. I'm starving."

"Come."

She led him to a room at the rear of the café. The room smelled heavily of perfume, a dressing table loaded with perfume bottles, powder puffs, lipsticks and rouge. A dozen dresses hung on a coat rail. There were two armchairs and two stools and a small table with a large bowl of fresh fruit on it. Kevin eyed the fruit; he had never seen so many different kinds of fruit in one place.

Jacqueline saw him looking at the fruit. "Help yourself."

"Thanks, miss." He selected a large peach. "I loved that song you were singing. Is it a French song? What's it called?"

"Yes, it is a very old French song. *Plaisir d' amour*"

"It was lovely, miss."

To his astonishment she began to sing softly, "*Plaisir d'amour me dure qu'un moment, chagrin d'amour dure toute la vie...,*" she sang him a few words of the song and then laughed pleasantly. "I'll bring you some food then we will talk. I'll see what we can do for you. I know why the British Consul have not been to the camp."

"Why?"

"Because Vichy France has just broken off diplomatic relations with Britain. The Consul and Vice Consul have been sent home."

"Oh, I didn't know that."

"Make yourself comfortable. I won't be long."

Kevin slumped down in the armchair exhausted, his eyes beginning to shut. He was abruptly woken by two young women barging into the room. Giggling, they came over to where Kevin sat and began fussing over him.

"You poor boy. Being shot at by the Germans and you so young," said the first girl. "You should be home with your mamma and papa ...in bed. What's your name, *mon cheri?*"

"Kevin."

"Kevin, *petite* Kevin. I'm Ruby, Ruby like my brooch." She touched a ruby red jewel pinned to her blouse. "And this is Fleur," Ruby said indicating the other girl. "Fleur, like Fleur de Lis." She pointed to a costume jewel Fleur de Lis brooch that Fleur was wearing.

Both girls had strong French accents, but their English was fluent.

Fleur squatted down beside him and took hold of his hand. "My sweet little boy. You are too young to be on a ship in war."

Kevin's head swam with the girls' heady perfume, he fought to keep his eyes away from the girls' bosoms that bulged over their dresses. He was enjoying the caring attention.

Jacqueline came back into the room with a tray of food. "Come, sit here and eat."

Kevin sat down at the table. "Wow, thanks." He took up a spoon slurping the soup. On the tray in addition to the soup there was French bread, olives and cheese. He cleared the lot.

The three girls left Kevin to eat, watching him discreetly, apparently pleased at having a young English boy in their care.

"Thank you, miss." Kevin said after finishing the meal, plus another peach and a banana.

Jacqueline could see how tired Kevin was. She said, "you must have a sleep now. I will contact a very good friend of mind. Lieutenant Garron, he will know what to do. His mother is English and he speaks fluent English, so he is friendly towards the British. He can be trusted. Come with me."

She led him upstairs to a bedroom. This room also smelled strongly of perfume. A roof fan cooled down the room. Next to the dressing table there was a double bed.

"Come, take off your clothes and get into bed."

"I must get back before it gets light," Kevin said without much enthusiasm.

"Not tonight, *mon cheri*. You sleep here tonight."

Kevin didn't argue. He removed his shoes, shirt and trousers and climbed into the softest bed he'd ever been in, a fleeting thought of the straw filled paillasse 'donkeys' breakfast' he slept on at the training ship *Cromwell*. Within two minutes he was fast asleep.

Kevin woke with the sunlight streaming through the window shutters. He looked around the room wondering where he was, the events of the night coming back to him. He reached for his shirt. Instead of his dirty old shirt there was a new American style T-shirt, new trousers, a new pair of socks and his shoes had been cleaned. He dressed and went downstairs to the bar. The bar was deserted except for four people sitting around one of the tables.

Jacqueline, Ruby, Fleur and a French Legionnaire officer. The officer looked vaguely familiar.

Jacqueline saw Kevin. "Good morning, *mon cheri*. Come and sit here."

"*Bonjour*, Kevin," Ruby and Fleur said in unison.

Kevin looked at the French officer.

"*Bonjour, mon ami*," the officer said.

Kevin's heart missed a beat. Had the girls turned him in to the police? Was he about to be taken back to the camp, or worse still, a Moroccan prison?

Jacqueline noted his expression of apprehension. "It's alright, *mon cheri*, come and sit down and meet Lieutenant Garron of the French Foreign Legion."

"Hello, sir."

Lieutenant Garron spoke in English, "Jacqueline tells me you were a sailor on a ship called *Alice Morgan*."

"Yes, that's right."

"How many men survived the sinking of your ship?"

Kevin thought about it, counting the men on his fingers.

"Fifteen…we had 20 crew and five of them were killed, including my friend Hector…"

"Erm, Fifteen? Tell me your name and where you were born."

"Kevin Fife, I was born in England."

"Where in England?"

"Blackstone."

"Who is your Prime Minister?

Kevin frowned at the line of questioning. "I don't know."

"Well then, which football team do you support?"

"Man City."

"Manchester City?"

"Yes, Man City."

"Do you like football?

"Yeah, course I do."

"Who won the FA Cup Final last year in 1939?"

Kevin thought for a moment. "Portsmouth. They played Wolverhampton Wanderers. Portsmouth won 4-1."

Garron turned to Jacqueline and said, "*Je crois le garcon*." He turned back to Kevin and said in English, "I was the officer who brought fourteen survivors of the Steamship *Alice Morgan* to Casablanca. And I do not remember a young boy being with them."

"That's because I wasn't counted."

"Not counted. Why was that?"

Kevin glanced embarrassingly at Jacqueline and the girls. "Err, I was behind a bush. Having a tom-tit."

"A tom-tit?

"Yes, a shit. I couldn't do it on that bucket in the police cell, in front of everyone. So, while you were counting the crew, I was behind a bush doing my business."

The officer smiled at that. "I had to be sure that you are who you say you are. Do you know what an '*Agent Provocateur*' is?

"No, sir"

"An '*Agent de Police*'?"

Kevin shook his head. "No."

"Never mind, Kevin. I don't think you are working for the Gestapo. The Nazi Gestapo are here in Casablanca, they are here to ensure we, the Vichy French, are abiding by the Armistice. However, my dear, sir, there are also Free French soldiers in Morocco. Should the police find out who are against the Vichy government, they would be arrested and shot as traitors. Including me. Therefore, I had to be sure you are who you say you are."

"Wow." Kevin was clearly impressed at being in the presence of a Free French soldier.

"I fear you British sailors may have to spend many months or maybe years in prison camps, until the end of the war. What exactly do your friends, your shipmates want me to do?"

"What do you mean?"

"Do they want to escape? Do they want me to help them escape?"

"Yes, they want to get back home. We all want to go home."

"Escaping will be dangerous. Are you sure your friends are prepared to face up to the danger of being shot while attempting to escape?"

"Yes... Yes, I'm sure they will do anything to get home. The camp guard said we will be sent to a labour camp to work 12 hours a day. The guard said the labour camp is a hell hole."

"Um," Garron nodded, pondering. "Well alright. You leave it with me to work out a plan.

However, in the meantime, you must stay here at Jacqueline's. You will have to stay out of sight of the police. You look like an Englishman, and, *bon ami*, you are an enemy of the Reich. The Vichy French have been ordered to defend our country against the enemy, and that includes the British. So, therefore, you must stay here for a while, out of sight. I have a lot to do to make plans. You may have to stay here for a few weeks even."

"A few weeks!?" Kevin looked around at his pleasant surroundings, at the beautiful Jacqueline and the two lovely young ladies. He grinned broadly. "Yes, sir. Anything you say, Lieutenant Garron."

~ * ~ * ~ * ~

For the next four weeks Kevin, hid out of sight of the café patrons only emerging during the day to help the cook and Abdullah to keep the place clean. In the middle of the twenty-eighth night laying up at the *Café La Belle France*, Kevin was woken by Jacqueline.

"Get dressed, Kevin. It's time to leave."

Kevin dressed, wondering what was happening. Jacqueline led him down to the café.

"Outside there is a taxi. You must leave in the taxi. Come, hurry."

Ruby and Fleur were waiting at the door.

"*Adieu, Kevin, bonne chance,*" Ruby said.

The girls each giving the bewildered Kevin a hug.

"Take this, *mon cheri*," Fleur said, handing him her fake jewel brooch. "You told us about your souvenir tin, if you get another tin, you can keep this to remember us here at *Café La Belle France*. The *Fleur de Lis* is an emblem of Free France. Sorry but it has little money value."

"I'm not bothered about money value, it's beautiful." Kevin held the paste to the orange neon sign gazing at the kaleidoscope of colours reflected by the foil behind the leaded glass. "Thanks, Fleur."

"You're welcome," Fleur said in English

Ruby was next to wish Kevin '*bonne chance*'. "My ruby has no value either, it is only red glass, but I want you to have it so you will remember me too."

Kevin took the jewel, glancing down at the tiny glass rubies made up in a floral design. "I'll never forget you Ruby. You have been so kind to me. Thank you so much for this treasure."

Jacqueline came over to give Kevin a hug. "Here, Kevin, you can also keep this in your tin box." She also gave him a gift. "Do you know what this is, Kevin?"

Kevin looked at the little silver cross in his hand. "It's a cross."

"It's not just a cross, it's the '*Cross of Lorraine*'. The symbol of resistance and the Free French Forces. Also, here is the photo Abdullah took of us. Keep this to remember the happy month you spent with us."

Kevin looked at the small black and white photograph of himself sitting at the table with three smiling women. "Thanks very much, miss Jacqueline. I've lost the cross my girlfriend gave me. I'll keep this photo forever."

"We shall miss you, Kevin and your cheerful face."

"I'm going to miss you all too. Especially you singing in the cabaret. I love those French songs."

Kevin was reluctant to leave the café. The month-long stay was the most pleasant time he had since leaving home in February. The three girls had mothered him better than his own mother had.

Outside in the deserted darkened *Rue de Rouen* a taxi waited.

Jacqueline hooked up with Kevin and escorted him to the waiting Renault, Fleur and Ruby following on behind.

"Trust the driver, he will take you to a safe place. And, Kevin, if you are ever back in Casablanca, in better times, when this war is over, come and see us. Until then, *mon garcon*, keep safe, *adieu, au revoir, bon chance*."

"I won't forget your singing, what's the name of them French songs again?"

"*Plaisir d'amour*… pleasing love and *Parlez Mou d'amour*, tell me about love or speak to me of love."

Then, to Kevin's astonishment, Jacqueline smiled at him and began to sing softly in French, "*Plaisir d'amour ne dure qu'un moment*."

Fleur and Ruby joining in, harmonising with Jacqueline, "*Chagrin d'amour dure toute la vie*."

As the taxi moved away from the kerb, tears wetted Kevin's eyes as the words of the song faded. Feeling as sad and homesick at leaving the cabaret singer and the two girls behind, as sad as he had at leaving his Mum and Dad, Jane, Maureen and Tommy nearly seven months ago.

Through the darkened streets of Casablanca and into the countryside, the taxi sped off deep into the rough country surrounding Casablanca. Through the night the taxi drove along metalled roads, then later turning off onto unmade roads and finally onto rutted dirt tracks not much wider than farm tracks. The taxi now climbing steeper hills. In the pre-dawn light, Kevin could see high mountains in the distance. The taxi's headlamps illuminating the bumpy dusty road, partially hidden by scrubby bushes on both sides. They finally arrived at a clearing in what appeared to be a forest of stunted bushes, the taxi stopping in a cloud of dust. The dust settled. Kevin looked around nervously. Out of the darkness a man emerged holding a rifle. Around his jacket upper arm, he had an armband showing the Cross of Lorraine. The soldier popped his head through the front window, checking out the passenger.

"Come." The soldier beckoned.

Kevin followed the soldier into a compound. There were a few ramshacled huts and outhouses. No lights showed. Kevin was led into one of the camouflaged huts. The barrack-like accommodation reminded him of the huts back at Arcaster, except these huts were covered in palm fronds and olive tree branches.

"Stay here. Lieutenant Garron will join you soon," the soldier said before leaving Kevin alone.

Kevin checked one of the beds, 'a bit rough', he thought, 'nearly as hard as the donkey's breakfast'. He lay down on the bed and fell asleep. He was woken by the sound of heavy vehicles outside. A couple of minutes later he was fully awakened when the hut door opened and in poured 59 sailors all talking in English. When they saw Kevin sat on the bed, an astonished gasp, followed by a cheer went up.

"Kevin! Hey, Peggie."

"Peggie!" Captain Abraham exclaimed. "What are you doing here? We thought you'd been taken by the police. We didn't know where you'd been for the past month. After a couple of weeks, we were sure you'd been captured by the police or the Gestapo."

The remainder of the three crews from the Casablanca compound gathered around Kevin, all asking questions, wanting to know where he'd been.

"What happened, Kev?"

"Where have you been? You've been gone nearly a month!"

"I've been staying at the *Café La Belle France* with Jacqueline, Ruby and Fleur."

Josh 'Stoker' White laughed, "you're a dark horse, Peggie. Living in a house of ill repute, a house of sin, a French Moroccan bordello."

"What do you mean a house of sin? *Café La Belle France* isn't a house of sin, it's a nice place."

"What did you do to pass the time, Peggie? Locked away with young ladies."

"Hey! Kev, you lucky dog," called Froggy Jackson. "No wonder you've got a smile on your face."

Other members of the crews chuckled, teasing Kevin.

Blushing a bright red, Kevin stammered, "I...I had to hide most of the time. I washed glasses and mopped the café floor and..."

"Did you manage to get through to the office in Cardiff?" Captain Abraham asked anxiously. "Let them know we are safe in Morocco?"

"Err, no, sorry, sir. Miss Jacqueline said something about there is no telephone link to England and letters to England are being opened by the Gestapo. So, no."

"That means our families still don't know that we are safe."

"Sorry, Captain Abraham."

"Never mind, son. You did your best. Do you know what this place is?"

"No, not really."

Captain Abraham nodded and left to talk with the other officers. Junior seaman Stan from the torpedoed *SS Markham Point* and Des the cabin-boy from the impounded *SS Devon Star* gathered around Kevin.

"How you doing, Kev? We thought you'd been captured. Here," Stan said, handing over Kevin's grab bag, "I brought this with me, just in case we ever met up with you again. I know your toffee tin is important to you. I was going to make sure your mum got it if we ever got back to England."

"It's not the tin, just what's in it. My souvenirs." Kevin took the tin out of the bag and opened it. All his treasures were intact. "Thanks, Stan." Kevin smiled as he added his Fleur de Lis brooch, the ruby red glass flower, the small silver Cross of Lorraine and the photograph to his other souvenirs.

"I'm getting quite a collection of crosses. I'm not even religious."

He showed the photo to the boys.

"Wow! Three beautiful girls. You look like the cat that got the cream."

"Yeah, Ruby, Fleur and Miss Jacqueline." He grinned.

"What are we doing here?"

"I don't know. Waiting for Lieutenant Garron, I think," Kevin said. "What happened to you?"

"About one o'clock this morning, two army waggons rolled up at the compound. This French officer woke us up shouting, '*Sailors, with your possessions, get onto the lorries you are being taken to Rabat.*' We were loaded on board and driven here. This place doesn't look like Rabat to me. The officer didn't say why or where we were going; I thought we were being sent to a different prison camp."

Stan's explanation was interrupted when Lieutenant Garron came into the hut.

"Gather round, gentlemen." Garron called. His English accent excellent with only the slightest trace of a French accent. "*Bonne journee, messieurs.*" He waited until everyone was gathered around the table and paying attention. "You may be wondering what is going on."

"You can say that again," Captain Scotton said.

"Well, my name is Garron, I am an officer with the French Foreign Legion. I am, more importantly, a Free Frenchman. The soldiers in this camp are also Free Frenchmen. First, I have some bad news for you men. You, *mes amis*, are now enemies of Vichy France. Great Britain is not very popular with the French people now, Vichy French and even the Free French. On 3rd July, your Royal Navy attacked the French Fleet at Mers el Kabirb. Many French sailors were killed. Battleships destroyed at their berth."

A moan of concern erupted from the British Merchant Seamen

"Why would they do that?"

"To stop the French warships falling into German hands. France has broken off diplomatic relations with Great Britain. Vichy France has bombed Gibraltar."

Another gasp went up from the sailors.

"You sailors are now enemies of Vichy France and could spend the rest of the war in a prisoner of war camp."

"Crikey, we didn't realise that."

"War is war and decisions have to be made. Our Free French leader

General Charles de Gaulle has been sentenced to death in Absentia. Any Frenchmen joining a foreign force will also be executed if caught. My question to you men is; do you want to spend the rest of the war as prisoners of war or would you want to escape back to Great Britain and your families?"

"We want to get home," all the sailors called.

"Willie Wilde chipped in, "yeah, we want to escape. Our families back home cannot live on fresh air. Our pay stopped the minute our ship was sunk."

"Well, when that young man there," Garron indicated Kevin, "told me of your plight, I thought of a plan to get you out of the compound and hopefully back to England. I'm sorry it took so long. I had to do a lot of work and planning to get you all here. Getting you all here is only the first part of the escape plan. The easiest bit."

The crews looked at Kevin with a mixture of surprise and admiration.

"Well done, Fifie, you did a great job," Captain Abraham called.

Kevin smiled self-consciously.

Captain Abraham turned back to the Lieutenant. "What happens next. Where do we go from here?"

"I got you out of the prison camp on forged papers on the pretext that you were being transferred to Rabat. It won't take the police long to realise that 60 British prisoners have just disappeared into thin air and that you must have escaped. They will be looking for you all at the ports, along the borders and searching the countryside for you... Nevertheless, I have a couple of suggestions for you to consider..." Garron looked at each sailor in turn. "One, is to get over the border into Spanish territory, Ceuta, and report as Distressed British Seamen and ask for asylum and a safe passage home. However, if you do manage to get to the border crossing, the Spaniards my not let you enter Spain. Although Spain is neutral, General Franco is not. He sympathises with Nazi Germany and he supports the Vichy government. So, there is the chance you may be handed back to the Vichy French. If you all split up into smaller groups you may evade the army looking and searching for you. I don't think you would evade them for long before you are picked up." Garron let the option sink in. "Or, secondly, I have a plan that might just work, and, in my opinion, the only way to escape out of Morocco is..." He paused, looking at Glover. "Is by ship... My suggestion is to retake your ship, Captain Glover, and sail it out of Morocco."

Glover's eyebrows raised in surprise. "Retake my ship! You mean retake the *Devon Star*?"

"Yes, the *Devon Star*. If you remember, captain, I escorted you down from Larache to Casablanca."

"Yes, I remember now. I thought I'd seen you before."

"Well, your ship is still in Larache. All the cargo has been taken off the ship and taken back into warehouses."

"Stolen you mean. My company paid for the cargo."

"Yes, stolen. I have it on good authority that your ship has been sold to a shipping company from Monrovia."

"Monrovia, where's Monrovia?"

"It's a port in Liberia, south of Morocco. There are some African sailors on board, I think they wait for officers. But anyway, the ship will be sailing away from Larache soon."

"In other words, if we do want to try to take the back the *Devon Star* we must act pretty quickly."

"Yes. If we retake it, your ship, we, you, could sail it to Gibraltar or Las Palmas, or some other neutral port. I am a soldier, my men are soldiers, we know nothing about the sea or ships. It will not be easy stealing a ship out from under the noses of the Vichy. And, for us Free Frenchmen, if we are caught, it's certain death for us and concentration camps for you 'Enemies of France'. But, as I see it, it's the only way."

There was a muttering amongst the crew as they discussed the options.

"I say we try and sneak over the border into Spain. It's less dangerous."

"I'd go along with Lieutenant Garron, and try to get our ship back."

"Me too. I think we should try to retake the *Devon Star*,"

"Me too."

"It's dangerous."

"Impossible you mean."

The crews chatted between themselves on the pros and cons of Garrons' suggestions.

"Let's take a vote on it," Captain Glover suggested. "All in favour of walking to the Morocco Ceuta border and asking the Spaniards for asylum?"

Four of the sailors raised their hand.

"Who is are in favour of taking back the *Devon Star*."

54 men, one by one, raised his hand. Kevin looked around at the others and then gingerly raised his hand.

"That's it then, there's a clear majority to take back my ship."

"There is one condition for our help." Garron looked at each of the three captains. "It is that you will transport the Free French soldiers here in this camp to England."

"Take Free French soldiers to England? How, why?"

"Our plan is to join General De Gaulle in England and fight the war from there. It is nearly impossible for us to escape in any other way from Morocco."

"That's no problem, we could take a dozen or so."

"No, I was thinking of more like 60 soldiers… and their families, and their children"

"Families! Wow, that's a lot of people. How do we get them all aboard without the authorities in Larache stopping us?"

"Well, that is the problem. All Atlantic ports are being reinforced against an attack from the ocean, so we will have to find a safer place to embark my soldiers. But, not only soldiers. In Morocco there are over 300,000 Jews and the Vichy government have ordered a census of Jews goods and property. The Sultan, King Mohammed the fifth, has refused, he told the Germans, '*We only have Moroccans in Morocco.*' We all know what's been going on in Nazi Germany for the last ten years or so with the Nuremburg anti-Jewish laws. Jews here are suffering the same fate '*Statut des Juifs*'. Jewish teachers not allowed to teach, Jewish doctors not allowed to practice, and so on. Some prominent Jews, that the Vichy government consider a threat, have already been locked up in prison."

Captain Glover frowned. "What about the Jews? We can't take 300,000 back to England."

"No, that is true. However, there are some other Jewish people who are on the Gestapo list for internment. If the Nazis capture these men, they most certainly will be sent to Germany. They are in hiding. We would also like to take them to safety. They are French citizens, academics and scientists, they will be important to help Britain win the war."

"How many people are you anticipating all together?" asked Captain Glover. "There is limited space for refugees on the *Devon Star*."

Garron wagged his head. "About 200."

"200!" Glover exclaimed. "How on earth do we embark 200 people, under the noses of the Vichy?"

"It will not be easy. I would take more Jews and Free French to safety if I could. There are so many proud free Frenchmen here in Morocco who would help Great Britain, free Europe from the Nazis. The only way to get them out of Africa … is by ship."

"Well, we certainly can't take all the Jews in Morocco, but we'll take as many as possible. Alright then, lieutenant, let's make a plan. How exactly do we take the *Devon Star* and where on the coast can we embark 200 people?" Glover paused for a moment before adding. "First, let's just concentrate how to get my ship back. How to get on the ship? How to deal with the African crew already on board? How to restart the engine? How to get nearly 200 people including children onto the ship? And, how to sail it out of the harbour and how to avoid getting sunk between North Africa and England or Gibraltar, by both the Germans or even by our own navy."

"And the Italians," Garron added.

"The Italians?"

"Yes. Italy has declared war on Great Britain. Their submarines are sinking British shipping. British ships in the Mediterranean around the Straits of Gibraltar are being attacked on all sides by Vichy France, German Kriges marine, and Mussolini's warships. Things are not looking good for Britain right now."

"Crikey, it might be safer to stay here in Morocco as prisoners of war," Josh White said.

Captain Abraham stared coolly at White.

"I'm only joking, Captain." White apologised. "I'm all for taking the *Devon Star* back to blighty if necessary. But it sounds like an impossible task."

"Alright, men. Let's get our heads around this plan and who does what. I agree with Josh, it looks almost impossible to sail out of Larache without being stopped by the enemy. Not to mention picking up 200 or so passengers and then taking them to freedom."

Kevin sat on the floorboards with his knees drawn up to his chest, his eyes wide open listening to the men discussing the plan. A buzz of excitement spread through the sailors as they sat around the table to discuss retaking the *Devon Star*, picking up 60 soldiers and their families and transporting them all to an Allied port.

Captain Glover, master of the impounded *SS Devon Star*, assuming himself to be the lead officer, addressed the seaman, the officers and the lieutenant from the French Foreign Legion.

"Stealing a ship and sailing out of an unfriendly harbour is not as far-fetched as it seems. I've done it before."

"Really! Where?"

"Back in 1930. My ship was impounded by the corrupt Port Authority, in Cartagena, Bolivar, Colombia, illegally I might add, on trumped up charges. It's a long story, but suffice to say, me and my crew took it back. Anyway, back to the plan. We can't all troop through the streets of Larache, I suggest a minimum crew retake the *Devon Star* and sail it out of Larache. A skeleton crew, two navigators, two engineers, two sailors, two oilers, a radio officer, and a cook."

"Agreed."

"Next, is to find a safe place on the coast to take on 200 people without being seen. Any suggestions?"

The sailors fell silent, pondering how to solve the problem of stealing a ship and then finding a place to embark over 200 people.

Josh White was the first to speak, "I know a place, captain. It's south of Casablanca on the Atlantic coast."

"Where?"

"Well, as I told you before I was trading with Silver Line down here for getting on ten years, taking iron ore to Middlesbrough. We used to use a port called Siri TanTan, well, not a port really, more like a jetty in the middle of nowhere. The ore came down from the mine by a long conveyor belt. The belt was always breaking down, it took ages to load 5000 tons of ore. We hated the port as there was nowhere near to have a run ashore, no bars, nothing. It's about 250 miles down from Casablanca. When the iron ore ran out in 1935, they just left the jetty and conveyor belt and the rolling stock to rust away."

"Do you know the jetty, Lieutenant Garron? Do you know Siri TanTan?"

Garron shook his head. "Sorry, no I don't. I've never heard of Siri TanTan."

"That's because it's not on the map," said White. "I remember the captain and navigators used to use landmarks to find the jetty. The port has no seamarks, no lights, and you can only get alongside during the day; the pilot wouldn't take you alongside at night."

"It sounds like an ideal place, a place out of the way. Somewhere we can load people without drawing attention to ourselves, but we have no charts. We don't know where Siri TanTan is. Do you have a chart of the coast?"

"Not a chart, but I do have an atlas. I'll get it." Garron got up and left the hut to find the atlas. The sailors waited for him to return. Five minutes later Garron came back into the hut holding a battered old atlas. The navigators gathered around the book studying the Moroccan coast from Ksar-el-Keir to Tarfoya. No sign of a Siri or a Siri TanTan or a TanTan Siri.

"The coastline along that stretch is as flat as a fart," White said. "Except just before you reach TanTan there is a hill, I remember the captain said it was called, 'One-tree-hill', like a bump with a palm tree on top, then it goes flat for about two more miles, then in good visibility you can see the conveyor belt and the jetty jutting out into the sea."

"Any other features?"

"No, not really. Hang on, there's a large town about 30 miles inland from TanTan. It's called Tiznit. We'd sometimes get a taxi ride to Tiznit. You drive through a large desert for about an hour."

Glover found Tiznit on the atlas.

"That reduces the area a bit. What direction was Tiznit from Siri TanTan?"

"Let me think." White scratched his head. "Easterly…maybe northeast. I remember the sun rising over the taxi's back window when we were getting back from Tiznit. I remember that because it shone in the rear-view mirror into the driver's eyes."

Captain Glover drew an imaginary line with his finger from the east through Tiznit to the coast, calculating a taxi travelling at 30 to 40mph for one hour. "There are charts on the *Devon Star* and there might be more info in the Almanac. But how do we relay the exact spot for the soldiers to muster? We can't have two hundred people wandering up and down the beach."

"Why not have someone on the beach at a point we can identify. We will send a code message by Aldis lamp and then you can follow the ship either north or south to Siri TanTan."

"Emm, that's a possibility." Captain Glover drew a small circle on the map. "I estimate the jetty is around here somewhere. Next job is to reconnoitre the *Devon Star*, to see how the land lies."

"Leave finding Siri TanTan from the land to me. You get on with finding TanTan from the sea, and hopefully we will meet up there." Garron produced a sheet of paper. "This is a rough drawing of Larache harbour. Here is the *Oued LoukKos*, the Loukkos River, and here, at the harbour entrance, is the Fort Al Kabibat." He pointed to the fort guarding the harbour entrance. "This is the problem, getting past this fort, from the river to the sea without being stopped or shot at. All movement in the river is controlled by the Port Authority, they let the fort know what ship is coming in and going out to sea. I can get you into Larache, but you will have to make plans to take the ship and get it out to sea yourselves."

"How will you get us into Larache?"

"I have papers, forged papers, for the police check-points. The order says you are prisoners of Vichy France, and we are taking you to the port for transfer to Marseilles on mainland France. I know a businessman in Larache. He too is a free Frenchman. Leave all that to me, and you make a plan how to steam out of Larache un-noticed. I will make my own plans how to find Siri TanTan and the transport for the evacuees."

Kevin, Des and Stan sat on the floor, mesmerised, listening to the seaman officers and Lieutenant Garron talking about the plan to steal a ship back from Vichy France and use it to transport Free French soldiers and prominent Jews to Gibraltar.

"Wait till I tell my pal Tommy about this adventure, it sure is more exciting than playing cowboys and indians."

"Yeah, but they won't believe us."

The three boys continued listening to the men.

"We will need to reconnoitre, the docks at Larache, to check out who is guarding the ship." Glover said. "We don't want any suspicious gendarme catching us spying on the port. Larache is under military guard. Spies are shot."

"I'll spy on the docks," Kevin volunteered. "No-one will suspect me."

"So will I," cabin boy Des said. "I know the port of Larache. I've been there three times, twice last year and once this year. Also, the *Devon Star* is my ship."

"Sorry, lads, it's too dangerous. You'll stand out like a sore thumb, you look like English schoolboys and you don't speak Arabic or French. You'll be picked up for sure."

"I can speak Italian," Junior seaman Stan said, standing up and raising his hand like a schoolboy answering his teacher.

"Really, what can you say in Italian?"

"I can say, *Buongiono* and *Buon poeriggio* and *Buona notte*."

"Anything else?"

"Err, no."

"Speaking a few Italian words isn't speaking Italian."

Stan sat down again, pouting.

"You know what, three young boys in Larache looking around the ships is less suspicious than three men spying on ships, and three boys, I think, is less suspicious than just one boy alone," Captain Scotton suggested.

The officers looked down at the three boys sat on the floor.

"I don't know, it's dangerous for anyone. Men or boys caught spying will be shot."

"Well, let's just think about it." Captain Glover said. "The boys can reconnoitre the port and give the *Devon Star* a closer examination. Let us know what's going on. We can finalise the plan when we get into Larache. There is an old army maxim; '*reconnaissance is seldom wasted*'."

With the sketchiest outline of a plan on how to escape from Morocco, along with over 200 men, women and children, the seamen settled down for the night in the Free French soldiers' clandestine camp.

20 hours later, with the hi-Jack crew selected, and a decision made to take the three boys along as potential reconnaissance scouts, ten men and the three boys stood by the army waggon waiting to climb aboard. They were surrounded by the remaining crews to be left behind with the Free French soldiers.

"Good luck, lads," Captain Abraham said to the men about to sneak into Larache. "And you too, Peggie, be careful. And we will meet up at TanTan in a couple of days."

"Okay, Captain Abraham," Kevin said while clutching his grab bag and a rolled up Djellaba Moroccan robe given to him by Garron. "I'll be careful, but just in case, let my mum know what happened here in Morocco."

"I will, but I'm sure you will be alright, just don't take unnecessary risks, like sneaking out of a prison camp to steal meat pies! And don't let anyone see your toffee tin, the picture of King George VI and Queen Elizabeth might attract attention to you. Why don't you leave the bag with us?"

Kevin looked inside his bag at the picture of the King and Queen on his 1937 coronation souvenir Thorne's one-pound premier toffee tin.

He grinned. "No, I'll hide my bag under this coat. It's got my good luck sheriff's badge and my mum's St Christopher medal. I want to keep them with me."

"Alright, suit yourself, just don't get caught."

"All aboard," called Garron

Captain Glover checked each man as they climbed up into the back of the truck; two engineers, one navigator, the ship's wireless officer, a cook, two stokers, two seamen and three boys. The captain last to climb aboard. Lieutenant Garron slammed the tailgate shut and climbed into the cab next to the driver. The waggon set off towards Larache.

The dawn was breaking over Africa as the four-tonner drove into the middle of Larache Town unchallenged. It appeared that the red and green and flaming grenade insignia painted on the doors and bonnet were enough identification to allow the vehicle to pass with no questions asked. The lorry drove into a gated courtyard at the back of a large two storey building. The gates were shut behind them. A man appeared out of the building's back door.

"All out, gentlemen," called Lieutenant Garron. "You are safe here for a couple of days and nights. Let me introduce you to Monsieur Lazard. Monsieur Lazard is the owner of this building, he is a friend."

"Hello, Monsieur Lazard," the men greeted the Frenchman as they climbed down into the courtyard.

"*Bonjour, les hommes.*" Lazard said.

"Mr Lazard will look after you and will help as far as he can. I must report back to my battalion, otherwise I will be marked as absent without leave, a deserter. Also, I have much work to do to organise our rendezvous at Siri TanTan. We will find TanTan from the land; you will have to do the same from the sea."

Kevin climbed down from the truck holding his meagre possessions.

Garron spoke to him. "In the morning, Kevin, dress up in the Djellaba and take a walk to the docks, report back here on what you see around the *Devon Star.*"

"Yes, I'll do that." He shook hands with Garron

"Bonne chance, mon garcon." Garron climbed back into the cab.

Kevin watched while the wagon reversed back out of the gate and drove away. Standing in the courtyard, he looked around at his surroundings. Listening to the sea birds squawking above, he thought, 'What the heck am I doing here? It doesn't seem like five minutes ago I was at school being called Five-foot-Fife!"

"Follow me," beckoned Lazard.

Lazard led the men down a flight of external steps into the basement. The basement storeroom was cluttered with odd chairs, 5-a-side football goal posts and nets, boxes of old curtains and bits of stage scenery. An internal staircase led up to the ground floor.

"Make yourselves at home," Lazard said in English. "I will get you some food and something to drink. The WC is there. If you need anything or information, let me know."

"We want information about the dock and the guards, any gunboats, etc."

"Since the war started, the port is swarming with soldiers, and Germans and the *'deteste'* Gestapo. They are arresting anyone who looks the slightest bit suspicious. So be very careful."

Kevin looked up at the noise coming from the floor above the high ceiling. "What is this place?"

Lazard, noting Kevin's curiosity said, "before the war it was a dance hall, and what do you call it in English? A place for people to come and enjoy?"

"Like a Community Centre?" suggested Glover

"Yes, that's right. The Vichy made me use it to house refugees. The main hall is now being used as dormitory for refugees. They are nearly all Jewish refugees escaping from Europe. You don't need to go up there."

Stan, rummaging through one of the boxes, pulled out a football.

"To me head, Stan," called Des.

Stan threw the ball across to Des, Des headed it back. The three boys began to dribble the ball around the floor.

Captain Glover watched them play for a minute then said, "I've got an idea. Lads playing football on that derelict space behind the dock fence won't arouse suspicion. I saw boys playing there when we were loading the grain. Why don't you boys take the football and play footie down by the dock and then report back what you see. In the meantime, get your heads down for a couple of hours."

Kevin found a corner to sleep in and slept soundly until mid-morning. He washed his face in cold water and waited until Des and Stan were ready to carry out a reconnoitre of the port. The three boys, all dressed like locals, left the basement. Outside, squinting in the bright sunlight, and kicking the football between them, the boys made their way down *Route d'Oujda* towards the docks.

"Follow me," Stan said leading them through the busy streets. "I know the way to the river."

None of locals seemed to pay any attention to three boys kicking a football down the road. They eventually reached the rough ground behind the dock perimeter fence. A group of three boys were already kicking a ball around in the dust. The ball rolled over towards Kevin's feet. He kicked it back.

"*Merci,*" the French-Moroccan boy said.

Kevin didn't answer. He just smiled and acknowledged him.

The Moroccan boy picked up the ball, tucking it under his arm. "*D'ou etes-vous.*"

Stan whispered to Kevin, "pretend we are Italians." He called over, pointing to his own chest, "*Italiano. No speaka French.*"

The boy beckoned, "*Viens Jouer au foot s'ie te plait.*"

"I think he wants us to play football," Stan said.

"Come on then, England against French Morocco," Kevin said enthusiastically.

"Don't tell them we are English for crying out loud. Pretend we are Italians. They won't know."

Without much more speaking and much more yelling of undecipherable words, the boys played a game of football.

"*Buongiono, buongiono,*" shouted Stan, passing the ball to the French Moroccan.

"*Buon poeriggio,*" called Des

"*Buona note,*" shouted Kevin not understanding what the words meant. Hoping the Moroccans didn't understand the words either.

Any thoughts of reconnoitring the port were gone as the six boys played football. A break from the war. Kevin, Stan and Des, all aged under 16, laughing and enjoying playing a game of football instead of worrying about being shot at dawn by the Gestapo. A jeep full of French soldiers stopped to watch the game, before driving off. After nearly an hour the Moroccan boy picked up the ball and indicated having to go.

"*Merci beaucoup. Nous devons partir. Au revoir.*"

Each of the Moroccan boys came and shook hands with the English boys.

"*Au revoir,*" said Kevin cheerfully. The game of football had cheered him up, making him feel genuinely happy again.

"Come on," Des called. "We've got to check out the port and then get back to report. They will be wondering what happened to us."

The three made their way towards the boundary fence looking around at the port, the ships in the port and the guards guarding the port.

"The *Devon Star* has gone!" Des sounded devastated. "We were over there loading wheat. The ship has gone. We're too late. Come on let's go down there and get nearer to the river." He kicked the football towards the fence leading down to the river. Kevin and Stan ran after him.

At the end of the dockyard, they could now see the opposite bank of the river.

"It's there, look. It's on the other side of the river."

Kevin looked across at the *Devon Star*. The cargo ship looked to be high and dry, sitting on the mud, leaning over on the rocky breakwater. The riverbed dropped sharply towards the fast-flowing river, six feet away from the ship's keel. "It must be low tide now. By looking at the barnacles on the rocks, I bet she won't float till nearly high water."

"Erm," murmured Stan, "I agree,"

"Me too," Des said. "I reckon we won't be afloat for more than two hours, or even less. If we leave it too late, she'll be back, sitting in the mud 'till daylight. That means another day lost, and the Africans may be taking her out of here tomorrow for all we know."

"Just look how fast the river is running, even at low water. It will flow even faster later; on the ebb tide."

They watched the ship for a few minutes in silence. Two men were working on the deck, a painting stage had been rigged on the funnel. A sailor using a pot of black paint, painted over the British shipping company's funnel markings. The red ensign on the ensign staff had been replaced by a flag showing a single star and red stripes, a flag that Kevin didn't recognise.

"There's no way I could swim across that river, it's flowing too fast."

"There is a bridge up stream, but that has soldiers on it checking people crossing."

"Is there a boat? To get over to the other side, we need a boat."

"Look at the big gun at the end of the sea wall. And another gun, over there, upstream."

The boys looked at the anti-aircraft guns. They looked across the harbour entrance towards the Fort guarding the port. Naval guns pointed seawards.

"There's no chance of getting a ship past that lot without being seen. Come on, let's get back and report what we've seen. I think we can give up on taking back the *Devon Star*."

The boys picked up the football and made their way back to the dancehall to report what they'd seen.

~ * ~ * ~ * ~

The officers gathered round the table looking at Lieutenant Garron's rough plan of the docks and river.

Des, using a pencil, drew on the plan. "The *Devon Star* has been moved to here, her bows are pointing upriver. On the end of this breakwater there is a big gun. I saw some soldiers near it. There is another Anti-aircraft gun here, near the bridge crossing the river."

"How many soldiers on the gun?"

"I saw three."

"The ship appeared to be careened over on the breakwater, and the river is flowing at a rate of knots," Kevin added.

"How many sailors did you see working on the *Devon Star's* deck?"

"Three. One man was painting over the company's funnel markings. Two other men were seen looking down the holds. The hatches were open, but the derricks were in their cradles."

"How was she secured? How many lines did you see?"

"Loads…I saw at least three lines going forward, and two lines out aft. We couldn't see the breast lines. But we calculated she won't be floating much more than an hour either side of High water."

"Even so, in the fast-flowing river she will need to be well secured." The Devon's star's chief engineer said thoughtfully, "You know once we are aboard it might take us an hour or more to get the engine warmed up and primed before we can let go the mooring lines. A ship is not like a car, you know, where you just turn on the ignition and drive off. We have to make steam."

The captain sucked in his breath. "Once we're on board we've go to get off as soon as possible, if we delay sailing the tide will run out and we'll be high and dry again."

"Just telling you skipper. The engine oil will be cold."

Captain Glover pulled on his ear lobe. "You know, the river could be to our advantage. Look at this." He pointed to the drawing. "At high water the tide will be fairly slack allowing us to cross the river. Then as the ebb starts to flow seawards, after high water, the river will be ebbing at around three knots. If we could let go her moorings, just say an hour after high water, the ship could just drift free out to sea."

"Drift?" asked the chief engineer sceptically.

"Yes, drift with no power. If we could drift out to sea that will give you time to warm up the oil."

"Yes, but she could also spin around and crash head or stern first into the breakwater or drift across the harbour entrance and hit the opposite shore. She might even crash into Larache Port over here. We'd look well sitting amongst the fishing boats with nowhere to go," the chief mate grumbled.

"Well, are we going to do it, or not?"

"Also, starting the engine before we sail will wake up the entire army," the chief engineer said. "I go along with Captain Glover's suggestion and cut the lines and drift out silently under the noses of the guards. We can fire up the main engine when we are well out to sea, the current runs out for over a mile; I know that from experience, it's a strong undercurrent."

"How do we get aboard?"

Captain Glover said, "I will climb up the gangway with Mr Jones and Mr Whittaker here, two strong men. I'll pretending to be the new captain joining the ship. Me wearing my uniform may fool the watchman. Once on board we will overpower the watchman and the rest of the crew will then take over the ship."

"What if the guard is armed?"

"Why should he be armed. Anyway, we'll have to cross that bridge when we come to it... Alright lads, that's the plan. We need to get a boat to cross the river. All agreed?"

The seamen nodded. "Yeah, what've we got to lose? We can't stay here forever. "What do we do with the African sailors onboard?"

"We take them with us."

"What if they don't want to sail with us?"

"We'll sling them overboard. They can swim back to Monrovia, wherever that is."

The men smiled.

"I'll go and see Monsieur Lazard and see if he can get his hands on a boat. We'll need a couple of axes too." Captain Glover looked around at the gathered crew. "All agree, no second thoughts?"

"No second thoughts," they all agreed. All of them desperate to get home to their families.

"That settles it then, chaps. I'll go and see Lazard about the boat and axes. The rest of you get some rest till night." Glover turned to the three boys. "Well done, lads. Your reconnoitre was well worthwhile. Thanks."

Kevin was too excited to sleep. As he listened to the bumps and sounds of movement on the floor above, he thought he'd go and have a nosey. *'I've never seen a refugee before,'* he thought. He climbed up the stairs to the ground floor. He pushed open the door and peeped through. He couldn't believe what he saw. Dozens of people, men, women, children and babies camped all over the floor and on the stage. Every available space taken. The noise and chatter and the smell of the huddled mass of people shocked him. Standing out amongst the masses, Kevin noticed a young girl sitting alone. He couldn't take his eyes off this pretty girl. She looked up and saw him peeping through the door, she smiled and gave him a friendly wave. Kevin smiled and waved back. He guessed the girl was about the same age as him, a bit older maybe. Kevin thought she was very pretty. He had not spoken to a girl of his own age since leaving home. She had long fair hair, braided in a single plait that draped over her left shoulder, and she wore a blue Alice band that matched the colour of her dress. Holding the hair band in place were two silver clips. Her dress was screwed and dirty, but Kevin didn't notice that, all he could see was a nice-looking, but sad face. He wanted to talk to her. How had a pretty European girl managed to finish up as a refugee in North Africa?

Against the advice of Mr Lazard, not to speak with the refugees, Kevin entered the hall and made his way over to the girl, who appeared to be on her own. Plucking up courage he sat down beside her.

She smiled and said, "*Bonne journee, Monsieur.*"

At close quarters Kevin could see just how beautiful her face was, her teeth so white and clean, her long eyelashes, her green eyes looking appealing but so sad at the same time.

"I'm sorry, I don't speak French. Can you speak English?"

"*Oui.* Yes, I speak a little English. Are you English?"

"Yeah, I'm a British seaman."

The girl frowned. "A seaman? You look too young to be a seaman." She glanced around nervously, unsure whether to believe him.

Kevin sensed her nervousness, "I'm not an *'agent provocateur'.*" Lieutenant Garron thought at first that I was an 'agent of the police', but I'm not. How come you are here?"

"I've nowhere else to go. My parents have been arrested; they are both in prison now. Our house near Casablanca has been taken over by the Vichy. All Jewish people in Morocco are being resettled in areas called *Mellahs*, you know, like ghettos."

"That's awful, why are they doing that?"

"I don't know why. It's the law now. All Jewish teachers, doctors and so on, here in French Morocco, Tunisia and Algeria are coming under the Nuremburg anti-Jewish laws and doctors are prevented from practicing. Our possessions have been stolen."

"That's terrible. What did your mum and dad do to get themselves locked up?"

"Nothing. They were arrested by General Nogues just for being French academics, professors at the University. Anyway, what are *you* doing in Morocco?"

"My ship was sunk by a German submarine. We were prisoners of Vichy France as well. Apparently, we are enemies of France too. We escaped."

"Escaped?"

"Yes, I'm not supposed to talk to you about it. But we escaped."

"I wish I could escape. But where to? I have no passport, no money, nothing. I depend on people here to help me. Monsieur Lazard lets me stay here. Although it won't be long before we are all forced out of here and made to live in the ghettos…the *Mellahs*. I'd hate it in there."

"Where would you go if you could get out of here, out of Morocco?"

"I would go to England. My mother has family in Cheshire, I have spent summer holidays in Chester. Do you know Chester?"

"Yeah, course I do. It's near where I live in Lancashire," Kevin glanced around the room. "Anyway, I'd better get back. I'm not supposed to be up here, Good luck. I hope you do manage to get out of here and safely to England."

"Thank you. What is your name?"

"Kevin."

"Thank you, Kevin. My name is Claudette."

"See you, Claudette."

Kevin made his way back to the basement wondering if Captain Glover could help the girl. He approached Glover who was sleeping and gave the captain a nudge.

"Eh, what the hell?" Glover woke up from a deep sleep.

"Sorry to wake you, Captain, but I've just been talking to one of the refugees on the dance floor."

"Dance floor, what dance floor?"

"The floor upstairs. There must be 100 people sleeping on the floor. They are mainly refugees from France, but there is a girl who is alone. Her parents have been arrested by the Gestapo and now she is all alone in the world."

"Well, what about it? What do you want me to do about it? The whole of Europe is one big refugee camp."

"Can we take her with us?"

"No."

"Why not?"

"Because I say not." Glover sounded grumpy. "It will be hard enough for us to get away, without a girl tagging along. It will make getting on the ship even harder."

"She's a Jewish girl. Things are not looking good for Jews. My captain, Captain Abraham is Jewish. He'd take her along."

"Don't try and blackmail me, Fife. Don't try and make me feel bad." Captain Glover sat up; his tone mellowed. "How do you know she will come with us. Her parents are here in Morocco. You haven't told her about our escape plan, have you?"

"No, I haven't."

"Look, Kevin, we can't take every Jew in Morocco."

"Alright, sir. Just thought I'd ask."

Kevin went and lay down on his blanket waiting for nightfall. He woke up hours later to a dimly lit room. Captain Glover was talking to Lazard. They looked across at the waking deck-boy.

"Kevin," Captain Glover called. "Come here a minute."

Kevin was amazed to see Claudette sitting alongside Lazard. He sat at the table next to the girl and waved bashfully at her. She smiled back at him.

"Right, young Fife, Monsieur Lazard and I have been talking about Claudette here. Monsieur Lazard agrees with you, he thinks her life may be in danger if she stays here in Larache. It has come to his attention that the Gestapo want to bring her in for questioning. Her parents are enemies of Vichy France, and as such, their daughter is a possible sympathiser with the British and a danger to the Vichy."

Kevin looked at the girl in wonderment. How could such an innocent looking girl be considered an enemy of Vichy France and Nazi Germany. He shook his head. What is happening to the world? A world which in less than 9 months has gone from a peaceful place to an ugly war, where little girls are considered enemies of the Nazis.

"We will take Claudette with us."

Kevin's face broke into a grin. "Oh, right," he said in surprise. "Thanks, Captain."

"Thank you, Kevin," Claudette said. "But for you, I wouldn't have got this chance to escape from Morocco. If I get to England, I will continue the fight against the Nazis."

One by one, the British crew began to stir, stretching and yawning.

"Get your things together," Lazard said to the gathered sailors. "I'm going to take you down to the river in three carloads. Fortunately, there is no curfew in Morocco at the moment. You will wait at the boat house and then my friends, when you are all together you will be on your own. If things go wrong for you and you are taken prisoners, please do not let them know about me or Lieutenant Garron, otherwise it's goodnight for us…If you know what I mean."

"I can assure you, Monsieur Lazard, we will not drop you in it. We will simply say we escaped from Casablanca and made our way to Larache to steal a boat and try to take back the *Devon Star*." Captain Glover reassured Lazard. "But we don't anticipate getting caught."

"Good, come on then. I'll take the boys and Claudette first."

Lazard drove his overloaded car out of the compound, through the streets of Larache and out of town heading up the river for five miles. The car pulled up outside a ramshackle building on the riverbank.

"Go inside and wait while I bring the others."

Kevin, Des, Stan and Claudette crept into the hut. It was pitch black inside. Moored alongside a derelict jetty there was an old rowing boat. The boat had seen better days but floated high in the water, there was one set of oars in the boat.

"It's going to be a tight squeeze all of us in that." Kevin muttered. "I hope it doesn't sink." He looked at the river. "You know, I think the tide has turned, look at the flow. I hope the others get here quick."

The four youngsters sat on the hard clay floor waiting anxiously for the rest to join them. By 1am the remainder of the crew had been transported to the rendezvous point.

Lazard shook hands with each of the sailors in turn. "*Bon chance, mon amees.*"

Carefully, one by one, they climbed into the boat, making sure it was well balanced. Kevin sat next to Claudette, his heart pounding both at the prospect of getting onto the *Devon Star* and partly at being so close to a young girl.

"Right, cast off," ordered Captain Glover. "Give way on the oars."

The river was ebbing fast now. Rowing on the river was easy, the current helping them float towards the sea. No navigation lights showed on the river. The night was moonless; the sailors struggling to see the riverbank, they were struggling to keep the boat in the middle of the river. After 30 minutes the lights of Larache appeared. The wharf and silos of the port could be seen outlined by the lights of the city. On the right-hand side of the river the outline of a ship could be seen.

"That's my ship," said Captain Glover. "Just where you said it would be."

"Be careful, Captain. There's a big gun this side of the ship, and other anti-aircraft gun at the end of the breakwater."

"Shush, everyone, stop talking, stop rowing. Let's drift past the AA gun."

They stopped whispering, the oarsmen resting on their oars. The rowboat drifted silently by, passing the first AA gun. No one moved around the gun. Kevin thought they'd all be sleeping with the chance of an air raid being virtually nil.

"Pull over, coxswain, ship your oars. Get ready to leap out, lads." Glover spoke to Jones and Whittaker, the two beefy seamen selected to overpower the watchman.

The boat drifted into the bank scraping its keel on the rocky breakwater.

Captain Glover stared hard at the water swishing around the bow of the ship. "I don't think she will be floating for long. We'll have to work fast." He stood on the gunnel waiting to leap ashore. The captain leapt ashore followed by his deckhands. Kevin and Stan followed the captain, holding onto the boat's painter to stop it floating off in the strong tide.

Glover whispered to his crew, "wait here, once we've taken the ship, I'll beckon you to follow us up the gangway."

The captain and his two strongmen disappeared into the darkness leaving the two boys struggling to hold the boat alongside the bank.

Three minutes later the captain returned to the boat.

"Big problem, lads," he panted. "There's no gangway. We can't get aboard."

The men in the boat moaned and muttered in dismay.

"What we going to do?"

"Don't know. What the f…"

Kevin looked at the tight bow lines as tight a bow strings leading up to the forecastle mooring bitts

"I could climb up the rope and get aboard,"

"What good would that do?"

"Me too, I can climb up the rope," Stan said. "We could lower the Jacob's ladder to you."

"That's a good idea, young man," Glover said enthusiastically. "There's a ladder in the forepeak… But it weighs a ton…"

"I can climb aboard too," Des the diminutive cabin boy said. "The three of us could lift the ladder."

Glover looked at his cabin boy. "Alright boys. That's the only way we can get aboard. Come on you two, get back in the boat."

The captain and the two sailors climbed back into the rowboat.

"We'll drift down to the bow and wait there till the ladder is lowered. I'm glad we brought you now, none of us men and the lassie here could climb the headlines. Good luck lads... And try and be as quick as you can. The water is running out fast and the current is getting too strong for us to hold the boat."

Des joined Stan and Kevin on the river bank. With the boys safely ashore, Captain Glover ordered the men in the boat to drift down stream to the bows of the *Devon Star*. The fast-flowing river swishing noisily between the ship's hull and the river bank forcing the bow of the ship outwards. As each minute passed, the ebbing tide grew stronger; the ship's forward mooring lines tight under the pressure.

"Come on," Kevin whispered.

The three boys crept down to the first of the mooring ropes. Kevin looked down at the river. "Don't fall in, you'll be swept away."

Des looked up. "Crikey, it's higher than I thought."

"I'll go first. Last time I did this was on the training ship *Cromwell* to become a *Crommie Boy*," Kevin whispered.

He glanced down the portside of the ship, he could just about see that the gang-plank had been removed. Without wasting time, Kevin grabbed hold of the headline with both hands swinging his legs over the rope. With his feet curled over the rope, Kevin shimmied, hand over hand, up the line to the fairleads. At the deck level he grabbed hold of the ship's handrail. With one mighty heave he leapt over the rail, landing silently on the ship's main deck. He lay flat waiting for Stan to join him. A minute later Stan landed on the deck beside him. They both looked over the side at Des, the cabin boy, struggling to climb up the rope.

"I can't make it," Des called, hanging onto the line like grim death.

"Don't fall off."

Kevin climbed back over the rails, reaching down, "Come on, you're almost there."

Des shook his head, "I can't. I'm going to fall."

"Hold onto my belt, Stan. I'll reach down to him."

Stan grabbed hold of Kevin's belt allowing him to reach down to the motionless cabin boy. Kevin gripped hold of Des's hand just as he was about to fall off the rope. Holding onto him with one hand, Kevin thought his arm would be pulled out of its sockets. He knew if he let go, Des would drop into the river and be swept downstream between the ship and the bank. He would surely drown.

With all his might and strength Kevin managed to grab hold of Des's other hand. Des's body now dangling down.

"Pull us up, Stan." Kevin puffed.

Stan did not have the strength to pull up the weight of two boys. He called down to Des, "Des, try and get your leg onto the line, my arms are dropping off."

Des kicked out, trying to reach the headline with his foot. He tried a second time, this time he managed to hook his foot onto the line. This took the weight off both Kevin and Stan. Kevin let go of one of Des's arms to grab hold of the handrail. Between them, Kevin and Stan pulled Des over the rails; all three flopped down on the deck exhausted.

After a few minutes, Des had regained his strength. "Sorry about that, I'm not strong."

"Don't worry, you did good."

"Come on, Captain Glover will wonder what's gone wrong. I'll show you where we keep the Jacobs ladder."

Des led them into the forepeak rope locker. The locker under the forecastle smelling strongly of tar and ropes. The heavy Jacobs ladder was coiled up on one side, it took all three boys to lift it and carry it to the starboard handrails. Kevin looked over the side and could see the rowboat below. The boat seemed to be struggling to keep station. The sound of the fast-flowing river drowned out the noise of the ladder as it was lowered over to the waiting men below. Kevin secured one side of the ladder to the handrail while Stan tied off the other side. Able seaman Jones, a giant of a man, was the first man to climb up the ladder. He carried with him the boat's painter. The ebbing tide, now getting stronger, trying to drag the small boat down river towards the sea. It took all the seaman's strength to stop the boat from drifting off to sea, carrying the captain and his crew and Claudette with it.

Jones, still holding onto the boat's painter, called to Des, "get a heaving line to help get the girl aboard."

Des ran back into the forepeak to retrieve a heaving line. He dropped the line to the captain. Glover tied a bowline to Claudette's midriff. Stan and

Kevin held onto the heaving line to help the girl as she climbed carefully up the dangling ladder. They helped her over the rails onto the main deck. One by one the remainder of the crew climbed aboard until they all mustered together out of sight in the forepeak. Jones let go of the boats securing line, dropping it overboard.

Kevin watched as the rowboat swiftly floated away into the night heading towards the sea. He whispered to Stan, "the river is faster flowing that I thought it would be."

"Um, yeah. I just hope Captain Glover's plan works."

The crew gathered around the captain in the darkness. "Right, lads, we need to check on the watchman, we need to find out if there's anyone awake, and how many are sleeping."

"I'll check on the watchman," Kevin volunteered.

"No, you stay here. Me, Mr Jones and AB Whittaker will deal with the watchman. Come on lads," Captain Glover said to his men. "Let's take back our ship and get the hell out of Morocco."

The three men disappeared down the darkened deck to sort out the skeleton crew of Africans. Kevin squatted down in the darkness next to Claudette. She took his hand and whispered, "This is so exciting, like a proper adventure story. I'm a bit scared what will happen to us."

Kevin moved closer to the girl and put his arm around her, Claudette in turn snuggled closer to Kevin, both waiting in anticipation for the captain to return. Kevin's heart beating faster. He wanted to kiss her but could not pluck up the courage to do so.

Ten minutes later the captain returned with a wide eyed and terrified African sailor in tow.

"This guy says there is no one else on the ship. The other sailors are ashore looking for women." Glover turned to the African sailor. "What's your name and where are you from?"

"Mi name is Winston, sah, like Mr Churchill." Winston saluted the captain. "I am Able seaman fro' Monrovia in Liberia."

"Right, Winston, I am your new captain, and these men," Glover indicated the crew. "are the new crew for this ship. Now you are sure there are no more men on the ship."

"Am sure, sah."

"That's a stroke of luck, no time to mess about. Chief, you go below check on the engine; get it ready for firing up. Chief cook, you go and check the galley, see what food there is."

"Aye, Captain." The chief engineer, second engineer and the two wipers left to go below to the engine room. The cook went to check that his kitchen was still serviceable."

"Sorry, Winston," Captain Glover said. "We're going to have you locked up 'til we get out to sea."

"Why dat, cap?"

"We can't risk you raising the alarm. When we get out to sea, we'll let you out."

"What 'bout mi frien' in port?"

"Sorry, Winston, they'll have to get another ship." Glover nodded to the mate to lock Winston in the mast-housing. "Right, you two go aft, you two go forward and when I give the signal, chop away the mooring ropes. Headlines first, then the stern line. Can't use the winches or windlass, the noise would wake up all of Morocco. Just cut the lines and we're off. And then, gentlemen, it's all in the lap of the God's. If my plan works, great, we'll drift out to sea. If it goes tits up, I'm afraid we'll be in deep shit." Glover looked at Claudette, "Excuse my language, miss."

Claudette smiled.

"Are we ready?" Glover checked his watch. "It's now nearly one hour after high water. The ebbing tide will be at its fastest for the next two or three hours. Here's hoping the tide will sweep us to safety."

The Captain looked at the men on the forward mooring line, one of the *Devon Star's* sailors holding an axe. "Right, cut away all the forward mooring lines."

The able seaman chopped at the headlines; they fell one by one onto the bank. With the stern lines acting like a fulcrum and the fast-flowing river rushing between the ship's port side and the breakwater forced the bow to swing out towards the middle of the river.

Glover gave a chopping signal with his hand, calling, "cut away the after lines."

Able Seaman Jones chopped at the rope, they too dropped onto the bank. With no donkey engines running to keep the noise to a minimum and without any steerageway the ship floated free, turning down the river towards the sea.

"We're floating, thank goodness for that. Everyone on the bridge, that's the safest place for us all to be; all in one place," called the captain. "There's nothing anyone can do now."

The captain, the radio officer, two sailors, three boys and the girl assembled on the bridge to watch as the *Devon Star* began to rotate 360 degrees. At one time heading for the sea stern first before slowly revolving back headfirst towards the sea. Everyone held their breath as the ship began to turn for a second time. This time in the opposite direction.

"Oh my God," Glover muttered as the stern quarter crashed into the breakwater right under the noses of the anti-aircraft gun located at the end of the breakwater. Kevin could see that the gun crew didn't seem at all surprised to see a ship appear out of the darkness. To everyone's relief the gunners didn't react, they just stood there, watching the ship glide past them. The out-of-control *Devon Star* cantered across the harbour entrance heading straight towards the fort on the other side of the river. The dark bulk of the fort getting ominously closer. Everyone on the bridge holding their breath expecting the ship to impact on the rocks or run aground.

"Come on, come on, please turn," the captain pleaded under his breath. "Swing round, swing to starboard.

The helm in the wheelhouse turned uselessly on its own with no power to turn the rudder. Just as if his prayer had been answered, the *Devon Star* turned once again towards the sea, less than twenty yards from the rocks at the base of the fort.

Kevin gawped up at the massive structure above, his heartrate dropping from around 150 beats per minute to somewhere round normal as the ship cleared the port entrance and drifted at three knots into the Atlantic Ocean.

Glover rang down to the engine room. "Alright chief, how's the engine, are you ready to fire it up?"

"Yes, Captain. Everything below is satisfactory. Not long now, the engine oil is warming up, fuel going into the injectors, fuel tanks full. We were all fuelled up and ready for sea, before we were taken prisoners."

"Thanks, chief. Give it another hour till we are well out to sea, then we'll start the main engine."

The cook came into the wheelhouse.

"How's the food situation, cookie?"

"Not good, Captain, the fridges have been robbed, the dry stores empty too. I managed to find some tea and I've brewed up."

"Good oh! Nothing like a brew in times of strife. Bring it up to the wheelhouse."

Claudette smiled and giggled.

"What's so amusing?" asked the captain.

"My father said, when things get tough for British people, they drink tea."

The men in the wheelhouse began laughing, mainly out of relief that they hadn't been challenged, shot at or grounded on the rocks. Captain Glover and the crew looked aft towards the port of Larache. The *Devon Star* caught on the tide, clearing the coast at a good rate of knots. There appeared to be no panic on the shore and the guns hadn't opened fire.

"How did you know the ship would drift out to sea?" Kevin asked.

Captain Glover grinned, "I didn't, but I've done the manoeuvre before. I took one of my ships back when it had been illegally impounded over in Colombia, right from under the noses of the Port Authority. I refused to pay them a $5000 bribe to get clearance. The harbour and river were pretty similar to this one."

One hour and 30 minutes later and three miles offshore the captain gave the order to start up the main engine and generators. The *Devon Star's* engines coughed into life, the steering gear primed, the captain rang down to the engine room for full speed ahead.

"We'll steam westerly out of range of the shore batteries then we'll head south looking for TanTan."

~ * ~ * ~ * ~

Two hours later steering towards the west. Captain Glover gave the order to change course and steam south.

Kevin, taking his turn on the helm, watched as the captain and the chief mate studied the chart of the west coast of Morocco.

The captain, holding a magnifying glass, muttered, "no Siri TanTan. However, there is a contour here, hardly worth noting. Although Tiznit is not on the chart, I estimate it's approximately here." He jabbed his finger on the chart. Using a parallel ruler, the captain drew a line on the chart. "If Josh White is correct about the bearings, the old jetty should be around here somewhere. ETA noon tomorrow."

CHAPTER 5

WEST AFRICA – SEPTEMBER 1940

KEVIN SAT ALONE ON THE foredeck staring out to sea. His sad eyes glistened. He didn't hear Claudette as she approached, she gave him a brief smile and sat down next to him. She looked at his eyes.

"Why are you crying?"

"I'm not crying," Kevin sniffed and tried to blink away the tears.

"What's that shoulder bag?" She pointed to the bag slung over Kevin's shoulder. "You always seem to be carrying it everywhere you go."

"It's my grab bag."

"Grab bag? What's a grab bag?"

"It's a bag with a few bits and pieces in it that I might need should I need to abandon ship again…in a hurry."

"What's in it?"

"Just a few essentials." He opened the bag to show her. "A water bottle, a few barley sugar sweets, my pen knife, my seaman's book, my ID card, a pair of socks and er…," he blushed shyly, "and a pair of undies…my torch, a fishing line, a toothbrush, soap and a flannel and my toffee tin."

"Toffee tin?"

"Yeah, there's no toffees in it just a few keepsakes. I'll show you." He took the tin from the bag and opened it. "My mum's St Christopher medal, a couple of letters, my pal Tommy's sheriffs' badge. He gave me that for good luck. A cross from my girlfriend, her dad's a vicar…other bits and pieces from my friends in Casablanca." He didn't mention that his Seaman's Discharge Book and his wallet were wrapped up in Board of Trade condoms.

"A tin of memories."

"Hmm, yes, I suppose so."

"Would you like a memory of me?"

He looked at Claudette and smiled. "Yes, of course I would... but you have nothing left in the world."

"I've nothing to offer...except this." She pulled the silver clip from her hair. "You can have this if you want...something to remember me by."

Kevin looked at the clip but didn't take it.

Overcome with sentiment, he said, "Oh, thanks, Claudette, you're really kind..., I'd like that, but that's all you've got that's pretty. I know from Monsieur Lazard that you had to sell your possessions, everything you had to survive in the refugee hall."

"It doesn't matter, I want you to have it. You have this one and I'll keep the other. They are a pair." She offered the clip again. "When you see the hairclip you will remember me, and when I see my clip, I will remember you."

Kevin studied the clip in the shape of a silver fern for moment. "Thanks, Claudette, I'll keep it forever." He carefully laid the clip in the tin box.

"That's a pretty box you have. Is that your king?"

Kevin nodded. "King George and Queen Elizabeth, on his coronation. I got it last Christmas for a present. Toffees are now on ration in England." He studied Claudette's face. "Why are people so awful to Jewish people? What have they got against kind people like you?"

Claudette thought for a moment. "I don't why, Kevin. Antisemitism has always been around; it never goes away. When governments fail, they look for scapegoats, someone to blame. The easiest people to blame are minorities, in Russian and Germany the Jews are in the minorities and are easy targets. When governments start anti-Jewish laws, the people will follow and turn on the jews and not on the government." She paused again. "Do you know what a scape goat is?"

Kevin shrugged, "I've heard of one, but I don't know what one is."

"A scape goat is a mythical beast that is ritually loaded up with the sins of others and then driven into the desert to carry away the sins of the community. Some people treat us Jews as scapegoats, blaming us for the sins of the world."

"I see." Kevin nodded. "I only know two Jewish people, you and Captain Abraham, and both of you are two of the kindest people I've ever met."

Claudette smiled at the compliment. "Captain Abraham. Who is he?"

"Captain Abraham is…was the captain of my ship; the *Alice Morgan*. He will be waiting at TanTan, I hope, that's if everything goes to plan and they are waiting for us. Anyway, I'd better get back to work, Claudette." He got to his feet. "We are sweeping up the grain left in the holds, the cook is grinding it into flour for bread. There's loads left in the scuppers and hold bottom." He was now feeling happier following his chat with a young girl his own age. "I'm glad this ship isn't a collier like the *Alice Morgan,* you can't eat coal dust."

Claudette made her way back to the accommodation; Kevin laid his grab bag by the hatch combing before climbing down into the hold to help Stan collect up more grains of wheat.

~ * ~ * ~ * ~

The *Devon Star* steamed south along the Moroccan coast all day and all night and half the following morning. Captain Glover now had all hands searching the coastline for what Josh 'Stoker' White called 'one tree hill'. The coastline according to Stoker White was miles of flat low sand dunes until a hill appeared. All hands now trying to locate this hill.

Kevin climbed to the foremast crosstree. The sun blazed down on him; visibility good for miles.

"Keep your eyes peeled for periscopes too," Captain Glover had warned him.

Shielding his eyes with the palm of his hand he searched the foreshore, occasionally glancing around at the shimmering sea. At a distance of about three miles to the southeast, Kevin spotted the hill. There it was, a bump on the landscape.

He shouted to the bridge. "There!" He pointed fine on the port bow.

Captain Glover raised his binoculars and studied the coast carefully.

A few minutes later, Kevin could see what he thought was a post on the top of the hill, then he saw the line of a conveyor belt disappearing inland. '*This definitely is one tree hill'*, he thought as he climbed down the mast to re-join the others on the bridge.

"From up there, Captain, I could see the jetty."

"Yes, well done, son."

One hour later with the ship slowed down to slow speed, the jetty was now clearly visible.

Through his binoculars Captain Glover studied the jetty. "I can't see anyone," he told the others on the bridge. "No one on the sand dunes, nobody on the foreshore." Kevin's heart sank. No Captain Abraham or his shipmates from the *Alice Morgan*, no Lieutenant Garron, no Free French soldiers, no refugees. "We'll go alongside and wait, any sign of danger, we'll go full speed astern and head back out to sea."

The *Devon Star* crept closer to the deserted jetty. With the main engine shut down, the ship gently approached the jetty. Suddenly, out of nowhere, a man appeared. He climbed from under the conveyor belt and onto the Jetty waving at the ship.

"It's Lieutenant Garron!"

Garron called to someone under the conveyor belt. Captain Isaac Abraham appeared and joined Garron on the jetty. Then almost unbelievably to Kevin, what appeared to be hundreds of men, women and children appeared from under the conveyor belt. They waved and cheered at the arrival of the rescue ship. Kevin jumping for joy at the sight of his captain and the crew from the *Alice Morgan*. The *Devon Star* now lay peacefully alongside the pier.

"Come on everyone, climb aboard," Captain Glover called.

Children and bags were handed over the handrails, French soldiers helping the women over the rails. The *Devon Star's* decks were soon crowded with people. Eventually everyone was onboard. Kevin watched as six men dressed in civilian clothing climbed over the handrails. Although their tropical suits were crumpled, Kevin thought they looked like what he imagined middle-aged college professors would look like. They had an air about them that was somehow different to the other civilians he'd seen in Casablanca. They stood alone from the others.

Captain Abraham and Lieutenant Garron, the last two to board the ship, climbed the steps up to the bridge; both men with beaming smiles.

"Are we all aboard?" Captain Glover asked.

"Yes, we're all aboard," said Abraham. "Ready to go when you are, Captain."

When Abraham saw Kevin, he came across and gave him a bear hug, nearly squeezing the breath out of the embarrassed deck-boy.

"Boy, am I glad to see you, safe and sound."

"I'm glad to see you too, Captain. When I saw the jetty deserted, I thought we'd gone to the wrong place or that you'd all been taken prisoners again."

"We've been hiding for nearly 36 hours. It's a long story, we got to the point of desperation, no food and the drinking water running out."

Kevin watched on as mothers poured water over their babies and children's faces washing off the sand, then taking sips themselves from the water bottles.

The ship's engines roared into life, black smoke belched out of the funnel, the propeller churned up the sand as it thrust the ship, stern first, backwards into the Atlantic.

"Where are we going, Captain Glover?"

"Don't know for sure. Let's look at the charts. Freeport, Las Palmas or Gibraltar?"

"How much fuel we got."

"Fuel and water's no problem, we took on bunkers just before we were taken prisoners, it's food we are short of."

"Oh, what I'd give for a cuppa. A decent cup of tea."

Claudette smiled at the British obsession with 'brewing up.'

"Tea's no problem, get the kettle on, Peggie," ordered a grinning Glover.

The three boys, laughing and joking, shot off below to brew tea for the officers. The dangers lurking under the sea and the dangers of Vichy French soldiers on the mainland forgotten for the time being.

With all the evacuees on board and the ship well clear of the Jetty, the officers gathered around the chart room table, the ship's logbook on the table.

Captain Glover, with pen in hand, said, "how many souls aboard?"

Garron checked his list. "59 soldiers, 30 women, 65 children, 6 Jewish refugees, one young lady from the dance hall, 62 seamen from the *Alice Morgan,* the *Markham Point,* and this ship, not forgetting Winston our Liberian deckhand, making a total of 224 persons in all."

Glover wrote in the logbook.

"Alright, gentlemen, the question is where do we go from here? I first thought Gibraltar, then had second thoughts about that with the Nazis on all sides, within range of Vichy shore batteries. I think sailing south to Freetown or west to the Azores, or to the Gran Canaria? What do you think?"

The captains of the *Alice Morgan*, the *Markham Point* and the *Devon Star* poured over the chart of the west coast of Africa, from Morocco to Nigeria.

"Las Palmas is nearest."

"How about sailing directly to the UK?"

"We've no food aboard. We have flour and water but nothing much else."

"Hmm, that's going to be a problem feeding 224 people. We have babies and youngsters; they can't live on bread and water."

"Well, Morocco, and all of French West Africa is under Vichy control," said Garron. "We cannot take on food on this coast. I suggest Gibraltar, that's the nearest Allied port. I'd forget Franco's Spanish ports and islands. They are supposedly neutral but they sympathise with the Nazis."

"Well, gentlemen, I'm steaming out due west. I want to be well clear of the African mainland; it's my ship, I will decide where we go..."

"U-boat! Dead ahead!" Screamed the lookout.

Everyone in the wheelhouse hurried to the bridge windows looking forward. They all saw the conning tower of a submarine.

"Blood hell," cursed Glover. "I don't believe it. "If they torpedo us, we're going to have a lot of people in trouble..."

"Captain the sub is signalling us on 500 kilocycles. It's a British submarine." Called from the radio cabin.

"Sir, the sub has dived," shouted the lookout.

The radio office came into the wheelhouse holding a slip of paper, he handed it to the captain.

Captain Glover shook his head, "What's going on!?" He read the cablegram, "Alter course and steam at full speed 180 true...You will be intercepted by British warship." Perplexed, Glover asked the radio officer "Is that it? What else did the sub say?"

"Nothing, captain. He used our call sign, it's as if he knew where we were. How does anyone know we are at sea? Nobody knew we were leaving Larache."

"Do you think it a ploy? Is it a trap?"

"I don't know. If it was a U-boat, why didn't it attack us?"

"It may have run out of torpedoes and shells... What do you think Captain Abraham?"

"I think we should sail south as ordered. A Nazi sub would not have surfaced to transmit a message like that."

"Alright, thank you, Issac." The captain turned to the helmsman, "Steer 180. Mr Jones."

The helmsman repeated "Steer 180, Sir." He turned the wheel and the ship headed south.

~ * ~ * ~ * ~

The *Devon Star* sailed south as directed. Kevin assisted the sailors to rig tarpaulins over the awnings to provide shelter for the soldiers from the blazing sun. Most of the women and children had been settled in the crew's cabins and sailor's mess room. The ship's small galley working overtime baking bread. Captain Glover, fearful of being torpedoed, preferred the evacuees to sleep out on deck rather than down in the holds. He gave orders to construct rafts out of timber shifting boards and had Jerry cans of drinking water lashed to the rafts just in case they did get attacked as the ship's two lifeboats were insufficient to hold 224 people.

"Ship approaching from the west bearing green four-five, Captain," called the lookout from outside on the bridge wing. "Warship, I think?"

Everyone piled out onto the starboard bridge wing to look.

Captain Glover raised his binoculars. "Oh God! It's a warship alright. If it's British like the submarine said we'll be alright, if it's German or Vichy, we're back in deep trouble."

"If it's Vichy, I'm a dead man," said Lieutenant Garron. "So are my soldiers."

"It's heading for us, Captain. No doubt about it."

"Alright. No need to turn and run, she'll be 10 knots faster than us and can blow us out the water with her armament."

The crew watched anxiously as the warship drew closer.

"I'm sure I can see the white ensign, Captain."

"I bloody well hope it is."

"Yes, I can see a white ensign flying off the yard arm. It's a British destroyer, I'm sure of it; I served on destroyers when I was in the navy." Jackson said.

A massive sigh of relief went around the assembled officers and men.

"Chief mate, do we have another ensign? Our Red Ensign has been stolen by the Vichy."

"There's a Union flag in the flag locker, Captain, I'll get it." The *Devon Star's* chief mate rummaged through the flag locker pulling out an old Union Jack.

"That'll do. Right lads," the mate spoke to the two deck boys. "Run out onto the boat deck and show this flag to the warship. It might stop them firing at us."

Kevin and Stan ran out onto the boat deck. They held the Union Jack flag between them, hoping the officers on the warship's bridge could see it. The warship approached at speed from just abaft the beam, Kevin could see officers on the destroyer's bridge examining the *Devon Star* with telescopes and binoculars. An Aldis lamp flashed out a signal.

"Sparky," called the captain. "The warship is signalling."

Donaldson, the ship's Radio Officer, hurried out onto the bridge wing holding an Aldis lamp. He plugged it into a socket and answered the warship, then started to read out aloud the Morse code message, "what ship?"

The radio officer replied in flashing Morse, "British ship *Devon Star*."

"Alter course to 185 true," replied the destroyer. "We are going to board you. Full speed ahead, do not stop."

Donaldson read aloud for his captain. Captain Glover said, "Acknowledge."

A bugle call from the warship resounded over the sea. Kevin watched as the warship's sea boat's crew hurried to man the boat. Within five minutes the sea boat had been launched and was speeding towards the *Devon Star*.

"Lower the starboard accommodation ladder on the lee side." Captain Glover ordered.

The ship's main accommodation ladder was lowered down to sea level. The navy's launch bumped up alongside the bottom platform.

The first man to climb up the gangway stepping onto the main deck was a Sub-Lieutenant from the Royal Navy.

Stan saluted him. "Follow, me, sir." He led the officer up to the bridge.

Kevin helped two more ratings step onto the ship.

"Hello, sonny, who are all these people?" asked a leading seaman. "Who are the soldiers? Frenchies?"

"Yeah, they are Free French soldiers and their families; we've just escaped from Vichy Morocco. Some are refugees, escaping from the Anti-Jewish laws. There's over 200 people on board."

"Blimey!" The leading hand seemed surprised.

"What ship is that?" Kevin asked, looking over to the warship and then at the letters HM DESTROYER on the sailor's cap tally.

"Can't tell you that, war time, you know."

"Why not? I'm not the enemy."

"Alright," the sailor grinned. "It's *HMS Eclipse*. A destroyer."

Kevin and the two Royal Navy ratings followed Stan up to the bridge while the *HMS Eclipse* steamed at full speed circling the *Devon Star* like a shepherd keeping the wolves away from a stray sheep. A meeting of the officers convened in the officer's mess, Kevin, Stan and Des were not invited. Following the meeting Kevin escorted the naval officer and the two ratings back to the gangway. To his surprise the six Jewish refugees were being helped down the steps by the naval ratings, they climbed onto the navy's launch.

"Are they leaving us?" Stan asked the officer.

"Yes."

"Why them?"

"Don't ask questions. I'm going back to the *Eclipse* and inform our skipper what's what here. A decision will be made what to do with you and the other civilians. I'll be back later."

"Bring some grub back with you, I'm starvin'," Stan said hopefully.

"And some fags." Kevin added.

"You're too young to smoke," the leading seaman said. He fished around in his shirt pocket and handed Kevin a packet of RN cigarettes. "Blue liners are pretty strong cigs so be careful."

"I will, thanks, mate."

The officer hesitated before stepping onto the accommodation ladder. "Which one of you is Kevin?"

Kevin frowned. "That's me."

The officer nodded and smiled but didn't say anything else.

Stan looked at Kevin, "I didn't know you smoked."

"I don't, but old Willie Wilde does, and I know he's gasping for a fag."

The two boys watched as the boarding party climbed back down into the sea-boat. The coxswain gunned the engine, put down the helm, and headed back to the warship at high speed, carrying six mysterious passengers.

"Why have the Jewish men been taken off?"

"I don't know."

"Strange."

Kevin and Stan made their way back to the bridge.

~ * ~ * ~ * ~

Later in the afternoon, the warship's motorboat headed back towards the *Devon Star,* this time there were six men in the boat and boxes of victuals. The sub-lieutenant clambered aboard followed by four naval ratings including a Chief Petty Officer. While the supplies were being lifted onto the ship's deck, the sub-lieutenant requested another meeting of the merchant seamen. They crowded into the officer's messroom. This time the boys were allowed to attend.

"Right, listen up, gentlemen," started the sub lieutenant. "This is what's going to happen, and these are orders from the Admiralty. The *Devon Star* is to be taken up from trade and will join the fleet. The French civilians are to be transferred to the Blue Funnel cargo passenger ship that will sail north in convoy to the UK, the Free French soldiers and the remainder of the merchant seaman are to be transferred to the Dutch liner *Westernland,* the French soldiers will join General Charles de Gaulle's 13th Demi Brigade, and the merchant seamen will sign articles and will be seconded to the Royal Navy." He looked around at the surprised officers and crew. "Anyone object?"

"Well, that solves the problem of where we go from here, the navy have made the decision for us. Do you know what we are expected to do, being pressed into naval service?"

"No, sorry."

"Where is General de Gaulle now?" asked Garron. "Where is the 13th Demi Brigade going?"

"I can't tell that either. You will of course be informed in more detail later. In the meantime, we are transferring some supplies to you to feed the babies and children while we wait for the liners to arrive."

"We're not going home then?" Kevin said.

"You are going home with the women and children, but not the rest of the merchant seamen. Not just yet. There's a war on, you know."

"Hmm," Kevin muttered, guessing that he was to be separated from Captain Abraham and the crew of the *Alice Morgan*.

With the meeting over, Kevin resumed his watch as lookout, scanning the horizon to the west. His mouth dropped open at the sight of a battle fleet steaming in line astern. Able seaman Jackson joined him looking at the ships on the horizon.

"Wow, look at all those ships."

Seaman Froggy Jackson said, "they are battleships. Something big is going down, I wonder what? Look over there…that looks like an aircraft carrier. Yes, it is, and a passenger liner, two passenger liners."

One of the larger merchant ships headed directly towards the *Devon Star*.

As the cargo ship drew closer, Jackson said, "that's a Blue Funnel boat. A bullshit company for sure, they run on naval lines, you know, a bugler on the gangway, all officers wearing uniforms. All their ships have Greek myth names, like Achilles and Diomedes."

The Royal Navy officer looked towards the Blue Funnel passenger cargo ship. He called to Garron, "Lieutenant Garron, get your families and children together. I'm afraid you are going to be separated for some time. All civvies and the young lads are being transferred to the Blue Funnel liner, boats from the liner will transfer the civilians. The Free French soldiers and merchant seamen from the *SS Alice Morgan* and the *SS Markham Point* will be joining the *Westernland*."

"Young lads," Kevin asked Stan. "Does that mean us?"

"I think it does."

Kevin frowned, holding up his hand he asked the officer, "Sir, why…why can't I stay with Captain Abraham. I signed on for 12 months, I should be allowed to stay with my shipmates."

"Sorry, lad, the merchant seamen are being taken up from trade, we need the men to man the merchant ships with the fleet. You need to be 16. How old are you?"

"Fourteen, but I'll be 15 the month after next."

"Hmm, sorry, son, you're too young."

The sub lieutenant shook hands with Captain Glover. "I'm off now, skipper. Chief Petty Officer Goodall here, will oversee the transfer. He will make sure the women are transferred to the Blue Funnel ship and the French soldiers and your seamen to the liner *Westernland*. Good luck. Can't say too much more, I do know there are other merchant ships attached to the fleet, mostly French. You will be assisting operations as directed by Admiral Cunningham."

"It looks like an invasion fleet to me," Captain Glover said, looking at the line of warships on the horizon and the passenger liner closing on the *Devon Star* at high speed.

"Hmm, keep a radio watch. The flag ship is *HMS Barham*, the flag officer will inform you of your role in this operation. Other than that, Captain, I cannot tell you anymore, sorry."

Kevin wandered across to Stan. "I'm not going with the women. I'm staying with Captain Abraham; I'm staying with the French soldiers."

"That's disobedience to orders. You can get shot for that."

"I'll plead ignorance, anyway, my dad said, *'Rules is for fools and the obedience of idiots'.*"

"My dad said something similar, like, rules are for the guidance of something, and the obedience of something else. I can't remember the rest of the saying. Alright, Kev, I'm with you. I'll say, *'Sorry, I got on the wrong boat'*. I'm staying with my captain too, bollocks to the navy."

"Go and get, Des. Tell him what's going on."

"I'm staying on the *Devon Star*, I'm staying with Captain Glover," Des said. "I do want to go home, but I'm staying put on the *Devon Star*. We have been through a lot this last three months and I'm not leaving my mates now."

Kevin and Stan agreed with Des.

The sea around the *Devon Star* churned with the wakes of three motorboats waiting in turn to take off the wives and children of the Free French soldiers. Kevin watched the soldiers take leave of their wives and children, some of the women were in tears, others looking down the accommodation ladder in apprehension. Then, in an orderly manner, they left the ship; women holding their babies and seamen holding children's hands, escorting them down the steps and onto the fast-moving boats.

'If one of them falls off the boat they will be swept away, Kevin thought, *but it's dangerous to stop the ship in case of a U-boat attack.*

Claudette was the last to leave, she walked over to where Kevin had hidden himself amongst the soldiers, keeping out of sight of the naval officer.

"Thank you, Kevin for helping me. But for you I would most probably be taken by the Gestapo. Now I have a chance to help England in some way to fight the Nazis. I hope to meet up with you again one day when this war is over. This is my aunties address in Chester." She handed Kevin a slip of paper.

Kevin took the note. "Me too, Claudette, I hope to see you again soon. Take care. If you get chance will you go and see my mum and dad and tell them I'm alright?"

"Yes, I promise. I'll easily find your family and friends in Blackstone; you've told me so much about them. Goodbye for now. May God look after you." Claudette kissed him on the cheek and then hurried to the gangway. Kevin watched her as she climbed down the gangway and into the motorboat.

"Come on, miss." The British sailor helped her into the boat before it peeled away from the gangway. Claudette waved back at the ship from the stern of the motor launch.

Not wanting to be seen by the Royal Navy Chief Petty Officer co-ordinating the transfer, Kevin joined Stan to hide among the soldiers waving goodbye to their families. With all the women and children disembarked, motorboats from the *Westernland* moved up to the gangway to take off the merchant seamen and Free French soldiers.

"All French soldiers get ready to disembark," shouted the coxswain of the first of the *Westernland's* motor launches to arrive at the foot of the gangway. Other boats from the Dutch liner waited astern ready to move up to the *Devon Star's* boarding ladder; three motorboats eager to take off the soldiers, yet mindful of Vichy French submarines or German U-boats lurking under the flat calm blue sea.

Kevin, with his grab bag slung over his shoulder, followed Stan down the accommodation ladder with the disembarking soldiers.

The naval rating in charge of the launch helped each man to step from the gangway onto the launch.

"Come on, son," he said to Kevin, "sit over on the starboard side."

Kevin breathed a sigh of relief at not being challenged, he sat down next to Stan and gave him a thumbs up. Soon the boat was full with a mixture of British merchant seamen and French soldiers. The cox gunned the diesel, put down the helm and headed towards the Dutch passenger liner, the *Westernland*. Kevin and Stan waved to Des, who stood by the *Devon Star's* handrail. Kevin was sorry to leave his friend behind. Someone had once said to him about merchant seamen shipmates; one-minute, good friends, living and eating together, going ashore together and facing danger from the sea and the violence of the enemy together, and then they become just 'Board of Trade acquaintances.' After 'paying off', never to be seen again. 'I wonder if I'll ever see my merchant navy friends ever again?' He thought about Wee Jock, sailing out of the Clyde and Harry Millward sailing out of Manchester and Crocker sailing out of London. As the launch approached the *Westernland,* what looked like a thousand French soldiers were crowding around the liner's handrails, looking down at the approaching boats. When the Free Frenchmen saw the soldiers, a loud cheer went up, *"Vive la France liber...Vive la France liber!"*

~ * ~ * ~ * ~

The crews of the sunken ships; SS *Alice Morgan* and SS *Markham Point* and Lieutenant Garron from the Free French, gathered in the cinema of the passenger liner. A tall handsome man dressed in tropical naval uniform with a double row of medal ribbons, climbed up onto the stage.

"Good morning, gentlemen."

"Good morning."

"My name is Hugh Hastings, I'm a Commander in the Royal Navy's Intelligence Department. But, before I start," he looked at Garron. "Lieutenant Garron, you are wanted on the bridge. I want you to meet an important Frenchman."

Garron frowned. "Who is this Frenchman?

"Well, if you go now up to the bridge you will find out."

Garron got to his feet and left the cinema heading up to the bridge.

Hasting waited until Garron had left. "Well, gentlemen, I'm here to answer as many of your questions as I can. I'm sure you have many questions for me. Firstly, you may think it was a coincidence that you ran into a battle fleet. Well, that submarine was standing off the coast,waiting for you to leave the port. Also, it was *HMS Eclipse* that came looking for you."

"For us!"

There was a muttering amongst the men.

"Yes, we came looking for the *Devon Star.*"

"How did you know about the *Devon Star*? How did you know we had sailed the ship out of Larache?"

"We have our sources in Morocco. Agents. Lieutenant Garron is one of our top agents. No need to say any more." Hastings said. "The six men taken off your ship yesterday are now on their way to England in that same submarine."

Another gasp from the gathered sailors. Kevin frowned, he had wondered why they had been taken to the warship and not to the passenger ship with the other women and kids.

"You obviously don't know the importance of these six men. They are six of Frances' top scientists."

"You mean the Jewish refugees?"

"Yes, they are Jewish, but that's not the reason they have been rescued from the Vichy. They are extremely important men and most valuable to the allied war effort. Our agents in Casablanca knew they were in hiding with the Free French. Mr Churchill had the submarine standing off the coast, ready to pick up the scientists, off the beach if necessary, that's how important they are. However, thanks to you and Lieutenant Garron, you saved the navy a dangerous mission. I have it from the highest authority to thank you and Captain Glover of the *Devon Star* for taking 60 soldiers and their families out of Vichy French West Africa, but most of all for evacuating the six scientists."

"Why are we on this ship and not with the others?" asked Captain Scotton of the *SS Markham Point*. "We are DBS's, Distressed British Seamen and really we should be repatriated to the UK."

"War is war, Captain. We need all the experienced seamen we can get. I suppose you are wondering where we are going and what we intend doing."

"Yes, we were wondering."

"I can tell you now. Now that the possibility of you being torpedoed again, taken prisoner back to Morocco, and you being forced to tell the Nazis what we intend doing, has passed. We are heading towards Senegal. We need the port of Dakar, because Freetown, the only Atlantic port in Allied hands, is too far to the south."

"Are you going to invade Dakar? Is that why we are on a troop carrier?"

"Hopefully, the marines on the *SS Pennland* and the French demi-brigade on the *Westernland* will be garrison soldiers. We hope to get Pierre Boisson, the governor of Dakar, to hand over power to the Free French without firing a shot. Unknown to the fleet, on this ship there are two very important men. One, a Frenchman, General Charles de Gaulle and the other is Mr Churchill's envoy to Free France, Major General Edward Spears."

Excited chatter spread through the seamen and soldiers.

"What if Boisson doesn't want to hand over power?"

"That's a good question. If Boisson refuses, we will take the port by force. I have to attend a ceremony with the French, I will tell you more of what we want from you later. In the meantime." Hastings looked at the two boys sat in the front seat. "Which one of you is Fife?"

"That's me, sir."

"Well, young Fife, what are you doing on this ship and not on the boat going home?"

"Err, sir, I got on the wrong boat."

"Hmm. A likely tale." Hastings laughed. "So, you are the pie thief?"

"Pie thief, sir? It was a fence and I didn't steal it. It was just lying there. I thought I'd put it to good use to help the war effort. The magistrates wouldn't believe me."

Hastings frowned, "no, I meant the pigeon pies. You are the boy who broke out of a prisoner of war camp and stole pigeon pies from the Vichy."

"Err, oh, yes, me and Stan and Des."

Again, Commander Hastings roared with laughter. "General de Gaulle heard all about you from our agents. De Gaulle also heard about you breaking out of the camp and finding your way to the café in Casablanca and establishing contacts with another one of our agents."

"Agents, sir? What agents?"

"Can't tell you that. Anyway, young Fife, and you, young man," Hasting indicated Stan. "If you'll follow me, please."

Wondering what was going on, Kevin and Stan followed Hastings out onto the liner's boat deck. Outside every available space on the deck was filled with soldiers, some sitting on the baggage hatch, some sitting astride derricks all the others squatted down on the timber decks under a canvas awning. A small band played French dance music, one or two of the soldiers danced to the music. Kevin reckoned there must have been over 1000 Frenchmen or more, all dressed in identical khaki green uniforms and pith helmets. A sergeant called the troops to attention and gave orders to fall-in. The troops lined up in ranks from the quarter-deck to the forecastle. Kevin was surprised to see a group of photographers and a cameraman with a movie camera.

"The men you see here are General de Gaulle's Demi Brigade. Stand on the end here," Hastings said to the boys. "General De Gaulle will be down shortly."

The boys stood at the end of the ranks of soldiers.

"Who the heck is General De Gaulle?" Stan asked.

"I don't know, I've never heard of him."

Two minutes later General De Gaulle, dressed in army uniform, his Aide-de-camp, a civilian and Lieutenant Garron, clattered down the ladder from the bridge. Garron joined the ranks with the Free French soldiers from Morocco.

A French officer ordered the troops, "*Attention.*"

The French soldiers who had been stood at ease, came smartly to attention.

General de Gaulle walked straight over to Lieutenant Garron.

Garron saluted the General.

Kevin couldn't hear what the General said to Garron, he just caught the odd French words that he didn't understand. De Gaulle then kissed Garron on both cheeks.

Kevin whispered to Stan, "I hope he doesn't kiss me."

"No, he's an ugly fucker, look at the size of his nose."

Hasting saw the boys giggling. "You will have to show the General some respect, boys, no giggling. The General is the leader of Free France, he has asked to speak to you two. When he speaks to you, call him sir, or General. He is the most important Free Frenchman currently; that man with him is Mr Churchill's personal envoy to the general. He too, may want to speak to you."

After inspecting Lieutenant Garron's men, De Gaulle spoke to the battalion. Kevin didn't understand the French, but he caught snatches of what he had to say, '*Merci soldats de France and Victoire la France*'"

The Aide-de-camp handed De Gaulle a medal. De Gaulle pinned the medal onto Garron's uniform jacket. The General kissed the lieutenant again on both cheeks.

"Crikey," whispered Stan, "the Frenchie's don't half like kissing each other, don't they?"

Kevin agreed, wondering what he was doing here with the French soldiers.

After addressing the troops, the General was directed towards Kevin and Stan.

The Aide-de-camp spoke quietly to De Gaulle, then handed over a medal.

De Gaulle laughed out loud, shaking Kevin's hand. He spoke to Kevin in English. "So, you are the boy who broke out of a prisoner of war camp to steal Pastilla, and you are the boy who met up with Free French agents in Casablanca."

Kevin looked up at the tall Frenchman, looking even taller in his French army pith helmet, and mumbled, "Err, yes, sir, General."

"*Bien fait, mon garcon,*" De Gaulle said as he pinned a medal to Kevin's shirt. He then bent down to embrace the boy-seaman and said in English, "this is a French honour medal, awarded to merchant seamen."

"Thank you, sir."

Edward Spears, Churchill's envoy, following De Gaulle came up to Kevin. He shook hands with him and said, "wear that medal with pride, my boy. You deserve it. This is the kind of sprit Mr Churchill admires and to be sure, I will be telling him all about you, how you met up with French agents in Casablanca and how you helped take back the *Devon Star*…and all about you stealing pigeon pies from the Vichy."

The General and the Major General repeated the ceremony for Stan.

After the medal awarding ceremony, De Gaulle and Major General Edward Spears returned to the bridge. The war correspondents took photos of Lieutenant Garron and the French soldiers. Just as Kevin and Stan were about to return to the ship's theatre, they were asked by the French cameramen to pose for photographs holding out their medals. Kevin grinned like an awkward schoolboy as he was photographed, first with Stan and then on his own. Back in the liner's theatre, Kevin examined the medal with its tri-colour ribbon. He carefully laid the medal on top of his other possessions in the toffee tin.

~ * ~ * ~ * ~

Commander Hastings returned to the meeting of the survivors of the two sunken merchant ships. The crews of the *Alice Morgan* and the crew of the

Markham Point gathered in the theatre of the Dutch liner *Westernland*. This time Kevin and Stan sat at the back, trying to keep out of sight of Hastings, they were still afraid that they would be separated from their shipmates and sent back home on account of their ages. Kevin leaned his head to one side to hear what Commander Hastings had to say.

"The Royal Navy have taken two Vichy French merchant ships as prizes of war. The Vichy French merchant seamen are now prisoners of the allies." Hastings looked around at the seamen expecting, and getting, a reaction.

"You will want us to man the French merchant ships then, Commander," Captain Abraham said knowingly.

"Hmm, exactly," Hastings answered. He looked down at his notebook. "The ships are the *SS Port Conakry* and the *SS Lily*. We have allocated Captain Scotton and the crew of the *Markham Point* to man the *SS Lily* and Captain Abraham and the crew of the *Alice Morgan* to crew the *SS Port Conakry*. Both ships are seaworthy, victualled and fully fuelled, both the *Port Conakry* and *Lily* are armed with a 100mm gun. We will provide gun crews for the guns."

"Err, excuse me, sir," Abraham interrupted the Commander. "I had five of my sailors killed on the *Alice Morgan*, so we are short of a cook and a radio operator."

"The Royal Navy will provide you with a cook and a radio operator and additional seamen to make sure your ships are fully manned. However, there will be strict radio silence from the fleet. We don't want to alert the enemy that we are approaching; most signals will be passed by lamps and flags. Also, you will be pleased to know, that the Admiralty in London have informed all your families that you are all safe and well, also the Admiralty have agreed to resume your pay, and have it backdated to the day your ships were sunk."

"Oh, that's great!" said Hemsworth. "My old lady will be pleased. Two months without a penny coming in and four kids to feed."

"That's good news, Commander Hastings. Thanks for telling our families that we are safe, and for reinstating our pay. It's a scandal that our pay stops the minute our ships are sunk."

"Yes, I agree, it is a scandal, I didn't believe it when I was first told about it. Anyway, back to your new roles and the situation here off the coast of Senegal. General de Gaulle is confident that the port of Dakar will join the

Allies. At this very moment De Gaulle's representatives are being taken by boat to carry out negotiations with Boisson."

"What if the negotiations fail?" Captain Scotton asked.

Hastings was reluctant to answer. "Hmm, well…if that happens, we will take the port by force."

"What's our roll in all of this?"

"As you may be aware, this ship, the *Westernland* and the other liner *Pennland*, are carrying troops, Royal Marines and the Free French. We are hoping these troops will be garrison troops, protecting the vital port of Dakar and not invasion fighting troops. If, on the other hand, Boisson refuses to hand over the port, then the Free French soldiers will invade."

"Frenchmen fighting Frenchmen?"

Hastings drew in his breath, "Er, well, yes, if need be. Let's hope it doesn't come to that. Err," Hastings coughed apologetically, "Err, this is where you come in. We cannot use the capital ships to land the troops. The Vichy have large shore-based batteries, guns that can fire a shell up to 12 miles. Our warships and the troop carriers will stand offshore while smaller ships land the troops in the ports."

"I guess that means us?"

"Yes, amongst other vessels. We have destroyers, armed trawlers and other merchant vessels under our command, the destroyers will escort you in. You will land troops either on the beach or directly in the port of Dakar. So, gentlemen, gather up your possessions you will be leaving for your new ships in the next two hours."

~ * ~ * ~ * ~

Kevin, with his canvas grab-bag slung around his shoulders, stood at the head of the *Westernland's* gangway watching as a motor boat loaded up with the crew of the *Markham Point*, cast off, heading towards the *SS Lily*, one of two merchant ships half a mile away on the port beam.

Junior seaman Stanley Windle waved up from the boat and called up, "so long, Kev, hope to see you around sometime."

Kevin grinned and waved back. "See ya, Stan. Be good." He looked around at the other ships in the fleet, hardly believing his own eyes. Massive warships in line astern; an aircraft carrier, two battleships, 10 destroyers, an armed trawler, two passenger liners and several merchant ships. On the other horizon, to his left, the coast of Senegal just visible. He looked up at the *Westernland's* bridge. General Charles de Gaulle, the leader of the Free French, stood studying the coast through binoculars. Alongside the General, Major General Spears, Winston Churchill's envoy to de Gaulle. Kevin shook his head in wonderment of the spectacle.

"My mum and dad just won't believe me when I tell them all about this," he said to himself.

"Alright, captain and the crew for the *SS Port Conakry*. All aboard the Skylark," called the Royal Navy coxswain of a warship's sea-boat.

Kevin followed Captain Abraham down the gangway, not wanting to look backwards in case he was stopped by Hastings for him joining an armed merchant ship at the age of 14.

Kevin's mouth dropped open as they approached the *SS Port Conakry*. Twice as big as the *Alice Morgan* and much cleaner. This was the type of ship he and Hector had wanted to sail on, back in Birkenhead. A single large funnel midship, with numerous rotatable vents towering above the decks, a large jumbo mast forward and a main mast aft. Three holds forward and one hold aft. A line of four lifeboats on the port side and a sea boat on the waist deck. The motorboat pulled up alongside the *SS Port Conakry's* gangway that had already been lowered.

"What a beauty," Kevin said to Captain Abraham.

"Yes, a nice-looking vessel to be sure. She's a cargo passenger liner. A bit different from the colliers I've sailed on in the past."

Kevin hung back while the crew of the *Alice Morgan* climbed up the ladder. He then climbed aboard his second ship.

The crew gathered in a group on the main deck looking around at their new home. A Lieutenant Commander from the Royal Navy climbed down the steps from the bridge followed by a dozen men; six navy ratings and six marines.

"Welcome aboard the *SS Port Conakry*," the officer addressed the crew. "My name is Timothy Conway, Lieutenant Commander Royal Navy, I will be the naval liaison officer on board this ship until the conclusion of Operation Menace."

"Operation Menace?" Abraham asked.

"Yes, that's what the top-brass have named this operation. You will be under naval orders of Admiral Cunningham until its conclusion, whenever that may be. When Operation Menace is completed you will sail this ship back to the UK. There, I expect the ship will be sold on to a new owner and renamed. You and your men will then be free to go home. The *Port Conakry* is a former passenger-cargo liner, about 14000 gross registered tons and will do around 15 knots." He then indicated his men. "My men, six Royal Navy ratings and six Royal Marines will also be staying on board until the admiralty say anything different. My men will show you and your men around, how things work and then when you are happy, we'll hand the ship over to you. The six marines are here to man the gun on the poop deck. If you follow me, gentlemen, I will give you a quick tour of the upper deck, the officer's accommodation and show you where the crew's quarters are." The crew of the former coal dust covered collier *SS Alice Morgan* followed Conway around the sun-bleached clean timber decks of the cargo passenger liner. Kevin, as usual, tagging on behind.

"Four large lifeboats on each side with a capacity for all the crew and passengers," he pointed to the davits on the waist deck. "That posh motorboat there was used to ferry the passengers from the anchorages to the ports."

Kevin looked over the lifeboats and the motor launch.

"Number one, two and number three holds forward. Number 4 hold aft." Conway said. Then indicating the masts, derricks and heavy lifting gear. "You merchant seamen will know more about the cargo handling facilities than I do, so I won't tell my granny how to suck eggs."

With the brief tour of the ship completed, Conway said, "take your possessions to your cabins, you'll be spoiled for choice on this ship. My men and I are accommodated in the passenger cabins.

Kevin followed Willie Wilde into a passageway named '*Logement de Marin.*' The bosun pointed to a name plate above a cabin door '*Maitre d'equipage.*'

"I think this is my cabin, you lads sort yourselves out." The bosun disappeared inside his cabin.

Kevin looked at the name plate above another cabin '*Matlot junior*'. "I think this must be mine," he said to Willie.

Inside the small cabin there was a single bunk, a bench settee and a small writing desk and chair. "My new home," he muttered to himself. "I wonder how long I'll be living here?"

He put his meagre possessions in a single drawer then decided to go back outside to wander around the ship. He examined the huge docking winch on the forecastle head, the winches, anchor chains, and the ship's bell mounted on a tripod. The bell was inscribed *SS Port Conakry 1935*. He wandered aft looking at the hatches, vents, masts and lifeboats until he finally reached the poop deck aft.

A 4-inch naval gun had been fitted on top of the poop. The Royal Marines gun crew were busy familiarising themselves with the mechanism of the French gun. Kevin's curiosity got the better of him and he wandered over to the poop.

"Can I have a look at the gun?" he asked the corporal in charge.

The marine corporal grinned at seeing the young boy. "Yeah, sure, son. Climb up."

Kevin climbed the ladder to the poop deck. "What type of gun is this?"

"It's an old French naval gun. 100mm. *Canon de 100mm*." He gave Kevin a good looking at before asking him, "what's your job on here?"

"I'm a deck boy."

"Deck boy. Right, what's your name?"

"Kevin."

"Well, Kevin, we're the gun crew to protect this ship." He pointed to each of the gunners in turn. "Marine Murphy, number two, better known as 'Ginge'."

"Hello, Ginge."

"Hi, kid."

"This is number three, Marine Kelly. Number four is Marine Sutcliffe and that scruffy fucker is number five, Marine Webster. That man there is number six, Marine Porter, Peter the Porter we call him."

"Hello, Kevin." said Webster, the other marines gave Kevin a friendly acknowledgement.

"And my name is Brian Smith. Corporal Smith, I'm number one."

"Hello, sir."

"No need to call me sir, sunshine. We are all equal here on this ship. Not like the Battleship *HMS Barham* over there." He pointed to one of the two battleships. "There's more bullshit on the *Barham* than in a farmyard."

"Why do you all have numbers?"

"The numbers are our position on the gun."

"Oh, right," Kevin said. "When do you suppose we'll take on board the soldiers?"

"Soldiers!? What soldiers?"

"Soldiers for the invasion."

Smith frowned deeply, looking at his colleagues. "Invasion? What invasion?"

"We are going to land troops on the beach."

"Bugger me! Land troops on the beach, are we? You know more about it than we do. This ain't a landing craft. So, young sir, how do we land soldiers on the beach? We were told to man the gun of this merchant ship, then we are to sail in convoy, north to England."

"I don't know how we will land soldiers on the beach, it's just what I heard."

"Maybe they'll have to dive overboard and swim to the beach."

"That'll be difficult, Corp, carrying a full pack and a rifle."

The marines laughed at the idea.

"Commander Hastings said if the talks break down the French and the marines would take Dakar by force. They won't bring the capital ships too close because there are shore batteries with 12-inch guns."

Smith looked at his men in astonishment. He turned to Kevin and said, "Commander Hastings, who's he?"

"He's the man giving the orders on the Dutch liner."

Smith shook his head. "Well, would you believe it, they certainly kept us in the dark. You seem to know a lot more what's going on down here than we do. What age are you, Kevin?"

"Fourteen and ten months."

"Fourteen! Well, I never. What else do you know?"

"I know General de Gaulle is trying to get the Vichy French to hand over Dakar, and if the man in charge, I think he's called Boyson or something that sounds like Boyson, refuses to parley, then you Marines will take the port by force."

"Well, well, well. Alright Kevin," Smith said slowly, unsure whether to believe the deck boy or not. "Thanks for telling us." Smith turned to his men. "Would you Adam and Eve it. A 14-year-old telling us what's going on." He then asked Kevin, "how come you are down here at war and telling *us*, what's going on?"

"Well," Kevin started, feeling important that grown men were asking him questions, not detecting the cynicism in Smith's voice. "We sailed out of Liverpool in May bound for Freetown with a load of coal from Cardiff. We got attacked by a bomber near the English Channel, but we drove it off with Mills bombs. Then we got attacked by a U-boat just off Morocco and got sunk. My best pal, Hector, he got killed. Then after seven days in the lifeboat we sailed to Morocco. There we were arrested and put in a prisoner of war camp. We escaped from the camp and then we stole a ship and drifted it out of a port. We were stopped by *HMS Eclipse*...and now we are seconded to this French merchant ship."

"Whoa, slow down. What do you mean by 'drifted out to sea'?" Smith listened to Kevin in disbelief shaking his head. "You can't just drift a ship out to sea."

"Well, we did."

"Em, well, you certainly have had some adventures for a 14-year-old. How do you drift a ship out of a harbour? You're not telling us porky pies, are you?"

"No. Why should I tell lies?"

"How come you went to sea at such a young age?"

"The magistrates sent me instead of getting the birch or going to Borstal."

Smith and the other marines listened to Kevin's story with their mouths open. "You look like butter wouldn't melt in your mouth, and here you are a war veteran. Why did the magistrate send you to sea? What did you do wrong?"

"The cops said I stole a fence, but I didn't. I thought nobody wanted it."

"A fence!" Smith and the other marines began to laugh.

"And I got a medal off General de Gaulle."

The marines burst into laughter. "Now we know you are bullshitting us. But a good story, Kevin. When you've got time, come back and we'll show you the gun."

"Alright, I will. Thanks." Kevin climbed back down the ladder to the main deck. He heard Smith say to the marines.

"A medal from General de Gaulle, my arse. A likely story, but he's a nice lad."

Kevin shrugged making his way back towards his cabin. On his way forward Kevin noted a line of motorboats heading towards the ship, the boats were loaded with French soldiers.

Able seaman Jackson called over, "when the Frenchie's are all on board, we have to string the boats aft, inline astern. Give us a hand with the boat's painters."

Kevin waited at the head of the gangway until all the soldiers had disembarked from the boats. The navy coxswains tied the boats from the stern of one boat to the stem of the other boats. Eventually six large motor cutters streamed in line astern. The last painter was passed to Kevin and with the help of three sailors the boats were tied off to the after bollards.

Kevin looked up at the marines who were watching the operation. He called up to Corporal Smith, "the soldiers won't have to swim ashore now Corporal Smith, we've now got landing craft."

Smith nodded and grinned. "Alright, son, my apologies." He indicated the 200 soldiers sitting around on the deck with their weapons. "It looks like we are going to land the soldiers on the beach after all. I shouldn't have doubted you. And, Kev, if you hear anything else when you are on the bridge, like how long we are going to be floating around here going nowhere, come and let us know. And later, I'll show you the workings of this old French cannon."

"Alright, I'd like that, see you later," Kevin smiled and continued working with the other sailors.

~ * ~ * ~ * ~

Finishing off cleaning out the sailor's mess room, Kevin made his way aft to the gun platform above the poop deck.

"Climb up, young Kev. Have you heard anything what's happening? I've asked the Frenchie's but they are as in the dark as we are, and the commander won't tell us anything.

"No, sorry, all I know is we have to stand here offshore waiting for orders."

"And from the little French we have between us, it sounds like these lads aren't so keen on fighting their fellow Frenchmen. Okay, then; come on I'll show you around this gun. This French 100mm naval cannon is nearly the same as our 4-inch naval gun. It's pre-1914 and who knows, it may have been used in the last war."

Smith showed Kevin around the cannon, pointing out parts of the naval gun. "Maine Murphy here, is the 'line layer', he will train the weapon left or right. Marine Kelly." He pointed to Kelly. "Is the 'elevation layer', he will elevate the gun up and down. My job is checking that everything is done safely. Marine Sutcliffe will open the breech here." He levered open the breech to show Kevin where the shells are pushed in. "The other marines, Webster and Porter, will be busy taking the projectiles and cordite out of the ready use ammo boxes."

Kevin looked around the cannon with interest. "Thanks for showing me how it works, can I be part of the gun crew?"

Corporal Smith grinned, "Sorry, sonny Jim. You are a bit too young to be around a gun when the shells start to fly. There could be a mis-fire and when the breech is opened the cordite might flash back, burning us all to a crisp."

"Never mind, I just thought I'd ask."

"I'll tell you what," Smith said as a conciliation to the disappointed deck-boy. "You could be our spotter."

"Spotter? What's a spotter?"

"A spotter gets eyes on the target and tells us where our shells are falling, you know, like 'over' the target, or 'short' of the target or to one side of the target."

"Yeah, I'd love to be a spotter, that's if Captain Abraham says it okay. Why would you want me to be a spotter?"

"Well, there are only six of us, and we've all got a job to do to load, aim and fire the gun. There really should be seven or eight of us to make up a full gun crew, so, we are short of a spotter. Come on, I'll explain." Smith pointed towards the sea. "Say there's a U-boat over there and we fire at it, you could be stood over there well clear of our gun and watch where the shell lands. If it goes over, you shout 'over' if it falls short you shout 'short' if it falls to the left, shout, 'train right so many yards and so on. Then when there's a hit in front and behind the Sub, you call, 'straddle' and we'll aim for the middle, hopefully hitting the target. Can you remember all that?"

"Yeah, I'm sure I can. Thanks Corporal Smith."

"You're welcome, son. Let's hope we don't have to use it."

Kevin left the poop smiling, hoping that one day he could be a spotter for the Royal Marines gun crew.

~ * ~ * ~ * ~

Gunfire from the British warships began without warning; Kevin jumped out of his skin as British shells screamed overhead on their way towards the Vichy coast. The action sent the Royal Marines tumbling towards their gun and set the French soldiers off chattering excitedly, looking towards the coast, towards where the British shells were heading.

The *SS Port Conakry's* engines throbbed loudly, the sea around the propeller churned as the former French merchant ship turned towards the coast, then suddenly, out of nowhere, a dense fog fell over the sea. Visibility dropped to less than 20 metres.

"Peggie, get up here on the helm," called Captain Abraham. "I don't want you on the open deck when the bullets start flying."

Kevin hurried up the steps to the bridge.

"What's going on, Captain?" Kevin asked as he took the wheel from Willie Wilde. "Where's this fog come from?"

"Don't know. It's unusual, I've never seen fog in this part of the world."

"I have," said Willie Wilde. "It's not common, but I've seen fog down here before."

The naval liaison officer emerged from the radio room. "Radio silence has been broken, now Vichy know we're here. The talks with General de Gaulle have broken down; we've just been ordered to land the Free French on the beach, or attempt to land them on the beach in this fog."

Captain Abraham and Lieutenant Commander Conway pored over the chart of the coast.

Conway looked at his notes. "This is the beach we've been ordered to invade. It looks wide and exposed. We've no idea where the Vichy shore batteries are located. Possibly here on these cliffs towards the port of Dakar."

Abraham checked the depth shown on the chart. He frowned at the depth shown and then looked at the spinning echo sounder.

"Here's the 40-fathom line, then look, there's a long sand bar before deep water again nearer the beach, it shallows to 2 fathoms at low water for up to two miles offshore."

"Two miles is too far out. You must get over the bar and get closer to the beach," Conway said. "No more than half a mile off shore. If the fog lifts and the boats are too far out to sea the Vichy guns will pick off the landing boats; there will be a bloodbath."

"Well, if we can sail over the sand bar and get back again before the tide runs out, we should be alright. On the other hand, if we get stuck on the bank we are in dead trouble. Either way it's going to get hairy; I fear. The shore batteries could blow us out of the water before we get anywhere near the beach. We were hoping the Vichy would hand over Dakar without a fight."

"I hope Cunningham and De Gaulle know what they are doing; we don't want another Dardanelles type cock-up on our hands.

"Slow speed ahead, Mr Todd, I'm not going to head for the beach at full speed in dense fog."

Todd rang the telegraph to tell the engineers to slow the ship. The *Port Conakry* continued heading eastwards towards the beach.

First came a bump as the ship hit the sand bar. Then an almighty scraping noise as the ship slid along the sand before coming to halt.

"Bugger me! We've run aground." Captain Abraham called. "I don't believe it. Either the charts are wrong or the Tidal Almanac is out of date, we should be in deeper water here. Half speed astern, Toddy, let's see if we can get off this bank."

The engines running astern churned up the sand, but the ship remained fast aground.

"Stop engines. We're going nowhere."

The engines fell silent.

The Royal Navy ships opened fire again. Kevin, scared out of his wits as the shells screamed overhead, crouched down behind the wheel.

Then as suddenly as the fog had appeared, the fog lifted. The sun broke through the cloud showing the beach about one mile away.

Captain Abraham looked at the coast in astonishment, then down at the chart. "The quicker you get the French soldiers ashore and off this sitting duck the better. Even if we float in the next few minutes, I won't be able to get closer to the beach."

"Alright, Captain, we'll embark the French into the landing boats from here."

Kevin blinked and flinched as more shells screamed overhead. It looked like all hell had broken loose. Warplanes from the aircraft carrier roared overhead, battleships major guns opened fire, sending 12-inch shells screaming towards the beach and cliffs. Explosions blasted sand and rocks 100 feet into the sky. Morse signals flashed between the warships and the merchant vessels. Signal flags were run up the halyards, battle ensigns on the warships were broken out. A destroyer, flying the French tricolour, bearing the Cross of Lorraine, steamed rapidly towards the SS *Port Conakry*, before hitting the same sandbank and coming to a crashing halt on the sand.

"The warship is aground too, Commander."

"Crying out loud, what a cock-up." Conway, standing on the bridge wing, shouted down to the coxswains waiting for orders. "Embark the troops now. Get them ashore ASAP."

The able seamen and the Royal Navy coxswains out on the deck began to pull the line of boats up to the lowered gangway. From the bridge Kevin could see other merchant ships disgorging the troops into invasion boats. He guessed one of them must be Captain Scotton's SS *Lily* with his pal Stan onboard. A small flotilla of landing boats were already speeding towards the beach.

Outside Commander Conway shouted orders to the Royal Navy seaman. "Come on, get them boats alongside."

The seamen pulled the motor launches up to the *Port Conakry's* accommodation ladder. The navy coxswains clambered down the steps, climbing into their boats. The French soldiers lined up on the upper deck waiting for orders to disembark the merchant ship and climb into the launches. Kevin could see now, by his naked eye, the flat sandy beach, where hundreds of troops had already waded ashore unopposed. Still the battleships pounded away at shore targets that Kevin could not see. Then to Kevin's horror, incoming Vichy shells began to explode around his ship sending columns of seawater and sand flying skywards. He'd never been so scared in his life.

"Alright, lads, down you come," called the first of the navy coxswains to the Frenchmen. The troops carrying back packs and their weapons climbed down the steps and onto the boats. One by one, the loaded boats cast off and headed towards the beach.

When all the boats had got away safely, Captain Abraham said resignedly. "Well, that's it for now, can't do any more until we float again."

Unable to steer the ship, Kevin left the wheel to see what was going on down on the beach. He could see that the Free French soldiers from the *SS Port Conakry* were now wading ashore. Shells began to explode sporadically in the sea close to the beach. The French soldiers dropped flat on the sand. A stray shell from the Vichy battery landed on the sandbank less than 20 feet from the *Port Conakry's* bow. The explosion rocked the ship and blasted sand over the bridge housing pitting and covering the bridge windows with wet mud. Kevin's face turned brown with the sand.

"Get back inside," yelled Captain Abraham. "Keep off the open deck."

Kevin scurried back into the wheelhouse, trying to blink the sand out of his eyes. "There's a ship burning up the coast, do you know what ship it is?"

"No, I don't, I don't know anything. I hope we float before they start shelling again."

No sooner than the captain spoke, a shell exploded on the *Port Conakry's* forecastle destroying the docking windlass and severing the portside anchor cable. The anchor plopped down into the sea and was lost. A second shell exploded in the sea close to the ship's bow.

"We're being deliberately targeted," called the captain. "Can you see who is firing at us? Where are the shells coming from."

"They are not shore battery shells," observed Commander Conway. "The explosions are not powerful enough. Possibly an artillery piece somewhere. A second shell hit the ship's side, punching a hole into number one hold.

The captain and the lieutenant commander searched the shore line with their binoculars.

"There it is!" called Conway. "I can see the top of what looks like a tank." He continued studying the sand dunes. A muzzle flash exposed a second tank. This second tank was firing along the beach, aiming at the soldiers wading ashore.

"There are two tanks, behind that dune, you can clearly see the turrets." Another shell from the tank exploded off the starboard side of the ship.

"Where's our escort? Where's that French destroyer?"

The destroyer had floated off the sand bank and had disappeared.

"She's gone!"

"Bloody typical, the navy are never around when you want them," Abraham complained.

"They have us straddled." Kevin called.

"Straddled? What do you mean?"

"They've got our range. The next shell will hit us."

As soon as Kevin had spoken, the ship was hit again on the port side.

"How the heck, do you know about range and bearing, Peggy?"

"The marines told me only yesterday."

Abraham and Conway looked aft towards the gunners on the poop deck.

"Our gun is out of line with the tanks, we can't train on the targets till we float again. Peggy, go aft along the starboard side, keep low and point out where the tanks are, behind that small sand dune over there."

"Right, Captain."

"And keep low."

"Yes, sir, I'll keep low."

Kevin hurried along the starboard side out of sight of the beach. He arrived at the poop, panting.

"Captain Abraham says can you fire at the sand dunes over there? There's a couple of tanks firing at us."

"What sand dunes? I can't see anything from here."

"You can see them from the bridge."

Smith looked towards the shore. The aftermost lifeboat and part of the boat deck obscured his view of the beach and sand dunes.

"We could shoot over the boat deck, but we need a spotter on the bridge to direct our fire."

"What, and use the telephone to tell you?"

"Problem is, young Kev, there ain't a telephone link from the bridge to the poop deck and it's too far to shout out orders."

"I could spot for you from up there." Kevin pointed to the main mast. I can see the dunes from there and shout down to you."

Smith drew in a sharp intake of breath and thought for a second about Kevin's suggestion. "Okay, Kev, do you remember what I told you about spotting, yesterday?"

"Yeah."

"Alright then. Let's do it…Stand to!"

The gun crew sprang into action.

"Train right, up ladder two."

The gun began to train and elevate at the same time. The barrel pointing skywards over the boat deck. Kevin climbed quickly up the mast, standing on the crosstrees. He heard Smith below.

"Range 5000, fire one. Shoot!"

"Fire!"

The 100mm shell screamed over Kevin's head heading towards the beach. He watched it explode behind the two tanks

"Over!" he shouted down.

Smith gave orders to raise the elevation. The marines had already reloaded, ramming the projectile and silk wrapped cordite into the breech. The breech slammed shut and a second round fired off.

The second exploded in front of the sand dunes.

"Short! Train right 20 yards." Kevin again shouted down from the mast.

Smith gave the thumbs up sign and re-trained right.

"Shoot."

"Fire!"

The old French Canon de 100mm spewed out fire and another explosive projectile screamed towards the beach.

Kevin shouted down excitedly, "straddle, straddle."

The gun elevation depressed slightly.

"Right, lads, let 'em have it!"

As fast as the marines could load the gun and fire, they rained shell after shell into the sand dunes.

Kevin could hardly contain his excitement when he saw a tank turret fly up into the sky. The second tank burning furiously. Smoke could be seen spiralling into the now clear blue sky.

"Check, check, check. Cease firing." Smith called and the firing stopped.

Kevin, dancing in excitement, came to an abrupt end when he heard Captain Abraham calling, "what the hell are you doing up there, Fife. Get down at once before you fall."

Kevin climbed down to the deck and returned to the wheelhouse.

"What were you doing up the mast, young man? You could have got shot or killed."

"I was spotting."

"Spotting? Spotting what?"

"Spotting the line of fire, Sir, at the tanks, I was spotting for the marines, they couldn't see the tanks from where they were."

Captain Abraham and Commander Conway, both lost for words, just shook their heads in disbelief.

Eventually Abraham conceded, "erm, well anyway, well done, Peggie."

"Yes, well done, son," repeated Conway. "The tanks have been destroyed."

Kevin, secretly pleased with himself, just nodded and smiled.

~ * ~ * ~ * ~

Two anxious hours after running aground, the ship rocked and bobbed about.

"We're floating."

Captain Abraham rang the telegraph, "Slow ahead. Starboard ten. Head out to sea."

The ship picked up speed heading westwards.

"Wow, that was exciting, Captain, unloading soldiers is a bit different from unloading coal at the Staithes, and firing at the tanks, that was exciting too."

The captain grinned, "yes, I didn't sign up for this malarkey."

"What's going on? What are the French soldiers supposed to do?"

"Who knows what they are doing? They are digging in, I think. The navy won't tell us what's happening. As far as our navy radio operator can tell us, the negotiations have broken down and our navy is shelling their navy, but that's as much as I know. We are to hold off here at a safe distance until the liaison officer gives us further orders." Abraham scanned the beach nearly two miles away, he could see smoke rising from different parts of the coast. "It all seems like a shamble to me...Brew up, Peggie, I need a cuppa."

Kevin left the wheel going below to brew a pot of tea. On his way back to the bridge, he heard the main engine start up. He carried the tray containing metal cups full of steaming tea into the wheelhouse. Willie Wilde was on the wheel.

"What's going on?"

Willie said, "you're not going to believe this, we're going back in."

"Back in! You're joking, why?"

"Don't ask me. We are taking the French off the beach."

"Why?"

"God knows, we just follow orders. It looks like Dunkirk out there. A merchant ship, up the coast has been hit."

As the ship's head turned back towards the beach and got closer, Kevin could see soldiers retreating to the sea line and wading out to the waiting cutters. One of the armed trawler's decks under water, and smoke poured out of a stationary merchant ship further down the coast.

Using the same boats that put the soldiers on the beach, the withdrawing troops had already motored away from the beach and were waiting for a tow. The *SS Port Conakry* took a dozen boats in tow, towing them well clear of the coast. Kevin looked over the beach that was now almost deserted of fighting men, it looked barren and devoid of any warfighting paraphernalia that he expected to see on a beach that had just been invaded by a thousand French soldiers. The only sign that an invasion had occurred, was a sinking trawler and a merchant ship on fire. The *SS Port Conakry* continued to tow the launches clear of the coast. When the boats were over two miles offshore, the soldiers climbed wearily up the accommodation ladder and spread out over the deck. The exhausted men flopped down in the shade of the hatch combings and ships superstructure.

Kevin hadn't a clue what was going on. Why had the soldiers retreated? Had they been in a fire fight? He asked Captain Abraham the question, "What's going on, Captain?"

Captain Abraham shook his head. He was equally in the dark on why they had to take the soldiers off the beach after less than four hours. "Don't know, son. The commander just got orders to evacuate the beaches. These soldiers are going back to the *Westernland*. Admiral Cunningham will let us know sooner or later no doubt."

The captured French merchant ship headed out to sea to join the main battle fleet and liners more than 10 miles away. Smoke poured out of one of the battleships.

"That ship, it's on fire," Kevin said to Willie Wilde.

"Um, I think it's the battleship *HMS Resolution*."

~ * ~ * ~ * ~

"Right, lads, it looks like the war is over in this part of the world." Captain Abraham addressed his crew, the six marine ratings, the naval ratings seconded to help man the ship and the Royal Navy coxswains. "We have just received orders from the flag ship. General de Gaulle is calling off the operation. The talks between him and Boisson have broken down. The Vichy have refused to parley. The war here is over. General de Gaulle has refused for Frenchmen to fight Frenchmen. You navy lads will take the French soldiers back to the *Westernland*, however, you marines are staying with us as gun crew. We're all going home."

There was a brief cheer from the former *Alice Morgan's* crew.

"Going home!" said the bosun sarcastically. "That'll be the day."

CHAPTER 6

SOUTH AFRICA – OCTOBER 1940

KEVIN FIFE STOOD WITH THE six royal marine gunners on the main deck watching as the Free French soldiers were transferred back to the passenger liner *SS Westernland*. The cheerfulness of the French soldiers dancing to the military band and singing patriotic songs that Kevin had witnessed a couple of days earlier, had vanished. The soldiers were now quiet and sullen.

"They look pretty glum." Kevin said to Corporal Smith.

"I'm not surprised. Travelling all this way, getting all excited and then withdrawing before a shot was fired."

"We fired shots."

"Yes, ironic isn't it, a British merchant ship, firing at Vichy French tanks. You did a good job, spotting for us. You could be part of my gun team any...."

"Royals, Peggie," Captain Abraham called down from the bridge. "All hands to muster in the officer's mess for a debriefing by Commander Conway.

Commander Conway waited until every member of the ship's crew, naval ratings and the marines had settled.

"Well, gentlemen, as you may have gathered 'Operation Menace' has been called off. The talks between de Gaulle's representatives and the Vichy governor has failed. Although some Free French soldiers have been killed or captured, and ships have been sunk or badly damaged on both sides, General de Gaulle has, in his wisdom, called off the operation. He said he doesn't want Frenchman fighting Frenchmen. Admiral Cunningham has reluctantly agreed to withdraw the British warships."

"Why, sir?" asked Corporal Smith, "our warships could blast Dakar to pieces, and I know the Royal Marines would have put up a better fight than the Free French have done."

"Yes, Corporal, you are right, but relationships between France, even Free France, and Great Britain is at an all-time low. What with our navy sinking most of the French fleet at Mers-el-Kebir, another battle down here in Senegal would only worsen relationships between our two countries. We still have hopes that other Vichy controlled countries in French West Africa will turn against Vichy and join the allies. So, here is what happens next, this ship, the *Port Conakry*, will sail south to Cape Town and will accompany the damaged warship that is being towed to South Africa.

"What ship is that, sir?"

"Erm, *HMS Resolution* has been damaged, she is listing. What we want is for you to be in close support, just in case."

"Just in case she turns over and sinks, or is torpedoed by U-boats?" Captain Abraham suggested.

"Yes, that's more or less right."

"We may also get torpedoed, stopping to pick up survivors, but we are more expendable than *HMS Ark Royal* or *HMS Barham* stopping to pick up survivors."

"Erm," Hastings didn't confirm what Abraham said. "Well, let's press on. The Royal Marine gun crew and the navy signalmen will stay on board here until Cape Town."

"Where do we go after Cape Town?" asked Corporal Smith.

"You will re-join your unit. That's all I know. The *Port Conakry* will still be under naval orders and, as I understand, after repairs to the forecastle and the shell hole in the hull has been properly patched up, you will take on a cargo in South Africa and will sail in convoy for England and maybe passengers to be repatriated to England."

"How many passengers?"

"I don't know. Sorry, I cannot tell you more than that."

"Thanks, Commander Conway." Abraham said. "Okay, men. Back to work. Mr Mate, lay a course to join the fleet sailing south."

"Didn't I tell you," moaned the bosun. "I ruddy well knew we wouldn't be going home."

The crew of the *SS Port Conakry* left the dining room chuntering about having to sail south to Cape Town instead of going north and home to Cardiff.

The nearer the *Port Conakry* got to the equator the hotter the weather. Sitting on number four hatch watching the marines and some of the navy ratings, Kevin fanned himself with a home-made fan. The marines had laid a rubber mat under the poop deck and were taking turns in bouts of wrestling.

"Phew, it's too hot to fight," Kevin called to the two marines who were wrestling in the shade of the poop deck.

"Marines fight in all weathers; hot or freezing cold," panted Marine Webster. "Cumberland wrestling is a tradition at sea, especially in the Royal Navy. Keeps you from getting bored and keeps you fit, you don't need much room to have a bout. Come on I'll show you a few wrestling holds."

Kevin shyly climbed off the hatch. "Maybe if I could wrestle, I wouldn't be pushed around so much."

"Why? Do you get pushed around?"

"Sometimes, because I'm so small people have bullied me."

Marine Webster, small in stature, sinewy, without an ounce of fat, said, "Come on, I'm not much bigger than you, and, I can tell you this, nobody pushes me around. We'll teach you how to defend yourself."

The other marines agreed.

"Yes, that's right, Kev," Corporal Smith said. "By the time we get to Cape Town you'll be an expert in self-defence, and able to kill a big man with a single palm blow to his head."

"My dad showed me a couple of self-defence tricks, but they didn't seem to work when I needed them."

"Come on, I'll show you the basic holds of Cumberland wrestling." Kevin joined Webster on the mat. "We start with a back-hold position. Chest to chest. Put your chin on my right shoulder."

Standing on the mat, Kevin swayed and shuffled self-consciously.

"Come on don't be shy. Grab hold of me, put your right arm under my left armpit." Webster bent his body so Kevin could put his chin on the marine's right shoulder. kv"That's it, now you have to unbalance me and trip me up, right?"

"Yes, I think so."

"Corporal Smith is the umpire, when he calls '*en-guard*', grab me round the waist and put your chin on my shoulder. He will then say, '*wrestle*' and you will then trip me up…easy. Alright, Corporal, ready when you are."

"*En-guard*," Smith called. Then two seconds later he called, "*Wrestle*."

In a Flash Kevin found himself flat on his back on the mat.

Marine Webster, laughing, pulled Kevin to his feet. "I'll show you how to do it."

Chest to chest and in slow motion, Webster taught Kevin two throws, "This is the Scottish throw." He demonstrated the Scottish throw. "And this is the Lancashire throw." Once again Webster showed Kevin how to unbalance his opponent. "Come on, let's try again. Okay Corporal."

Corporal Smith called, "*En-guard*…Wrestle."

Kevin stuck his leg between Marine Webster's legs, pulled him backwards, twisted and fell on top of the marine. A cheer went up from the onlookers.

"That's it, Kev. You actually threw me."

"No, you let me throw you."

"Honest, you actually knocked me off balance. I think you're going to be a natural wrestler."

Kevin smiled. "Thanks."

Marine Sutcliffe took to the mat, holding a bayonet. He tossed the knife to Kevin. "I'll show you how to defend yourself if you should ever get attacked by someone with a knife."

Keven looked at the bayonet. "It's a real bayonet."

"Yes, that's right. Come on, try and stick it in me."

Kevin looked down at the dagger again. "It's sharp."

"Yes, it's sharp alright. Come on, attack me with it."

Kevin hesitated.

"Come on, Fifie, if I get that knife off you, I'm going to gut you like a pig. So, stick it in me, up to the hilt. Don't hang back. You'd better kill me, or you are a dead man."

Kevin, knew the marine was taunting him, but he felt his hackles rise all the same. If this was a real situation and he was facing a man determined to take the bayonet off him and gut him with it, he'd better learn how to stop it happening. Kevin took up an attacking stance, holding the knife tight, he stalked around the marine, then lunged. Like a flash, the marine parried the blow, spun Kevin like a top and disarmed him. Kevin finished up flat on his back, with the marine's knee on his chest and the bayonet pointing at his Adam's apple.

"Blimey! What happened?" Kevin gasped.

Grinning, Sutcliffe stood up, helping Kevin back on his feet.

"I forgot to tell you, Kev.," Corporal Smith said laughing. "Marine Sutcliffe was a former policeman in Shanghai. He'll teach you the skills he learned at close quarters. Hand to hand combat and how to wrest a pistol from an assailant before he has time to fire it. However, Kev, first thing to learn is don't get into a fight unless you can't help it," Corporal Smith said. "It's better to walk away than finish up with a stab wound or dead. The second thing to learn is always to be alert. If you feel trouble is brewing, just be alert, don't let your mind wander or be distracted. Most important, keep your distance. Don't get in too close for starters, that gives you time to think and react to the situation. If you come back tomorrow, we will show you close quarter combat, toe to toe, two handed grip, single handed grab, leg catch, sweeps, blocks and chokes."

Kevin looked at Sutcliffe with a new respect. He looked a lot older than the other marines who were in their early twenties. Sutcliffe looked to be around forty.

Sutcliffe said, "Remember this; go for the ears, eyes and testicles."

"Okay, I'll try and remember that, thanks, I already feel better prepared to defend myself."

"Alrighty, Kev." Smith pointed to the 100mm naval gun. "We'll also teach you about firing that gun; even let you work it."

"Thanks, lads, I'd better get back to work." Kevin started to return to the sailor's mess to prepare tea and toast for the off-coming watch.

"Hey, Kevin," Smith called after him. "Sorry we took the piss out of you the other day about General de Gaulle giving you a medal an' all. Captain Abraham told us about your adventures in Morocco. Well done, son."

Kevin smiled briefly, nodded and went back to work.

~ * ~ * ~ * ~

Kevin, sitting at his little desk began to write a letter home.

Anchored just off the South African coast. 1ˢᵗ November 1940

Dear Mum and Dad.

As you will know today is my 15ᵗʰ birthday but I didn't get a birthday cards or any presents. I hope this letter finds you well. I am well and enjoying my life at sea. At the present time I can see Table Mountain off to the port side. We have been anchored here for ages waiting for a berth. It seems we spend a lot of time at anchor waiting for a berth, or for the convoys to form up, 'swinging around the pick', Willie calls it. We had to escort a warship to Cape Town. I don't know the name of the ship as they won't tell us, but my friend Willie say's it's a battleship. The ship got damaged in a fight off a place called Dakar. Did you get my last letter, I gave it to a girl called Claudette. She promised to post it for me in England. As you may know my first ship the Alice Morgan got sunk by a German U-boat. I am now on a ship called Port Conakry, a very nice ship, a cargo passenger ship but we don't have any passengers at the moment. I don't know where we're going after Cape Town, maybe we will be coming home. I hope so as I am missing you all. Captain Abraham is a good man and he said he will promote me to Junior Ordinary Seaman now that I am 15 years old. We have some Royal Marines sailing with us. They are manning the gun we have on the poop deck. Yesterday, they showed me how the gun works, all about loading and firing it. We had to fire it in Dakar. I say my prayers every night and I pray that the Germans don't bomb Blackstone. I've been away from home 9 months now and as yet I haven't had a letter off you. Your loving son Kevin. PS. I met a Frenchman called Dee Gowl I don't know how to spell his name. He gave me a medal.

~ * ~ * ~ * ~

The following day the SS Port Conakry sailed into Cape Town. Kevin stood by the ship's handrails looking over the docks.

"What are you looking at, Kev?" Kevin's daydream was interrupted by Corporal Smith.

"Them little tanks," Kevin pointed to a long line of armoured cars waiting to be loaded onto ships.

"Erm, more like armoured cars rather than tanks. That's a Vickers machine gun if I'm correct," Smith said, pointing out the single gun on top of the vehicle. The six Royal Marines were standing at the head of the gangway waiting to disembark.

"Well, Kevin, time to say so long. We have to re-join the Fleet."

"Yeah, I know."

"Here. A little memento for your collection." Smith handed over a cap badge.

Kevin examined the badge, "thanks, Corporal Smith."

"Do you know what it is?"

He turned the badge over. "No, it looks like a globe."

"Yeah, that's what it is. It's the Royal Marines badge, known as the Globe and Laurel."

"Oh, thanks."

"Yes, mate, so you will remember us by. By the way. Happy Birthday for yesterday. Captain Abraham said he promoted you to Ordinary Seaman."

Kevin grinned. "Yeah, Junior Ordinary Seaman. Two bob a month extra."

"Well, that's it. Come on lads, let's get back to the bullshit brigade," he called to his squad. One by one the departing marines shook hands with Kevin.

"See you, mate," they said in turn, before clambering down the gangway to a waiting 4 tonner waggon. They climbed over the tailgate. Kevin watched as the waggon drove off towards Simon's Town naval base. As the wagon moved away, Kevin noted a man leaning against one of the tanks, watching as the armoured cars were being loaded. The man dropped his cigarette butt and screwed it into the ground with his foot before walking off towards the port gates.

"Fife." Captain Abraham called from the bridge. "Come up here for a meeting."

Kevin climbed the steps up to the officers' dining room. Inside the room, all the ship's company had gathered. Commander Conway sat next to the captain.

"Sit down, Fife."

Kevin found a chair next to Willie Wilde.

Conway started, "Captain Abraham tells me you all have agreed to stay on this ship until it returns to the UK. I cannot tell you when that may be. At this point in time, the war isn't going too well for us. To get back to England the ship will have to transverse either the South and North Atlantic or the Indian

Ocean via the Suez Canal through the Mediterranean, both are dangerous places for Allied shipping. This ship is to be taken up from trade and will be renamed, '*Empire Orion*'. You will be asked to sign Form T124 Merchant Navy Serving Under Naval Command. You will be under Admiralty orders, therefore what you see, where you go and what cargo you carry will be classified. You are to sign new orders. Any questions?

"Yes, sir," said Willie Wilde. "Where are we going from here?"

"You will load tanks of the 1st South African Light Tank Company and take them to Mombasa, in Kenya. Along with some South African personnel."

"Why Mombasa, Commander?"

"I'm not telling you anything secret when I say the British Army is fighting the Italians in Abyssinia and Somalia. Forces of the British Empire are attacking the Italians from the south, British forces are attacking them from the north. That's all I can say. Lt Bates has the T124s. Sign the form and you will be under naval orders."

One by one the sailors signed the T124 Articles. Kevin last in line to sign, picked up the pen.

"How old are you, son?" asked Bates quizzically.

"Seventeen, sir"

Bates gave Kevin a longish look before saying, "okay, young man, sign here."

Kevin signed the T124.

After the meeting with Lieutenant Commander Conway and Lt Bates, the crew dispersed back to their duties on deck, in the engine room and the cook left for the galley to prepare lunch.

~ * ~ * ~ * ~

The following morning, Kevin and Willie Wilde were sitting on a painting stage that had been hung over the passenger/cargo liner's bow. Kevin looked down at the 20-foot drop to where the Cape Town shipyard engineers were fitting a new anchor to the end of the severed chain, replacing the anchor shot away during the skirmish off Dakar. Kevin carefully painted over the letter C with black paint, covering over the original ship's name of *Port Conakry* in readiness for renaming the ship, *Empire Orion*.

Kevin gripped the painting stage gantline tightly with his free hand.

"Relax, Fifie, you won't fall off."

Kevin looked again at the twenty-foot drop to the water. "I don't like swinging about like this, I don't feel safe." He continued painting over the word 'Conakry'

The newly named ship was now tied up alongside the Cape Town docks, stevedores were busy loading the armoured cars into the ship's holds. Other shipyard workers were welding steel plates over the damaged hull

"Excuse me, gentlemen," a voice with a strong Irish accent, called from the dockside below.

Kevin and Willie looked down at the man standing on the dockside.

"Top of the morning to you," the man called up.

"Morning," Willie replied. "Can I help you?"

"Yes, maybe you can. I'm a DBS… A Distressed British Seaman, survivor of a Dutch merchant ship, sunk by a German raider in the South Atlantic. I'm looking for a ship going home."

"Where you from, mate? You sound Irish, are you from Belfast?"

"Oh, dear God, no. I'm from the republic, to be sure. I signed on the SS *Goede Hoop* in Rotterdam before the German occupation. All Dutch ships that escaped the Nazis are now under British command. Therefore, I'm classed as a DBS."

"Oh, right," said Wilde, "what can I do for you?"

"I was hoping you might sign me and a couple of me mates on as crew."

"You'll have to see the captain about that."

"And what be his name, the captain of this fine ship?"

"Captain Abraham."

"Abraham," repeated the Irishman. "Can I come on board and speak with Captain Abraham?"

"Yes, alright, I'll take you up to his cabin. Kevin, you continue on here while I take this gentleman up to see the skipper."

"Yes, I'm alright on my own," Kevin looked down at the Irishman. "I've seen you before. Yesterday."

"I don't think so, young sir. I only arrived here in Cape Town from Durban this very morning."

Kevin frowned. "I'm sure I saw you yesterday, stood over there, by the tanks, watching as the marines disembarked."

"No, I'm sorry, son, that wasn't me, for sure. Anyway, what's a young pup like you doing working on this big ship. You should be at home with your mammy."

Kevin resented being called a young pup. "I'm fifteen and I've not seen my 'mammy' for nine months now."

"Fifteen, are you? Quite a young man now to be sure. Why are you painting over the ship's name?" asked the Irishman.

"Err, we're changing her name."

"Well, well, is that so. And what are you going to call this ship now?"

"Empire…" Kevin hesitated, remembering Commander Conway's order not to tell anyone anything about the ship, what she was carrying and where she was going to next. "Err, I don't know the new name. You'll have to ask Captain Abraham."

"Alright, it doesn't matter. Do you know where you are going next? Home to England, I expect?"

"Don't know where we're going. They won't tell me anything," Kevin lied again.

The Irishman pointed to the welders. "It looks like you've been in the wars."

"Erm," Kevin was non-committal, he continued painting over the letters on the bow.

When he looked down, two other men had joined the Irishman. They spoke together in low tones; Kevin couldn't hear what they were saying. The three men wandered off, up to the gangway, waiting to be invited aboard. Kevin continued working until all the letters had been painted over. He clambered back up the Jacobs ladder onto the forecastle head. Sitting in the shade of the combings he wiped the black paint off his hands with a ball of cotton waste, watching as the small armoured cars were lowered into number one hold. Twenty minutes later Willie re-joined him.

"You've done a good job there, Kev."

"Thanks, Willie. What's happening with the three men?"

"I think the skipper will sign them on as crew. The other two are Dutchmen, they said they were attacked by a German pocket battleship. They seem okay and we need the crew. Hey up, here comes the bosun."

The bosun approached the two sailors, he glanced over the side. "Well done, lads. Just been talking with Captain Abraham. He has signed the two

Dutchmen on as stewards. The Irishman says he was an Able Seaman on the ship sunk in the Indian Ocean."

"Atlantic Ocean."

"No, he said the *SS Goede Hoop* was sunk by a pocket battleship off the coast of Port Elizabeth. Apparently, the Royal Navy sent three warships off to search for the battleship."

"I'm sure he said they were sunk in the South Atlantic."

"Well, it matters not where they were sunk, the two oceans meet here off the Cape. They are classed as shipwrecked sailors. I've put Paddy on the mate's watch and the two Dutchmen to work in the passenger's dining room as stewards. They can look after the soldiers when they come."

"More soldiers?" Willie asked

"Yes, South Africans. Six are joining us here, senior officers I believe. Soldiers of the infantry division will board at Durban. We're taking them with their tanks and aircraft to Mombasa."

Kevin asked, "where's Mombasa?"

"Kenya. As far as I can gather, they will join up with the British forces to fight the Italians who are invading Kenya from Abyssinia. That's all I can tell you. If you go ashore tonight, don't go spreading that around in the pubs. You know what they say on the posters? Walls have ears." The bosun pointed to the hold. "When they have finished loading number one hold, batten it down for sea. They are going to load aircraft onto the hatch covers. I'll get Paddy the Irishman to help you.

Four hours later, Kevin, Willie, Froggy Jackson and Paddy Dimmock watched as the Cape Town stevedores finished loading the last of the light tanks into the ship's hold. The four deckhands began to cover the hold opening with heavy timber hatch covers. With all the hatch boards in place they began to roll out the canvas hatch coverings. Dimmock kicked the Trapline into place and began to roll it across the hatch.

"That's the wrong way around," Kevin said to the Irishman.

"What you mean, wrong way? There's no right way or wrong way."

"Yes, there is," Willie said. "You have to have the seam facing aft."

"And what difference will that make?"

"Sea water will get through the seam and tear the stitching," Kevin told him.

"Hmm, you're a clever little fucker, ain't you," Dimmock said tetchily.

"I'm only saying what I was told at the training ship," Kevin mumbled quietly, looking at Willie.

"Come on, let's get it covered. They are waiting to load the aircraft."

The seamen finished covering the hatch boards then battening the canvas in place ready for sea.

"Smoko!" called the bosun.

Kevin and the three sailors followed the bosun down to the crew's mess room. The two Dutchmen were already sitting at the long table. They nodded a greeting towards the Irishman.

Willie Wilde sat nursing a metal cup of tea. "What are you lads called?"

"De Jong," said the first Dutchman

"Jan Bakker," said the other.

"Where were you torpedoed?"

"About 100 miles east of Port Elizabeth. But we weren't torpedoed. There are no U-boats in the Indian Ocean. We were sunk by a German pocket battleship…The *Admiral Graf Spee.*"

"It can't have been the *Graf Spee*, that was sunk by the Royal Navy last December."

The two Dutchmen glanced at each other. "That's British propaganda," De Jong responded abruptly.

"No, it's not. Why should anyone lie about that? It was in all the papers."

"Well, you shouldn't believe everything you read in the papers. Anyway, it was a pocket battleship."

"How many survivors?"

"Just us three," Dimmock said

"Okay, lads, back to work, called the bosun.

With 'Smoko' over, the stewards returned to the passengers' accommodation. Kevin, Willie, Jackson and Paddy Dimmock returned to complete their work on the deck.

~ * ~ * ~ * ~

The newly named ship *Empire Orion* sailed from Cape Town with a new windlass, a new port anchor, a patched-up hull and three additional crew members. As the ship sailed further north, the weather grew hot again. Although Paddy Dimmock was on the chief mate's watch and Kevin was on the second mate's watch, the two often worked together on the deck, chipping off old paint and re painting. Kevin had taken a distinct dislike to the Irishman, who had from day one started picking on him.

On the second day out of Cape Town the sailors worked on the upper deck parts. The sun blazed down on their heads. The mid-day temperature hitting 90 degrees.

"Hey, boy," Paddy Dimmock called to Kevin who was painting the hatch combings.

Kevin stopped painting and looked over at Dimmock. He resented being called 'Boy'. He resented Dimmock's patronising attitude towards him, always pulling rank.

"Yes, Mr Dimmock."

"Go down to the passenger's galley and bring me a jug of ice-cold water. I'm dying of thirst here."

Kevin frowned and looked down at his blackened hand, '*Flipping heck*', he thought, '*he's only been onboard five minutes and he's already giving orders.*' He said, "go and get it yourself. Can't you see I'm busy."

"Don't give me a mouthful of cheek, you fuckin' young pillock! You bloody well do as I tell you. I'm senior to you, so get your little arse midships and bring me a jug of iced water."

Kevin remained sat down and continued painting.

"Did you fuckin' hear me, you little twat?"

"I heard you."

"Well, then if you don't want a clip around your ear, you go and get me the water. Have some respect for your elders."

Kevin gave out a long sigh. Without saying anything, he laid down the brush, wiped his hands and walked off to bring the water. He returned with a metal jug full of cold water. He put the jug down by the Irishman and resumed his painting. After a few minutes, Kevin stood up, stretching, he walked over and picked up the water jug.

"Put that down," Dimmock said snappishly.

"Eh? What do you mean put it down? I want a drink of water."

"You can fuck off. If you want a drink go and get one from the galley."

"I brought that jug. Why can't I have a drink of it?"

"Listen, you little English puff, if I get any more lip off you, I'll beat the shit out of you."

Kevin gave the Irishman a longish stare before deciding not to aggravate him further. Dimmock was nearly six feet tall, muscular with a brutish face. Kevin continued painting, muttering under his breath. This was the first time since joining the crew of the *Alice Morgan* six months earlier, had he had any bullying from a crew member. Even the captain, chief mate, chief engineer and the bosun had been friendly towards him. Kevin decided he didn't like the Irishman at all.

The *SS Empire Orion* had left Cape Town fully loaded with war apparel and was now steaming up the eastern coast of South Africa. The warm southern hemisphere sun shone on the calm sea. Kevin watched the flying fish scoot across the surface, breathing in the sweet air before doing his trick on the helm. He walked into the wheelhouse to take over the steering from Willie.

"Steer north east by east and three quarters east," Willie said, "She's taking a little starboard wheel."

"North east by east and three quarters east," repeated Kevin.

The *SS Empire Orion*, loaded with 24 light tanks, six aircraft sitting on the hatches, 500 tons of ammunition and six army officers, was steaming, unescorted, north-easterly at 15 knots and heading towards Durban.

Kevin struggled with the large mahogany helm, trying to keep a steady magnetic compass course.

"*I hate this magnetic compass,*" Kevin muttered to himself, almost having to stand on tiptoes to see the compass card inside the large brass binnacle. '*Keeping to these quarter points is hard work. I much prefer steering by a gyro compass,*' he thought, constantly glancing up at the bridge clock. The minutes on the helm dragged on for what seemed like hours. *Ten more minutes and the Chief Mate's watch will take over steering,* "I can't wait," he murmured to himself.

"Fife."

Kevin blinked out of his daydreaming and looked towards the captain. "Yes, sir."

"I'm afraid you will have to an extra hour on the wheel."

Kevin's head dropped. "Err, yeah, alright, captain. What's happened to Mr Dimmock?"

"The chief mate set him on painting the forecastle. Mr Chapman says Dimmock's steering is all over the place."

'Tut,' Kevin muttered under his breath. "Yes, alright, I don't mind."

Sub Lieutenant Richard Crowe RN, the ship's new radio officer, came into the wheelhouse from the radio room. He stared through the windows at the sea ahead, then strode outside onto the starboard wing, looked aft and walked through the wheelhouse to the port wing scanning the sea all around and behind the ship.

"What are you looking for, sparks?" Captain Abraham asked.

"There's a signal breaking in on my transmissions. It sounds like the sending station is close by. You can tell when another nearby ship station is transmitting, it sounds like clicks. It blocks out other signals."

"I think we're alone, Sparky. No ships in sight, the lookouts haven't reported another ship all day."

"Alright, thanks, skipper. It could be a station on the coast somewhere. The signals are not standard naval signals. No call signs or any recognisable preamble." He looked down at his writing pad. "All in code except this person's name, 'Marmon Herrington'."

Captain Abraham frowned. "That's not a person's name. It's the type of armoured car we are carrying."

"Hmm, that's strange."

"Yes, odd. Keep me posted if you pick up any other strange or unusual signals, Sparky."

"Alright, Captain. Will do." He returned to the radio room.

Captain Abraham looked over at Kevin. "Lifeboat and fire drill this afternoon, Fifie. We haven't done a drill since the one we did after sailing out of Cardiff. Are you ready for it?"

"Yes, sir. I passed my lifeboat ticket on the training ship *Cromwell*, but I haven't seen these types of davits before."

"Most davits are more or less the same. You'll soon learn the drill."

An hour later Kevin handed the helm over to Able Seaman Hemsworth of the chief mate's watch.

"Thanks for doing the extra trick on the helm, Fifie," Hemsworth said. "I'm having to do an extra hour because of that useless fucker Dimmock, he says he never had to use a magnetic compass before and can't get his head around the quarter points."

"I'm struggling with them too. See you later." Kevin left the wheelhouse to attend the lifeboat drill.

Outside on the starboard boat deck a crowd of sailors had gathered. Stacked up on the deck in a neat line were lengths of fire hose, fire branch nozzles and lifejackets. The mate held a clipboard, calling out the names.

"Jackson."

"Here, sir."

"Fife."

"Here, sir."

"Wilde."

"Here, sir."

"Stoker White."

"I'm here, Mr Chapman."

"De Jong."

No answer

"De Jong? Anyone seen De Jong? No."

"Bekker."

"Bekker's not here."

"Anyone seen the Dutchmen, De Jong and Bekker?"

Fife looked around. "No."

"Dimmock."

"Not here, Mr mate."

"Where's Dimmock and the two Dutchmen?"

"Don't know, sir."

The mate turned to Kevin. "Fifie, go and find the new lads and tell them to get up here at the double. They knew there was a boat and fire drill today."

"Will do, Mr Chapman."

Kevin set off to the crew's mess room. Tony Dimmock, De Jong and Bekker were sitting at the table drinking coffee, Dimmock looked up when Kevin entered the messroom.

He said to the Dutchmen in English, "here he comes, the captain's pet. The little English puffta with his shoulder bag. Cocky, like all the Brits. All Brits are bastards. What do you want now, boy?"

Kevin ignored the insults. "The chief mate wants you on the boat deck. There is lifeboat and a fire drill on now."

"Tell him to fuck off."

"You what?" Kevin frowned.

Dimmock stared down into his cup for a moment. "Never mind, we're coming."

The three men got up slowly from the table, finishing off their coffee and followed Kevin up to the boat deck.

The mate looked at his watch. "In your own time, lads," he said sarcastically. "Where've you been? You were told about the drills."

"Sorry, sir," Dimmock apologised. "We forgot."

"Okay, fall in. Line up."

The boats crew lined up.

"These davits are the same as British built ships, a bit old fashioned. The boat must be lifted off the blocks before we swing the boat outboard. Dimmock you tend to the gripes. Fife you are number one, you will get in the bow and work from there." The chief mate detailed all the crew their allocated duties in launching the lifeboat.

When the mate was satisfied that all men knew what they were supposed to do, he called, "drill as detailed – Launch the boat."

The British sailors without talking jumped to their duties in an efficient manner. The two Dutchmen and the Irishman on the other hand were less familiar with the mechanism. Kevin climbed up into the boat, he watched as Tony Dimmock began to remove the inboard gripe.

"Don't take that one off first. Take the outboard off first."

Dimmock glared at Fife. "Who the fuck, do you think you are talking to, Fife? I was launching lifeboats before you were born."

"Sorry, but…"

"What's the problem here?" the mate intervened.

"That little puff is trying to tell me what to do. I'm an Able Seaman and I was at sea before he was born! And he's just a snotty deck-boy, a bloody mess boy."

"I'm a JOS," Kevin corrected him. "Sir, if he lets go the inner gripe first before the outer gripe and the boat lurched it would knock him over the side."

"Fife's right," the mate said to Dimmock. "Let go the outer gripe first then the inner."

Dimmock gave Kevin a look that could freeze blood. "I'll fuckin' knock you over the side, you little shit," he mouthed so that the mate couldn't hear him.

~ 214 ~

After an hour of boat drill the mate was satisfied that his men knew the procedure. The seamen then practised fire drill for an hour using the smoke hood and squirting the hosepipes out to sea.

"Knock off and make up the equipment." Chapman gave the order to end the fire drill.

Kevin squatted on the deck coiling the smoke hood breathing hose back into the box. Dimmock came over to him.

"Listen to me, Fife. If you try and show me up once again, I'm going to wring your fuckin' neck. Do you hear me?"

"Well, I'll tell you what, able seaman Dimmock, I'm not going to stand around and let you do it."

"Are you trying to threaten me?..." He stopped short when the mate approached.

"Everything alright here?"

"Yes, sir." Kevin said quietly.

Dimmock mumbled, "Yes, all cool." Before walking off the boat deck back to the seaman's accommodation.

The chief mate could see the tears of frustration in Fife's eyes.

"You did well today, young Fifie, and don't let that man get you down."

"I'm not afraid of him, sir, I seem to spend half my life fighting off bullies. I loved being on the *Alice Morgan* and this ship, until he came aboard. He never stops ordering me about and he's always calling me a little English puff and that I murdered Irish babies. I've never even been to Ireland... And I'm not a puff."

The mate hesitated before saying, "erm, yes, the Irish have long selective memories of history. Don't worry about it, not all Irish folk hate the English."

~ * ~ * ~ * ~

After rounding the Cape of Good Hope, and having sailed up passed Port Elizabeth and East London, the *SS Empire Orion* now stood off Durban waiting for the pilot to take them into port. The pilot boat putt-putted out of the harbour. Kevin replaced the *'I require a pilot'* flag with the *'I have a pilot aboard'* flag. He then hoisted the South African courtesy flag before joining Todd and Willie by the stern mooring lines as the ship entered Durban docks.

Holding a heaving line, he looked down at the hundreds of soldiers milling around on the dock side.

"There must be 1000 men there," he said to Willie, "they can't all fit on this ship, can they?"

"No, look over there. There's a passenger liner, a troopship."

"Right, Fifie, heave the line down to the dockers."

Kevin threw the line down to the waiting stevedores and the heavy mooring ropes were pulled down onto the dock and the ship was tied up alongside.

With the ship securely tied up, Kevin looked around at the other ships in the Port of Durban.

"Look over there at that ship." Kevin pointed to a ship on the far side of the harbour; it looks like it's been in the wars."

Willie Wilde looked at the damaged ship. "Wow, take a look at the size of the hole in her side, she looks to have been torpedoed."

"Are there U-boats in the Indian Ocean?"

"There must be."

"De Jong said there are no U-boats in the Indian Ocean."

"What does he know about anything?"

"This is a busy port. Have you been here before?"

"No, never been this far south before."

Their conversation was interrupted when the captain called for another of his regular meetings.

Once again, the captain waited until all the ship's company had assembled in the officers' dining room.

"As promised, men, I'll keep you posted what's going on with the war, as far as I can. We are taking part of the South African Light Armoured Division to Mombasa. We will be sailing in convoy and escorted by ships of the Royal Navy's Eastern Fleet; if you go ashore tonight do not talk about this. Careless talk costs lives. And if there are U-Boats operating in the Indian Ocean we don't want them to know when the convoy sails or where we are going."

"Where are we going after Mombasa?"

"After we disembark the troops, we are sailing home to Blighty."

There was a cheer from the gathered crew.

"We will also be taking a cargo of tea from Mombasa to Liverpool."

Another cheer went up from the sailors.

"100,000 sacks of tea will keep Britain supplied in brews for a long time," the captain joked. "Finally, I have to inform you gentlemen, we have been tasked to take 200 Italian prisoners of war to England."

"Why take POWs to England? Why not keep them in Kenya?" De Jong asked.

"They are needed for the labour, shortages of farm workers."

"That's against the Geneva Convention. It's called slave labour," Dimmock complained. He added quietly. "But just about right for the Brits."

"Who'll look after the prisoners? 200 prisoners could easily overpower us if they rioted."

"The army will be their guards. Army cooks will feed them. In the meantime, the South African troops will be boarding shortly. We sail in convoy tomorrow for Kilindini."

"Kilindini! Where's that? I thought we were going to Mombasa." De Jong sounded troubled.

"Does it matter where we go as long as we get the troops off safely. Anyway, Kilindini is near Mombasa."

De Jong shrugged, glancing briefly towards Bekker.

"That's it then, lads. Enjoy your run ashore tonight, it may be the last you get for a while. Don't get too drunk and don't forget, be like dad, keep mum."

Kevin followed the crew back to their accommodation, looking forward to a night out in Durban.

Kevin, not having boys of his own age on the ship to go ashore with, tagged on with Willie Wilde and Froggy Jackson, his fellow watchkeepers as they wandered up the Durban Point Waterfront. Kevin enjoying his first run ashore in a friendly country since sailing out of Cardiff seven months earlier.

"Where are we going?"

"You won't be allowed in the bars, so we'll have a couple of beers in the seaman's mission."

They stopped at the kerb waiting to cross the road. A taxi drove past. Kevin looked inside at the passengers.

"I wonder where they are off to?"

"Who?"

"The Dutchmen and Dimmock, they are in that taxi."

"I don't know. They are a strange bunch. They keep themselves to themselves."

"I don't like Dimmock. He's always picking on me."

"If he picks on you again, let me know and I'll sort him out."

"Erm," Kevin smiled at that.

"Here we are. The Flying Angel. Come on, let's go on inside and have a couple of beers."

Inside the seaman's mission they found themselves a table in the crowded lounge. The mission chaplain spotted the newcomers and came across to their table smiling.

He introduced himself, "*Welkom by die seeman se missie.* Welcome to the seaman's mission. I am the mission padre, Father Van de Westhuizen."

"Hello, Father Westhuizen."

The padre gave Kevin a long look. "Hello, my boy. What ship are you off?"

Kevin frowned at the question, *'here we go again'*, he thought, *'being called 'my boy'.*

He said, "I'm not allowed to say what ship I'm off."

The padre laughed, "that's alright, we are at war and you never know who's listening to our conversations. What's your name?"

"Kevin."

"*Welkom by Durban*, Kevin," the padre said in Afrikaans. "What part of the world are you from?"

"Blackstone… in England."

"Blackstone? Where is that?"

"Near Manchester."

"Rainy old Manchester."

"Yes, it rains a lot in Manchester. Have you been there?"

"No, I come from the Free State…Bloemfontein. Err, how are you finding sunny Durban?"

"Yes, it's nice. I wouldn't mind living here."

"There are lots of British people living here in South Africa, also many people of Dutch origin, like me."

"We have two Dutchmen sailing with us." Froggy said. "Their ship was attacked by a German battleship and sunk."

"Really. What ship were they off? We had a couple of seamen staying here at the mission, their ship was sunk too. What was the name of their ship?"

Kevin thought about it. I'm not sure. "Do you know the name of De Jong's ship?"

Willie scratched his head. "Err, no. I've forgot, it had a Dutch name, sounded like Good Hope."

"*Goede Hoop*?"

"Yes, that was it."

"Did you say De Jong?"

"Yes."

"Ah, yes, Mr De Jong, stayed with us here. But they are not Dutch. They are Afrikaans. I thought they would be going home to Bloemfontein. So, they are sailing with you? They must be gluttons for punishment, going back to sea so soon after being shipwrecked. I'm so pleased they are sailing with you. Where did you say you are going next?"

"We didn't say," Willie said.

"Oh no, that's right. I keep forgetting we are at war. I am just naturally curious about the seamen who visit my mission - where they come from? - where they are going?"

He turned to Kevin, "I bet a young man like you are also interested in ships, eh? Have you been on your ship since leaving England?"

"No, this is my second ship. We, shipped out of Cardiff on a collier called the *Alice Morgan* ."

"Well, well, so how did you find yourself on another ship in Durban?"

"It's a long story. We..." Kevin stopped talking when a fight broke out near the bar. The padre left to sort out the trouble.

"Don't tell him too much, Fifie. You don't know who's listening to our conversations. Do you want a beer? You are old enough to have one beer."

"I've never tried beer. My mum wouldn't like me to drink beer."

"One beer doesn't hurt anyone, and your mum is miles away from here."

Froggy brought the beers to the table. Kevin nursed his glass watching the sailors from many nations getting more and more inebriated, including Froggy Jackson and Willie Wilde. The padre never came back to their table. Two hours later, walking back down the Durban Point towards their ship, a taxi carrying the two Dutchmen and the Irishman, pulled up by the gangway. The six sailors climbed aboard together.

Kevin looking over the decks of the *Empire Orion* was amazed to see so many soldiers. The soldiers sat around on the hatches smoking; one played a guitar, others squatted under the aircraft wings playing cards. All the soldiers appeared to be cheerful, laughing and talking loudly. Already canvas tarpaulins had been stretched between derricks to make awnings. The smell of cooking meat wafted on the warm breeze. Kevin noted that the soldiers had cut an oil drum in half, top to bottom and filled it with burning wood chippings. A soldier was grilling meat and sausages. Kevin wandered across to the improvised cooker.

"Hi, mate," the soldiers said to him while turning over the meat. "How, ya doin'?"

"I'm good thanks."

"Do you work on the ship?" The soldier had a strong South African accent.

"Yeah, I'm a deck hand. What you doing there?"

"Having a braai, mate."

"A bri? What's a bri?"

"What's a braai? A barbi, a barbeque."

"A barbeque. I've never heard of a barbeque."

"Aw, we have braais, roasts, social gatherings all the time in South Africa. Where you from?"

"England."

"Don't you have barbies in England."

"No, I don't think so."

"Here try this." The soldier speared a sausage with the fork handing it to Kevin.

"Thanks very much." He took a bite out of the hot sausage. "Oh, tasty, thanks."

"You're welcome."

Wandering amongst the troops, Kevin decided he liked the easy-going South Africans. He noticed two officers chatting to some of the soldiers, they looked like senior officers to him. They had shoulder epaulettes full of rank markings. The officers gave Kevin a glance as he passed them by as he made his way back to the junior seaman's cabin to turn in for the night.

CHAPTER 7

EAST AFRICA – NOVEMBER 1940

THE SOUND OF MUSIC, MILITARY music, coming from outside on the dockside woke Kevin.

"Turn to, sunshine," called the boatswain, knocking on Kevin's cabin door. "We're leaving."

Kevin made his way aft to tend to the after mooring lines. Soldiers were lined up along the handrails waving at the people on the quay. Kevin looked over the side at the band. A small army band were boisterously playing, '*We'll Hang Out the Washing on the Siegfried Line*'. There were a few women and children on the shore waving up at the soldiers.

"Let go aft," called Captain Abraham from the bridge. The second mate signalled to the Durban stevedores to cast off the lines. Kevin helped winch in the mooring lines up onto the quarterdeck.

The ship's horn gave a single toot as the ship's head fell away from the dock and started moving to starboard. As the *Empire Orion* manoeuvred clear of the dockside the band began to play, '*Auld Lang Syne*'.

The *Empire Orion* sailed out of Durban harbour carrying 200 troops, part of the 1st South African Infantry Division and 20 airmen of the South African Air Force. Well clear of the harbour, the ship, escorted by warships of the Royal Navy's Eastern Fleet, turned northwards heading for Mombasa.

As Kevin took over steering the ship, he noticed the two army officers outside on the bridge wing talking to Captain Abraham.

"Keep a steady course," Jackson said, handing over the wheel, "the navy go mad if you drift off course while in convoy."

"I'll try. Who are them officers?"

"I'm not sure who is who, the one on the left is a Brigadier the other chap is a Colonel."

Kevin looked out over the sea. Ahead, a large troop carrier, several smaller merchant cargo ships and tankers, out on the periphery of the convoy, a British warship patrolled.

~ * ~ * ~ * ~

Three days out of Durban, while Kevin stood lookout on the bridge wing, he heard someone shouting from below.

"Make way, make way." He looked over the windbreaker and saw the South African colonel, red in face, pushing his way through the throng of soldiers gathered on the upper deck. Taking the bridge ladder two steps at a time he breathlessly reached the wheel house.

"Captain," he called to Captain Abraham. "Captain Abraham. The Brigadier has gone missing!"

"Missing? How do you mean he's gone missing? Are you sure?"

"I'm sure. He didn't turn up for a meeting, two hours ago, his batman has no idea where he is. We've searched all the accommodation, all the passageways, all over the ship; he's nowhere to be seen."

"Crikey, when was he last seen?"

"Last night. Private Canning, his batman, said the last time he spoke to the Brigadier, was last night around midnight. He didn't report him missing until this morning, he just thought he was out talking to the troops."

"Shit," Abraham said, looking aft at the *Empire Orion's* wake. "I hope to God he hasn't fallen overboard." Glancing up at the ship's clock, he added, "eight or nine hours, if he fell overboard at midnight, there's no chance of finding him in the sea. The navy ordered the convoy to alter course at daybreak, then again an hour ago."

The worried colonel shook his head. "Can you put out a message on your ship's intercom. If he doesn't answer to that, what else can we do? He's one of the Empire's most experienced soldiers. A *very* important officer."

Abraham gave a polite cough. "You don't suppose he's in someone else's cabin, do you, Colonel Flodwyn?"

Flodwyn frowned. "What do you mean?"

The captain shrugged a little uneasily, "You, know…in a cabin with someone."

"No, definitely not. Jan Van Riebeeke is above reproach in such matters."

"Alright," said the captain. "I just didn't want to embarrass the Brigadier in his private affairs. I'll try the Tannoy, if there is no response from the Brigadier, there's not really a lot I can do about it. I can't drop out of the convoy and go searching for him without the Admiral's permission." The captain picked up the large black telephone and switched on the ship's internal intercom. "Attention. Brigadier Jan Van Riebeeke. Please report to the bridge. Brigadier Jan Van Riebeeke, please report to the bridge, immediately." The system sounded throughout the ship.

Five minutes later Captain Abraham repeated the call. There was no reply; the Brigadier had gone missing.

"Get your radio operator. Send a message 'man overboard'. Inform CinC about the Brigadier, send it in code, I don't want the whole fucking fleet to know we've lost the Brigadier."

"Alright, Colonel, I'll get the message coded up and sent to the flagship marked 'urgent' requesting guidance."

The signal was transmitted to the Eastern Fleet flagship. The captain and the colonel paced up and down the bridge waiting for a reply.

Ten minutes later, the ship's wireless officer handed Captain Abraham a cable. "From the Admiral, sir."

Abraham read the telegram out to Colonel Flodwyn, "'*Maintain position in convoy Stop I will despatch a corvette to carry out a search of the estimated area of sea covered by convoy last eight hours Stop Continue your investigations on board Empire Orion Stop Am sending naval intelligence officer over to you by sea boat Stop Report findings to CinC Eastern Fleet'*. End of message colonel."

"Thank you, Captain."

The agitated army officer left the bridge.

"What more could we do," Abraham said to no one in particular. "If he's gone overboard the sharks will have had him for dinner."

Kevin's eyes looked upwards. He continued steering the ship.

The radio officer, about to return to the radio room, hesitated. He asked the captain, "Sir, what was the name of the Brigadier?"

"Jan Van Riebeeke."

"Erm, that's odd. Do you remember as we left Cape Town, I got strange signals breaking in on my transmissions? Transmitting WT right through the silence period. At the time I thought it must be a shore station not familiar with marine radio procedure. Well, I got the same transmissions again last night, just as I was coming off watch at midnight. I was going to tell you about it but you had already turned in for the night. The loud clicking signals, as if the transmitter was next door."

"You mean, like on this ship?"

"Erm, yes. The transmissions were in code, gobbledegook, except one name in plain language … Jan Van Riebeeke."

"Erm," the captain pondered. "Erm, strange. Right, sparks, draw up a coded message, to the flagship. Make the signal marked 'priority' for the CinC Eastern Fleet. Tell him in as much detail as you can remember, word for word, of the two transmissions you received. When the navy's Intelligence Officer arrives, we'll ask him what he makes of the signals, if anything. In the meantime, keep me posted, especially if you get any more of these strange signals. You know, Sparky, no one ashore knows which ship is carrying what senior officer. There's a Brigadier and Colonel with us, a Major General on another ship and a Lieutenant General on a warship and so on. They are spread out just in case one ship is sunk. They don't want their senior officers all going to the bottom of the sea together. So, it is strange that Brigadier Jan Van Riebeeke's name, not an altogether common name, is being bandied about on the airwaves."

"Right, sir. I'll do that." The radio officer returned to the radio room to have the captain's request transcribed into naval code and sent to the flagship.

"Fifie," the captain said to Kevin, "you overheard what the sparky said. For the time being, don't you repeat anything you've heard on the bridge today to the crew or any of the soldiers."

"Right, sir. I won't."

Twenty minutes later at the end of Kevin's trick on the wheel he was relieved by Tony Dimmock.

"Steering north-north-east and taking starboard wheel." Kevin handed over the ship's wheel.

Dimmock, looking at Kevin with contempt, snatched at the wheel. He muttered under his breath, "go on, you little English fucker, get the fuck out of my sight."

Kevin, with his hackles rising, stopped in his tracks and turned his head. "Try and keep steering a straight course you Irish t...," he refrained from swearing. "The navy go mad when *you* go off course..."

Fuming, Dimmock stepped away from the wheel, his fist balled to punch Kevin in the head. Kevin saw the blow coming and took one step to the side. Dimmock's fist brushed Kevin's right ear.

"What the fuck you doin', Dimmock?" shouted the chief mate. "Get back on the wheel. You too, Fife, you go below."

Kevin left the wheelhouse listening to the mate chastising Dimmock for leaving the wheel. He heard Dimmock saying, "I'm not having a snotty kid talk to me like that, calling me an Irish twat. Who the..." Kevin didn't hear what else Dimmock had to say. He just wondered why the Irishman had taken such a dislike to him and why Dimmock was such a nasty person and what had he done to upset the Irishman.

~ * ~ * ~ * ~

Kevin Fife standing with Froggy Jackson watched as a navy motor boat pulled up alongside the already lowered accommodation ladder.

"A lieutenant commander, no less," Jackson, a former royal navy seaman, informed Kevin.

They waited until the commander stepped onto the deck.

"Welcome aboard, sir," Froggy Jackson said.

"Good morning, gentlemen. I'm from the flagship."

"Yes, sir, we were told you would be joining us. Your cabin is ready."

"Yes, thank you. I'll be staying with you until you return to the UK. Can you get my bags off the cutter?"

"Yes, sir." Kevin climbed down the accommodation ladder to the motor cutter. A rating passed across a heavy naval grip. Stencilled on the canvas bag the officer's name. Lt Cdr A E Bateman (NID). Kevin lugged the bag up the steps.

"Shall I take your bag to your cabin, sir?" Kevin asked.

"Yes, thank you." The officer turned to Jackson. "Take me up to see your captain. What is his name?"

"Captain Abraham. Isaac Abraham."

"Also, please will you ask Colonel Flodwyn to join us."

Jackson escorted Bateman up to the captain's cabin and then went seeking Colonel Flodwyn. Kevin took the grip to the captain's sea cabin.

Later, Kevin re-joined Jackson in the crews' dining room.

"Why do you suppose he's staying with us for so long? From here to England?"

"I don't rightly know, Fifie. I guess he will want to interrogate the Italian POW's when they join us. But the main reason I suppose, is to investigate the missing Brigadier."

"I think he should start with Paddy Dimmock. I don't trust him."

"Why do you say that? Just because you don't like him?"

"No, there's something fishy about Dimmock. He contradicts himself. He said he was a survivor off the *SS Goede Hoop* with the two Dutchmen. Yet the padre in Durban said there were only two survivors off that ship, and they were not Dutchmen, they were Afrikaans. Dimmock says he's an Able Seaman, but I know more about seamanship than he does and he knows it. That's why he picks on me, because I show him up."

"Erm, well Fifie, you should be a ruddy detective. I do know the captain checked up on the two Dutch sailors with the port office, and they confirmed De Jong and Bekker were survivors of the *Goede Hoop,* they've been given temporary British Seaman's Cards. They may be Dutchmen just living in South Africa. Did they confirm they were from Holland, and what about Dimmock? Tell you what, when you get chance, tell Bateman about your concerns."

"I will. Anyway, I'm off to get my head down for a bit."

Kevin retired to his cabin to rest before starting his next spell on watch.

At midnight, after spending his 8 to midnight watch alternating between steering the ship and keeping lookout, Kevin was pleased that his relief was Able Seaman Pickard, his friend from the *Alice Morgan,* and not Tony Dimmock the Irishman. Outside, the fragrance of the tropical night wafted on the warm offshore breeze. Kevin stood for a while breathing in deeply the fruity aroma and perfume of African rainforests.

"On nights like this it's good to be alive," he said to himself.

He looked over the bridge wing windbreaker at the forward deck, most of the South African soldiers had bedded down for the night, one or two soldiers sat on the bollards talking quietly amongst themselves. A perfect, peaceful night; the war seemed to be a million miles away. The convoy had not been attacked. '*Was it possible that there were no U-Boats in the Indian Ocean?*' Kevin wondered. He looked over the after decks noting they were dark and deserted. Not a soul moved. He made his way down across the open boat deck, heading for the seaman's accommodation. Stopping by one of the portside lifeboats he looked up at the canvas cover, not wanting to go back to his stuffy cabin, he decided to climb up onto the lifeboat and lie down on the canvas and do some stargazing. The ship was now only a few hours away from Kilindini, he looked towards the land. No land or lights showed. The sky was cloudless and jet black. Once again Kevin was astonished looking at the billions of stars, shining like crystal. He sighed, remembering the night in the lifeboat with his friend Hector, how they had both laid on their backs staring up in wonderment at the galaxy. Once again, he felt the rising sadness overcoming him. The despair he felt when he thought about Hector, and the night Hector died in his arms. He drifted into sleep.

Someone talking quietly below the boat woke him. He listened to the whispering without moving. '*Were they talking in Africana,*' he thought. '*Not English.*' The South African soldiers were not supposed to wander onto the out-of-bounds boat-deck. The hairs on the back of his neck rose when he heard Dimmock's Irish accent. The voices faded. Kevin didn't hear or understand what they were talking about. He lifted his head to look over the dark boat deck and could just about make out the silhouette of three men huddled together by the handrails. What were the two Dutch stewards doing up in the middle of the night? And why were they climbing up onto the aftermost lifeboat?

"Crikey! If they look forward, they will see me."

Kevin slid off the canvas and climbed down the davit, hiding under the boat, undecided whether or not to go and see what they were up t or sneak away unseen back to his cabin. Maybe they are just sleeping outside in the fresh air rather than in their stuffy cabins.

Just as Kevin decided to make his way back to his cabin, he jumped a mile when a hand gripped his shoulder, another hand slapped across his mouth.

"Keep quiet, son." The voice had a strong South African accent.

"Wait till they start transmitting," the whispered voice belonged to Lieutenant Commander Bateman.

Kevin saw that Bateman was holding a pistol, two other soldiers with him held rifles.

Bateman whispered to Kevin, "go quietly, back to the bridge, go on."

Kevin scared out of his wits nodded vigorously. The soldier released him. Kevin crept back to the ladder leading up to the bridge. Another soldier knelt behind the bulwark, holding a rifle. Back inside the wheelhouse Kevin was surprised to see the Captain, Colonel Flodwyn, Mr Chapman the mate, the second mate and the radio officer. The helmsman still steering the ship maintaining position in the convoy.

"What's going on?"

"Naval intelligence is onto the two Dutchmen." Captain Abraham said quietly. "Just keep out of sight. We didn't expect you to go and sleep on the lifeboat. You could have put a spanner in the works if you'd spoke to them before they set up their transmitter."

"Sorry, I didn't know."

"We are just waiting until they start transmitting. Catch them red-handed, so to speak."

Suddenly the radio in the radio cabin began to transmit loud clacking Morse code. The radio officer wrote down the message.

"Now!"

The captain hit the boat-deck floodlight switch. The whole deck illuminated up brightly. The two men on the lifeboat stared horrified at the lights.

"Get your hands up," shouted Bateman pointing his pistol at the Dutchmen.

The soldier hiding behind the bulwark, stood up pointing his rifle at the two stewards.

Kevin unable to contain his curiosity, peeped out of the door. He saw one of the Dutchmen throw a box over the side before he slowly raised his hands. The other Dutch steward, standing on top of the lifeboat also put up his hands. The boat was surrounded by a half dozen soldiers, all pointing their weapons up at the two stewards. Bateman indicated for them to climb down.

"Where's the Irishman?" Kevin wondered.

Tony Dimmock had disappeared off the deck.

The two captured Dutchmen were bundled up towards the bridge. "Where is Dimmock?" Bateman questioned Bekker.

Bekker shrugged, but he didn't answer.

"You, where is the Irishman?"

De Jong shrugged. "I don't know any Irishmen. Why you capture us? We just sleeping on top of the boat. It too hot in the cabin. You let me go, I am a Dutch citizen."

"You are no more Dutch than I am. You, my friend, are a South African Afrikaans. You are members of *Ossewabrandwag,* or in English, the 'Ox Wagon Sentinel."

Bekker could not hide his shock at what Bateman had just said. He stammered with less confidence, "*Osswa…Osswabrandwag*! I never heard of this word."

"You were transmitting to the Nazis."

De Jong scoffed. "To transmit you need a transmitter. Where is this transmitter?"

"I saw them throw a box over the side, Captain." Kevin whispered to Captain Abraham.

"Yes, I saw them throw something over the side. Whatever it was it will be at the bottom of the sea now."

"Get the Irishman; he can't be far away. Have the ship searched. I want to speak to Dimmock now. Captain, I need a space or strong room to keep these two men locked up."

"The best place is the rope locker. No portholes, a steel door with a strong lock, one key. You'll need a blow-torch to cut open the door without the key."

"Great. I've no need to tell you, these three men are dangerous Nazis."

"I feel guilty, signing them on in Cape Town." Abraham said. "I believed their story, that they were DBS's wanting to be repatriated to the UK and Ireland."

"It's not your fault, Captain, if we'd known earlier the three would have been picked up in Bloemfontein. Their story about the sinking of the *Goede Hoop* is true, but they have never been to sea. The Irishman was working on a farm in Bloemfontein. He deserted a British ship ten years ago…as a boy seaman."

"How do you know all this?" Abraham asked.

Bateman smiled. "Can't tell you that, Captain, suffice to say, British Naval Intelligence is superior to German Naval Intelligence Service, in German, *marineenachrichtendienst*, let's leave it at that. I can tell you that *Ossewabrandwag* or known in English as the 'Ox Wagon Sentinel', is an anti-British, pro German organisation who oppose South Africa's participation in the war. We too have spies in Bloemfontein. The two men have been on our radar since 1939. When they disappeared, we suspected they would try and get aboard a British ship to spy on convoys. We didn't know which ship or where they had gone, that is until the Brigadier went missing. We checked your crew list given to the Port Authority in Cape Town, when we saw that you had signed on De Jong and Bekker, we knew then the *Ossewabrandwag* were aboard your ship."

"How?"

Bateman hesitated momentarily. "Because, Captain, De Jong and Bekker were found murdered in Bloemfontein."

"Oh, crikey. Who are the Dutchmen then?"

"We don't know their names yet, but we *will* find out."

"What will happen to them?"

"Not sure yet. They will get a fair trial. We believe they are responsible for Brigadier Riebeeck's disappearance. When we got your report that the Brigadier had gone missing from this ship and that you were picking up unidentified signals, it aroused our suspicions at NID. We did some investigations about you and your crew, saw that De Jong and Bekker had signed on in Cape Town... that's a miracle as the two shipwrecked seamen, De Jong and Bekker, as I said, were found murdered near Bloemfontein."

Kevin's brow furrowed, something that Bateman was saying was wrong. He spoke to the captain. "When we were in the seaman's mission in Durban, the padre said he knew De Jong and Bekker. I'm surprised he didn't hear that they had been murdered."

"That's right," confirmed Jackson. "Surely he should have heard about the murder of two seamen?"

"Right, young Fifie, I'll tell that to Lieutenant Commander. You never know if it's important."

"The vicar was a nosy parker asking about ship's movements and what we were carrying, where we were going next."

"Really? I'll let Bateman know that. But anyway, that's what vicars are like, wanting to keep up with their flocks, pretending to show an interest in their lives."

Kevin watched as soldiers took the two stewards down to the rope locker. Dimmock had disappeared. A search of the ship from stem to stern failed to find the Irishman.

~ * ~ * ~ * ~

Standing by the handrails, Kevin watched the South African soldiers disembarking. They clambered down the gangway with their rifles and packs. He looked out at the warehouses and cranes of Kilindini Harbour at Mombasa. A dockside crane was already lifting the aircraft off the hatches and lowering them onto waiting flatback waggons. The soldiers lined up in ranks on the quayside before marching off to the local barracks. The decks of the ship were strangely empty, hardly any evidence that over 200 soldiers had been occupying the decks and passenger cabins for a week. Kevin missed the friendly soldiers, he wondered how quickly they would be fighting the Italians. He glanced at the rope locker door. The two prisoners were still locked inside. Their military guards had already gone ashore with the other soldiers. He met up with Froggy Jackson and the bosun.

"Who's going to guard the two prisoners?"

"British soldiers, when they arrive. They will be on board guarding the POWs including these two. Commander Bateman is sailing with us to the UK. He will be interrogating the Italians."

"I wonder what happened to Tony Dimmock? He just vanished into thin air."

"I reckon he jumped over the side to avoid capture."

"Why would he do that?"

"I don't know. Bateman said there is a new law in Britain called 'The Treachery Act' aimed at Nazi spies or saboteurs being caught. Apparently, they cannot be treated as traitors, if they are not British. So, if they have not committed murder they cannot be executed. Churchill wants spies to be executed. So, they have just brought in this new Treachery Act. There's only one sentence in the act and that's death!"

"So, Paddy Dimmock could be executed just for being involved in assisting the enemy?"

"Yes, that's right. Anyway, that's what Bateman told the captain. That's why I think Dimmock jumped over the side."

~ * ~ * ~ * ~

After the Kilindini stevedores had finished lifting the aircraft off the hatches, Kevin assisted the other sailors to remove the tarpaulins and hatch boards. The men spent the next two hours removing the shifting boards fitted to stop the armoured cars from moving while the ship was at sea.

The bosun called down to the men working in the holds, "when you have finished down there the captain wants to talk to you about the Italian POWs."

An hour later the entire crew assembled in the officers' dining room. Lieutenant Commander Bateman also in attendance.

"Well, gentlemen," Captain Abraham started, "what a voyage we have had. You will all be boring your grandchildren to death with the stories of our exploits so far. As we all know life at sea can be pretty mundane at times."

"Not for me, Captain, sir," interrupted Kevin holding his hand up. "It's been a bit too exciting for me."

The crew laughed.

Abraham smiled and continued, "I've spent most of my seagoing career taking coal from Newcastle to the Thames on dirty old colliers. Now here I am the skipper, err," he coughed "Captain, Royal Navy Volunteer Reserve, no less, of this fine ship. A magnificent passenger cargo ship. However, our next passengers will not be paying passengers. They are Italian prisoners of war. As soon as the war cargo has been unloaded, we will start taking on board the prisoners. Commander Bateman will tell you what's going to happen."

Bateman stood up. "Thanks, Captain. We are taking on board about 200 Italians, officers and men. They will be accommodated in the former passenger cabins under the guard of British soldiers, Lancashire Fusiliers, I believe. The army will be responsible for guarding and feeding the prisoners. Any attempt of them trying to escape, they will be shot. We need tight control of them, however, the trip from Kenya to the UK is a long one and we cannot keep the POWs cooped up in stifling heat, they will need to come out on deck for exercise and fresh air at least once per day."

"Does that include the two Dutch prisoners?" asked Josh White.

"No, they are traitors to South Africa, they are going to be sent back to Bloemfontein where they will go on trial for murder as well as treason. If they are found guilty, they will be hanged in Bloemfontein. That's the judicial capital of South Africa. They will remain locked up on board here until the Kenyan police take them ashore."

"When will that be?"

"Your guess is as good as mine but sooner rather than later...I hope."

"What about the Irishman?"

"If he is ever caught, he will be transported back to the UK for trial there."

"On what charges?"

"Treachery."

~ * ~ * ~ * ~

Night fell and still the Kenyan police had not turned up to take the two South African traitors ashore.

Kevin and Jackson were sitting at the crew's dining table drinking tea.

"Have you ever been night watchman in a foreign country before, Fifie?"

Kevin thought about the question. "No, no, this is the first time."

"Not much to do, except make sure the locals don't sneak onboard stealing ropes and whatnot. If you do the first hour patrolling the decks, I'll do the second hour, while you get your head down, okay?"

"Yeah, okay, I'll do the first watch." Kevin drained his mug and got up to do the rounds of the upper decks.

Outside the decks were now deserted. All the cargo had been discharged and all the soldiers had long gone. The off-duty crew had turned in for the night. Kevin looked over the docks, no one or anything moved. The cicadas chirped loudly and there was a heavy scent of the tropics in the air. Dozens of insects buzzed around the dim deck lamps. He walked up to the rope locker door and checked the handle. The door was locked, he put his ear up to the metal door listening. No one inside the temporary prison spoke.

He turned to continue the rounds and came face to face with Dimmock. Dimmock pointed a knife at Kevin's eye.

"Where the heck did you come from!?"

"Never mind where I came from. Just do what I say or I'll fucking gut you, like the fucking English pig you are."

"W…what do you want?" Kevin stammered.

"The key. I want the key."

"What key?"

"The key for this locker, you idiot."

"I don't know where it is."

"Listen, sunshine, you bloody well do know where it is." Dimmock snarled, at the same grabbing hold of Kevin's shirt and almost lifting him off his feet. "You better find it pronto or I will kill you right here."

Kevin swallowed. "I think it's on the bridge, in the key locker."

"If it was there, why the hell would I ask you? It's not there. You better find it or you will be over the side feeding the sharks. Go on." Dimmock, pushed Kevin towards the bridge. "Move. Don't try any funny business or I'll stick you."

Kevin nodded, tamely leading Dimmock up to the bridge. He knew the key was on a hook inside the captain's sea cabin.

"It's with the navy officer, in the captain's sea cabin."

"Alright, I'm right behind you, any funny business I'm going to shove this knife in, right up to the hilt."

Kevin felt the knife point pricking his abdomen. He led the way up through the wheelhouse to the captain's sea cabin. The sea cabin door was held open with a cabin hook.

"Go on, get it." Dimmock said in low tones. "If the officer wakes, you're both dead."

"Alright, alright." Kevin felt blood trickling down his back. "You've already cut my back with that knife." He carefully lifted the hook and quietly opened the door. Reaching inside, he lifted the rope locker key off the hook handing it over to Dimmock. Dimmock took hold of the large key and dragged Kevin backwards into the wheelhouse.

"Right, you little shoulder bag carrying puff. I'm going to teach you a lesson. You won't be showing me up again. I'm gonna cut out your gizzards and feed them to the fish."

Kevin took one pace back before leaping forward, high kicking Dimmock in the face, almost removing Dimmock's nose. Blood poured down the Irishman's chin."

"Wow, Brit. Where did that come from." Dimmock wiped the blood off his face with his hand while taking up an attacking stance. Kevin kept his eye on the knife firmly gripped in Dimmock's hand. They circled each other.

"Say bye-bye, Fife, because now I'm gonna take off your fuckin' bollocks…"

Remembering what Marine Sutcliffe had told him earlier about going for the ears, eyes and testicles, Kevin sprung a second time kicking Dimmock hard in his testicles.

Dimmock groaned bending over in pain. A split-second later Kevin lashed out with his foot again kicking the Irishman hard in his left ear. Dimmock squealed loudly, but still held tightly to the knife. Shaking his head from side to side and wiping the blood, still pouring out of his nose with his free hand, he lunged again at Kevin.

Kevin danced to one side. "Come on then, Paddy, let's see what you can do." Kevin taunted the Irishman.

This enraged Dimmock further. With his angry brutal face grimacing and covered in blood, he snarled, "I'm gonna gut your fuckin' English…"

A gun shot blasted in Kevin's ear, cutting off Dimmock's threat. A small hole appeared in Dimmock's forehead; a look of astonishment on his face, a trickle of blood ran out of the hole. Dimmock fell down with the back of his head blown off.

Kevin turned and stared at Bateman, standing in just his underpants, and at the automatic pistol he was holding.

"You alright, son?" Bateman said.

Kevin was speechless. He just stared down at Dimmock as blood spread from under his shattered head. Kevin just nodded before throwing up.

"I heard him," Bateman said. "I was asleep in the captain's sea cabin. I couldn't believe hearing the Irish accent and the threats, by the time I found my pistol and got out here you'd kicked the shit out of him. Wow, where did you learn how to do that?"

Kevin eventually found his tongue. "The marines, sir. The Royal Marines showed me self-defence." Kevin bit his own bottom lip, fighting back the tears.

The shot had woken the captain. He wandered sleepily into the wheelhouse looking in disbelief at Dimmock's lifeless body, Dimmock still gripping a knife in one hand and the blood covered rope locker key in his other hand.

"What the...What happened?"

"This young man, here, has just prevented Dimmock from releasing our two traitors."

"How? What? Well done, young Fife. Well done indeed."

Kevin was still in the state of shock. Too upset to respond to the compliment.

Jackson arrived on the bridge panting.

Kevin just looked from the captain to Bateman and then at Froggy Jackson. Looking down at the body, slowly shaking his head, he said quietly, "I want to go home."

"Come on, Fifie. Let's go and have a brew."

Jackson, with his arm around Kevin's shoulder, led him back to the seaman's messroom.

~ * ~ * ~ * ~

Timber pallets full of sacks of tea swung over the decks and down the three forward holds. The loading of tea for Liverpool had been underway all morning.

Kevin faced the warm sunshine.

"How you feeling, mate?" asked Jackson.

"I'm alright now, thanks." Kevin said solemnly, as he watched the two South Africans being taken ashore by the Kenyan police. The two Africana's were unceremoniously bundled into the back of a police van. The back doors slammed shut and the van driven away. Kevin looked away as a rough pine wood coffin containing the body of Tony Dimmock was swung ashore on a pallet. The coffin was loaded into a black hearse.

"War is terrible, Fifie. It brings out the worst, and the best in people. I feel sorry for you, you are too young to be involved in all this...

As the hearse drove away from the docks, the sound of singing came from behind the dock warehouse interrupting Jackson. They both looked over the docks. Marching around the corner of the warehouse came a column of scruffy soldiers. The soldiers were singing in Italian.

"Hello, here come the POWs."

The singing grew louder as more and more marching soldiers appeared from around the warehouse.

"Crikey, there's a lot of them," said Kevin.

The prisoners marched up to the gangway.

An Italian officer called, "*Arresta!*" The three columns halted and the singing stopped. Some of the POWs glanced up at the ship. "*svolta a sinistra.*" The prisoners turned into line. "*Stare a proprio agio.*" The soldiers stood at ease.

Although the soldiers' uniforms were scruffy and soiled with sweat, the Italians stood upright and proud. The soldiers wore similar desert grey uniforms, but some wore forage caps while others wore sun-helmets with their regimental badges. All the uniforms had a large red disc sewn on the jackets and one leg of their trousers. They all looked tired. A dozen British soldiers, armed with Sten guns, guarded the prisoners.

"Poor beggars," Kevin said sadly.

"Well, the war is over for them. Have you noticed, Fifie, they're nearly all officers?"

Kevin noted their rank markings. He also noted how young the Italians were, one boy in particular didn't look much older than 15 or 16 years old.

After standing in the sun for nearly an hour, the prisoners were ordered up the gangway. Kevin returned to his work on deck until Freddy Todd the second mate called down to him, "Fifie, another war conflab. Officers' dining room."

"Alright, Mr Todd, I'm coming."

Kevin made his way along the boat deck and up the ladder to the officers' dining room. As usual at the daily war update meetings, the room was crowded and noisy. All the ship's company had gathered, waiting for the news. Commander Bateman, sitting with Captain Abraham, puffed on his pipe.

"Good afternoon, gentlemen." Captain Abraham greeted his crew. "Lieutenant Commander Bateman is going to brief us on the POW situation. Commander."

"Thank you, Captain. Before I start, I must mention the incident last night. I had no choice but to shoot Dimmock. He was just about to stab our lad, young Kevin Fife, there."

Kevin blinked and nodded.

"War is war, as they say. Dimmock was a spy, he and his conspirators had been gathering intelligence and transmitting the information to someone, don't know who yet. We believe it was the *Abwehr*, the German Intelligence Service. Also, I am convinced they murdered the Brigadier and threw his body overboard. We believe they also murdered two survivors of a sunk ship, a Mr de Jong and a Mr Bekker, and took on their identities. The courts in Bloemfontein will deal with them. Any questions about them?"

There was no response from the crew.

"Okay, then. Now, about the POWs. Firstly, I told you earlier that we would be taking about 200 prisoners back to the UK. Well, that number has now increased to 250, 100 officers and 150 other ranks."

"250! Where are they going to sleep?"

"We'll have to make room for them."

"Sir, counting us and the army personnel that means we will have getting on over 300 persons on board. We don't have sufficient lifeboats for 300 people, what happens if we get attacked and torpedoed?"

"We are going to have Carley floats provided."

"Where are we going to accommodate 250 POWs?" Jackson asked again.

"Well, the 100 officers will be accommodated in the passenger's cabins. The 150 other ranks will sleep on the tween deck in number 4 hold.

"Down the hold! Is that allowed? Why are we taking 250 Italians back to England, anyway? Why not leave them in Africa?"

Bateman was silent for a moment. "At the beginning of the war our government was reluctant to use prisoners of war for slave labour. Firstly, there was high unemployment in the UK and secondly the British trade unions objected to prisoners doing work that could be done by British people. However, things have changed. We now need workers on the land. So, the 150 other ranks will be employed on farms. The Geneva Convention prohibits using POW officers for work unless they volunteer to do the work, you know, for extra rations. I can tell you this; all the prisoners will be treated well."

"So why take the officers to England?"

"The officers will have valuable information that may help us win the war. They will be interrogated by me, and then when they are in the UK our British Intelligence agents will be chatting to the officers, listening to them talking between themselves. It's surprising what information you can glean from them when you treat them well. We don't pull finger nails out or torture our prisoners. Name rank and number is all we require.… Everyone happy?"

"Erm, yes, alright," the crew agreed.

"Right oh, now down to logistics. The Army Catering Corp will provide victuals and cook the food for themselves and the POWs. The army will be in charge of security. Any prisoner trying to escape, *will* be shot. We cannot keep 250 men cooped so they will be allowed up on deck in batches."

"What happens if they jump overboard, or riot?"

"We, the Royal Engineers, that is, are going to build a compound around the quarter deck. What you call the poop deck."

"The gun is on the poop."

"The POWs won't be allowed on the upper poop deck. The wire cage roof will be under the gun level. Finally, we don't want you merchant seamen fraternising with the prisoners."

Kevin leaned over to Jackson and whispered, "what does fraternise mean?"

"It means talking to the prisoners or making friends with them."

"Okay."

"Can you tell us anything else about how the war is progressing?"

"We are beating the Italians here in east and north Africa taking many prisoners and the Greeks are beating the Italians in Greece. The RAF have bombed Berlin…"

"Lieutenant Commander Bateman." Kevin put his hand up. "Sir, is there any chance of getting letters from home? I haven't heard from my mum since we sailed out of Cardiff last May."

"I hope we get mail in Alexandria. Alright, gentlemen, that's it for today. We'll have another briefing tomorrow."

~ * ~ * ~ * ~

Kevin dropped his hook, line and sinker into the sand-coloured harbour water, he tugged gently on the line hoping to catch a fish. In the warm sunshine, he watched as the engineers finished off fixing wire mesh around the after part of the ship. On the other side of the ship an officer from the Catering Corp was supervising the loading of stores for feeding the POWs and feeding the army guards.

"Come on, get this chocolate out of the hot sun."

Kevin heard the officer. "Chocolate!" Kevin said to himself. "I haven't tasted chocolate since last Christmas."

"Officer's mess. Those boxes are for the officers. Take them down to the fridges," the officer said to his cooks. Telling them what stores were for the officers, what were for the other ranks and what victuals were for the prisoners of war.

"Those sacks of pasta are for the Italians."

Kevin looked at the victuals on the pallet. Giant size tins of jam and marmalade, large jars of Marmite, packs of bottled HP brown sauce and Lea and Perrins Worcester sauce. Culinary items he had not seen since before being sent to the training ship *Cromwell*.

The fishing line gave a jerk. "Oh, wow, a bite!" Kevin pulled up the line. He was disappointed to see a tiny fish flapping on the hook. "Flipping heck, the hook's bigger than the fish's mouth." The fish flopped around on the deck, jumping and turning. Kevin tried picking up the slippery fish, it slipped out of his grasp. He tried for a second time to pick up the fish. He unhooked the hook from the fish's mouth, the small fish shot out of his hand and dived overboard back into the water.

"Damn," he said under his breath. He heard laughing and turned his head to look. A small group of Italian prisoners inside the improvised compound were watching him trying to catch the fish.

"*Un pesce scivoloso e difficile da tenere*," the young Italian prisoner called cheerfully.

Kevin, not understanding Italian, just smiled embarrassedly. He gave the boy a shy wave, rebaiting the hook and dropping the line and sinker back into the muddy water and continued fishing. He looked again at the POWs. He noticed the young prisoner talking to an officer.

'He doesn't look much older than me,' Kevin thought.

He glanced at the officer. The Italian officer wore a white doctor's coat with a stethoscope poking out of the coat pocket and wore a red cross armband.

The fishing line gave a strong jerk in Kevin's hand. "Wow! Wow, I must have caught a shark." The line tightened in his grip. "Maybe it's caught on the bottom." He pulled on the fishing line. Slowly, hand over hand Kevin pulled up the line. He looked over the side to see what he had caught. "An eel. I've caught a green eel!" The eel fought on the hook, curling and thrashing about. Kevin pulled the fish over the handrail onto the deck. The green reptile slithered and thrashed on the end of the line. "I'd better unhook it; I'll use the eel for bait. I'm not going to eat it," he muttered to himself.

Kevin lifted the curling and twisting reptile by the line. He was just about to grab it by the neck when the Italian boy shouted, "*Fermare! Arrestare! Serpente, serpent*e!"

Kevin looked at the prisoner and frowned, "What?"

The boy called to the doctor, "*Dottore, per favore, vieni!*"

The doctor came over to the wire mesh and looked at the green snake.

The doctor shouted in English, "do not touch, it is a snake!"

Kevin dropped the line and reeled back in horror. "I thought it was an eel."

"No, it's a green mamba. Very venomous. One bite and you will be dead in less than one hour!"

"Oh, wow! Thanks for telling me."

"Yes, they can also reactive strike, even when dead. Do not touch."

Kevin stared at the snake coiled in the scupper, hissing and snarling. He looked around for a stick, there was a brush propped up against the mast housing, using the long handle he flipped the snake back over the side. He watched as the green mamba dived back under the water with the hook still in its mouth trailing three yards of fishing line.

He turned to the Italians. "Thanks very much, I owe you one."

"That is alright." The doctor and the young soldier gave a brief wave and smile, then continued exercising around the poop-deck.

"Phew, that was close." Kevin coiled up his fishing line and retired to his cabin thinking about chocolate and Marmite on toast.

~ * ~ * ~ * ~

Kevin looked around to see if anyone was watching him. He peeped inside the passenger's galley. The army cooks had cleaned away for the night, the galley flat was deserted.

A short staircase led down to the cold stores and freezers. He leaped down the steps two at a time, and tried to open the cold store door. "Damn it's padlocked." he noticed the large Chubb padlock locking the door. "Keys...Where do they keep the keys?" He said under his breath. He searched around the flat, no keys. He crept back up the steps into the galley and looked around. "There they are," he said gleefully. He took the bunch of keys off the hook. Back down by the fridges he found the key to unlock the padlock. He walked inside the large walk-in cool room.

"Wow, Aladdin's cave," he said to himself. He eyed the boxes on the shelves. "Erm, Terry's Dark Chocolate, Ex-Lax chocolate, never heard of that. Marmite, I haven't had Marmite for ages. He piled the Ex-Lax box on top of the Terry's dark chocolate box and a tray of marmite jars on top of the Ex-Lax. The three boxes were heavy. He carried them out, put them down on the floor next to the stairs and re-locked the cool store door. With the booty on his shoulders, he scurried back towards his cabin, hanging the keys back on the hook. Passing the sailors' mess room, he looked inside and saw Jackson sitting at the table. "Hey, Froggy. Look what I've got."

"Blimey! Where did you find that lot?"

"In the army officer's fridge."

"You naughty boy, Fifie." Jackson said as he checked the boxes. "Don't eat too much of that chocolate though, Fifie, you'll have the tomtits for a week."

"Tomtits, why?"

"Because Ex-Lax is a laxative. For constipation. If you ate a full bar you could shit through the eye of a needle at twenty paces."

"Laxative, I've never heard of a laxative."

"Well, you can eat one or two small pieces, but no more than that. Tell you what, put the Ex-lax and Terry's dark chocolate in our fridge. We'll share it out with the other watches. Don't let the captain or Commander Bateman know or you'll be in trouble." Jackson licked his lips. "Marmite, I love Marmite. Come on, let's get the toaster on."

"Good idea, you do the toast and I'll put the chocolate in the fridge, there's enough bars in the box to last us till we get back home."

"Yes, sailing in the morning. Liverpool here we come."

CHAPTER 8

DECEMBER 1940 - HOMEWARD BOUND.

THE *SS EMPIRE ORION* SAILED out of Kilindini without fuss or fanfare heading for the Suez Canal. The watches were put back on a war footing. No one was sure whether or not U-Boats were in the Indian Ocean or if pocket battleships were prowling.

Kevin inched his way towards the prisoner's compound and towards the guard on duty. "Hi, mate. Where you from?"

"Accrington," said the fusilier.

"I know Accrington. My dad supports Accrington Stanley. I support Man City, myself, but Stanley is my second-best team. Are you looking forward to going home?"

"You bet, I don't like being at sea." He looked out at the ocean. "A torpedo could come steaming in at any minute, no warning. I don't know how you put up with it. I'd have joined the ruddy navy if I wanted to be at sea."

"Do you mind if I give that Italian some of my chocolate ration. That one there. He saved my bacon the other day, he warned me about a snake I was just about to pick up. I thought it was an eel; it was a green mamba water snake."

The guard sucked in his breath, "well, it's against regulations to give the prisoners anything, but seeing as your dad supports my team, go on. I won't look."

"Thanks." Kevin went up to the compound wire. A batch of prisoners had been allowed up on deck for exercise and fresh air, the teenage soldier was amongst them.

"Hiya," Kevin called.

The young soldier saw Kevin and smiled. "Oh, *Ciao*."

"Here, I've got some chocolate. He pushed the bar through the wire.

The youth looked pleasantly surprised, "*Grazie mille*. Thank you."

"Do you speak English?"

The boy screwed his nose, "a little, I speak little of the English."

"I know some Italian words too, I can say, *Buongiono* and *Buon poeriggio* and *Buona notte*."

"Any more?"

"No, sorry."

The Italian laughed. "I show English to ski. So, I know some word."

"Ski, what's that?"

"Don't you know?"

"No, never heard of it. What's your name?"

"Nino. Giannino Lombardo."

"Hello Nino Lombardo. My name's Kevin. Kevin Fife. Where you from Nino?"

"From Bolzano."

Kevin laughed, "Nino Lombardo from Bolzano, it rhymes."

"Why you laugh?"

"Ninooo, Lombardooo, from Bolzanoooo."

Nino frowned, "I'm from South Tyrol. North Italiano."

"Alright, sunshine, you've talked long enough," called the fusilier, "You'll get me in trouble letting you fraternise with the enemy."

"Nino's not my enemy."

"Nor mine, but rules is rules, you know. And if you are seen giving them chocolate, I'll get it in the neck."

"Alright, I'll keep away."

He muttered under his breath as he walked away, "and my dad supports Burnley FC not Accrington Stanley."

The ship sailed north to Suez without incident. Kevin once again asked the fusilier if he could chat with the Italian prisoner of war.

"Go on, five minutes."

Kevin saw Nino sitting on a bollard looking out to sea. Nino looked sad.

"Nino."

"*Ciao, Kevin*."

"What's the matter, mate, you look so sad."

"It's nothing. I wanna go home."

"I wanna go home too. How old are you?"

"I'm sixteen."

"I'm only fifteen, I hate this war."

"Me too."

"How come you're in the army at sixteen."

"It long story. I join as boy. Now with war I cannot get home."

"Did you enjoy the chocolate?"

"No, he steala mi cioccolato." Nino looked towards a rough looking soldier leaning up against the bulkhead. "Him. Risso."

"He stole your chocolate?"

"Si. He steala ma things. He eata ma cioccolato, like so..." Nino gave the impression of someone gobbling down the chocolate bar in one go.

Kevin looked across at the thief. "I know his type; I hate thieves and bullies. I know now how to deal with a bully. Let me think about it, I'll be back in a minute."

Kevin wandered off knowing quite well how to pay back Risso the chocolate thief.

Back in his cabin Kevin carefully unwrapped a bar of Terry's plain chocolate and replaced it with a bar of Ex-Lax chocolate. He hurried back to the compound before the prisoners were sent back down the hold.

"Nino, here." Kevin called. He waited until Risso was watching before passing the chocolate through the fence to Nino. "Do not eat this chocolate. Pretend to hide it, but make sure Risso sees you do it. But, Nino, *do not* eat this chocolate."

"*Si,* Kevin. I understand."

"Next week, I'll get our cook to make a chocolate cake and chocolate sauce. And don't eat that either."

Nino smiled and nodded.

Just before the guards ordered the prisoners to go below, Kevin heard Risso call to Nino, "*Vieni qui piccolo merda...chi cosa hai li?*" Risso pulled Nino to one side, pushing him hard up against the bulkhead. He robbed him of the chocolate bar. Risso disappeared down the hold ladder already biting into the chocolate. Nino turned to Kevin and gave him the international thumbs up sign.

~ * ~ * ~ * ~

The *SS Empire Orion* dropped its anchor in the Bay of Suez waiting to transit the Suez Canal. Kevin stood next to the wire compound talking to his new friend, Nino. They were watching a motor boat from Suez take off a seriously ill prisoner of war. Risso the chocolate thief, laid out on a stretcher, looking very sorry for himself.

"I think we over did it with the chocolate pudding, Nino."

"Nino grinned, "Si. He very sick. How you call it? *Diarrea. Sospello caso di dissenteria.*"

"Yeah, suspected dysentery. The shits. He won't be bothering you anymore."

"No, that is good."

They watched as the motor boat carrying Risso and two more prisoners requiring hospital treatment, as it disappeared towards the Port of Suez.

"Here, Nino, an early Christmas present; a tin of Nuttall's Mintoes, Commander Bateman's own personal supply. I'm sure he won't mind you having them." Kevin squeezed the tin through the wire.

"*Grazie mille, buon Natale*, Kevin."

"*Prego*," replied Kevin.

"Your Italian is very good."

"Yes, I now know ten Italian words. Commander Bateman says you will be kept down the hold while we transit the canal. I'm sorry. Bateman said that you will be working on a farm in England. That's not so bad. Josh White said the farm girls like a roll in the hay."

Nino laughed. "I teach English girl some Italian too."

"I bet you will. See you later, Nino, I must get back to work. I'm not allowed to steer the ship through the canal."

Nino, not understanding all the English words waved, "*Arrivederci*, Kevin."

The *MV Empire Orion* safely passed through the Suez Canal and sailed onto Alexandria and arrived in the harbour 20th December 1940. The ships agent came on board carrying mail from England.

~ * ~ * ~ * ~

The chief mate sporting a homemade beard made out of cotton waste, came into the Seamans' dining room dressed up like Father Christmas, carrying a sack. Captain Abraham followed, carrying two bottles of Navy Rum. Chief Engineer Andrew Hollander, the two engineers and the second mate and the radio officer followed on.

"Ho, ho, ho," said the chief mate, "An early Merry Christmas everyone. Early Christmas prezzies and letters from home."

A cheer went up from the sailors. The mate began to distribute the mail and little bags of nuts and raisins.

"Fifie," He sniffed at one of the envelopes. "Lavender." He grinned, raising his eyebrows. He handed over three letters.

Come on lads. Let's charge up our glasses for the loyal toast. Are we all here? Most of the *Alice Morgan's* crew and our replacements comrades from the Royal Navy. Let us drink the toast now in the safety of the harbour," said the captain, who did not allow his crew drinking alcohol while his ship was at sea and on a war footing.

The rum bottles were passed from sailor to sailor.

Kevin glanced at the bottle; British Navy Pusser's Rum 100 proof.

"Go on, Fifie, a wee tot for Christmas."

Kevin was given a small tot of rum.

"Well gentlemen, let's not forget out lost colleagues and toast to them," the captain holding a glass of rum, said, "Jeb Habbard, John Burch, Otto Alfredson, Mr Cameron our cook, and, last but not least, young Hector Davis-Davidson, may they all rest in peace, safe in God's arms. Lost friends."

The captain raised his glass.

"Lost friends," answered the crew.

Captain Abraham raised his glass again. "The loyal toast. The King, God bless him"

"The King," they all answered

Copying the others, Kevin swallowed his rum in one. His face turned red, the veins in his neck dilated and he nearly choked on the spirit. Coughing and spluttering he gasped, "how do you manage to drink that without choking!"

The sailors laughed at him.

"When we have refuelled and resupplied, gentlemen, we sail with the convoy though the Straights of Gibraltar, up to Ushant, there we will sail independently to England, non-stop. I say non-stop, we are to disembark the POWs in Falmouth before sailing on up to Liverpool. We should be back in home-waters around 1st or 2nd January. With our diesel engines and our superior speed, it will be safer sailing independently than being in position 13 on the portside column of a slow-moving convoy. We can zig-zag during the day, and get our foot down in the hours of darkness to..."

"Liverpool!" the crew called loudly in unison.

Kevin couldn't wait to read his three letters; he opened the first from Jane.

Dearest Kevin. Thank you so much for your two letters from Cape Town and Durban. It was so good to hear that you are safe and well. I cried every day for two months when we were told your ship the Alice Morgan had been sunk. We all thought you had been lost at sea. Daddy had a special service dedicated to you and a Sunday service dedicated to all those who serve at sea. We sang, 'Almighty Father Strong to Serve'; the sailor's hymn. Then our prayers were answered, when your mum got news you were safe. And Kevin, we saw you on the Pathe News, I couldn't believe it! Flogger Links yelled out, 'that's Five-foot-Fife!' at the top of his voice in the cinema. Then Tommy said, well, shouted, "it's Kevin!' The whole cinema stood up clapping. It was so wonderful...'

Kevin frowned, "When was I on the news?" He read on.

'Getting a medal off General de Gaulle, we are all so proud of you. I don't mind telling you, I gave Flogger a good telling off for shouting, 'Five-foot'. What has size got to do with anything. You are a much bigger and braver man than he will ever be. Your mum said she also got a letter from a girl called Claudette. I felt really jealous, I hope she isn't your new girlfriend because I still love you and want to be your sweetheart when you return home. I still pray for your safe return every single night. Maureen and Tommy send their love and they cannot wait until the Cobden Gang are back together again. And guess what? Blackstone got bombed. Yes, a German plane on its way to bomb Manchester was being chased by a spitfire. The bomber dropped its bombs so it could fly away faster. The incendiary bombs fell on the allotment and on Johnny Clegg's hen hut. The hut and all the pigeon coops were blown to pieces but thank God no one was hurt. I will end this letter sending you all my love and kisses. Be safe and God bless you. Lots of love from your girlfriend Jane XXXXXXXXXXXXXXXXXXXXX.'

With a broad smile across his face Kevin counted the 20 kisses. He placed the letter in his toffee tin and opened the letter from his mother.

My Dear Son. Thank you for your letters from South Africa. We are so sorry that you didn't get our other letters, we wrote to Cardiff Coal and Coke shipping offices. They returned our letters when they found out the Alice Morgan had been sunk. Dad and me thought you'd been lost at sea. Your dad was devastated, and me too, but your dad took it very badly. However, our prayers were answered when we got news from the Admiralty that you were safe. You seem to have seen a lot of action. We were told you had been on the news at the Olympia cinema, so next day, we all went to the pictures to see you. Granny Fife and Granny Malone, your Aunty Martha, Uncle Alex, all your cousins, we all went to see you. And there you were, getting a medal off Charles de Gaulle. We were so proud and all the people in the cinema clapped and cheered for our little Kevin, we were so proud of you. I noticed a tear in your dad's eyes...

Kevin grinned, '*my dad's more sentimental than mum*', he thought. He continued reading.

'*We were so sorry to hear that your friend Hector had died and the other men on your ship being killed, it's all so sad that this war continues. We pray for you all and all those brave men who go down to the sea in ships, every day. Everyone here sends their love. I saw Miss Frost the other day; she sends her love too. Your pal Tommy often calls and so does Jane Black, she is such a nice girl. Keep safe Kevin my dear boy and we will see you when your ship returns to England. Don't forget to wrap up warm, it's very cold here now. Lots of love from your Mum and Dad XX*'.

He finished reading the letter for the second time before placing it in his tin box. The letters made him even more homesick. "I can't wait now to get home," he said to himself.

Kevin didn't recognise the handwriting on the third envelope. When he opened it, he gave out a little exclamation of joy, "Oh, it's from Claudette."

He read the letter, '*My Dear Friend Kevin. I hope you don't mind me writing you. Your mother gave me the navy's address for your ship. I got to England safely and now staying my aunty in Chester. As promised, I called at your maman et papa's house to pass your message. They are kindest people and I know they miss you much. I think about you often, how you met me at M. Lazard's dance hall. I was so lonely and sad. When I saw your happy face, it cheered me up too. Thank you for speaking on my behalf to Captain Glover. I found out the Gestapo wanted take me to prison camp. I convinced now you saved my life. Thank you so much mon doux garcon. One day I hope we meet again. Until then I will pray for you. L'amour de Claudette X.'*

Before Kevin put Claudette's letter in the tin, he took out her silver hair clip and blue hair ribbon. He touched the ribbon to his lips. He then carefully replaced them and the letter in the toffee tin with his other treasures.

Six hour later, one week before Christmas day, the SS *Empire Orion* sailed out of Alexandria Harbour homeward bound for Liverpool.

CHAPTER 9

NEW YEAR'S EVE – 1940 – THE NORTH ATLANTIC.

2355, FIVE MINUTES TO 1941, Kevin glanced up at the bridge clock for the umpteenth time. "Five more minutes and I'll be off duty."

Reminiscing on the uneventful eleven days, 3600 nautical mile trip between Alexandria and the Bay of Biscay, he calculated how many more hours he would have to do steering this ship between here and docking at Liverpool in two or three-days' time. Five minutes to midnight. Five more minutes on watch. Five more minutes to a new year. Kevin looked out of the bridge windows at the scant moonlight reflecting on the breaking white waves, relieved that for the first time since leaving Alexandria there were no other ships around, and no strict position to maintain in the convoy making steering a straight course less pressurised. They were now sailing alone; the slow London bound convoy had departed company at Ushant, the main convoy turning towards the English Channel while the *Empire Orion* headed north towards the Irish Sea unescorted.

The *SS Empire Orion* pitched and rolled in the heavy Atlantic swell. Waves crashed over the bows, spray hitting the bridge windows. The warm seas of the South Atlantic, Indian Ocean, the Red Sea and the Mediterranean were becoming a distant memory. Snow flurries and sleet blew down from the north. Number four hatch had been battened down and covered with a tarpaulin to keep the foul weather off the Prisoners-of-War camping on the decks below. Most of the Italian soldiers were sea sick. Kevin glanced up at the clock again waiting for his relief at midnight. The chief mate was already on the bridge examining the charts.

Captain Abraham scanned the dark sea and the last quarter of the waning moon with his binoculars. Satisfied all was well, he came back into the wheel house and looked at the ship's clock. Midnight.

"Happy New Year, Mr Todd," Captain Abraham said. "Happy New Year, Mr Fife."

"Happy New Year, Captain," they replied.

"It's tradition that the youngest member of the crew rings sixteen bells at midnight on New Year's Eve but I'm not sending you forward in this weather. I don't want you to be washed over the side."

The captain turned to the second mate, "I think it's safe to stop zig zagging, Toddy. When the convoy departed, I thought it best to keep well off the coast. Much less chance of being torpedoed now, a dark night and rough seas."

"Aye, sir. It's pretty dark outside. We saw a Sunderland flying boat earlier. Tomorrow we should have air cover." He spoke to Kevin, "Steer nor', nor' east, Fifie."

"North, north east, sir," Kevin turned the wheel watching the lubber line. "Steering north, north, east, sir."

"Well, Toddy, 1940 has been an eventful year, a terrible year, let's hope 1941 is going to be better for us," the captain said, gazing out of the window watching the waves break over the bow. "And it's been an eventful year for you too Fifie, for a 14-year-old. You are too young to have seen the things you've seen since we left Birkenhead last May. Being torpedoed, seeing your pal die and that fight you had with the Irishman, Dimmock. You will be telling your grandchildren these stories in years to come."

Kevin just smiled and murmured, "erm, yeah...But I don't think they will believe me." He handed the helm over to his midnight relief. "Steering north-north-east, she's taking port helm."

"Thanks, Kev." Able seaman Hemsworth took over steering the ship.

Kevin stood next to the captain looking out of the bridge windows.

He heard the captain say, "It's nasty weather tonight, Toddy, sleet and snow this far south is unusual. Not to worry, two more days and we'll be home. Two more days and..."

A massive explosion ripped through the ship knocking the captain off his feet. The second mate, thrown in the air by the explosion, landed on top of the captain. The ship lurched to starboard then rolled over to the port side.

Kevin staggered, hitting the telegraph. His mouth wide open in horror at the sight of the forward hatches being blown high into the sky followed by flames. Ten seconds later a second deafening roar and explosion right under the bridge. Flames issuing out of the passenger's accommodation two decks below. There was no doubt in Kevin's mind that they were being torpedoed as a third torpedo slammed into the port quarter. The smell of burned cordite heavy in the air.

Captain Abraham, scrambled to his feet and ran out onto the port bridge wing, looking aft. "Oh, my god!"

The ship began to list over to port. Abraham returned to the wheel house. "We are on fire from the boat deck to the stern. Toddy, ring down, stop engines. Sparky!"

The radio officer had rushed up from his cabin holding a life-jacket. "Yes, Captain,"

"Send out an SOS SSSS attacked by U-boat, give them our position."

"Okay, Captain, I'm onto it." The radio officer rushed back into the radio room to transmit the distress signals.

By this time the chief mate and the chief engineer were on the bridge. The main engine had stopped throbbing.

"Colin, go below and assess the damage. I'll dump the confidential papers." The captain was already packing the canvas sink bag with the Admiralty sailing orders and code books. "Report back. See if we can fight the fires below decks. Andrew, go below, check the engine room, see if we can stabilise the ship. Get the squaddies to help."

"Okay, Cap. Leave it with me." The chief engineer said calmly before setting off to go back down the engine room.

Kevin, still hanging onto the telegraph, open mouthed, amazed at the efficient way everyone acted. No one panicking.

Commander Bateman arrived on the bridge panting. "What do you want me to do, Captain?"

"Unless we can stabilise the ship and fight the fire we're going down sooner or later. Three torpedoes! On a shitty night like this could not be worse. If you can get the fusiliers to help my lads fight the fires, and if the worst comes to the worst, help us swing out the portside lifeboats."

Captain Hargreaves of the Catering Corp also stumbled up the steps to the bridge.

"Captain Hargreaves, can you get your lads to get the Italians out on deck and mustered by the Carleys? Get the Carley floats ready for launching. Stay onboard as long as possible, until I give the order to abandon ship. If we can save the ship it will be better than launching into these waves."

Captain Abraham looked at the terrified Kevin. "Well, my lad, I want you to go into the sea-cabin and grab yourself my jumper and oilskins, they are in the locker." He spoke calmly and slowly, "put them on, put on a life jacket and then go and assist Mr Chapman. And, Fifie, stick by him. You will be alright. Go on son…and God be with you."

"Thanks, Captain Abraham, good luck to you too."

Kevin found the captain's oilskin and jumper. He dressed quickly, donned the lifejacket and finally slung his canvas grab bag over his shoulder. Outside on the deck he could not believe his eyes, it looked like the entire ship was on fire. The sacks of tea in the forward hold burned furiously showering the night sky with millions of tiny sparks. Kevin ran down the steps to the main deck to assist the chief mate who was trying to organise a firefighting party; a mixture of sailors and fusiliers had run out the fire hose.

"Fife," called the mate. "Water on! Turn on the valve."

Kevin opened the fire hydrant. Water surged through the snaking hose pipe; the jet aimed at the fire burning furiously in the midships accommodation.

The screams of the trapped Italian officers adding to the distress. One or two of the Italian officers staggered out onto the open deck with their clothes on fire. The mate trained the water jet onto the burning prisoners. Then, two minutes later, the engine room fire pumps stopped working. The fire hose flattened.

"No use," the mate said in disgust. "Okay, boys, let's get up top to the boat deck and get them lifeboats ready to launch."

The soldiers and sailors threw down the hosepipes and hurried up the steps to the lifeboats.

Half blinded by the swirling smoke, Kevin looked out at the rough seas, at the sleet lashing down and then at the fire burning inside the ship. He was already struggling to stay on his feet on the tilting deck. The chief mate had disappeared in the smoke. The fierce heat from the inferno drove Kevin down the passageway towards the shouting and terrified POWs that had managed to escape from the fire. Kevin felt scared and useless, not sure what to do. He stared at the turmoil on the after deck, watching the Italian prisoners struggling to climb out of the smoke-logged hold. The screaming of the Italian officers, trapped in the former passenger cabins, that were now well alight, added to the night of terror. Fire pouring from the cabin portholes and licking up to the boat deck above, setting fire to three of the portside lifeboats. The ship groaned and sank down another few more feet. Kevin instinctively knew the ship was doomed. He looked amongst the prisoners of war crowding around the Carley floats in utter confusion, looking for his friend Nino. There was no sight of him. He saw Dr Baldini, trying to calm down the Italians.

"Doctor," Kevin called. "Have you seen Nino?"

The doctor shook his head. "No, I think he is still below."

Kevin looked aft at number 4 hold. The hatch covers and the compound wire fence had been blown off by the third torpedo strike, smoke poured out of the hold opening. Kevin made his way aft on the crazy angled deck, made worse by the high waves lifting up the ship then dropping it down with a crashing noise. Snow flew in his face, sea spray blown off the waves by the near gale force winds lashed him. British soldiers were helping injured Italians. *There are no enemies in situations like this*, Kevin thought, as he struggled to reach the open hold. When he looked down at where nearly 200 POWs had been sleeping, he gasped in horror at the glowing fire below the thick curling smoke and the screaming and shouting emanating from below. One or two of the prisoners were climbing up the raking ladder emerging from the smoke.

He shouted down, "Nino."

The ship gave a sudden lurch to port, the main deck scuppers were now already under water.

"Abandon ship!"

Kevin looked up towards the bridge, the captain, using a megaphone shouted once again, "Abandon ship!"

Kevin knew there was little time left before the whole ship would heel over and capsize.

"Nino!", he shouted again.

"Kevin....*Aiutatemi!* ... Help me!" the voice came out of the smoky hold. "*Aiutatemi!*"

Kevin ran over to where the ladder appeared from the hold. Nino's head emerged from the smoke, struggling to climb the ladder. The man behind Nino was trying to climb over him, trying to pull Nino off the ladder in an attempt to get into the fresh air. Kevin grasped hold of Nino's hand and pulled him upwards with all his strength. They both collapsed down on the deck, both of them gasping for air.

"Come on, Nino, let's get to the lifeboats."

They made their way past the fusiliers who were helping the Italians throw the Carleys overboard. Some men had already jumped into the sea and were swept away.

Kevin looked on in horror as three of the four portside lifeboats were in flames.

"Come on, Nino, let's see if we can get into that boat. We've more chance if we do."

Todd, the second mate, Froggy Jackson and Willie Wilde, had managed to wind out the unaffected boat to the embarking position. The boat's keel already touching the sea, rising and falling on the waves.

"Come on, Fifie, get in," called Todd. "Try and release the disengaging gear."

"Get in." Kevin pushed Nino into the boat. Nino, not knowing what to do, crawled under the thwart seat. Kevin grabbed hold of the bowsing line, waiting for the order to release the falls.

"She's going over!" cried the second mate still standing on the ship's boat deck

"Mother of God!" Kevin gasped as large ventilator broke free crashing over the ship's side not more than six feet from where he stood. The heavy lifting gear masts accelerating the capsize.

Nine minutes after the first torpedo struck home, the *MV Empire Orion* overturned, tipping hundreds of men into the sea. The force of the capsize wrenched at the falls tearing them away from the davits and the lifeboat slewed sideways away from the hull. The resulting wave knocked Kevin overboard. He sank down below the waves for what seemed like an eternity. With his lungs bursting and his heavy clothing weighing him down, Kevin began to rise slowly to the surface. Spluttering and gagging on seawater down his throat and in his eyes, he saw the lifeboat ten yards away floating upright, the rope falls hanging over the gunnels. He struck out towards the boat managing to grip hold of the trailing lines. Pulling himself up to boat's lifeline and grabbing hold of it he hung on for dear life, knowing it was too high for him to climb out of the water into the boat. The boat rose high on a wave before crashing down, nearly crowning the struggling boy. He called for help.

A petrified Nino looked over the gunnel.

"Nino!... Help me!... Give me a hand, Nino." Kevin gasped, holding up his hand. Nino reached down, gripping Kevin's wrist with his two hands, assisted with a rising wave, he pulled Kevin over the gunnel into the boat. They both lay on the bottom boards exhausted.

The lifeboat rose and fell on the waves with monotonous regularity. Sleet lashed down covering the boys in a thin covering of snow. The pounding waves, the screaming wind and the driving snow continued all night long.

Dawn on New Year's Day saw sea spray flying into Kevin's face; he looked down at the huddled, shivering Nino. Kevin tried to stand up. The sea was still rough. He peered over the gunnels, no sign of the *Empire Orion*. He could see a couple of upside-down Carley floats. Also, he saw bodies floating in the sea. They had frozen to death during the long night. Kevin was horrified to see the only two people in the lifeboat were Nino and himself. It was impossible to step the mast, there was nothing they could do but wait for rescue.

"You, alright, Nino?"

Nino nodded, "Si, Grazie." Nino was freezing, he huddled himself back under the seats. Kevin himself was saturated and cold. He knew from Bosun Heygate at the Sea Training School that hypothermia was a killer of shipwrecked sailors. Heygate had told the recruits how sailors who survived the shipwreck were only to die, quite quickly, of hypothermia.

Kevin opened the sail bag pulling out the lifeboats main sail and jib sail. He used the sails to covered Nino. He looked out over the sea again. The sea was empty now as far as the eye could see. No lifeboats, no Carley floats, no rescue ships. The two boys huddled together, under the sails trying to keep warm. Night came, freezing cold. Kevin opened his grab bag.

He took out a bar of Terry's chocolate and broke it in half. "Here, Nino."

Nino, smiled briefly, "*Grazie*, Kevin. When war is *finita*, I teach you ski. South Tyrel. It *Bellissima, molto bello* in mountains."

"When the war is over, and you are free again, Nino, I'll teach you how to fish in the Manchester Ship Canal. There aren't any green mambas in the Ally-Ally-Oh," he said weakly.

The weather was unrelenting; raining, sleeting, snowing and then raining again. It took all of Kevin's strength to peep over the gunnels to see if there were any sign of life or a rescue vessel. The sea was empty of ships, no sight of Southern Ireland.

Night fell again, two days and three nights of constant sleet and raining, Kevin's strength was failing, all he wanted to do now was sleep. He couldn't get warm; the sails were stiff and wet, his clothes were saturate. He thought about home, his mother's cooking, the warm fireside, his dad smoking a pipe in his armchair. Drifting in and out of sleep he opened his eyes when he thought he heard friendly chatter. Lifting himself slowly up on one elbow, he looked at a group of boys sitting on the thwarts. The boys stopped talking and looked at Kevin, all the boys were smiling happily.

"Hello, Kevin."

"Hector! Where did you...?"

Kevin looked at the other boy, sitting next to Hector. He said feebly, "Wee, Jock! How did you get here?"

"Hi, Kev. My ship was torpedoed too, just outside the Clyde. All hands went down with her, I'd only been at sea two days."

Kevin noticed other boys behind Hector and Wee Jock. "Who's that?"

Hector and Jock moved apart to show more young boys sitting on the midship thwart.

"Crocker!"

Crocker nodded, "yeah, my ship was blown to pieces in mid Atlantic, no one had a chance."

"And you, Stan?"

"My ship was shelled when we invaded Dakar. The invasion is still top secret. My mum doesn't know yet that I was killed."

Kevin looked beyond Stan, the boat was full of boys, some of them sitting upon the gunnels, others trailed their fingers idly in the sea. One boy stood at the bow, scanning the sea. Kevin didn't know any of them. He began to drift back to sleep. He heard Hector say, "you will be alright, Kevin. Come with me, I will lead you to Fiddler's Green, to a sailor's Valhalla."

"Valhalla?" he repeated faintly.

"Yes, a place where only those who have died bravely are received." Hector's voice faded.

One by one the boys vanished. Kevin smiled briefly looking at the empty boat. The snow and rain clouds cleared leaving a cloudless sky. The temperature plummeted. Kevin and Nino huddled together for warmth, both lay on their backs, staring up at the stars. Once again, the stars shone like diamonds.

Just before the pre-dawn light, Nino's eyes closed. He moaned softly and died.

Kevin, with his head on one side, looked at his dead friend. He touched Nino's cold hand with the back of his fingers and whispered, "*Arrivederci, Nino*, God bless and look after you."

"Are you coming, Kev?"

Kevin looked at Hector who was standing on the path running alongside the River Welland. Primroses growing in green grassy bank waved on the gentle breeze. The warm sun causing the ripples on river to sparkle like silver ribbons. The sky was clear blue and cloudless.

Hector turned again, beckoning. "Come on, Kevin."

"Wait for me, Hector," Kevin called. "I'm coming."

With a happy smile on his face, Kevin, following his friend to Valhalla, passed away peacefully in his sleep.

Three nights and two days after the *Empire Orion* had sunk, Kevin, the British deck boy, and Nino, the Italian prisoner of war, huddled together as friends, not enemies, had died of the cold and exposure.

EPILOGUE

BLACKSTONE VILLAGE - 1ST FEBRUARY 1941

MRS FLORENCE FIFE, WASHING UP at the sink, looked through the kitchen window. A taxi pulled up in the street outside her front door. Her heart sank as Reverend Black and his daughter Jane climbed out of the car; both their faces saddened. Jane gave a brief smile, her face was wetted by tears.

Wiping her hands on her pinafore she went to the door. With the vicar, another man, wearing a small silver cross in the lapel of his black suit, followed them.

"Hello, Florence," said the vicar. "Can we come in?"

"Hello, vicar. Hello Jane, come on in." Florence knew instinctively that they were bringing her the worse possible news. "Jimmy," she called to Kevin's dad. "Jimmy, Reverend Black and Jane are here."

James Fife came into the room; he looked at the three, his face grim, his knowing eyes reflected his grief.

"This is Mr McCabe, he's from the Seaman's Mission in Liverpool."

"Hello, Mr McCabe. Have they found him? Have they found my boy?"

McCabe nodded sadly, "Yes, Mr Fife. There were no survivors, I'm afraid. A terrible tragedy. Over 300 men went down with Kevin's ship."

"We knew that the ship had been torpedoed a month ago, on New Year's Day, but you know, we just hoped Kevin may have survived."

"No, I'm sorry. A lifeboat was found by *HMS Amethyst*. Your boy and another young lad were in the boat, but they had both died. I'm really sorry to tell you that they both had died from the cold. They were found huddled together, trying to keep warm."

Mrs Fife began to cry uncontrollably. Jane put her arms around her shoulder to comfort her.

"We know it was Kevin as he was carrying this canvas bag," McCabe said as he handed over the bag to Florence.

She took the bag, fingers white from the pressure of her grasp, and held it to her cheek. "It's still damp," she said softly.

"Yes."

"Where is Kevin now?"

"He was buried at sea. *HMS Amethyst* was on war patrol, hunting U-Boats. They had picked up a couple of Carley floats from the sinking, all people on the floats had died from exposure. The navy had to bury them at sea."

After a few minutes of small talk, condolences and sympathies, Reverend Black, his daughter Jane and the man from the Seaman's Mission got up to leave.

Chaplain McCabe hesitated by the door, he turned and said, "You know, Mr and Mrs Fife, the men at sea in the Merchant Navy are fighting a battle, just as violent and fierce, as any soldier fighting in the fields. These men and boys who go down to the sea in ships, in wartime, are very brave men indeed."

He carefully closed the door leaving Florence and Jimmy Fife alone sitting at the table with their memories.

Mrs Fife opened the bag. She took out an empty Terry's chocolate wrapper, a pen knife, a fishing line minus its hook and sinker and an empty water bottle and a torch.

Jimmy picked up the flashlight and pressed the switch. "The batteries are dead...I gave this to Kevin on his 10th birthday." Next, Jimmy Fife took out the toffee tin. "We gave him these toffees, Christmas 1939." He opened the tin and laid out the contents on the kitchen table. A small bundle of letters, Kevin's ID card and seaman's book, still wrapped in a Board of Trade condom. The St Christopher medal his mother had given him, a tin sheriffs' badge, a small silver cross. Next Kevin's dad unfolded a sheet of paper. He read the note. "This is a crew list of the *Alice Morgan*." He turned the sheet over and read aloud, "*The position where Alice Morgan sank 30th June 1940 - 33.34.11 N 11.03.31W.*"

He picked up the small photograph. A photo of Kevin, looking very happy, sitting at a table with three beautiful young ladies. He studied the photo for a long time. "I wonder where this photo was taken?" he said to himself. "And what was our little Kevin doing with these ladies?" Turning the photo, he read the inscription written on the back. "There's a message written in French, not Kevin's handwriting." In hesitant French he read aloud, *"Avec amour de Jacqueline Ruby et Fleur. Plaisir d'amour, Parlez-mou d'amour."*

He then gently touched each item on the table, the Cross of Lorraine, the small Fleur-de-lys brooch and the ruby flower.

Frowning, he picked up the photograph again, noting that two of the girls were wearing the same brooches in their blouses. "Em," he murmured, "I wonder why these ladies gave my boy their brooches... if only these gems could speak."

Once again Kevin's mum nodded in agreement but she didn't answer just staring through her tears at the two jewels.

Jimmy Fife pondered for a moment before looking at the other items; a *'HM Destroyers'* cap tally, a Royal Marines cap badge, a piece of blue hair ribbon with a silver fern hairclip attached, and a French naval medal with a tricolour ribbon.

"Look, Florrie, this is the medal that General de Gaulle gave him."

Florrie took the medal and looked at it. She simply nodded, laying the medal on the table and smoothing out the ribbon with her finger.

"I think this is Italian," Jimmy examined the Italian army pith helmet badge. "I wonder where he got this from?"

The last two items he looked at were two silver badges; a reef knot encircling the letters MN.

"I suggested Kevin should collect little souvenirs of the places he visited during his voyages. I wonder how Kevin came to own all these? I think there must be a story connected to each item."

Florence nodded again but didn't answer.

Finally, a letter addressed to Mr and Mrs Fife. Jimmy handed the letter to Kevin's mum. The ink on the envelope had run but the letters were still readable.

She pressed the envelope to her lips. "Will you read it for me?"

Kevin's dad opened the envelope and slowly and sadly read the letter aloud.

"Dear Mum and Dad. Thank you so much for your letter that I got here in Alexandria. It was the first letter I have had from you while I have been at sea. I also got a letter off my girlfriend Jane and a letter from Claudette, the Jewish refugee I told you about. Jane told me she often calls at our house to see you. We celebrated Christmas a week early in port as captain Abraham does not allow drinking rum while we are at sea. Captain Abraham is a good man, as are all the officers and men on this ship. We are all looking forward to getting home and seeing our families again. I was going to post this letter in Egypt but I missed the post. I will post this letter in Falmouth. That is where we go from here to put the Italian prisoners of war ashore before heading onto Liverpool. I made good friends with one of the POWs, Nino, he is not much older than me. After the war he has invited me to his house to meet his mum and dad and all his brothers and sisters. He is so homesick missing his mum. Let's hope the war ends soon so he can go home. I just can't wait to be home again and wear my pyjamas and sit with you around the fire listening to the radio. See you in a few days' time. Lots of love from your son Kevin. XX" PS Please will you make me a meat and potato pie when I come home.*

The End

THIS NOVEL IS ALSO DEDICATED to the hundreds of young boys aged between 14 years and 18 years who served in the Merchant Navy during the wars 1914 – 1918 and 1939 – 1945 many of whom lost their life at sea. They have no graves but the sea.

Printed in Great Britain
by Amazon